## PASSION'S PRISONER

"I hate you," she spat.

White Wolf's eyes held hers. There was no indication that he had understood or even heard her. Yet that icy gaze held her fast, flicking to her mouth then back again to chain her eye. That look of possession which had become so familiar to her sent a tremor through her body. He lowered his head once more, but before he could kiss her again, she jerked her head away.

In surprise, Rachel felt his lips gently graze across her jaw to her ear. Softly his tongue tickled there, then down the column of her throat. She was enjoying the sensations . . . but how could she? This was indecent, beneath contempt. She was English, a white woman; he was a savage. He was her captor; she was his prisoner.

He was sweeping her away with these sensations, and she found herself letting him do as he wished. She did not know what spell he had cast over her, but suddenly she did not care . . .

Amy Christopher

CAPTIVE KISS

**ZEBRA BOOKS**
**KENSINGTON PUBLISHING CORP.**

*To Mom,*
*my first editor,*
*with love*

ZEBRA BOOKS

are published by

Kensington Publishing Corp.
475 Park Avenue South
New York, NY 10016

First printing: February, 1992

Printed in the United States of America

# Chapter One

*1704*

A large group of men stole almost to the edge of the forest and halted. Their clothes and demeanor showed signs of the many weeks they had been travelling down from the north, of the hardships they had endured crossing the mountains. They settled themselves among the trees, for they would have to wait before they could take any action. Some gathered in small groups and held quiet conversations; some huddled beneath the trees to sleep. All were hungry, for their supplies had run low the last few days; all were cold, but on this night there would be no fires for warmth that would give away their presence.

One man detached himself from the group and slowly made his way to where the trees thinned. Crouching in the shadows, he turned back to look at his fellow travellers. A frown crossed his features. Even after all this time, the men still divided themselves into two groups. Only their common goal had held them together.

His eyes swung around to the scene before him. Beyond the forest lay snow-covered fields, and beyond, on a small rise, the tiny village. A stockade surrounded a few dwellings, but most were outside the protective walls. The houses clustered together like a crown atop the plateau. A dog, perhaps scenting the presence of strangers, began barking furiously, but was quickly silenced. A few lights still gleamed softly in the houses at this late hour. As the man watched, two lights blinked out. Even those who would not or could not sleep were retiring to their beds to huddle beneath the warmth of blankets and quilts.

Silently, the man moved along the edge of the forest, making sure that he remained within the shadows of the trees. He stopped beneath a towering pine and once again studied the village across the open fields. The houses raggedly lined a lane. A light bobbed its way towards him, then stopped before the last house. He saw a man cradling a musket in one arm and swinging a lantern with the other. Beside the man was a woman. She turned to her escort and spoke a few words, then watched as he moved back in the direction he had come.

The woman pushed back the hood of the cloak she wore and turned towards the forest. The man in the shadows stiffened. He knew he could not be seen, yet all the same, the sense of her eyes on him made him hold his breath. She was magnificent, this woman. Her carriage was straight and tall; she held her head proudly. She reminded the man of his young mother, now gone to her ancestors. In the dark, the man smiled coldly. The woman before him would make a fine captive. Revenge, this night, would be sweet.

* * *

A bloodcurdling scream rent the predawn silence. Rachel jerked awake from her deep slumber. With a groggy mutter about cocks that would not sleep, she plumped her pillow and settled back into it. This was — had been — her first full night's sleep in almost a week. She had been working furiously on a wedding gown for Prudence Whitson, who would be wed in another seven weeks, and the gown for Prudence's mother, who was a hard taskmistress. Rachel was exhausted. Visions of what she would like to do to the cock that decided to wake early ran deliciously through her head.

Just as she got comfortable, an odd sound slowly thrust itself upon her consciousness. Rachel lifted her head and listened. Had she heard screams and musket fire from the other end of the village? The wind soughed around the corner of the house. She shook her head at her imaginings and lay back down. It could not possibly be an Indian attack. It was still winter; at least three feet of snow blanketed the ground.

Rachel's head jerked up again as a distinct musket shot came to her ears. The eerie, savage cry of an Indian war whoop raised the tiny hairs on the back of her neck. Within seconds, the noises of an attack flowed closer to her house, threatening to engulf it.

Rachel knew exactly what to do. Her father had drilled her in this a number of times. Jumping out of bed, she ran to the hook where her cloak hung and flung it about her shoulders. Next, she thrust her bare feet into her shoes. Her father had always told her that she would not be any good fighting off an attack by Indians if she froze to death. Racing to the hearth in the main room of the tiny house, she pulled the musket from its place above the mantel. Four breaths later, she had the musket loaded and aimed at the door. Amazed at how her fingers had accomplished their task in spite of their trembling, she congratulated herself for being so coolheaded. Her mouth set itself into a determined line. No Indian was going to get her.

Her eyes travelled to the narrow bed over against the wall where her father had once lain. She wished for his quiet strength now. Tears suddenly blurred her vision at her memory of him. She would remember him as he was when they had moved to the village of Deerfield in the western part of the colony of Massachusetts seven years ago—strong and handsome and always smiling. The man she had buried last autumn had only been a shell, small and shrunken from the wasting disease. Yet his last words to her echoed inside her head as if he had just spoken to her: "Be brave, Rachel, and remember that your mother and I will always love you."

Screaming and yelling were now very clear and very close. The orange glow of burning houses tinged the snow outside the narrow window. She would be brave. In spite of her determination, her knees were quaking. A loud thud rattled the door. Then another. And another. Rachel gripped the musket tighter. The door could not stand much more hammering.

With a last complaining screech of splintering wood, the door gave way. Rachel brought up the musket and sighted down its barrel, just as her father had taught her and she had practiced many times. This time, instead of having a tree or haystack in her sights, she had a large, menacing, savage redman. There was a tiny moment when he hesitated while he searched for victims. Just as his eyes met Rachel's, she pulled the trigger.

Through the smoke that hung in the air from the

musket's discharge, she saw his eyes widen, and he looked down at his chest where a black hole was slowly being surrounded by an oozing stain. He took one step towards her, then two. In shock, she watched him topple forward onto his face. Behind him, another Indian came forward into the house. With tomahawk raised, his face, painted half black, half yellow, was a mask of rage. There was no time for Rachel to reload. With a sound between a sob and a scream, she threw the musket at the Indian and dashed into the room behind the kitchen where she usually slept.

Rachel headed for the one window in the room. Her fingers were stiff and trembling clumsily as she tried to open it. A cry of anguish and rage came from the kitchen and prodded her feverishly. Grabbing a stool, Rachel flung it with all her strength against the window. A fleeting twinge of regret washed through her as she watched the valuable glass window shatter into pieces. Gathering her nightdress and cloak about her, she scrambled after the stool.

Her one thought was to get to the woods where she might be able to hide. Despite the expanse of open fields between the house and the forest, she felt that was where safety lay. There was no escape towards the village. Flames licked the black sky, and dark figures swarmed around the burning houses.

The cold air seared her lungs as she plowed through the deep, crystallized snow. If only she could get a footing on top of the crust, she would be able to run. Finally, she found a hardened spot and pulled herself up. As she made her way across the back of the house, she heard the Indian come through the window behind her. One, two more steps, and she would be out of sight. She glanced over her shoulder just as she turned the corner of her house. The Indian had seen her.

Then she hit something with all the force of her body. It was hard and warm and smelled of woodsmoke and leather. Two strong hands gripped her upper arms for balance. When she was able to draw a breath, she opened her eyes and looked up into a face chiselled from shadows. Two streaks of red warpaint slashed down across each cheekbone. The scream that had been building in her throat died instantly.

She stared up at this redman, and he stared back. His mask of a face did not reassure her in any way that he would not butcher her right then and there. Yet, his hold on her was not cruel, only firm and unrelenting. Flames crackled from the roof of the house next to hers and threw odd light across his features. Rachel's breath caught in her throat when the light touched his eyes.

The Indian who had been chasing her rounded the corner of the house and stopped behind her. The man holding her slowly raised his eyes to look across the top of her head. Words were exchanged between the two savages. Rachel listened to the strange language, and even though she could not understand a word of it, she knew somehow that the two men were arguing about her.

The fingers about her arms tightened painfully. The Indian who held her spat out one word, dropped one of his hands from her arm, turned and stalked off, dragging her after him. Rachel tried to dig in her heels to resist, but the icy crust on the snow made it impossible. She plucked at the iron grip about her arm with her fingers. As she passed the front corner of her house, she reached out and grabbed the wood. Her captor pulled

10

her free with a jerk. Rachel pounded on his arm with her free hand.

"No!" she yelled. "I am not going with you! No! No!"

The Indian turned, shook her, snarled several of his strange words at her, then kept on going. Rachel had caught a glimpse of his eyes again when he faced her, and terrorized, she immediately quieted. Silently, she stumbled along after him.

They moved unerringly down the street that cut through the center of the village. Rachel hoped she might find help from her fellow villagers, but as she was pulled along, that hope died a very quick death. Houses burned on either side of them. Small, tragic vignettes played themselves out at intervals along the street. At the Stebbins house, some villagers fought valiantly to ward off the assault. Several Indians ransacked the Catlin house whose inhabitants were nowhere to be seen. Matthew Brodie and his wife and children were huddled together beneath a tree as their captors whooped and celebrated around them. All along the street there were bodies lying in the snow. Rachel tried not to look too closely. She did not want to know who they were.

When they passed the stockade, she saw that not even the few houses enclosed within it had escaped the attack. And she saw why. The snow had drifted to within a few feet of the top of the north side and had given the Indians easy access over the wall. No one had thought the snow, which should have hindered an attack, would have made one easier. Rachel swallowed against her despair and fear.

Her captor turned towards the house of Ensign John Sheldon. Outside, several invaders stood guard. The Indian who held her said something to them in his strange language as he passed, then dragged her inside. He pulled her to a corner of the room and stopped before a roughly hewn, ladderback chair. Unwinding a narrow strip of rawhide from his arm, he bound her wrists together. His warm fingers against her icy skin made her clench her fists in longing for him to chafe some heat back into her hands. The idea made her gaze fly up to his face to see if he could read her shocking thought.

He finished tying the rawhide, and he raised his eyes. A tiny gasp escaped Rachel's lips. What she had seen twice before but had not truly believed was vividly apparent in the dim light of the house. His eyes were an incredible, bright blue.

Rachel could not tear her gaze away from them. They held her captive as surely as his hands. One moment, she wanted to shrink into herself and never look at them again, and the next, she wanted to lean into his warm body and bury herself against him. A flush crept into her cheeks at the preposterous idea. There was no warmth in those eyes, only a savage hunger that sucked the strength from her limbs. When he put a hand on her shoulder to push her down onto the chair, her knees had already begun to give out beneath her.

A slight narrowing of those eyes and a barely perceptible twist to his lips conveyed the unmistakable message that she was his property. As he crouched before her to tie her ankles together, his long, dark hair, bound only by a thin strip of rawhide across his forehead, brushed against her knuckles. It was surprisingly soft and warm. Despite her unnatural desire to feel it between her fingers, she pulled her hands back into her lap.

The Indian rose to his full height and stood before

her. The top of his head barely cleared the rafters of the ceiling. She realized when she had been standing she had been forced to look up at his face, something quite unusual for her. Because of her own height, she usually looked down at people.

With one last possessive glance, the Indian turned and walked away. Rachel averted her face. In shock and shame, she slumped in the chair. How could she want to touch that savage who had probably killed many of her neighbors and friends in the village of Deerfield? He was a heathen, a barbarian, an inhuman killer of women and children. She was the worst kind of shameless Jezebel for harboring such lustful thoughts about him.

"Rachel. Rachel. Rachel Linton."

The voice finally penetrated her thoughts and she looked up. Mistress Catlin, a kindly, middle-aged woman who had helped Rachel with her father's burial, stood before her. Rachel wanted to ask the woman where the other members of her family were, but she refrained, fearing the answer she might get.

"Are you all right, dear?" Mistress Catlin asked.

Rachel's face flamed from her inner shame, then paled. "I'm fine, Mistress Catlin." Rachel hoped her guilt was not evident to the woman.

"Would you like a drink of water?"

Rachel shook her head.

"You sure? You're the only one of us that's tied up."

Rachel glanced around the parlor. What the woman said was true. Young, sixteen-year-old Mary Sheldon and her two younger brothers huddled in a corner on the floor. Hannah Sheldon, the children's sister-in-law, sat with one quite swollen foot propped up on another

13

chair. Several other women moved about freely. A wounded man lay on the bed across the room, and from his clothes, Rachel realized he was an officer in the French army. Three other French soldiers stood guard about the perimeter of the room. So, the attackers had not just been savages. She should have known the despicable French were involved in something as ghastly as this attack on an innocent village.

Rachel looked back at Mistress Catlin. "Perhaps just a small sip of water would help, thank you."

The woman went to fetch it and brought it quickly back to her. As she placed the cup in Rachel's hands, she whispered, "That savage who brought you here. Did he hurt you?"

Giving a tiny smile, Rachel handed the cup back to her. "No, he didn't touch me."

Mistress Catlin took the cup and searched Rachel's face before she gave a small nod and turned to attend to Hannah's swollen foot. Rachel leaned back in the chair and lowered her eyes to her bound hands. She had felt little fear since she had fled through the window of her house. Even now, when forced inactivity had allowed her mind to think about the consequences of this attack, she realized she was not afraid. What she felt was an overwhelming sense of shame. The strange, primal urges that had swept through her when she had been with her captor confused her, frightened her. How could she feel such things with a savage?

Silently, she repeated her words to Mistress Catlin: No, he didn't touch me. Didn't he? With only a glance from those frigid blue eyes, he had reached into her inner being and ravished it. He had somehow taken possession of her. No, he didn't touch me.

Shock, she told herself. That's what it was. It was just the shock of the attack. The next time she saw that savage, she would hate him for what he had done to her home and her friends and for what he was. She already did hate him. She could feel it growing inside her. Or was that the beginning of fear?

The trembling started around her knees and slowly worked its way up her body until her teeth were chattering. Mistress Catlin came and pulled Rachel's cloak tighter about her body. Bending over her, the woman murmured soothing words and rubbed Rachel's back. Rachel was barely aware of what the woman was doing. The horror of the night descended on her like a pall. Yet the screams and war whoops and crack of muskets and tongues of fire were like an awful haze around the edges of her mind. All she could see was the Indian who had dragged her through the village, who had tied her up and looked at her with such cold possession. Who had raked her soul with his blue eyes.

Tears streamed down her face. Vaguely, Rachel was aware of an order coming from a man at the door to the house and people moving about and leaving. Someone, a shadowy figure, sympathetically patted her shoulder. When Rachel was able to stop crying and dried her eyes with the backs of her hands, she realized she was alone. Gazing about the room, she saw that there were no prisoners, no guards, no injured officer on the bed. Except for the hiss of the dying embers on the hearth, the room was silent. From the other end of the village, she could hear a battle still raging.

Rachel sat unmoving for a long time while she waited for something to happen, while her brain slowly came back into focus. It did not seem right that she should be left behind when all her neighbors had been taken captive by the French and Indians. The thought that she might be the only living person left in the village frightened her more than anything that had happened so far. The sound of musket fire from down the road told her that at least some of her neighbors still fought valiantly.

With her teeth, she began worrying the knot of rawhide which bound her wrists. She had to untie herself if she was not going to sit there and freeze to death. The small goal of getting herself untied seemed to help clear her thoughts. She was concentrating so hard on the knot that when the door opened, she jumped.

The Indian who had chased her through the house, the one whose face was half black and half yellow, stood just inside the door and stared at her. Rachel dropped her bound hands into her lap and stared back. She did not know what this savage meant to do to her, but she was not going to be cowed by him. He approached her slowly. When he stood above her, he jerked a large hunting knife from a sheath at his waist. With his free hand, he reached out and grabbed her hair.

Rachel was sure she was about to be scalped. She had heard grisly tales of bodies that had been discovered in the forests by settlers, bodies whose heads had been skinned so that the Indians could prove to their French allies that they had been victorious. She looked up into the painted face of this savage. His was a proud face with dark, gleaming eyes and high cheekbones, but it did not compare with the wild beauty of the man who had captured her. As if summoned by her thoughts, that redman suddenly appeared at the door.

His glance took in the scene before him and his face darkened in anger. He spoke a few short, sharp words, and the Indian who held her answered in the same tone, the same language. The grip on her hair tightened painfully. After a quick, heated discussion, he released her.

Able now to turn her head, she looked from one Indian to the other. They glared at each other across the small room. She could feel the tension and animosity between them like something tangible. Surreptitiously, she began to try again with her teeth to undo the knot tying her wrists. It was only when she had success that her blue-eyed captor realized she was almost free. With a growled word, he stalked to her. Rachel expected to be clubbed, stabbed, beaten, but instead, he pulled his own hunting knife from its sheath and bent down to cut the bonds tying her ankles together. As she stared at him with her mouth open, he freed her wrists, dragged her to her feet, and began to propel her towards the door. He tossed a few words over his shoulder, and the other Indian followed.

# Chapter Two

Rachel was surprised to see that during the time that she had been in Ensign Sheldon's house, the sun had risen. It was going to be a bright, late winter day. She squinted against the light and tried to keep up with her captor's long strides.

The village they passed through was desolate, with fires burning hungrily in several of the houses. Ahead of her, at intervals across the snowy fields, she could see other captives being herded in the same direction she was going. There was no one behind her; she was the last.

Several times, she tripped on her cloak, or her shoe got caught in the snow and came off. Each time, her captor tugged on her arm and urged her forward. Finally, just before they reached the Connecticut River that ran across the bottom of the meadows, Rachel tripped and fell flat on her face. Her Indian captor dragged her to her feet and was about to start off again, but Rachel wrestled out of his grasp and planted her feet solidly.

"Look, you heathen savage," she fumed. "I can only walk so fast and no faster. I am obviously your hostage, but I would like to be treated with a bit more respect."

Panting, she stood a few feet away from her captor. She did not know if he understood her, but she thought her tone of voice might reveal her ire. In the light of day and with some distance between them, she discovered the spell of his eyes to be not quite so potent, although far from calming.

After her little speech, she found herself waiting for some monstrous thing to happen to her. He stared at her quietly for some moments, then he turned to the other Indian and spoke a few words to him in that strange language he used. Rachel thought she saw a tiny glimmer of amusement in those blue eyes, but when he turned back to her, whatever had been there was gone.

As Rachel's captor decided what to do with her, another man approached them. He was dressed strangely, in a fur coat that reached almost to his knees and a fur hat with flaps that turned up at the front and sides. About his shoulders he wore a bright red woolen scarf that hung down to the length of his coat. His legs were encased in deerskin leggings, and these disappeared into high moccasins. His hair, as long as the Indians', straggled wildly about his shoulders, and the lower part of his face was obscured by a thick beard. Rachel could not tell if he was old, young, or somewhere in between. After greeting the Indians in their language and exchanging a few words, he turned to Rachel.

*"Bonjour, mademoiselle,"* he greeted her in French. "Is zhere a problem?"

Rachel hated the French for what they had done to her, but realized that this man had no part in that. He had greeted her politely enough. The thought flitted through her head that here, at least, was someone civilized; then her anger at the redmen and her situation asserted itself again.

"A problem? How can there be a problem?" Rachel seethed. "My village is attacked in the middle of the night by these savages, I am chased by them, captured by them, tied up by them, and now they are racing me across the snow in only my nightdress and shoes and cloak. It is an outrage!"

The Frenchman nodded his head sympathetically. *"C'est dommage,"* he agreed. "I zhink it would be best, *mademoiselle,* if you did not complain too much," he told her. "You see, zhese warriors will not put up wizs much complaints. Zhey will kill you if you give zhem much trouble." He shrugged. "A live hostage or a scalp, it is all zhe same to zhem."

"Well, could you please ask them to slow down just a little? Tell them I promise not to complain any more if they will only do that."

The Frenchman shrugged again. "If you wish, but it will not do much good."

Without waiting for a translation, Rachel's blue-eyed captor spoke to the Frenchman quickly, and the Frenchman translated.

"Zhis one, *mademoiselle.*" The Frenchman pointed with his thumb at her captor. "He says zhat he can tame wildcats and complaining women. I zhink, perhaps, you would not like his ways, *mademoiselle.*"

Rachel glanced at her blue-eyed demon, and a shiver that was not from the cold ran down her spine. Tearing her gaze away from those hypnotic eyes, she pulled her cloak tight around her.

"Tell him," she said to the Frenchman, "that I will not complain any more."

As the Frenchman was translating, the other Indian, the one with the black and yellow painted face, impatiently pushed between them and shoved Rachel from behind. Grabbing her elbow with a jerk that nearly pulled her arm from her shoulder, he dragged her along. Rachel cried out from the pain, but said nothing else. Her impudence, masquerading as bravery, had given out at her captor's comment about wildcats and women.

They crossed the frozen river and entered the pine forest. There, the invaders allowed their captives to rest for a few minutes as they gathered the packs they had left buried in the snow while they had attacked the village. Rachel found a fallen log and wearily sat down. Shivering, she pulled her cloak about her.

Mary Sheldon approached and handed her a woolen bodice and skirt. "You're to put these on, Rachel," she said. Her voice shook with nervousness. "That savage over there says to." She nodded vaguely at a group of Indians who were digging packs from beneath the snow and adding plunder to them.

Gratefully, Rachel took the clothes and stood up. She realized with a start that they were her own clothes she was putting on. In fact, they were her warmest. She donned them right over her nightdress. When her head was free, she asked, "Which savage gave these to you, Mary?"

Mary did not answer. With frightened eyes, she shook her head a little indicating her reluctance to speak.

"It's all right, Mary," Rachel soothed. "They're not going to murder us for having a conversation."

"I'm so frightened," the girl admitted.

"I'm frightened, too," Rachel told her. "We all are."

Mary's eyes widened in surprise. "But you seem so calm."

Rachel gave the girl a tight little smile and went on fastening her bodice.

Mary looked around furtively, then she leaned forward a little and whispered, "The tall one, the one with the blue eyes. He gave me the clothes."

Rachel looked for him in the group Mary had indicated, but he was not there. As she glanced away, she saw him standing apart from the other savages with his arms folded across his chest. His blue gaze was fixed coldly on her. Ducking her head to avoid those eyes, she fussed with her skirt. A hot-cold feeling had swept through her at sight of him. She did not like the feeling, nor the confusion in her head that it caused.

Mary held out a pair of woolen stockings. "He said to give you these, too."

Rachel took them and sat down on the log to put them on. Several questions sped through her mind as she pulled a stocking over her frozen toes. Why had the blue-eyed savage given her the warm clothes? Why had he taken the time to gather her warmest things? What did he want from her besides her obvious use as a captive? She asked aloud the one question that Mary could answer. "Did he speak English to you, Mary?"

Mary shook her head. "No, he told that man with the funny hat what to say to me." She paused a moment, thinking. "He's scary. You know, more than the other savages."

Rachel had finished with one stocking and shoe. She glanced up at the girl and gave her a weak smile. "I know."

An Indian came over then and spoke angrily to Mary.

Roughly, he pushed her away from Rachel. Rachel watched helplessly as the girl was herded to the far side of the clearing and forced to sit down on the snow. The other captives, men, women, and children, were spaced about the clearing singly or in small groups of two or three. There were not many of them. In fact, Rachel realized that there were not many attackers, either.

As she wondered about the small numbers, an order was given, and the captives were rousted from their rest and moved off through the woods. The Indian who had chased her through the house, the one whose face had been painted black and yellow, walked behind her. The blue-eyed demon was not in sight.

As she plodded along, Rachel wondered about the generosity of her captor. She would not call her gift of warm clothing a kindness. She did not believe he could be kind. Those eyes belied any speck of softness in the man. He was heartless and cruel and cunning. That was it. It was only cunning and greed that prompted him to give her the warm clothes. He would have no hostage to turn over to the French if she froze to death on the journey to wherever they were going.

They moved through the forest quietly. Several of the women sobbed, and the few children that were in the group either cried or had been shocked into silence. They were not allowed to speak to each other, and they were separated by the Indians. Before her, Rachel had a young brave who swaggered along proudly; behind her, she felt the overbearing, menacing presence of the dark-eyed savage.

They followed some invisible path among the trees. Unerringly, they travelled north. Rachel knew that much from the position of the sun and from watching the moss on the trees. She had been taught that moss always grew on the north side of tree trunks. It was a piece of information that she had learned from her father upon moving to Deerfield, in case she ever became lost in the woods. Now, it was no longer a mere curiosity, but a vital indication that told her in what direction their fate and final destination lay.

They were a strange, pathetic group. The Indians moved along almost silently in their high moccasins; the few soldiers with them were a bit noisier about trudging through the snow; the captives grunted and panted and cried as they slogged along. After almost an hour, they came out upon an open space at the foot of a tall hill. A group of captors and hostages was already there. Rachel assumed that the attackers had split up upon leaving the village, and this was their gathering spot. They were made to sit as before, singly or in groups of two or three. Rachel saw many of her neighbors in the group. Among them was the Reverend John Williams and his wife, Eunice, newly delivered of a child only a week before. The woman rested heavily against her husband. Her face was pale and drawn from weakness and exhaustion. Several of the smaller children huddled against the adults and slept. Rachel was made to sit alone.

Pulling her cloak about her, she leaned against the trunk of a tree and clutched her knees to her chest. The cold wind traced her bare cheek with its icy hand. Shivering, she hunkered down further into her cloak. It had been a hard winter. The snows had been fierce and long. Today was the last day of February, and there was no sign that spring would be coming in a few weeks. Rachel listened to the wind as it moaned through the trees. The sound carried a desolate message of despair. Fighting back tears, she forced herself not to dwell on her misery.

She should be giving thanks, she told herself, that her father had died before the Indians had swept through their village. There were many others who were grieving also, who had lost husbands or wives or children in the massacre. Closing her eyes, she dropped her head to her knees. She was so tired.

Sensing the approach of someone, her head jerked up. The dark-eyed Indian, the one whose face was painted half black, half yellow, stood above her. His eyes gleamed viciously. Reaching out, he grabbed a handful of her hair. Rachel flinched away from him, but his grip prevented her from moving. She watched his expression become fascinated as he felt her hair between his fingers. He bent down and sniffed it. Rachel did not dare breathe, much less move. It was all she could do to keep from screaming hysterically. Terrified, she watched him unsheathe his hunting knife.

An angry voice interrupted whatever the savage had meant to do. Straightening, he stared at the blue-eyed Indian who stood several feet away. He snarled something, but he still did not release his grip on Rachel's hair. Short furious words were exchanged between the two men. In one quick motion, the dark-eyed Indian turned and sliced off a lock of Rachel's hair. Holding it triumphantly up before the blue-eyed savage, he gave a short bark of laughter then stalked away.

With a gasp, Rachel's hand flew to her head where the short strands fluttered in the cold breeze. Then she looked up at her blue-eyed monster. His face, as always, was hard. He returned her look, then swung about and left. She watched the fluid grace of him as he moved away. Something close to gratitude rose up in her. She thought, perhaps he had saved her from being scalped.

The Frenchman who had translated for her before had been standing not far away and had seen everything. He moved a few steps closer and crouched beside her. For some reason, Rachel's hatred of the French did not extend to him. She sensed he was innately kind.

"You are very lucky, *mademoiselle*," he observed. "You have caught zhe eye of two of zhe most powerful redmen wizs us."

Rachel made a face of disgust. "I wish they would just leave me alone."

"*Non, non, mademoiselle,* do not say zhat. Zhey will keep you alive on zhe journey. It will be very long and very hard."

"Where are we going?"

The Frenchman looked at her a moment before replying. Finally, he said shortly, "Mont Réal."

Rachel's mouth dropped open. "But that is hundreds of miles from here!"

"Shush. Not so loud. You are not supposed to know zhat yet." He grinned and exposed a gap on the right side of his smile. "You see? You have even brought me under your spell."

Beneath the man's rough charm, Rachel was forced to smile back. "Why are we going to Montreal?" She used the English pronunciation of the name of the French settlement on the St. Lawrence River.

"Because zhat is where zhese French soldiers wish to take you. And zhat is where zhese Indians will get rewards for zhe prisoners." He shrugged. "Zhat is all I know, *mademoiselle*."

Rachel allowed that information to sink in a bit. Now she knew the reason for the attack on Deerfield. Perhaps, if she survived the trip, she would be able to exact her own bit of revenge. "Will you be going to Montreal with us?"

The man shrugged again. "Perhaps, perhaps not. I do not come to fight, only to translate and track. I do not like zhis fighting. I am *le coureur de bois*. I hunt and trap zhe animals for zheir furs." He winked at her. "But wisz you on zhe journey, maybe I go all zhe way to Mont Réal, eh?"

In spite of the man's obvious flirting, Rachel was not afraid of him. On the contrary, she found his presence comforting in an odd sort of way. Perhaps it was because he was the only one of the attackers who seemed to have any decency about him.

She smiled at him. "If you are going to be on the journey for that long, perhaps I should know your name, sir."

"Ah, forgive my manners, *mademoiselle*. I have been too long in zhe woods. I am Claude Donat, at your service. And you, *mademoiselle*. Who is it who honors me wizs her conversation?"

"Rachel Linton."

"Ah, Rachel. A wonderful name."

At that moment, the prisoners at the opposite end of the clearing were being roused from their rest and herded together. Rachel saw the blue-eyed savage bearing down on her.

"I zhink we are moving out, *mademoiselle*. I must leave your charming company," Claude told her as he got to his feet. "Your master would not like me talking to you."

The cold look in the blue-eyed monster's eyes pinned Rachel where she sat. When he stood before her, she could only stare up at him. A mysterious force seemed to emanate from him. It reached out and played along

27

her nerve endings. He spoke sharply and motioned with his hand for Rachel to get up. Slowly, she rose to her feet. Tilting up her chin in defiance, she met his icy gaze. Without taking his eyes from her, he spoke to Claude in his Indian language.

Nervously, Claude cleared his throat. *"Mademoiselle* Rachel, he says zhat you are not to try to escape. If you do, he will track you until he finds you. Zhen he will give you to his friend."

Rachel paled at the threat of being handed over to the dark-eyed savage, but she did not lower her gaze. "Tell him, *Monsieur* Donat, that I will not try to escape. He has destroyed everything that I would escape back to."

Claude translated, but even before he finished, Rachel saw a tightening around the Indian's mouth. Could this man understand what she was saying?

With a jerk of his head, he indicated that the Frenchman was to leave them, then he held something out to her. Rachel looked down at the odd things in his hand. They were flat, oval frames, about the size of a large meat platter, with an open weave of twisted hemp within the curve of wood. Puzzled, Rachel glanced up at him. He pushed them closer to her, obviously wanting her to take them. Glancing past him, she noticed the other captives strapping these odd contraptions to their feet.

Rachel took them and placed them on the ground, then she placed one foot in the center of one of them. The blue-eyed demon crouched before her and tied the frame to her shoe with strips of rawhide. When she placed her other foot on the second frame, he tied that one, also. The nearness of him, the sight of him crouched before her, the soft touch of his fingers on her feet, did strange things to her breathing. Only when he

28

stood once more before her was she able to take a deep breath.

Surprisingly, with these things strapped to her feet, she did not sink into the snow. In amazement, she looked up at him.

"Thank you," she said.

He grunted at her words, then with a last narrowing of his gaze, the Indian turned on his heel and stalked off. Rachel watched him go with great relief. Why, she asked herself, was she so unfortunate as to have this cold-eyed demon as her captor? Why had he chosen her to torment? As she was herded together with the other prisoners, she put him out of her mind. She could not worry about herself. There were other friends and neighbors who could use her help on this long journey ahead.

The clearing where they had gathered was on higher ground than the village. When Rachel stood up, she could see fires still burning in some of the homes. A few tiny specks that must have been villagers who had escaped the attack moved about the flames. With a silent farewell to her father who was lying in the small cemetery, she moved off with the other prisoners as they began the long trek into New France.

The thought of ending up in French territory sent a surge of emotions racing through her. Since the death of her mother, she had dreamed of invading the land of her enemy. Her father had cautioned her against such hatred, saying that it did no good and only brought anguish to the person who hated. Even though she would enter New France as a prisoner, the thought of being that close to the root of her feelings made the blood run quicker through her veins in exultation. Once in Montreal, she would find a way to throw off her bondage and seek her revenge. There was no doubt in her mind about her surviving the journey. She knew she would.

Rachel found herself walking beside Prudence Whitson, the girl whose wedding gown Rachel had been sewing. Prudence was a few years younger than she and had been planning to marry a young man from Hatfield at the end of April. Rachel and she had never really been friends, although in such a small town as Deerfield, it was hard not to be constantly thrown together at social activities. Prudence was the envy of every girl of marriageable age in the village and for miles around. Her thick golden hair curled charmingly about her heart-shaped face, and her pale blue eyes were surrounded by a heavy fringe of lashes. She never failed to use those eyes to her advantage to get exactly what she wanted. As a result, Rachel thought of her as vain and spoiled. Next to her petite frame, Rachel felt like a giant.

"Oh, Rachel," Prudence sniffed now. "I am so glad you're here. I just don't know what I'm going to do. I'm so frightened."

Rachel told her the same thing she had said to Mary. "We're all frightened, Prudence."

"I know, I know, but I lost my beautiful wedding gown that you were helping mother make for me. I saw some savage tearing it to pieces. And I so wanted to show it to Aldridge when he came to visit me next week. I'm so worried about him. He will be so upset when he discovers what happened to me. Do you think he'll come after us? Maybe he'll rescue me."

Rachel hid a smile. Aldridge was Prudence's betrothed. The girl believed he could do almost anything, including rescue her single-handedly from the three hundred or so Indians and French soldiers who had captured them. Aldridge was a big, muscular young man, but Rachel doubted even he would be foolhardy enough to try to fight so many of the enemy.

"He might try, but I don't think he'll have much success," Rachel said. "It will be difficult for anyone to follow our tracks. Did you see what the Indians did when we left the clearing?"

Prudence looked at Rachel with her big, blue, innocent eyes. "No, what did they do?"

"They took branches and swept the whole area, any place where someone had walked, and then they swept behind us on the trail. There aren't many men who can track an Indian, let alone one that covers his trail."

"Oh, Rachel," Prudence sighed in despair. "You're so practical. Mother always said that was your best feature. She always said that it should have been enough to lure some young man to ask for your hand despite your being so tall and that awful dark red hair. Mother always said that good looks hooked a man and practicality reeled him in. At least you have the practicality."

Rachel ground her teeth in exasperation. Prudence had developed little of the quality that her name implied.

The girl was oblivious to Rachel's feelings as she tried to smooth her disheveled hair. "I must look a fright. How can I possibly travel through the wilderness in these clothes? Why, those savages did not even give me time to bring along a brush! What will Aldridge think when he sees me? I don't think I'll ever see him again." She began to sob quietly.

Rachel tried to ignore the sniveling that was going on beside her. Actually, Prudence's comments had started Rachel's mind down a path she purposely tried to avoid.

She knew she had been the subject of gossip for the past year or so. Being twenty-two years of age and still unmarried with no likely prospects was enough to cause speculation among the matrons of the village. No young man in the area was comfortable enough with a woman who towered over him, and who could outrun him, outshoot him and out-think him, to ask for her hand in marriage.

Having no mother and a father who was slowly dying had brought out the pity for Rachel in just about all the villagers, but not enough to encourage their sons to marry her. Her father had been too ill to arrange a match for her, and she had been too involved in caring for him to bother to look for a husband.

She was almost too old to be included in a gathering of the younger, single people, and she was too young to be included in the older married group. At the moment, she was a social misfit. The raid, as horrifying and tragic as it had been, could not have come at a better time in her life.

Prudence stumbled on her clumsy snowshoes, and Rachel reached out to steady her. The line of captors and hostages came to a halt ahead of them. Several Indians moved along the line, picking out children and shoving them into the arms of the nearest adult. Some of the children were almost too big to be carried, but it was obvious they were tired and had been slowing the progress of the group. The adults themselves were suffering from shock and were near exhaustion, and Rachel wondered how the Indians expected them to move any more quickly carrying the burden of a large child.

The dark-eyed savage who had snipped Rachel's hair approached them with little three-year-old Elspeth Brodie in his arms. Rachel had not seen Elspeth's parents since she had been dragged through the village. She wondered what had happened to them. The savage held Elspeth out to Prudence, who took the child fearfully. His eyes raked coldly over Rachel's face, then he moved down the line. Prudence hefted Elspeth, who was just about asleep.

"Why in the world did he give this child to me?" Prudence complained. "I can barely walk myself. My feet are cold and wet and my dress is soaked at the hem. These stupid Indian shoes keep getting in the way. How am I going to keep from tripping if I have a child in my arms?" She plunked the little girl back onto her own feet. "Here, you walk beside me, Elspeth, and I'll hold your hand." Elspeth started to cry. "Oh, for heaven's sake!" Prudence wailed.

With a swift glare of anger at Prudence, Rachel reached around her and swept Elspeth up into her arms. Pulling her cloak around the little girl, she soothed, "It's all right, Elspeth. I'll carry you. You put your arms around my neck, and we'll keep each other warm."

The dark-eyed savage had begun to make his way back up the line from the rear. When he reached Rachel and Prudence, he stopped. He stared meaningfully at Prudence, then at little Elspeth in Rachel's arms, then back at Prudence. He stalked away, but returned after only a few minutes. Dropping a large, deerskin pack at her feet, he said something and pointed at the pack. Prudence looked questioningly at Rachel for help.

"I think he wants you to pick it up and carry it," Rachel told her.

"What does he think I am, a beast of burden?" Prudence exclaimed.

"Prudence, pick it up," Rachel said between clenched teeth. "Do you want to get us killed?"

With a vexed groan, Prudence bent down and lifted the pack. She immediately let it drop again. "I can't lift it. It's too heavy."

The Indian uttered several angry words.

"Prudence, I think you'd better try," Rachel warned her.

With a look of utter dislike at Rachel, Prudence lifted the pack. She moaned as she clamped her arms around it. The Indian gave a grunt of satisfaction, then moved away.

"I'm going to have Aldridge beat him to a pulp when he rescues me," Prudence panted under her load. "Imagine, having me carry this heavy bundle!"

Rachel remained silent, repressing the urge to shake the girl until her teeth rattled. As the line began to move again, she glanced to her left. Several feet back from the trail, the blue-eyed savage stood with his arms crossed at his chest. His look was inscrutable as he watched Rachel trudge past. She wondered how much of the little scene between Prudence and the dark-eyed savage he had seen.

Late that afternoon, the captors called a halt to the march. The hostages were all exhausted, and most were barely able to stand. It had been a terrifying, gruelling day. The spot where they had stopped was devoid of trees, and appeared to be the flood plain of some river or other. Rachel guessed that since they had been travelling north, they must have been loosely following the Connecticut River which flowed down from the north. She wondered if they were anywhere near Greenfield, a village about five miles north of Deerfield. The thought of escape slipped enticingly through her head.

Before she could give the idea any concrete planning, she, along with Prudence and the other women and children, were herded together. They were made to sit on the snow, and guards ringed them about. Actually, she was grateful for the enforced rest. She had carried Elspeth just about all afternoon. Although the little girl did not weigh much, her arms felt leaden.

The men were marched off back towards the forest under the watchful eyes of many Indians. Many of the women whose husbands or sons were in the group cried out. They were sure the men were about to be massacred. After several minutes, the Indian and French guards brought the women under control after conveying the message through sign language and the interpretation of Claude Donat that the men had only gone to cut tree boughs for beds.

Rachel glanced about for her blue-eyed captor. She had not seen him since that incident with Prudence and Elspeth and the dark-eyed savage. She told herself she just wanted to be sure she knew where he was so that he would not sneak up on her and do something awful to her. Yet, she could not deny the twinge of disappointment that ran through her when she did not see him. It was relief, she tried to convince herself. Why ever would she be disappointed that a savage was not about to watch her every move with those monstrous blue eyes?

# Chapter Three

As darkness fell, small fires were lit by the Indians and the French soldiers. The captives huddled miserably beside the warmth of the flames in little groups. Rachel sat on a pile of pine boughs and stared into the fire near her. Absently, she rubbed her shins to ease the ache in them caused by wearing the awkward, uncomfortable snowshoes — what Prudence had referred to as Indian shoes. Beside her, Elspeth slept the deep sleep of an exhausted child. Rachel still had not seen the little girl's parents. She tried not to speculate about their fate.

The hostages had eaten sparingly, for the captors wanted to ration their supplies for the long trek back into New France. Rachel's stomach growled emptily. She had been given a piece of hard bread and salted beef for her meal, but had not had the strength to eat. When Prudence had eyed the food hungrily, she had given it to the girl who had wolfed it down. Rachel was amused at the unladylike manners that the girl was suddenly displaying. After finishing every crumb, Prudence had curled up and gone to sleep several feet away. She had not even complained about not being able to indulge in her evening toilette before she had curled up on her pile of boughs.

A figure approached Rachel and broke into her reverie. She recognized the bulky form of Claude Donat. As he came closer, the murmur of several men captives not too far away suddenly ceased. Rachel had the impression that they had been plotting some sort of escape.

As Claude crouched beside her, a shadowy form emerged from the darkness, a very familiar form. Rachel and the Frenchman watched as the blue-eyed savage forced the whispering men apart. His movements were not cruel, only firm with authority. He placed each of the men with a group of women guarded by one of the French soldiers. One man, he left where he was, by himself. He bound the man's wrists and ankles, then left him alone and melted back into the shadows.

Claude Donat whistled softly between his teeth. "He is a smart one, zhat."

With her eyes, Rachel probed the darkness beyond the firelight where the savage had gone. "What do you know about him, *Monsieur* Donat?"

"Please, *Mademoiselle* Rachel, you must call me Claude. Zhe journey is too long for formalities."

Rachel grinned at him. "All right. Claude. What do you know of the blue-eyed savage?"

Claude shrugged. "I do not know much, *mademoiselle*. He does not talk much to Claude. He does not talk much to anyone. He is dangerous when he is angry, and even when he is not. Zhey say he can hit a buck wizh an arrow from a mile away. He can run as fast as zhe deer and stalk like zhe mountain lion. He has killed a bear wizh only zhe tomahawk. I, Claude Donat, have seen zhis wizh my own eyes. His proof is zhe necklace of bear claws he wears. Zhey say he has killed a hundred men. He is a crazy man."

"But he saved me from being scalped by that other savage," Rachel pointed out. "Surely he can't be all bad."

Claude grinned at her from the tangle of his beard. "You are his hostage, *mademoiselle*. You are Dark Eagle's hostage, too. Zhey want you alive."

"Then why did Dark Eagle want to scalp me?"

"He did not. He wanted your hair. He zhinks it is strong medicine."

Rachel put a hand up to the short hairs that now fell across her forehead. "Why would my hair be strong medicine? It's just like everyone else's."

*"Non, non, mademoiselle,"* Claude chuckled. "Not like everyone else's. It carries zhe fire, but is not hot. It is dark and bright all at once. Zhese Indians have never seen anyzhing like it."

Puzzled, Rachel frowned. She had never considered her dark auburn hair anything unusual. In fact, she thought it was a great hindrance. It was too thick and heavy and therefore not easily kept neatly in the bun that she put it in every morning. Dark hair was definitely unfashionable. All the women said so. Yet, here was some savage who thought her hair was some sort of magic talisman. What, she wondered, did the blue-eyed devil think of it?

As if her thoughts had conjured him up, he suddenly appeared before her. Claude rose to his feet. A short conversation ensued that Rachel did not understand. At the end of it, Claude moved away several feet and settled on a pile of boughs.

The blue-eyed savage crouched before her. Taking her cold hands in one of his warm ones, he bound her wrists together with a strip of rawhide. When he had finished, he did the same to her ankles. Rachel craved the warmth that emanated from him. He seemed to have retracted the icy armor that he had kept around him all day. A gentleness pervaded his motions as he attended to his loathsome task.

Tears burned the backs of Rachel's eyes at the glimpse she had of a strange compassion in him. The desire to cuddle next to him almost overwhelmed her. With an effort, she forced herself to be realistic. This man was her captor. He could do as he wished with her. After what Claude had told her, she knew him to be a violent man. She had no reason to think he would show her any mercy or kindness.

Gently, he pushed her down sideways onto the bed of boughs. Picking up Elspeth, without waking her, he laid her against Rachel. They could keep each other warm in the coming night. Shaking out a deerskin that he had with him, he laid it over them both. He straightened quickly and disappeared once again into the shadows.

For a few bemused moments, Rachel lay quietly. Then, in a whisper, she said, "Claude, what is his name?"

"He is called White Wolf, *mademoiselle*."

The man called White Wolf stood with his feet planted apart and his arms crossed at his chest. His gaze lifted above the dark forms of the sleeping hostages and their captors spread out before him. The sky was beginning to pale in the east. Soon, it would be time to roust his friends and their captives from their sleep. But for now, he cherished the solitude of the last watch of the night.

39

Across the dark shapes of sleeping bodies, he could see Dark Eagle crouched on his haunches. He was motionless, just as White Wolf was. A predawn breeze fluttered the lock of hair he had snipped from the woman. It hung from the end of the bow he had slung across his shoulder.

White Wolf knew that the eyes of Dark Eagle had strayed often to where he stood during the watch, just as his own eyes had sought out the figure of his brother. They were not brothers in the sense that they came from the same mother and father, but they had sworn an oath in blood to each other when they had been children. How long ago that seemed now. Regret at what had come between them welled up in White Wolf's chest. That rift would never be healed.

An owl glided past silently above his head. It would be dawn soon. Then they would begin the journey home in earnest. He wondered how the woman would fare on the march, if she would be able to cope with the hardships. His eyes searched out her sleeping form. She seemed strong enough, and certainly showed courage. Satisfaction seeped through him at his good fortune. When he had set out on this journey, he had not the least idea that such a woman would be waiting to be taken.

He saw her move beneath the deerskin he had placed over her and the little one, and a frown creased his smooth brow. Why had he bothered to cover her? he wondered to himself. Did she have some strange power that forced him to protect her? No. It was because of the little one. She had been brave during this ordeal. Such bravery in such a young one deserved respect. Yet, there was something about the woman, some force that drew him to her.

He brought a picture of her to mind, of her standing defiant before him as he dragged her towards the river. She was taller than most white women, and not as fleshy. Yet, she curved pleasantly in all the right places. Her skin, when he had touched it to bind her, was smooth and soft. It had taken a great deal of restraint for him not to run his hands up her arms and legs to feel more. Her eyes were the color of the blue spruce, and he thought perhaps they had the ability to change shade depending on her mood. And her hair, her most glorious feature. It hung, thick and heavy, well past her waist. Dark in the shadows, an inner flame kindled within it when the light touched it.

He felt a stirring between his thighs and frowned to himself. It had not been his purpose to come all this way to have a woman entice him, especially not this woman. This woman was with him for a different reason.

Across the humps of bodies, he saw Dark Eagle stand. It was time to waken the others. The gaze of the two men locked. This woman who had invaded his serenity would become another wedge in the rift between himself and Dark Eagle. If he had known that, he would have left her in the village. As he moved to waken the French leader, he realized he was lying to himself. He would never have left this woman behind.

The French commander, Hertel de Rouville, came awake the instant that White Wolf shook his foot. He was a good soldier, this Frenchman, and a good leader. Sitting up, he rubbed the sleep from his eyes with the heels of his hands.

"Morning already, eh, White Wolf?" he remarked in his native French. He glanced up at the brightening sky. "Looks like some bad weather coming in. Maybe it will

41

hold off till nightfall. I want to put some distance between us and that village today. I don't want any Englishmen tracking us."

"No English will track us," White Wolf commented flatly in the Frenchman's tongue.

At that moment, a disturbance erupted at the other end of the camp where Dark Eagle had been waking the others. Glancing up, White Wolf watched as his brother wrestled one of the French soldiers to the ground. They rolled over several times before Dark Eagle overpowered him. Straddling him, the redman raised his tomahawk, prepared to smash the soldier's head. White Wolf gave a shout and hurried to the spot.

"My brother, what has this man done, who calls himself friend?" he asked in the language of his mother's people.

Without taking his eyes from the Frenchman beneath him, Dark Eagle growled, "He is no friend. He has allowed a captive to escape."

"How do you know he allowed it? Perhaps it was one of the others who was on watch."

"The captive was in his area. It did not happen while you and I were on watch, did it, brother?" Dark Eagle glanced meaningfully up at White Wolf.

White Wolf looked down at the trembling white man. His eyes bulged and droplets of sweat beaded his forehead and upper lip. Even if the escape had happened during the man's watch, they could not afford to fight among themselves. There were too many captives to control.

White Wolf shrugged. "Perhaps it did happen while you and I watched. It does not matter. The man is gone and on his way to find his friends. We have to move swiftly, before he returns with them to attack us."

Dark Eagle's eyes narrowed angrily as he looked up at his brother. He stared at him a moment, then turned back to the white man. "You will regret your mistake," he snarled. Although the white man could not understand his words, it was evident he did not miss their meaning. Dark Eagle's tomahawk chopped down into the snow beside the man's head.

White Wolf saw the tomahawk bury itself in the snow up to Dark Eagle's wrist. If it had hit the man, his head would now be lying in two cleanly split pieces. Dark Eagle climbed off the man and stalked away. White Wolf knew that his brother would not forget this incident. With an inward sigh, he went to untie the woman.

As he approached, he saw her eyes were open and watching him. She nudged the little one sleeping against her and spoke quietly to her. Yawning deeply, the little girl sat up. When she saw White Wolf, she scrambled over the woman to put her body between herself and White Wolf. The woman struggled to a sitting position and spoke soothingly to her.

White Wolf crouched before the woman and untied her wrists. Her hands had swollen during the night from being bound. He heard the woman's quick intake of breath as the blood painfully surged back into her hands. Taking first one hand, then the other, he firmly massaged them until the initial pain passed. He sensed her perplexity at his actions, but she said nothing and allowed him to do as he wished. He repeated the process with her feet after untying her ankles.

When he had finished, he glanced up and met her gaze. Her eyes betrayed her open emotions—her fear, her gratitude, her want. He surmised that she did not even realize she was showing him her inner thoughts. The need to touch her flashed through him, but he suppressed it immediately. He had not brought her for that. Angry with himself for allowing such weakness, he stood up swiftly. He saw the hurt which came to the woman's eyes and which she quickly hid. It pleased him that he should affect her so, yet, at the same time, he wanted to make the hurt go away. This was not good, he thought. He had to get away from this woman. Motioning for her to get up, he turned quickly and moved away.

Rachel watched White Wolf stalk away from her. His bearing, even in the snow, was tall and proud. He moved lightly, like some sort of cat. She had never seen a man walk with such grace. Most of the men she knew plodded along as if it was an effort to put one foot before the other.

She wondered why he had suddenly looked so angry. Certainly, she had done nothing to cause his mood. Well, she was not going to allow the tantrums of some savage to bother her. If he wanted to get angry over absolutely nothing, it was none of her affair. Her problem was just trying to stay alive.

Stiffly, she struggled to her feet. After taking a few experimental, hobbling steps around the pile of boughs where she had slept, she discovered the pain in her feet was slowly fading. She glanced up and across the milling captives to where White Wolf was speaking with the French commander. Still, she would like to know what had caused his anger.

After only a short time, just long enough for the captives to awaken and gather themselves, they started out on their march once again. Rachel held little Elspeth by the hand. She had promised the little girl that she would carry her later on. She could see Prudence up ahead. Once again, she struggled with the large deerskin pack. Although Rachel felt sorry for the girl, she also had to chuckle. Dark Eagle had discovered the perfect punishment for Prudence's disobedience of the day before.

Behind Rachel were Reverend Williams and his wife, Eunice. Eunice did not look well at all. Her face was deathly pale, and she leaned heavily against her husband. Each step for her appeared to be a struggle. Even after a night's sleep, she seemed exhausted.

When Rachel offered to help support her, the Indian walking near them made it quite clear he did not want that. Helplessly, Rachel listened to them labor along. Finally, she could not stand it any longer. Moving in beside Eunice, she slipped under her arm and supported her about the waist. Elspeth clung to Rachel's skirt. The Indian once again motioned vehemently that she was not to help. This time, Rachel was not about to let him bully her.

"I am going to help this woman whether you like it or not," she told the savage firmly. She did not care if he understood her, or even if he beat her.

As the Indian began to move angrily towards her, a deep voice from behind her stopped him. Glancing back, she saw White Wolf. Had he been there all along? she wondered. The two Indians held a short conversation in their own language. At the end of it, the savage who did not want her helping Eunice lapsed into sullen silence.

She took a quick peek at White Wolf. His face was expressionless, but she felt that he was somehow amused. She could not imagine what he would find amusing in such a terrible situation. His reaction, or what she perceived to be his reaction, only confirmed her idea that he was truly a savage. Why she had found him at all attractive was a mystery. How could she have been drawn to such a being?

The pace that the captors set that morning was gruelling. The word had travelled down the line of hostages that anyone who dallied behind would be left. It went unsaid, but they all knew that no one would be left behind still alive. The implication spurred them on.

Rachel had deduced the reasons for the urgency. She was sure the French commander wanted to put as much distance as he could between themselves and Deerfield and any rescuers. Also, the sky was heavily overcast. A storm was coming. They had to find some sort of shelter that they could use for a period of time in case the storm lasted more than a few hours.

It was midday when they were finally allowed to rest and have something to eat. Rachel watched Reverend Williams speaking to the French commander as she gnawed on a chunk of stale bread. Finally, the reverend motioned for his flock to gather about him. He said a few inspiring words and a short prayer, then one of the Indians made him sit down.

Rachel was next to two of the men from the village, Enoch Cooper and Israel Putnam. Enoch was a middle-aged widower whose children were grown and off on their own; Israel was a younger man who had wed only the year before. The young woman had been spared the horror of the attack because she had been visiting her sick mother in Greenfield. As soon as Reverend Williams finished speaking, Israel and Enoch began a quiet conversation. Being so near, Rachel listened.

"Do you think Jackson made it to Greenfield?" Enoch Cooper asked.

"Don't know," Israel Putnam answered. "I sure hope so."

"I think someone else should try. We can't be certain about Jackson."

"You can't try to escape," Rachel quietly exclaimed. "Didn't you hear the warning the savages gave to Reverend Williams? If anyone else escapes, we will all be burned!"

The two men looked at each other, then back at Rachel.

"They don't mean that," Enoch said. "If they did, they wouldn't have any hostages left to sell to the French."

"They don't need hostages, Enoch," Israel told him. "They can take our scalps. Maybe Rachel is right. Maybe we shouldn't try another escape."

"Hmph. So what are we going to do? Follow these savages like lambs to the slaughter? Who knows what they mean to do to us between here and New France? Don't you want to get back to that young wife of yours?" Enoch turned his calculating gaze back to Rachel. "Two of them seem taken with you. They're always having words over you. Maybe you can get them to fight over you, create a disturbance. Then one of us can slip away."

Rachel frowned. "I don't —"

Her words were cut off by the sudden appearance of Dark Eagle. He motioned for her to get up. When she did not move fast enough to suit him, he grabbed her hair and dragged her to her feet. Tears sprang to her eyes at the pain. With angry words and motions, he ordered her away from the rest of the villagers. Glancing back at Enoch and Israel, she saw Enoch nod at her with

47

encouragement. Quickly, she looked away. Didn't he realize what a dangerous thing he was asking her to do? she wondered. What if something went wrong? What if the two savages fought to the death? What if Dark Eagle won the fight? A shiver ran down her spine. She did not want to contemplate her fate if she was left with Dark Eagle as her only captor.

The savage pulled her to a spot away from the others and forced her to sit. Squatting beside her, he took a handful of her hair and began to examine it. He turned it this way and that, watching how the light changed its color; he felt it between his fingers and weighed it in his hand; he sniffed it.

Rachel did not know whether to be frightened or to laugh. Finally, she decided she was just annoyed with the Indian's strange antics. Reaching up, she started to pull her hair away. With a growl, Dark Eagle closed his fist about the hank of hair he held and yanked it, making her head snap back on her neck. He raised his tomahawk and held it before her eyes.

Rachel stared up at him and swallowed. "Please, don't hurt me," she pleaded. "You can look at my hair all you want."

At that moment, a call to start moving again came from the French commander. Dark Eagle ignored it. The thought ran through Rachel's head that this was the end. This would be where she would end her life, on some cold, snowy trail in the middle of nowhere. Out of the corner of her eye, she saw the others moving away.

It seemed she and Dark Eagle remained frozen in one position for a long time, but it was really only a minute or two. Without letting go of her hair, Dark Eagle stood and pulled her up. He motioned for her to start walking.

It was difficult for Rachel to move with his hand twisted in her hair. She stumbled along as best she could. After they had travelled for quite some time, White Wolf appeared beside them. A heated discussion sprang up between the two Indians. Even though Rachel did not understand their words, she knew they argued about her. Each time Dark Eagle gestured, Rachel's head was jerked painfully on her neck. Finally, with a violent shove, he sent her flying to land face down in the snow.

White Wolf and Dark Eagle stopped and waited for the woman to regain her footing. They watched her struggle to her feet. White Wolf saw the glint of hatred in her eyes as she stood before them.

"She may come and kill you as you sleep one night, brother," he observed to Dark Eagle in the language of their mothers.

"I will kill her first," Dark Eagle replied. "I want her scalp. It is strong medicine."

"No. I want her alive. I will have my revenge."

Dark Eagle spat. "It is always what you want, what you need. What of the needs of the People? Do you forget she killed Deer Stalker? The woman is my captive, too."

"I know she killed your mother's son. She must be punished for that, but she is brave and a worthy enemy. What good will she do us if she is dead? Will the English want her back then? No. She is to be kept alive."

"One day, my brother, you will discover that you do not have the wisdom of the Great Spirit." Dark Eagle spat again, and with a baleful look, moved off.

White Wolf watched him go, then turned his attention back to the woman. She stood, unmoving, waiting. Her eyes held no fear, only defiance. Such spirit this woman

49

had! He wondered fleetingly what it would be like to have this woman lie beside him in passion. With a silent rebuke at himself, he angrily motioned her to follow the others.

# Chapter Four

Rachel trudged along through the snow. She could hear the soft muffled movement of White Wolf behind her. Except for a few Indians who watched the rear of their group, they were the last in line. Elspeth had been given into the care of one of the other women. Dark Eagle was beyond her line of sight.

This last incident with Dark Eagle had both terrified her and enraged her. What right did these Frenchmen and Indians have to swoop down out of the north, to invade their village and take them captive? Yet, here they were, being herded along like sheep. The only one who had shown any courage had been Douglas Jackson, the man who had escaped. She thought about the plan of Enoch Cooper and Israel Putnam. It did not seem so ridiculous now.

A bramble bush caught her skirt. White Wolf came forward, and without giving her a chance to untangle it, ripped it from the thorns. The bottom of one side now hung in shreds. Rachel was furious.

Turning on him, she yelled, "Why did you do that? I could have untangled it without ripping it! This is the only skirt I have! You stupid lout!" Lunging at him, she began to pound on his chest with her fists. "I'm going to pay you back for what you did! One day, I'm going to kill you!"

White Wolf grabbed her arms and held her away. Shaking her, he spoke one fierce word, one that Rachel did not understand but that clearly conveyed his meaning. Rachel's anger dissolved into tears of frustration and exhaustion, but they lasted only a moment. Sniffling, lifting her chin, she stared directly into those cold, blue eyes. Her resolve hardened. Soon, she would find a way to help Enoch and Israel, even if it meant spending the rest of her life with this blue-eyed monster, or worse. Jerking out of his grasp, she turned and followed the line of the other unfortunates as they wound their way through the wilderness.

The rest of the afternoon, Rachel mulled over different ways she could create a disturbance and attract everyone's attention while either Enoch or Israel escaped. Nothing she could devise seemed sufficiently troublesome enough to make everyone, French and Indians alike, pay heed. If one of the villagers acted up, his or her captor would handle the discipline. No one else took any notice.

By the time they stopped for the night, she still had not decided on a plan, but she knew she had to do something that night or not at all. If she were to wait another day, they would be too far into the wilderness for either man to find his way to civilization and help. She told Israel that she had decided to help him, then she went to sit on her pile of pine boughs.

This night, they were camped in the clearing of a forest at the foot of a mountain. Outside the light of the fires, the trees and blackness closed in. It had begun to snow lightly late that afternoon. Rachel knew that before morning everything and everyone would be covered in a blanket of white. The Indians had shown the villagers how to build tiny shelters using evergreen branches, but these were for sleeping. The captives huddled together about the fires for warmth and companionship; even the Indians sat together in a few large groups.

Across the clearing, she saw White Wolf and Dark Eagle. Their faces were bronzed by the light of the fire. Before she could think about what she was about to do, she stood and began to move towards them. She could feel eyes watching her as she progressed closer to her captors.

When she passed Reverend Williams, he called out to her. "Rachel, where are you going?"

She stopped, but did not look at him.

"Rachel?" His voice was heavy with concern.

Before she moved away, she turned and gave him a tremulous smile. "It's all right, reverend. Don't worry."

"God go with you, my child," he replied. She realized he suspected what she was about to do.

There was a small opening in the circle of redmen around the fire, and she stepped through it. All conversation ceased. Steadily, she made her way across the snow to where Dark Eagle sat. Stopping before him, she stared down into his dark, fathomless eyes. She could feel the stares of all the Indians, but most especially, that of the blue-eyed demon. Praying that the one called White Wolf would do as she expected, she raised her hand and slapped Dark Eagle across the face. The sound of flesh against flesh echoed across the clearing. Before she turned away, she saw shock become rage in Dark Eagle's eyes.

Rachel took one step, then two, then three. That was as far as she got before a cry of wild animal fury raised hairs on the back of her neck. A powerful body crashed into her and flattened her against the snow-covered ground. As she twisted onto her back and fought for her very life, images flashed across her eyes — the tomahawk raised above her head, the feral sneer on Dark Eagle's lips, the firelight glinting off his metal-hard face.

One of her hands was free, and she reached up and dragged her nails down his cheek. The tomahawk swished downward. She dodged out of the way just in time. Biting, clawing, punching, she fought with the abandon of a madwoman. Dark Eagle, with his superior strength, finally was able to straddle her. His weight bore down heavily on her middle, squeezing the air out of her. His free hand seized her throat and forced her head into the snow. Rachel pushed ineffectually against his chest.

Again, the tomahawk began its swift, terrible descent, but it never reached her head. Instead, a single, strong hand clasped the wrist of Dark Eagle and held it unmoving. Muscle and sinew stood out as Dark Eagle strained against the constriction. Rachel looked beyond her would-be murderer and breathed a sigh of relief. White Wolf stood restraining him.

Dark Eagle looked back and up at White Wolf with a mixture of disbelief and anger. Snatching his arm out of White Wolf's grasp, he jumped up to face him. White Wolf calmly met his blazing eyes.

"You have interfered once too often, brother," Dark Eagle raged in the language native to him. "The woman is as much mine as yours. She insulted me. I have the right to punish her as I see fit."

"To punish her, yes. Not to kill her." White Wolf stood

perfectly still. In his present mood, Dark Eagle was quite dangerous.

"If that is the punishment I decide she deserves, then I will do as I think right," Dark Eagle informed him coldly.

"Not if it means denying me my hostage."

"I think you want her for more than a hostage," Dark Eagle sneered. "Does she appeal to your white blood, *brother?*"

White Wolf's eyes flickered at the insult, but he did not give any other indication that it had made any impression on him. "Perhaps we should let others decide this dispute," he suggested.

Dark Eagle stared hard at the man before him. He had loved him like a brother, even more so. They had laughed and played together when they had been children; they had hunted together as they grew older. Dark Eagle had foreseen his friend becoming the chief of their tribe and himself as a trusted warrior, respected by all because of the respect in which White Wolf held him. But then White Wolf had been sent away by his father for many seasons. When he had returned, he had somehow changed. Dark Eagle saw that his friend, his brother, might no longer become chief of the tribe. He could not understand the change in White Wolf; he resented it. Yet he remembered their love, and because of that, he gave up his rage.

"Perhaps," Dark Eagle said, "we should let the Great Spirit decide the fate of the woman."

White Wolf hesitated only an instant before he bowed his head in agreement.

At that moment, a cry of pain could be heard from the woods on the other side of the clearing. There was some commotion, then two of the warriors emerged into the

55

firelight with one of the hostages held between them. An arrow stuck out of the captive's left shoulder.

Rachel, who had not dared move while the two savages argued above her, now propped herself up on one elbow to see what was happening. When she saw Enoch Cooper between the two Indians, she groaned aloud in frustration. Immediately, Dark Eagle dropped to one knee beside her and raised his tomahawk threateningly above her head. His eyes blazed in fury as he jabbered something at her. Rachel did not need an interpreter to understand what the Indian wanted.

Pretending ignorance, she remained silent. Inside, her heart had sunk to her knees. What she had done had been for nothing. Enoch had not been able to escape to find help for them. The Indians would be furious that one of their captives had tried to flee. It was very likely the savages would carry out their threat and burn them all. She was sure that before that happened, she would be subjected to some sort of exquisite torture.

Claude Donat was summoned to interpret. With a look of concern at Rachel, he crouched beside her on the snow. Dark Eagle spoke rapidly while Claude listened, then the Frenchman turned to Rachel.

"Dark Eagle asks, *mademoiselle,* if you knew of zhe plan of zhis man to escape." Claude's eyes were sorrowful, as if he already knew what her fate was to be.

"What difference does it make, Claude?" she asked. "They will kill me anyway."

"Please, Rachel." It was the first time the *coureur de bois* had used her Christian name without putting *"mademoiselle"* before it.

Dark Eagle growled something and waved his tomahawk menacingly at her.

Swallowing the lump in her throat, Rachel said, "No. I knew nothing about the escape."

Claude translated for the Indian.

Rachel felt Dark Eagle's stare. She was sure he did not believe her. Her eyes flicked up to White Wolf standing over them. Did he believe her? she wondered. He gave no indication one way or the other. His face was expressionless; his blue eyes were as cold as a clear winter sky.

There was silence for a moment as her two masters studied her and decided her fate. Finally, Dark Eagle stood and spoke to White Wolf. Claude told her what was being said.

"Zhey are discussing what to do wizh you, *mademoiselle,*" he said. "Dark Eagle wishes to burn you before zhe ozhers, to make an example of you. White Wolf does not agree. He suggests zhey leave you in the hands of zhe Great Spirit, as zhey had decided before. Dark Eagle says zhat zhe Great Spirit will be confused by your strong medicine, your hair. He says you must have great powers, for how else were you able to walk into zheir circle tonight and strike him wizhout being seen or stopped first. He says you must be destroyed or zhey will never reach zheir home. You will call down zhe evil spirits on zhem."

Rachel listened to Claude with a mixture of amazement and fear. She almost felt flattered that these savages held her in such high esteem that they should be afraid of her. Yet, because of that fear, they would kill her. Did they not realize she was only a human woman and incapable of doing any of these magical things?

The two men stared intently at each other. Rachel felt that the fact that White Wolf was protecting her was only a result of some deeper, unknown tension between him and Dark Eagle. Yet, for now, that was enough. At least it was keeping her alive. Finally, White Wolf spoke.

Claude translated, "White Wolf suggests zhat zhey leave you to zhe wolves. Zhat way, you will be a lesson to zhe ozhers and will be punished. If zhe wolves do not want you, zhen it is up to zhe Great Spirit to find you and take you."

Rachel watched Dark Eagle pause after the suggestion, then nod his head in agreement. Her insides froze. She was glad she was lying on the ground at that moment, for she did not think she would have been able to stand. Her fate was worse than being burned. She would be torn to shreds and eaten alive by the voracious wolves that roamed the forest. White Wolf and Dark Eagle had found a bridge over their disagreement. Her protector had turned his back on her.

Dark Eagle bent over and grabbed Rachel by the arm. Dragging her to her feet, he raised his tomahawk and yelled to get everyone's attention. Rachel saw the faces before her blur, and her knees began to buckle beneath her. All she wanted was blessed oblivion. Seeing her sag, White Wolf took hold of her other arm. His touch, his complicity in the savagery that was about to take place, was more than Rachel could bear. Her mind closed down into blackness.

When she regained consciousness, she found herself sitting on the snow-covered ground with her back against a tree. Her arms had been tied back around its trunk, and her legs, bound together at her ankles, stuck out straight before her. Strips of rawhide dug painfully into her chest where they held her tightly in place against the tree. She was alone in the forest. It was so quiet that she could hear the snow falling.

In the odd light that occurs sometimes during a snow-fall, when the world appears lit from inside, she strained her eyes for any sign of the group of captors and hostages. There was none. Footprints, which were fast becoming obliterated by the falling snow, led away from her into the dark.

Tears sprang to Rachel's eyes at her desperate situation. Already shivering from the cold, her trembling increased as she allowed her fear to take hold of her. How much pain would she be in when the wolves began to devour her? she wondered. Or would she already be dead from exposure when they came? No, she could not think of those things. She had to think about something pleasant.

She brought up memories of her mother and her father. Of the last Christmas they spent together in Boston, before her mother was killed. Of summer rides in their carriage through the town and out into the country. Of her father's proud face when he completed their house in Deerfield.

Was that movement she saw over there? Rachel strained her eyes to see. Did she hear something on her other side? She whipped her head around so she could look. A dark shape skulked before her amongst the trees. Then there was another. Several pairs of yellow eyes stared at her. Rachel dared not move. The wolves were all around her now. She counted six, then eight, then nine. One, perhaps the leader and bolder than the rest, slunk forward a few steps. Its tongue lolled between sharp teeth from its open mouth. A few of the others, emboldened by their leader's actions, began to close in.

With a whimper, Rachel pulled her knees up and tried to make herself small. She twisted at her bonds. The wolf leader approached closer. Frantic, Rachel kicked snow at it. It jumped back a little only to advance again, this time growling.

"Oh, please," she cried as she yanked and pulled at the rawhide strips tying her. "Please don't let them get me." Rachel knew her pleas were a waste of energy, but hearing her own voice gave her some courage. Perhaps yelling would drive them away, she thought. "Help! Help, please!"

A low snarling started among the pack. These wolves were hungry, starving creatures. Food was not easy to get in the winter. They would not be denied this easy meal.

The leader rushed in suddenly and nipped at Rachel's foot. She screamed as she kicked out at it. Her shoe caught only air. Another wolf attacked from the other side. His teeth snapped at her leg, but missed. He got only a piece of her skirt. Rachel squeezed shut her eyes and screamed again, and again, and again. She could not stop screaming. The noise seemed to flow out of her on its own.

Something firm and warm suddenly clamped itself over her mouth. It took a moment for her to realize that no noise was escaping beyond her lips. Opening her eyes, the first thing she saw was a deerskin-clad arm. Her gaze travelled up the arm to the face above. Looking down at her were the ice blue eyes of White Wolf. His face, as always, was impassive.

Motioning silently, he had her look to one side. What she saw made her close her eyes again and swallow. One of the wolves was lying on the snow with an arrow sticking out of its side. The others were devouring it.

When she was able to face the horror, she opened her eyes again and looked back at White Wolf. He placed his finger across his lips to indicate that she was to remain silent, then he slowly took his hand away from her mouth. When he saw she would be quiet, he pulled out his hunting knife and cut her bonds.

With a little assistance from White Wolf, Rachel stood on shaking legs. As the strength returned to her numb limbs, White Wolf quickly tied the end of a length of a rawhide strip to one of her wrists and the other end to one of his wrists. She noticed he glanced up frequently to check on the wolves. When he had finished attaching himself to her, he motioned her to follow him. They slipped into the forest away from the blood-crazed animals.

The snow had let up, and now big, fluffy flakes drifted down from the dark, metallic sky. Rachel was trembling violently from the cold and the aftereffects of shock. The chattering of her teeth sounded like the drilling of a woodpecker inside her head. The noise finally made an impression on White Wolf, and he glanced back at her.

They travelled for several more minutes before he made her stop beside him. As she hugged her arms about herself, she looked up at him. What, she wondered, was he going to do to her now? She was grateful he had saved her from the wolves, but she did not think she could take any more of his help only to have him turn cruelly on her again.

He wore the hide of a silver wolf as a cape over his deerskin tunic. Unfastening it, he took it off and placed it about her shoulders. It still held his warmth, and she pulled it about her tightly. For some reason, it made her want to snuggle against him, this man who held her captive. Fighting the ridiculous impulse, Rachel stared up at him.

He gazed back at her, holding her immobile with his eyes. Reaching up, he pulled the skin tighter around her neck. Puzzled at his strange behavior, Rachel remained unmoving, barely breathing. As he looked into her eyes, she thought she saw a tiny twitch at the corner of his mouth that could have been the start of a smile.

"Thank you," she said.

Immediately, his face darkened. With a jerk on the rawhide that connected them, he started off through the forest.

Rachel was forced to follow. Stumbling along behind him, she wondered what had made him save her from the wolves. It had been his suggestion to leave her to them in the first place. What cruel torture would he put her through now?

After travelling for quite some time, Rachel realized they were not heading back towards where the others were camped. They should have arrived there by now. Where was he taking her?

By the time Rachel could barely put one foot before the other, he motioned for her to crawl beneath a tangle of brambles that he held up. With a suspicious glance from the brambles to his face and back again, she shook her head. Growling, he placed a heavy hand on her shoulder and pushed her down to her knees. She was too exhausted to argue any further. She crawled under the branches.

Beneath the knot of branches, she was surprised to find a natural shelter. There was much less snow on the ground and the cover shut out the icy breeze. White Wolf ducked down so she could see him, and he motioned for her to stay. Then, untying the rawhide from about his wrist, he moved away, letting the branches fall back over her.

Rachel sat with her knees hugged to her chest while she pondered the Indian's strange behavior. It was almost as if he had saved her for his own purposes. They obviously were not going to return to the large group of his friends, unless they planned to meet with them further along. She thought perhaps he had betrayed Dark Eagle. But why? It was too much to figure out. She let her head rest on her knees.

With a jerk, her head came up again. What a fool she was! Of course she knew the reason for his saving her and taking her away from the others. He was going to use her for . . . Oh, dear God! He was going to . . .

Rachel was no prude. She had kissed plenty of boys, some of them even on the lips, but what this savage wanted her for was indecent. It was for married people, and certainly not for a white woman and a savage. Oh, she knew there were women who were not married and did that sort of thing, but they were shunned, not even a part of society. She remembered the way he made her feel when he looked at her, and she shivered. No savage was going to do *that* to her.

Determined now that she would prefer to die from starvation and the cold, and maybe even to be eaten by wolves, she pushed up the branches to crawl out of the little shelter. It was difficult to do by herself, without having White Wolf hold the branches up for her. She got just about all the way out when she saw two moccasined feet in front of her nose. With a groan of frustrated despair, she looked up at him.

He was watching her impassively. Without a word, he

held the branches up so she could crawl back under them. When she was all the way in, he passed her several pine boughs he had cut from the surrounding trees. After the last one, he crawled in beside her. He arranged the boughs across the floor of their little shelter, then motioned for her to lie down. When she had, he pulled a large deerskin from his pack and covered her with it. Tying the free end of the rawhide strip to his wrist once more, he lay down beside her beneath the deerskin blanket.

They were so near each other that she could feel his body heat. With one arm, he pulled her back against his chest. Rachel's eyes opened wide in surprise, but she dared not protest. Besides, he was warm and she was very cold. She could feel his warm breath stir the hairs across her ear. The rhythm of his breathing soothed her. Before another thought formed in her head, she was asleep.

# Chapter Five

Rachel slowly awoke. The snow of the night had given way to a bright, sunny morning. The deerskin still covered her, and she was quite comfortable and warm, but White Wolf was not with her. The rawhide strip tied to her wrist lay unattached to anything. She realized immediately this could be her chance for escape. Throwing off the deerskin, she began to crawl beneath the brambles. Once again, after struggling partway through, the branches were suddenly lifted from her. Once again, moccasined feet were planted only a step away from her nose.

Biting down on a moan of dismay, she climbed the rest of the way out and stood. White Wolf gazed impassively at her a moment before he ducked under the bush, retrieved the deerskin and put it in his pack. Rachel felt trapped by that cold, blue gaze. She did not dare to move. When he again stood before her, he held out his open hand. In his palm were several small, irregularly shaped, brown balls. Not knowing what he expected of her, Rachel looked from his hand to his face and back again. White Wolf took one of the little balls and popped it into his mouth. She watched skeptically as he chewed and swallowed.

Again, he held out his hand with the little balls. Taking one gingerly in her fingers, she examined it. Glancing up at him, she noticed that he suffered no ill effects from eating one of them. Since it appeared that these things were going to be the only food she was going to get for a while, she decided to try it. Hesitantly, she nibbled at the one she held. It was dry and the texture was not particularly appetizing, but it was palatable. It seemed to be made of dried, ground meat with ground up, dried berries and nuts mixed in. She popped the rest of it into her mouth and chewed. When White Wolf saw that she would eat, he put several more into her hand. She gave him a weak little smile of thanks. When he turned away a moment, she slipped them into her pocket. She was not hungry enough to attempt to eat them all.

White Wolf handed her a pair of the strange Indian snowshoes that kept her from sinking into the snow. She watched a moment as he attached a pair to his own feet, then she bent down and, with cold fingers, attempted to do the same with her own. For some reason, she could not get them to stay on her feet. Impatient with her clumsiness, White Wolf crouched before her, brushed her hands away and fastened them for her. The graze of his fingers across her ankles sent wisps of weakness curling up her legs. Strange, she thought, she had never been ticklish there before. She was relieved when he finally stood up.

Remembering suddenly that she still wore the wolf pelt and not wishing to be indebted to this savage any more than she had to, she pulled the warm fur from about her neck and held it out to him. He gazed at her a moment with those demonic blue eyes, then slowly reached out and took hold of the fur.

"Thank you for loaning it to me," she murmured, even though she knew he could not understand her.

An odd expression crossed his face at her words, but it was quickly gone, replaced by his usual stern demeanor. Tossing the pelt across his shoulders, he quickly tied it about his neck. As a cold breeze swept through the trees, Rachel sorely missed the warmth the fur provided, but she suppressed her shivering. She would not give this redman any indication of weakness.

Grabbing the loose end of the strip of rawhide still bound to her wrist, he tied it to his own, then with an unnerving glance of possession at her, he set off. Again, Rachel was forced to follow. She paused only long enough to scoop up a handful of snow to wash down her breakfast.

After travelling for many minutes, it became quite clear to Rachel that her captor was not going to give her time to relieve herself. The further they walked, the more imperative it became for her to stop. Afraid of offending White Wolf and making him angry at her, she held on for as long as she could. Finally, she could wait no longer. Catching up with him, she tapped him on the shoulder.

"Excuse me," she said politely, "Could you please stop?"

White Wolf stopped abruptly and swung about on her.

"Please, I have to . . . Please, I . . ." At a loss at how to explain her need delicately to this savage, she pointed to the woods beside her.

White Wolf stared hard at her a moment, then he gave a curt nod and motioned her to go. Without wasting another moment, Rachel hurried behind a huge pine tree. So intent was she that she did not consider the strip of rawhide that bound her to her captor. When she finally turned around, she saw that White Wolf stood just behind her with his back facing her.

Furious that he should so invade her privacy, she flounced about to stand before him. "How dare you!" she railed. "You savage! You heathen savage! Have your people no manners? Do you think it is fun to spy on people in their private moments?"

White Wolf gazed down at her from his great height. His eyes, frosty as the snow underfoot, bored into her. Beneath that unwavering gaze, Rachel fell back a step. She was still angry, but decided it would not hurt to be a bit prudent. After a long moment, one in which she thought perhaps she might breathe her last breath, he finally gave a low grunt, pushed past her, and started off. Rachel followed when the rawhide strip tugged at her wrist.

As she trudged along behind her captor, she silently called him every vile name she knew. What right did he have to spy on her in her private moments? What right did he have to drag her through the forest? What right did he have to come sweeping down onto her village and kidnap her?

She watched the broad shoulders and proud head of the man before her as he walked along. His powerful legs moved rhythmically, effortlessly through the snow, while she, who had prided herself on her strength and agility, found every step an effort. It was not fair. The man was superhuman. He was some sort of spirit. He was a devil.

All morning Rachel's anger kept her silently fuming at her captor and helped her keep up with his long, even strides. All kinds of delicious, painful tortures which she might inflict on him ran through her head. Those, she knew, required that their roles be reversed, that he be her captive. There were other, more immediate punishments she could inflict on him. She wanted to rake her nails down across that wildly handsome face. She wanted to punch him until he was black and blue. She wanted to kick him.

So intent was she on her imagined conquest of her captor, that when he stopped short directly before her, she walked right into him. Swinging about on her, he took her by the arms and forcibly moved her back a step.

"Pardon me," Rachel muttered to that closed face. "If you had given me some indication you were going to stop, I would not have bumped into you."

Ignoring her words, he swung about again to look at something in their path. Around the broad back of the man who blocked her view Rachel craned her neck to see what it was he watched. When she did, she gasped in pleasure. Before them, not fifteen paces away, stood a huge bull moose. Its head was as high as White Wolf was tall; its spread of heavy antlers was as wide as the reach of a man's open arms.

Moving up beside White Wolf, she waited for him to shoot the animal. When he did nothing but stare at it, she became impatient, then suspicious. Was the man afraid of the animal? Is that why he hesitated? She decided to nudge him along.

"Kill it," she whispered loudly.

White Wolf ignored her, but the moose swung its ponderous head around to stare at them.

"Kill it," she whispered again, more urgently this time, as she motioned as if to shoot an arrow. "We can cook the meat and eat it."

The moose took a step towards them. White Wolf's

arm suddenly whipped around her. His hand closed over her mouth at the same instant that he clutched her close against his body to keep her still. Rachel was shocked into immobility. Like an inanimate doll she leaned limply against the hard muscles of the man who held her.

The moose took another step towards them and bellowed. Rachel was not sure which frightened her more — the prospect of the moose charging them, or the warm, tingly, uncomfortable feeling she experienced at such close contact with her captor. She could feel his chest rise and fall with each even breath. His heartbeat drummed slowly in her ear. She could smell woodsmoke, and deerskin, and the faint tang of pine. With a start, she realized he smelled clean.

Rachel all at once wanted to be anywhere but where she was. Embarrassed at how she must smell after three days of captivity, she wanted to back quickly away from the man who held her. Since she could not move because of his tight hold on her, there was nothing for her to do but endure her embarrassment. She prayed that the moose would decide soon to move off into the forest.

The moose bellowed again. There was a distant answering bellow from deep within the woods. The animal's head swung about towards the noise. It took a tentative step in that direction. In silence, unmoving, Rachel and her captor watched and waited. The moose bellowed a third time. The answer came from somewhat nearer. Then another moose bellowed from a different direction. The animal before them listened a moment as it sniffed the air, then it plunged noisily into the undergrowth.

White Wolf waited the space of ten heartbeats before he released Rachel. When he did, she backed quickly away. Covering her embarrassment with anger, she glared at him.

"Why didn't you shoot it?" she demanded. "We could have had meat for our dinner." She made motions as if she were shooting a bow and arrow, then as if she were eating. "You know. Shoot. Eat."

White Wolf watched the woman a moment. Her color was high in her cheeks and those blue-green eyes snapped angrily. Marvelling at her courage for being brave enough to be angry with him, her captor, at the same time, he found himself fascinated by his need to touch her full, parted lips. Mentally shaking himself, he forced those thoughts from his mind.

He knew what she wanted. He debated a moment with himself if he should take the time to explain to her. He knew she must be very hungry, for she had eaten little since he had taken her. Coming to his decision, he hunkered down where he stood and began to draw in the snow. When the woman did not follow, he took her wrist and pulled her down beside him.

Rachel watched first in exasperation, then in fascination as he explained in drawings and motions that the moose had been too large for just the two of them to consume. It would have been wasteful for him to shoot it unless it had threatened them. Because the two other moose with the bull were female, it would have charged them if it had felt threatened. Therefore, he had made no movement to frighten it.

When White Wolf had finished, Rachel stood and looked down at the snow pictures. "Still, it would have been nice to have fresh meat for our supper," she murmured.

White Wolf stood beside her. Giving the rawhide strip

which bound them together a tiny tug, he turned and started off once more. He would not be enticed by this woman again. Yet, he heard the wistful note in the woman's voice and knew of her hunger. She had not complained of her empty middle before this. For some reason which he could not understand, he promised himself that she would have meat before she slept this night.

Rachel followed her captor meekly as they moved along. The thought of moose meat, freshly roasted over an open fire, made her mouth water. It had only been three days since she had had a decent meal, but she felt as if it had been a lifetime. Having understood White Wolf's explanation of why he had not shot the moose, she found herself wondering if it had been only a convenient excuse. Thus far, she had not seen him use any kind of weapon. Perhaps he had been afraid of the moose. Perhaps he was inept at hunting. Perhaps they would starve before they reached civilization.

She began to think about food and the wonderful things she and her father had eaten together. She thought about fresh bread with blackberry preserves, cornbread with honey, apple fritters with maple syrup. A chill breeze skipped along the ground and up under her cloak. Rachel shivered.

"Some mulled cider would be nice."

She did not realize she had spoken aloud until White Wolf stopped and swung about. Giving an embarrassed little laugh, she backed up a step.

"Well, it would, you know," she said. "Hot, mulled cider."

White Wolf stared at her as if she had lost her mind completely.

"Well, for heaven's sake! Since you never speak to me, I

72

have to speak to myself. I can't trudge for miles and hours without end and not speak to someone."

Without a word, White Wolf turned and started off again. He felt the woman's hunger and fear and loneliness in her tone. Those emotions were not foreign to him. He had felt them himself at one time in his life. They were strong, raw feelings that could turn a person into nothing, an animal. For this woman to keep them to herself and try to hide them from him proved once again that he had chosen correctly. She was truly worthy. Before she slept this night, he vowed she would have fresh meat.

Rachel remained silent for the rest of the day. Not wanting to annoy him any further, she stopped obediently when White Wolf stopped and walked when he bade her. She could hardly believe that she had spoken her thought aloud as she had. Always before she had kept complete control over her tongue. Perhaps, she thought, she was losing her mind. That would certainly make her situation easier if she was unaware of what was happening to her. Then she would not care if she starved or if this demon who strode so proudly before her had his way with her. Her eyes raked over his strong back. No, she decided, she wanted to be aware if he touched her. She would fight him until she breathed her last breath.

It was the middle of the afternoon when White Wolf found a suitable spot for them to camp for the night. It was earlier than when they had stopped with the large group of prisoners and captors, but Rachel was not about to argue with him. She was glad of the respite. He had her sit on a bare rock where the sun's rays bathed her face. Then tying his end of the rawhide strip to a nearby branch, he disappeared into the woods.

Rachel had no idea where her captor had gone. She wondered briefly if he had decided to leave her in the woods to die from starvation or the wolves. Just as quickly she dismissed that idea. He had gone to too much trouble to save her only to abandon her now. Her eyes travelled along the length of rawhide. He had tied his end to a spot that was easily accessible. Rachel could simply walk over and untie the knot and slip away into the forest, but she did not. His act had been a symbolic gesture, meant to make her understand that she was still his prisoner and that he could track her easily if she escaped.

With a sigh, Rachel absently scooped up a palmful of snow. She watched as it melted from the warmth of her hand and stripes of clean skin appeared where the water dripped through her fingers. It took her a moment to understand exactly what had taken place. Excitedly, she scooped up more snow and rubbed it between her hands. When she looked, her hands were clean. Quickly, she rubbed the snow over her face and used her skirt to dry herself. She wondered why she had not thought of this before. Clean. She was going to be clean.

When she had finished washing as much of herself as she could, she broke a green twig from a nearby branch. Mashing one end of it on the rock, she used it to clean her teeth. Then she combed her fingers through her hair to get out the tangles. With her hair being so long and thick, she was engrossed in this chore for a long time. The sun had almost set by the time she had finished her impromptu toilette. Now that she had nothing else to occupy her, she began to wonder where White Wolf was.

It was twilight and he still had not returned. A twig snapped in the forest across the clearing. Expectantly, she gazed in that direction. Nothing appeared. She began to get cold and think of wolves prowling in the dark. A shiver ran through her.

Suddenly, something landed in her lap. With a yelp, she jumped up and at the same moment, she realized White Wolf was standing beside her.

"Don't frighten me like that," she huffed.

He pointed to the thing that had fallen to the ground when she had stood. Looking down, she saw two small rabbits.

"Rabbit!" she exclaimed happily. "You killed rabbits for our supper!"

White Wolf walked to the branch where the rawhide strip was tied and undid the knot. Then he untied the strip from her wrist. He tossed it to where his pack lay on the other side of the clearing. Facing her again, he pulled his hunting knife from its sheath and held it out to her, handle first.

Rachel looked from the knife to his face and back again. He was telling her many things with that simple gesture. He was saying that it was her job to skin and clean the rabbits. He was saying that he expected her not to use the knife to stab him in the back and escape. He was saying that he trusted her.

Slowly, Rachel placed her hand on the knife and closed her fingers about its handle. The idea of killing this devil and escaping did flit enticingly through her head, but the more tangible thought of fresh roasted rabbit made her stifle her first impulse. It had been too long since her last decent meal to contemplate outwitting this savage. Picking up the rabbits, she moved to the edge of the clearing where she proceeded to skin and clean them.

While she was occupied, White Wolf started a fire and cut fragrant cedar branches for their beds. Then he fashioned a spit and two brackets to hold the rabbits over the fire to cook them. By the time he had finished, Rachel had completed her job. Picking up the rabbits and the knife, she walked to where her captor tended the fire. She gave him the rabbits and watched as he threaded them onto the spit.

Once again, the idea of escape slipped through her mind. She had the knife. It would be easy to stab it down into his back while he was occupied. Then, she would be free. He had no reason to trust her, no reason to believe that she would not kill him. Yet, he had trusted her. He had given her the instrument of his own death and turned his back on her. She did not know why he had done that. She only knew she could not break that trust. Standing quietly, she waited as he placed the spit holding the rabbits over the fire.

When he had finished, he looked up at her. Their eyes met and held. Rachel was drawn into that fathomless gaze. She was unable to move; her breath lodged in her throat. A strange, giggly sensation erupted in her middle. After what seemed an eternity had passed, her brain began to function once more. Blinking and taking a deep breath, she remembered why she was standing there. Handle first, she held out the knife to him.

He reached out and took hold of it. His fingers overlapped hers. Lightning shot through her hand and up her arm when his warm skin touched hers. As if she had been burnt, she jerked her hand away. In the suddenness of the movement, her thumb scraped across the blade and a thin line of blood appeared. The pain surprised her, and giving a little cry, she stared stupidly at the tiny cut.

Before she could think, her captor took gentle hold of her thumb and put it to his mouth. His lips surrounded her wound and his tongue softly washed it. In shock at his action, Rachel remained motionless. The pleasure of his touch overwhelmed all her other feelings and erased the discomfort of the cut. When he removed her thumb from between his lips and placed a lump of icy snow against it, she finally came to her senses. Pulling her hand out of his grasp, she held the snow against the cut herself.

"I am perfectly capable of tending my own wounds," she told him primly. "You need not concern yourself."

She thought she saw amusement flicker in his eyes. With a sniff of disdain, Rachel swung about and returned to her side of the fire. She told herself those odd feelings she had felt were a result of her hunger and fatigue. Why else would such strange emotions overwhelm her in the presence of a savage?

As she sat tending her cut and trying to deny what she had experienced at the touch of White Wolf, the smell of the roasting rabbits wafted through the air and made Rachel's mouth water. It was almost more than she could bear to wait until they were cooked. When they were finally done, White Wolf pulled them both off the spit. He allowed one to fall into the snow; the other, he broke in half and gave one piece to Rachel.

Rachel thought she had never tasted anything so delicious. She savored every bite. Licking her fingers, she looked expectantly to White Wolf to break the other rabbit in half, but instead, he picked it up and placed it in his pack. Then he gathered the skins and rolled them up and put them in his pack also. He had Rachel retrieve the entrails from where she had cleaned the animals and place them along with the bones near the fire. Sitting before the small pile, he began to methodically toss the pieces onto the flames.

77

While he did so, he sang something in a low, rhythmic tone.

Rachel listened to the melodic baritone of the man's voice. She thought she had never heard anything so strange yet so wonderful in her life. The soft, primitive melody wrapped her in its cocoon and transfixed her where she sat. The play of firelight on White Wolf's features gave him the appearance of some unearthly creature, come to entrance her and spirit her away to his world.

When his song finished, he raised his eyes and met hers across the fire. Rachel blushed hotly for staring and allowing herself to be so swept away by such a savage. Quickly, she averted her face.

Stupid, she chided herself. He is your captor, a redman. You are only worth the price of the ransom he can get for you. He will take what he can from you and leave you to suffer the consequences. He is a heathen, a savage.

But his song was so beautiful.

# Chapter Six

Rachel suspiciously watched her captor. She was determined not to be frightened. He had enthralled her during his little performance, but it was over now. Whatever gods or wraiths he had called upon would not take her unaware. She was not some insipid female who knew nothing of the world. There were no spirits who would rise out of the fire and possess her. Her father had taught her French and Latin; she had read Plato and Socrates, Shakespeare and John Donne. No heathen was going to befog her wits. He would not have his way with her.

She was going to escape from him. Somehow, she would find her opportunity and dash off into the woods. They had not travelled that far during the day. She thought she could find her way back to the other captives. At least with them and the other redmen she would be safe from this devil's eyes. Even remaining with Dark Eagle was preferable to enduring captivity with this man. Perhaps she might even stumble across a settlement where she could find help. The villagers could help her rescue the others from those savages.

Yet, she had to struggle to remain alert. The warmth

from the fire, her full middle and the exertions of the day made her eyelids heavy. She shifted position often to stay awake. Several times she found herself drifting into sleep and jerked herself upright and awake. She had to watch. She had to.

White Wolf saw the woman's efforts to fight sleep. Amusement at the irony of the situation seeped through him. She did not know that it was not his purpose to lay with her. Yet, the only fear he felt from her was of him touching her as a man touches a woman. With all her womanly courage, in this she was still a child.

Her reaction to his tending her small wound had been swift and deep, a sign that she had known no man intimately. The thought that he could be her first caused a tightening in his loins. He wondered again what it would be like to have this woman lie with him in passion. Would she be wild, like the cougar, or gentle, like the rabbit? No. It did no good to wonder about such things. She was not for that. With an effort, he brought his body once more under control.

He knew she had been enchanted with his song to the Great Spirit, and he knew she thought he was trying to bewitch her. She did not understand that any part of an animal that had been killed and would not be consumed was to be returned to its spirit brother or sister. If he had wanted to bewitch her, there were other ways.

He watched her head slip forward onto her knees and her glorious hair fall like dark fire around her. She had cleaned herself while he had been hunting. It was the first thing he had seen when he had returned to her. He wondered if she understood her own want. Her head jerked up and her eyes opened wide. She was afraid he would touch her in the manner of men and women. He could not. She was not for that purpose. Yet, his fingers itched to lose themselves in that mysterious hair that glowed with its hidden flame.

Fool, he scolded himself. The woman is your revenge.

The campfire was beginning to die. The night was too young to allow that to happen. White Wolf knew the woman would not add more wood. She needed much training in the ways of women. Resignedly, he rose to his feet to stoke the flames.

Rachel rubbed her eyes and shifted her position once again. She had almost fallen asleep for good, and she could not allow that to happen. That blue-eyed devil sat so smugly there on his cedar branches. He thought he could sing strange songs and weave his spells about her, but he was wrong. She was stronger than he.

She watched as he gracefully rose to his feet. Preparing to jump up and run if he made any threatening movement towards her, she was relieved that he only picked up some wood and fed the fire. He crouched beside her and a little in front of her. The handle of his hunting knife stuck out invitingly from the sheath which hung at his waist.

It took Rachel a moment to realize that this was her opportunity, the one she had been waiting for. All she had to do was take the knife, stab him, and run. She blinked as the enormity of what she was about to do washed through her. Once she had killed him, she would be on her own and free. Free. Although it had only been a matter of days since she had taken that word for granted, it felt like an eternity. She felt as though she had always been in the power of this blue-eyed demon. But soon, soon she would be free.

Not wanting to think about it any longer or consider the consequences of her actions, she took a deep breath.

Slowly, she reached out her hand. The hilt of the knife was just out of reach. Her captor had not moved; he did not realize what she was about to do. Letting out her breath softly, then holding it again, she inched forward. Don't let him hear me, she prayed. As she stretched as far as she could, her fingers touched the knife. There, she had it.

No sooner had her fingers closed around the bone handle, than White Wolf's arm shot out, catching her across her chest and shoulders. The force of that hard, muscled limb threw her down and back onto the ground. Her breath whooshed out of her. Before she could breathe again, White Wolf's body covered hers. He flattened her with his weight, pushing her down into the branches. No! she screamed silently, too frightened and too disappointed to make her voice work.

In the next instant, she realized all was not lost. Miraculously, his knife had slipped out of its sheath and remained clutched in her fingers during her fall. It was her only chance of survival. She flailed wildly at him.

As her hand swung in its deadly arc, a band of steel wrapped itself about her wrist and checked her movement. A cry of dismay emerged from her throat as a thin whimper. He forced her arm back down to lie limply on the branches above her head. Easily, he slipped the knife from her weak fingers and tossed it away over his shoulder.

Rachel pushed and pounded on his chest with her free hand. Terror made her struggles blind and ineffectual. "No," she panted. "You won't touch me. You won't."

Capturing her other wrist, White Wolf pulled that arm above her head, also. She was trapped. The muscular weight of his thighs held her legs immobile; his body pressed her down onto the branches; his hands kept her arms pinned above her head.

Rachel gazed up into those frosty eyes. Her breath rasped in and out of her throat. The heat of him burned along the length of her body, weighing her down, making her feel as if she were drowning. Yet she did not have time to be afraid. Before she could formulate a thought, his mouth swooped down and captured her lips in a kiss like none she had ever experienced. It ravished her mouth. It was savage in its intensity. It was cruel and punishing. It proclaimed who was master. It proved her weakness.

When he raised his head finally, Rachel was thoroughly shaken and humiliated. She felt used, abused, dirty. She wanted to crawl into a hole and never again see the light of day. She wanted to take the knife and cut his graceful, muscular body into ribbons.

"I hate you," she spat.

White Wolf's eyes held hers. There was no indication that he had understood or even heard her. Yet that icy gaze heated until she felt she might be burned to ash where she lay. His eyes flicked to her mouth and back again to chain her gaze. That look of possession which had become so familiar to her sent a tremor through her body. He lowered his head once more, but before he could kiss her again, she jerked her head away. She would not allow him to punish her again.

In surprise, Rachel felt his lips gently graze across her jaw to her ear. Softly, his tongue tickled there, then down the column of her throat to where a pulse throbbed. With each heartbeat he sucked until the rhythm quickened.

Rachel swallowed convulsively, and he raised his head. Her eyes searched his in confusion. What was he doing? she wondered wildly. Before she could form an answer, his lips were once again on hers, softly gliding back and forth across her mouth. His thumbs slowly caressed the inside of her wrists and sent tendrils of exciting sensations shooting down her arms. Her eyelids slipped closed; her lips parted. One of his hands released her wrist and slipped into the mysterious depths of her hair to tangle there. It was a gesture both of gentleness and bondage. His kiss deepened, slowly forcing her awareness to center only on him. His tongue probed gently between her honeyed lips. Instinctively, she allowed him entrance.

All thought fled from her mind as he caressed her lips with his tongue. Slowly, he invaded her mouth, teasing, tormenting. Rachel let him do as he wished, awash in feelings that were new, disturbing, overwhelming. Her mind was paralyzed by what he was doing to her. She could not have formed a coherent thought if she had wanted to.

His hand trailed from the web of her tresses down her throat. The clasp of her cloak and the ties of her nightdress were magically undone by his fingers. He cupped one perfect breast in his hand and brushed his thumb back and forth across its rosy tip. It hardened into a tight little bud beneath his touch.

Rachel was swept away by the sensations he aroused in her. Wonderful, rhythmic pulsing throbbed deep in her middle. Weakness invaded her limbs while at the same time she felt more alive than she had ever felt before. She did not know what spell he had cast over her, but she did not care. She only wanted it to go on forever.

Then his lips were no longer on her mouth. They traced down her throat to her shoulder, then lower until they covered the tip of her breast. Sensations like lightning radiated out from where he touched to every part of her body. Even her fingertips tingled. His tongue ran wet circles around the dark pink aureole, then his mouth covered it. He sucked and licked until she was mindless. Her breath

84

came and went in tiny gasps; her blood raced through her veins like fire. She had not known it, but it was exactly what she had wanted him to do. A low moan escaped her throat. She wanted more. Throbbing heat centered between her thighs. There was something else . . . something else . . . Without realizing what she was doing, she rubbed her hips up against him.

Suddenly, his face was above her. Rachel blinked in surprise. It took a moment for her to bring him into focus. The shuttered, cold look in his eyes shocked her back into awareness. The icy stiffness of his body froze her. What had she done?

In one fluid movement, he was off her and standing. As he strode away into the forest, he stopped only long enough to bend down and retrieve his knife where he had tossed it. He jabbed the knife into its sheath as he disappeared among the trees.

Like someone just coming out of a deep sleep, Rachel stared at the spot where the tall figure of White Wolf had been swallowed up by the blackness. The chill night air caressed where his warmth had been. As if they belonged to another person, her hands moved to knot the ties of her nightdress and fix the clasp of her cloak. The bare skin beneath her fingers brought her mind sharply into reality. What had she done?

The shock of the truth made her clutch her cloak spasmodically. She had allowed him to kiss her, to touch her, to arouse heathen, demonic emotions in her. How could she have let him do those things to her? He was a redman, a savage. She had vowed he would not touch her, yet she had let him. Worse than that. She had lain open and acquiescent beneath him.

With a wordless cry of anguish, she curled up into a ball

as she tried to shut out the vivid memories of what had just taken place. She was a shameless Jezebel for allowing him to take such liberties. She was a sinner. Mortification and humiliation washed over her.

It could not happen again. He would not touch her again. He would not kiss her, nor suck at her breast. He would not turn her insides to molten fire. He would not.

But you enjoyed it, a tiny corner of her mind protested.

"No!" she sobbed aloud.

She covered her ears to block out the noise of that little voice. How could she enjoy it? She was English, a white woman; he was a redman, a heathen, a savage. He was her captor; she was his prisoner. She was indecent, beneath contempt.

The memory of his hands and lips on her stole through her brain. A tremor ran through her body. When he had touched her, she had been transported into another world. It was almost as if . . . as if he had cast some spell over her. That was the reason for this aberration. It was not her fault that she had succumbed to him. He had brewed something magical when he sang over the fire.

Idiot, that voice argued. You enjoyed his touch.

Rachel sobbed and curled tighter into her ball. That tiny voice would bring her to ruin. What she had felt was unnatural. She did not enjoy it. She did not. She did not.

You did, that tiny voice nagged. You wanted him to touch you, to make you mindless. You want him to do it again.

Rachel pressed her hands tighter against her ears. It was wrong. Wrong. She could not have enjoyed what he had done. It was impossible. They were from two separate worlds. He knew nothing of hers, of living in frame houses, of London fashions, of table manners, of Sunday services, of courtship and marriage before God. She knew nothing of his, of his heathen gods, of his savage ways. They were different, so different. His touch had done nothing to her. Nothing. Nothing. Nothing.

White Wolf swung himself up into the bare branches of a maple tree and made himself comfortable. Leaning back against the trunk, he stretched his long legs out along the branch where he perched. He was deep enough into the forest that the light from the fire did not penetrate here, yet from where he sat he could see the woman curled up on the cedar branches.

He knew he could not stray far from her and leave her unprotected. That self-imposed restriction weighed heavily on him. What he wanted to do was run through the forest until he dropped from exhaustion, to wipe out what he had just done — with the rhythmic pounding of his feet against the ground, the mindlessness of racing the wind. He wanted to forget that he had broken his vow to himself. But he could not. His honor did not allow it. Since that was impossible, he had chosen the next best thing and climbed into the welcoming arms of a tree.

Unfamiliar emotions assailed him. Always before he had held strict control over himself. It was the way of his mother's people. Yet, this woman had caused him to betray his brother and unleash the passion burning in his heart. He did not know what had possessed him to touch the woman as he had. He knew it had been what he had wanted from the first time he had seen her, yet he also knew it was not to be. She was his prisoner, his revenge.

He heard her cry out her denial, and his heart contracted in his chest. She was an innocent with men. He had sensed that from the first, had learned it anew when he had tended her cut. He had used it to make her open her passion to him. What he had done was dishonorable.

He closed his eyes against the guilt. He was piling wrong upon wrong, and this woman was at the root of it all. Hunting Dog, the wise one, had been right. Before coming on this journey to the village of the English, he had gone to the shaman for advice and to discover what the journey would hold—whether it be good or ill. Hunting Dog had told him that a woman of cold fire would cause him great pain and great joy, that she would be the cause of change in his life and the resolving of opposite forces.

White Wolf shook his head. He did not see how one insignificant woman would make all that come about. He understood how she could cause the pain. He was experiencing that now, for his heart ached with what he had done, both to her and to his brother, Dark Eagle. But the changes she would cause were beyond his understanding. The People had been in existence since before memory. Their ways, his ways, were a deep part of them all. It was not possible for this woman with the hair of hidden fire to have such power over them or over him.

Yet, perhaps he had changed. The control he held over himself seemed to vanish in the presence of this woman. He did things and thought things that surprised him, things that he would not ordinarily do. It was as if she held some strange power over him, as if she were some witch-woman. Perhaps Dark Eagle was right. Perhaps her hair was strong medicine.

He rubbed his fingers together lightly remembering how her hair had felt. Strong medicine. The woman invaded all his senses. The memory of those honey lips and that smooth skin made his heart leap within him. He smiled into the darkness. Perhaps the woman would bring him great joy. What he had sensed from the beginning had proved true. Besides having the courage of a worthy enemy, the woman held the fire of passion within her.

He gazed through the trees to where she lay curled up into a tight little ball. She was afraid of him, as she should be, for he was her master; she, his hostage, his revenge. But she was also afraid of herself. She was afraid of her feelings and what they might reveal to her. That was something a brave warrior learned to face first. For without knowing himself, a warrior could not know his enemy. Perhaps, on this journey they took together, he would teach her to know herself better, and thus, to know him, her enemy, better.

Hunting Dog was rarely wrong when he gazed through the sacred smoke into the sacred fire. The journey with the woman was long. Not even the Great Spirit would find fault with him if he followed his destiny.

Rachel awoke the next morning stiff and cold and still curled into the same tight little ball. It was barely dawn and gray clouds blanketed the sky. Across the cold ashes of the campfire, White Wolf sat cross-legged and immobile. His blue eyes gazed impassively at her. Quickly, she averted her own eyes. Her mortifying reaction to that man's touch on the previous night was too fresh and painful to even acknowledge his existence. She wondered how long he had been sitting in that position watching her, if he had slept at all or merely stared at her sleeping form as he tried to devise his next attack.

When he saw that she was fully awake, he motioned impatiently for her to rise. At some point during the night, he had covered her with the deerskin. She wanted nothing more now than to pull it over her head and never have to look at his handsome face again. Instead, she climbed stiffly to her feet.

He pointed to the woods beside her, and she assumed he meant for her to attend to her needs. She was a little surprised when he did not follow her, but she was grateful for at least that small amount of privacy. When she emerged back into the clearing, he motioned at the deerskin and then at his pack. With a tiny sigh of resignation, she folded the deerskin and put it away.

Fleetingly, she wondered why he seemed so angry. Certainly she had done nothing to put him in such a dour mood. He had gotten what he wanted. If anything, he should be gloating that he had been able to have his way with her.

When she had finished with the deerskin, he motioned that she was to scatter the ashes of the fire. As she did so, her temper started to rise. He had done nothing to help break their camp except sit and order her about. Did he think she was his slave? Did he believe that because she had been foolish last night he could make her do everything—or anything?

Straightening from scattering the ashes, she glared at him and said, "Would you like me to fetch your morning clothes for you, my lord? Which would you prefer—the blue velvet or the gray wool?"

Rachel knew he would not be able to understand the sarcasm, but at least by saying something she felt better. When White Wolf stood, she thought perhaps she had overstepped her bounds. She retreated a quick step as those demonic blue eyes slid over her. Instead of punishing her, he picked up his pack, his bow, and quiver of arrows and started off into the woods.

Rachel was undecided. He had not tied her with the rawhide strip, so she was not sure if they were again starting on their journey. Perhaps he meant to leave her there to fend for herself and find her own way back to civilization. Even though last night she had tried to escape, in the cold morning light, the thought of finding her own way frightened her.

As she stood there, unmoving, White Wolf emerged from among the trees. With an angry, impatient gesture, he ordered her to follow. Meekly, Rachel did as she was told. As she trudged along after him, she wondered why he had not tied her with the rawhide. Perhaps he thought since she had acted so stupidly the night before, the invisible chains which bound them were stronger than anything which he might use to link them.

At that thought, Rachel's chin came up. He would not touch her that way again. She would make sure of that. For now, she would follow him, but she would be aware of any chance she might have to escape. She might have passed up a chance that very morning, but she was more determined now. The rest of her life would not be spent with this blue-eyed demon.

# Chapter Seven

A week plus two days passed of cold and gloomy weather. Rachel followed obediently along after her captor. She stopped when he stopped; she walked when he walked. She gathered wood, cleaned and cooked the game he caught, and tidied up their campsite before they left it. In all, she was a model prisoner.

Yet, despite this, there was a deep unease between them. Rachel still felt a stab of embarrassment and humiliation whenever she happened to meet those devilish blue eyes. Her guilt tormented her during her every waking minute. White Wolf, on his part, was even more implacable and impassive, if possible, and his impatience with her was more frequent. Rachel wanted to scream at him that if he had not captured her in the first place, he would have no cause to be angry with her. But she did not. Resolutely, she pressed her lips together and swallowed her words. Soon, she would find the opportunity for her own revenge.

This day, they were high in the mountains and the weather was not so dark. They had stopped to rest and to eat the remainder of the squirrel which White Wolf had caught and she had cooked the night before. Occasional breaks in the roiling clouds overhead allowed sudden shafts of sunlight to brighten the day.

Rachel finished her meal and stood up. Walking towards the edge of the precipice where they had stopped, she gazed out across the valleys and mountains. She could see for miles. In the distance, the silvery ribbon of a river wound its way across the valley floor. Below her, the trees looked like fluffy cushions that would gently break her fall if she jumped into them. The sun chose that moment to peek from behind the clouds, and its rays flooded the near side of a mountain across the valley.

"It's so beautiful," she breathed.

A tinkling sound from below where she stood drew her attention. Moving to the edge of the rock, she leaned over and out to find the tiny underground stream as it emerged from the bowels of the mountain. Before she had a chance to see the stream, a hand grabbed her by the arm and jerked her back from the edge. Rachel glared up into White Wolf's frosty eyes.

"What do you think you are doing?" she demanded. "Unhand me this instant, you beast! Do you think you can manhandle me any time you wish?"

She yanked her arm out of his grasp and stepped back. Once again, his hand snaked out, this time catching her about the waist. Lifting her bodily from the ground, he moved her to a safe distance from the edge of the precipice and put her down. Rachel struggled out of his grip and flounced several paces away.

"Keep your hands to yourself!" she huffed. "I will not be jounced about like some rag doll!"

Fighting to keep his face expressionless, to keep his anger and amusement hidden, White Wolf bent down and picked up his pack and his bow and quiver of arrows. Tossing his pack to the woman to carry, he slipped his bow over his shoulder. When she had settled the pack on her back, he motioned her to follow.

He knew she had not realized he had grabbed her to save her life. The edge where she had been had not been safe because of the underground stream. With the spring thaw, the ground was not solid and could have given way beneath her at any moment. It did not bother him that her reaction was so wild, that she thought he was touching her in the way a man touches a woman. Eventually, she would learn that his self-control had returned. What had happened between them would not happen again.

Yet it had pleased him to see such anger in her. It proved that she was still confused about what had happened, and her confusion proved that her want was still there inside of her. Despite her cold eyes of days past, her passion ran deep. He was satisfied that his actions had not doused the flame of that passion. He would have been disappointed if this woman's heat had turned to ice.

Rachel dogged White Wolf's steps as they descended into the valley. Instead of being quiet as she usually was, she muttered angrily with almost every step. She had had enough of this redman's arrogant ways. For over a week he had tolerated her presence. Imagine! He had *captured* her and now he *tolerated* her presence. Then he pushed her about with no thought of asking her permission or apologizing. How dare he think he could put his hands on her whenever he felt the urge? Just because she had been overcome by his heathen spells did not mean that she would allow him to do as he wished to her any time he felt the need to do so.

And she had been overcome, she had decided. It had

not been her fault that she had let him touch her as he had. Well, she was not about to let *that* happen again. And this last breach of manners . . . It was too much to bear. When she reached civilization, she would teach him a thing or two.

"Arrogant savage," she muttered. "Wild heathen." She stepped over a log. "No manners. No manners at all." She ducked a low branch. "Who does he think he is? Pushing me about like that." She huffed her way through a deep snowdrift. "Just because I'm his prisoner doesn't mean that he can do what he feels like doing to me."

White Wolf stopped before her and Rachel waited in exasperation for him to go on.

"He's probably looking for some fiendish way to torture me now," she mumbled.

Suddenly, White Wolf launched himself at her, dragged her to the ground and rolled with her beneath the undergrowth. His hand clamped over her mouth, and one word emerged from deep in his throat.

"Quiet."

Rachel's eyes opened wide as she stared at the man above her. The fact that she was lying on the cold, wet snow in an uncomfortable, compromising position with the man she had just been berating did not even enter her consciousness. What riveted her attention was that he had spoken to her — in English!

She was not sure how long they lay together motionless before she finally heard what White Wolf had noticed long before. The sounds of men moving through the forest drifted to her ears. Yet, the impact of that fact was very small in comparison to her newfound knowledge that White Wolf had understood everything she had ever said to him. Heat suffused her face as she remembered all the insults she had spoken. Embarrassment tinged heavily with fear made her squirm beneath him. A shake of his head and a glance from those blue eyes stilled her immediately. His hand tightened in warning on her shoulder.

The movement made her mind shoot off in another direction. Who were these men who travelled through the forest? Why was the brave warrior White Wolf hiding from them? Would it not be better if they continued their journey in the company of others?

The group of men passed very close to them, but did not notice that a man and a woman hid from them in the undergrowth. Rachel could not see them, but she knew from their quiet steps and then from their intermittent words that they were redmen, like her captor. They moved off deeper into the woods, but White Wolf held her still long after she could no longer hear them. When he was finally satisfied that the men had gone, he rolled off her and stood.

Rachel scrambled to her feet and faced her captor. "You speak English," she stated.

White Wolf gave a curt nod.

"You speak English!" she accused.

"I speak many languages," White Wolf said shortly.

"You speak English!" she nearly yelled.

"Hush, woman, the hunters will hear you," he warned.

"I don't care."

"You will care if they return."

Rachel ignored his statement. "How dare you make me believe you could not understand me?"

"I never led you to believe I could not understand you."

"But you never spoke to me. You always had Claude Donat translate for you or you used sign language."

"I felt it was better if we did not speak."

"Better? Better!" she sputtered. "You arrogant cad! Better! I was frightened and alone and you thought it was better if we did not speak?! You overbearing savage! That is the cruelest, most heartless, most vicious thing you could have done!"

White Wolf's eyes turned icy. At his look, Rachel backed up a step. She sensed she might have said too much.

"What I have done, I have done to keep you safe," he told her coldly.

"Safe?" she countered. "How can I be safe with the man who attacked my home and dragged me off into the forest?"

Immediately, Rachel wished she could have snatched her words back out of the air between them. A pulse throbbed rapidly in White Wolf's jaw as his face turned murderous. Staring at her with those devilish eyes, he finally drew a slow breath and released it.

"That is enough," he said, straining to keep his voice even. "Come. We have wasted enough time *speaking*." With that, he turned and stalked off.

Rachel watched his retreating back for the space of two heartbeats. Then, with a sigh that was a mixture of anger, fear and relief, she followed. She knew she had made White Wolf angry with her accusations, and fear insinuated itself into her brain. Apprehension about what might happen to her once they made camp that night made her consider trying to follow the trail of the group of hunters who had just passed them. She wondered again why White Wolf had hidden from them. If he had wanted to avoid them, perhaps she should, too. She gazed at his broad back and sighed again. What other secrets did those demonic blue eyes conceal?

That afternoon when they stopped for the day, White Wolf was just as taciturn as he had always been. His anger, if he was still angry, was well hidden. Although his commands were spoken rather than signed, he used as few words as possible.

Rachel remained silent and went about her usual chores with no comments. She realized her stupidity of that afternoon had almost cost her dearly. And she knew White Wolf was capable of punishing her in ways that were more effective than inflicting physical pain, ways that bared her soul and took her very self away from her.

With her nerves stretched thin, she sat quietly and waited for whatever punishment he decided to inflict on her. Finally, when they had finished their meal of the quail which White Wolf had caught, and the fire danced and crackled between them, Rachel could stand the silence no longer. Summoning her courage, dismissing her fear and anger, she decided to try to talk to this man who frightened yet fascinated her at the same time.

"Are you angry at me?" she asked in a quiet voice.

His blue gaze narrowed on her from across the fire. "Your tongue is too sharp for one who should not speak," he said coldly.

"I am sorry. Sometimes I say things I regret later."

"Regret does nothing but make a man weak." He returned to his work on a rabbit skin.

Rachel watched him in silence for a long time. She wanted to talk to him, find out about him. Finally, summoning her courage, she swallowed and opened her mouth. "Mister White Wolf, sir?" she ventured timidly.

White Wolf's head snapped up. His eyes bored into her across the fire.

Rachel cleared her throat nervously and tried again. "Mister White Wolf, sir?"

"Since the loose tongue of Claude Donat has spoken my name to you, please use my name correctly. It is White Wolf, no 'Mister', no 'sir'."

A deep blush stained her cheeks at the rebuke. Speaking with this man was going to be more difficult than she had thought. "I am sorry," she mumbled.

He grunted and returned to what he was doing.

"Please, don't be angry," she said. "I just want to talk with you."

He heard the wistful tone in her voice and tamped down his irritation. As he had first thought, it would have been better not to speak to this woman. Speaking revealed many things about a man's spirit. It was not part of his plan to reveal his spirit to this woman. He berated himself for the weakness that had seized him and made him speak to her. Yet, he knew she must be very frightened of all that had happened to her, even though she had shown little fear since he had taken her, except of course for that one night when he had touched her in passion. Her courage persuaded him to answer her.

"What is it you wish to talk about?" he asked.

Rachel gazed at him a moment as she tried to decide what she should ask him first. Finally, she decided that she should start with something impersonal.

"Why did we hide from those hunters in the forest today?"

White Wolf fought for self-control as anger surged through him. Was this woman questioning his bravery? He, who had killed a bear with only a tomahawk, who had led the warriors of his mother's people on many successful raids? He searched her face. No, she was only questioning something she did not understand.

"They are our enemies," he said.

"Why are they our . . . your enemies?"

"They have always been our enemies. The why of it does not matter."

"But you told me that I would care if they came back and found us."

"They are of a different nation. They are called *Megwah* by my mother's people. By others, they are called *Mohowauock*. It means 'coward' or 'he who eats man'."

Rachel stared at him. "You mean that they eat *people?*"

He shook his head impatiently. "Perhaps, at one time. Now, symbolically, they eat their enemies, those who have shown great courage. They feel that by eating their enemies they will gain their enemies' bravery. It is strong medicine for them."

"Oh my," she breathed. "Oh my goodness. But why does their name also mean 'coward'?"

"Among the People it is felt that a warrior who must eat his enemy to gain courage must not be very brave."

His answer led Rachel to believe that his people did not eat their enemies, but she felt she should ask anyway. After all, if her fate was that she would be eaten by a group of savages, she decided she would rather run off into the woods and die of starvation. "Do your people eat their enemies?"

White Wolf gazed at the woman. A mischievous spirit took hold of him as he answered, "Only if they are women with hair of hidden fire."

It took a moment for Rachel to realize that he was referring to her. She stared at her captor as she tried to decide if he was serious. Then as she watched, his eyes

100

softened and one corner of his mouth twitched ever so slightly upward. Just the notion that this taciturn, silent man had joked with her was enough to make her speechless. She finally realized he was doing just that. A tiny smile curved her lips. Despite the fact that he had plucked her out of her home, she suddenly felt more comfortable with him. After all, he had saved her from Dark Eagle and the wolves even if it had been for his own purposes. She wanted to discover everything she could about him.

"Tell me about your people," she said.

White Wolf gazed at the woman as he tried to decide what to tell her, if anything. His instincts warned against telling her too much, against sharing any part of his life with her. Somehow he felt that giving her any part of him would lead to trouble. Yet, his heart warmed to her and felt the need to reach out to her. This is wrong, he told himself. This woman was with him only to fulfill his revenge. There was no need to share anything of himself with her. He should have kept his tongue silent as he had first decided to do. It would have been simpler that way.

Rachel saw the slight frown crease White Wolf's forehead. Afraid she had somehow insulted him by asking him about himself, she immediately apologized, "I'm sorry. I did not mean to intrude."

White Wolf was surprised by the woman's words. He had not expected her to be so aware of his feelings. She was not like other white women who poked at his thoughts until their curiosity was satisfied or his patience had ended. This woman was different, worthy of his consideration. Perhaps it would not be wrong to tell her of the People so that she would understand them.

"The People live in a place where the river flows on

101

rocks," he began slowly. "To others, we are known as 'Penobscot'. We live in our village by the river until the cold paints the leaves many colors and they fall from the trees. Before the snows fall, we scatter to the forest to trap animals for their meat. The furs, we trade for guns and cooking pots."

Rachel looked pointedly at White Wolf's bow and quiver of arrows where he had hung them from a branch.

"It was a promise I made that prevented me from bringing the weapon of the white man," he explained. "The People have lived without the white man's weapons since before memory. It is only since the white man has come that the People feel the need to use their firesticks. Since the white man has come, the People must go farther and farther away from their village in the winter to find food."

Rachel suddenly felt very guilty about being a resident of Deerfield. She felt like a trespasser on land that did not belong to her. "That is terrible," Rachel said. "Is that why your people attacked my village?"

"There were many reasons why your village was attacked. Each man had his own reason."

"What was your reason?" she asked quietly.

White Wolf stared at the woman. With one question she could lay bare his thoughts if he allowed it to be so.

"Enough, English," he said brusquely. "My reason does not concern you. It is time for sleep."

Rachel silently disagreed with him. She felt it concerned her a great deal since she had been captured by him and she was now alone with him in the forest. She watched as he pulled the deerskin about his shoulders and lay down on his pile of pine boughs. She was not in the least bit sleepy. Too much had happened that day, too many unanswered questions roiled around in her head for her to even consider sleep. She wanted to know more of the conflict between White Wolf's people and the ones he called Megwah; she wanted to know more about his people, the Penobscot; she wanted to know more about the man who lay on the other side of the fire.

After some minutes of silence, White Wolf said quietly, "Come here, English." He lifted one side of the deerskin.

She did not move for the space of one heartbeat. Her mind teetered between acquiescing and refusing. She wanted no repeat of that shameful night when he had kissed her. Yet, the invitation he was extending to share his warmth was so appealing. She had not been warm at night since they had slept together beneath the brambles after he had rescued her from the wolves. Without any more thought, Rachel rose from her own pile of boughs and walked around the fire. She vowed to herself that if he tried to kiss her again, she would find some way to kill him.

She lay down beside White Wolf and held herself stiffly away from his body. He dropped the deerskin over her and his arm fell across her middle. With little effort, he pulled her back against his hard body.

"It is to keep warm that I told you to come, English," he murmured in her ear. "If you lie away from me like a stick, you will be as cold as if you had slept alone."

Rachel thought she heard a hint of amusement in his voice, but she did not care. His warmth enveloped her and the slow, regular beat of his heart soothed her. She felt protected and cared for in a way she had never felt before. Instinctively, she knew that he would not attack her in her sleep. With a sigh, she realized just how tired she was. She was asleep in the space of two breaths.

When Rachel awoke the next morning, a light drizzle was falling. Even though the temperature had risen enough so that the precipitation was not snow, still the air was raw and damp. White Wolf no longer shared the deerskin with her. She felt his absence keenly. She got up and went in among the trees to take care of her needs. By the time she emerged, White Wolf had returned. When he spoke, it was evident he had been scouting the area.

"The Megwah hunters are still very close," he told her as he hunched before the cold ashes of the fire. "It is strange for them to come this far. Their people must be very hungry. We must move quickly and quietly as the wind. The men will be hunting for food. If they find us, it will not go easy for you. Sport with a white woman would lighten their spirits."

"Won't it be worse for you if they find us?" she asked.

He raised those devilish blue eyes to her face as she stood on the other side of the remnants of their campfire. She saw a look of surprise and gratitude flash quickly in them before he masked his feelings.

"A warrior meets his death bravely," he said. "I will not hide like the timid rabbit when it is time for me to meet my ancestors."

"Well, that is very noble of you, but I think we should move out of their hunting ground as quickly as we can, don't you?"

White Wolf ducked his head to hide his smile. In the time it took to breathe in and breathe out, the woman had surrendered to his authority yet had made it clear that she could think for herself. Once again controlling

104

his features, he stood up.

"You speak wisely, English," he said. "There will be no cooking fires until we have safely left the Megwah hunters behind."

"But we had a fire last night," Rachel argued.

"The Great Spirit watched over us and kept us safe," he told her. "We should not presume on the Great Spirit's goodwill. No cooking fires."

Rachel sighed. "How long before we can light one?" Already she missed the heat from a fire. The drizzle and cold penetrated to her very bones.

"Maybe two, maybe three suns," he said. "The hunters will not be foolish enough to venture much farther into the land of the Abnaki."

"Who are the Abnaki?" Rachel asked.

"The People of the Dawn. They are our cousins. The People live where the sun rises. The Megwah live where the sun sets."

"Then I guess the sooner we get started, the sooner we'll be able to light a fire and get warm again," she said with a shiver.

"You will be warm enough by the time we have stopped to eat," he told her. "Come, we must break camp and set out on our journey."

For the first time since her capture, Rachel set to scattering the ashes of the campfire and doing the other small tasks assigned her with enthusiasm. She had no wish to fall into the hands of the Megwah and be their meal. It was not long before she was once again following behind White Wolf as he led her through the forest.

# Chapter Eight

The wet weather continued for two days. During that time, Rachel slogged along silently behind White Wolf as he led her away from the Megwah hunting party. Her disposition quickly deteriorated into sullen grumpiness. In her head she railed against the wet and the cold and particularly the unfeeling arrogance of the man she followed. Her gentler feelings towards him dissolved in the rain. He moved through the dripping forest as if he were simply taking a walk in the summer sunshine. Nothing — not the cold, not the dampness, not the soggy, slushy ground — nothing seemed to affect him.

Her captor, as he had said, allowed no fires. Therefore, their meals consisted of those small, dried up little balls which he had first offered her. She discovered they were called pemmican, but knowing what they were did not make them any more palatable. It was one more thing in a long list that she held against him.

The idea of escape flitted through her head from time to time, but she was so miserable she did not have the energy to try any feats of bravery. It was not until the gray dawn of the third day that she realized just how stupid she had been. If the Megwah were enemies of White Wolf's people, and his people were allies of the French, then the Megwah must be allies of the English, she reasoned. If she escaped to the Megwah, they would probably return her to an English settlement.

As she lay huddled on her pile of pine boughs at dawn of the third day without a fire, she watched from beneath half-closed eyelids while White Wolf made his regular, early morning survey of their camp. There was no sign that he suffered any ill effects from sleeping in the cold and damp on the ground. Rachel hated him for that, because she was stiff and very uncomfortable. When he finally moved off into the forest to attend to his needs, she waited a few moments to be sure he was far enough away before she scrambled to her feet. He had left her covered with the deerskin, and she decided she would take it with her. At least one of them would keep relatively warm. Without another glance around, she headed off in the opposite direction from her captor.

She had no real plan. All she wanted was to come across that group of hunters that White Wolf had been so anxious to avoid. She thought that if she just wandered about she would eventually run into them.

Even though the snow underfoot was wet and heavy and difficult to move through, her spirits suddenly soared. She had finally escaped the man who had captured her, and in so doing, had escaped the fate of being thrust into the bosom of the French whom she despised so much. If the snow had not prevented her, she would have had a bounce in her step. She was free, and soon, she would be returning home.

Towards midmorning, the drizzle stopped and the wind changed. A while later, the clouds broke up and disappeared. The sun was warm on her back when she was out in the open. Rachel felt the change in the weather was a good sign, and she picked up her pace. After two miserable days, she would finally be relatively dry.

Not having any definite destination in mind, she was not particularly upset when she came out onto a narrow flood plain and a swiftly moving mountain stream confronted her. Walking to its bank, she surveyed the rushing water. It was too deep to cross where she stood, so she moved upstream to find a place to ford. With the spring thaw, the stream had swollen to twice its normal width and depth. There was no place to cross. Moving back downstream, she again found no place shallow enough that would allow her easy access to the other bank. With one last glance at the roiling water, she gave a sigh and turned back in the direction she had come. She decided she would duck into the treeline and follow the path of the stream. Someone, she thought, must use the stream for drinking water and cooking. Eventually, she would stumble upon them.

After taking only a few steps, a small rustling in the bushes ahead of her made her stop. She strained to see what had caused the noise. The disturbance had been too small to have been caused by any large animal like a deer or moose — she hoped. When all remained quiet and nothing emerged into her path, she moved on. As she passed the bushes that had first rustled, something else moved ahead of her. Again, she could see nothing. When the same thing happened a third time, she became truly frightened. Perhaps she had run into the Megwah hunters. The idea of joining up with them and the actual fact of meeting them were entirely different, she discovered.

"Hello?" she called timidly. "Is anyone there?"

There was no answer.

"Hello?" she called again.

There was still no response.

A shiver ran down her spine, and she glanced back over her shoulder. She had the uncanny feeling that someone, or something, was watching her. Not seeing or hearing anything else, she shook her head at herself.

"You silly girl," she scolded herself aloud. "It was probably just a bird."

As she finished speaking, the cry of the bluejay came from just ahead.

"There, you see?" she said. "It was only a bluejay looking for something to eat."

As she passed beneath an oak tree, she glanced up into its branches to see if she could spot a bright flash of the blue feathers of the bird. When she lowered her gaze to the path, a dark figure blocked her vision. With a scream, she jumped back. White Wolf stood in her path with his arms crossed arrogantly across his chest.

Furious that he had found her and scared her so, Rachel immediately attacked. "You!" she accused. "How dare you frighten me so!"

"You are easily frightened, English," he said quietly. "Speaking aloud will chase away the animals, but will only amuse the Megwah. A silly white woman will make a good slave."

"You are just trying to make me afraid of them," Rachel scoffed.

"As you should be."

"Well, I'm not. And I'm not going any farther with you," she announced. "I am not your prisoner any more."

As she spoke her last word, she swung around and fled

back the way she had come. He was not going to have her as his prisoner any longer. He was not going to keep her around to satisfy his savage urges as he did on that awful night when he had kissed her. He was not. He was not.

She repeated those three words to herself as she tried desperately to outrun her captor. Branches reached out and tugged at her clothes; trees put themselves in her way; the wet snow and mud underfoot sucked at her feet and slowed her steps. When she finally broke free of the trees, she ran along the bank of the stream. She could hear White Wolf behind her. His running steps were easy and rhythmic. While she panted in her urgency to escape him, his breathing was not in the least labored.

Finally, she found she could go no further. She was on a small rock outcropping which rose many feet above the stream. Before her was a drop to the stream bed twice as high as she was tall. Behind her, White Wolf blocked the path back into the trees. Her breath rasped in her throat and her lungs burned. She was winded and trapped. She turned to face her captor.

"I am not going any farther with you," she repeated. "I will find my own way back to my people." She took a step back.

"You will die in the forest before you reach them," White Wolf told her. "You will come with me."

Rachel shook her head. "No." She stepped back again. Pebbles scuffed beneath her feet. They rolled away off the rock and fell to the stream below.

"There is no choice, English."

"There is." Desperate for escape, afraid of what her captor might do to her, fearful of her own shameful reaction to him, she felt her eyes fill with the tears of weakness. Stepping back again, she reached the edge of the rock. "I will jump into the stream and drown," she threatened.

Amusement flickered across White Wolf's face. His frosty blue eyes turned warm. "You will not drown, English."

"Don't laugh at me!" she raged.

Her anger came not only from being mocked but also from the odd, delicious tremble she felt in her middle at the softening of those devilish eyes. He was a cad, a savage, a heathen. He would not have her again. Before she could think about it, she stepped back again into the air.

The thin scream which escaped her lips as she plummeted down was cut off abruptly as she hit the rushing water. Its iciness stole her breath and its swiftness pulled her under as she fought for a foothold. The strength of the current dragged her along, and she bounced painfully off the rocky bottom. As she gasped for air, her fingers clawed at anything that would keep her from being swept away. The terrifying thought came to her that she really was going to drown. Finally, she came to rest against a boulder near the edge of the stream. Sitting on the bottom, clinging to the rock, she pulled in huge lungfuls of air.

The frightful experience had left her limbs with no strength to heave herself up. The cold had numbed her to the point of paralysis. She watched as White Wolf strode to the edge of the stream and stood with his hands on his hips. His lips quirked slightly upward in what could almost be a smile.

"Of course you're going to just stand there and watch me like an idiot," she mumbled through stiff, blue lips. She floundered about in the water as she tried to stand against the icy, rushing current. "Could you please help?" she yelled in exasperation.

He enjoyed her plight a moment longer before he waded out knee-deep into the water. She took his proffered hand, and he hauled her to the rocky bank. Her clothes were leaden and clung to her body in frigid folds. The cool breeze felt like icicles against her skin.

"I said you would not drown, English," he reminded her. "Perhaps you only wished to bathe?"

Even with chills shaking her body and her teeth chattering madly, she threw him a murderous look. His smugness made her blood boil, although not enough to get her warm at the moment.

"I n-need-d a f-f-fire," she stuttered through her chattering teeth.

"No fire."

"P-Please," she pleaded. "I'm f-f-freezing."

"Undress," he told her.

"I b-beg-g your p-par-d-don?" She was not sure she had heard him correctly.

"No fire, English. Take off your clothes to get warm."

She hugged herself and shook her head vehemently.

"You can only get warm if your clothes are dry."

Rachel backed up a step and shook her head again. "N-No."

He sighed in exasperation. "English . . ." His voice trailed off. "English," he tried again, then stopped. He stared at the woman shivering before him. The idea of having her remove her clothes made his blood sing. He wanted to see her in all her glory without those hideous coverings. He wanted to feast his eyes on the swell of her breasts, the curve of her hips. Fool, he told himself. What he wanted was impossible.

Getting himself under control once more, he said quietly, "What you are afraid of will not happen again."

Rachel stared at him while she tried to decide if he was telling the truth. Nothing in his manner revealed what he was actually thinking, whether he would keep his word or attack her as soon as she was vulnerable. So far, except for that one instance, he had been honorable. She felt that in spite of his being a savage, she could trust him.

With a tiny nod, she agreed. "All r-right-t. T-T-Turn around."

He tossed her the deerskin she had dropped in her flight and the wolf pelt from his back. Without another word, he turned his back to her.

Rachel also turned her back and stripped the sodden clothes from her body as quickly as her cold, trembling fingers allowed. Not wishing to be completely naked, she left on her nightdress, then wrapped herself in the deerskin and threw the wolf pelt about her shoulders. When she was satisfied that she was well covered, she turned back to White Wolf.

"All r-right," she said. "Y-You c-can t-turn around-d n-now."

He turned to face her and his eyes travelled the length of her body. Shaking his head in exasperation, he told her, "I said all your clothes, English."

"I d-did."

He pointed to where her nightdress fluttered soggily against her ankles.

"I w-wish to k-keep it-t on," she announced with a defiant tilt to her chin.

"Off." He took a menacing step towards her.

Rachel scampered back, fearful he would rip the nightdress from her body. "All r-right," she muttered. "T-Turn around-d. I'll t-take it off."

When the nightdress lay in the pile with the rest of her clothes, White Wolf scooped them up and began laying them across bushes in the sun. Rachel stood shivering and hopping from one foot to the other as the cold from the ground seeped into her bare soles.

When White Wolf had finished, he said, "Come," and strode away. Rachel followed meekly. Sitting in the shelter of the outcropping of rock where the breeze was blocked but the sun shone brightly, he motioned for Rachel to sit beside him. Carefully, she sat almost an arm's length away. With a sardonic lift to his brow, he easily shifted her so that she sat cuddled next to him in the protection of his arm. He tucked her feet beneath his thigh and spread her wet hair across her shoulder so that it would dry.

Despite Rachel's first impulse to scuttle away, the need to be warm again overcame her trepidation at being in such close contact with her captor. As much as she did not want to, she had to admit she felt comfortable in this man's embrace. Slowly, between the warmth of the sun, the warmth of the man near her, and the heat from her own body, Rachel's shivers stopped. The necessity for her to be so close to White Wolf disappeared, yet she was reluctant to move away. For once, she did not feel any negative feelings emanating from him. There was no anger, no wall of reserve, no cloak of sarcasm. He seemed content to merely sit in the sun with her.

White Wolf was very aware of the woman's body as she cuddled next to him. He felt her shivers slow and stop, and knew he should release her and move away. Yet, he was at ease, and for once, the demons which haunted him had receded. This woman with the hair of hidden fire surely had strong powers to be able to give him such a feeling of contentment, even if for a short time.

He found that he enjoyed her company as they journeyed through the forest. When he had first seen her that night — so long ago it seemed — in her village and known she would be his revenge, he had sensed there was something special about her. Now, he knew he had not been wrong. Each day she proved herself worthy of him. She complained little of their hardships, and when she did complain, he was usually forced to swallow his laughter. Her spirit was strong and free and cheerful. He wished to prove himself worthy in her eyes. He wished to prove himself brave and strong. It was not wise, he knew. She was his revenge. Yet to see in her eyes her respect for his courage would make his heart full. If he could bring her safely to the village of his mother's people and then to the village of his father's people, he would be content.

Although he knew he should not reach out to her, he wanted to know about her. She would leave him at the village of his father's people. He would no longer be her protection from death. Yet, he needed to hold something of her thoughts in his heart. When she left him, that memory would be enough.

"Tell me about your family."

Rachel had been so comfortable in the crook of White Wolf's arm that she was half dozing. Hearing his voice murmur its request startled her into full awareness. She should not be cuddling so near to him. It was not right for her to feel so content in this man's embrace. Sitting up straighter, she tried to ease away from him, but his arm tightened about her shoulders.

"Tell me about your family," he repeated.

Forced to lean against him once more, she decided that it was infinitely more comfortable than shivering in the cool breeze. She felt safe and protected, feelings that were contradictory with her situation of being this man's captive. Giving her head a mental shake at such odd sensations, she realized she had not answered him.

"My family," she said slowly, "are all dead."

There was silence from White Wolf, and she sensed he felt that she was accusing him.

"My father died last autumn from the wasting disease," she explained. "My mother . . . died when I was fifteen, seven years ago."

"Are there no brothers or sisters?" White Wolf asked.

Rachel shook her head. "There is no one, at least, no one close to me. I have an uncle who lives in Boston, but I have not seen him since my father and I moved to Deerfield."

"Your mother was already dead when you left Boston?"

Rachel turned her head and looked away across the stream. "Yes." Her voice was muted when she answered.

White Wolf sensed the deep pain of the woman's loss of her parents, but there was also anger in her feelings when she spoke of her mother. She was holding something tight in her heart.

"How did your mother die?" he asked.

Rachel swung around to face him. Gazing straight into those bright blue pools, she announced furiously, "She was murdered. By the French."

The only sign of White Wolf's shock was a slight flickering of his eyelids. He felt that if he showed her the least bit of pity or compassion, the brittle shell which dammed her heart would collapse and she would be unable to continue their journey. Better that she should feed on the anger until he could get her to his mother's people where she

116

would be safe from hunger and the Megwah. Then would be time enough to discover the truths in the woman's heart.

"She is at peace. She has gone to the Great Spirit," he stated.

The woman made a hissing noise and straightened stiffly away from him. "I needed her more than the Great Spirit," she said angrily. "I plan to find and kill the Frenchman who murdered her." She looked deep into White Wolf's eyes. "Not you nor anyone will stop me."

White Wolf felt an odd thrill run through him at the woman's statement. He knew she meant what she said. When the time came for her to strike at her enemy, she would do it swiftly and bravely like the hawk. Truly, this woman should have been born a warrior.

Rachel finally broke her eyes away from the blue gaze of her captor. Heat rushed into her face at what she had just revealed. She had never said that to anyone before, not even her father. Somehow, this man, her captor, had made her open her soul.

"My clothes must be dry by now," she mumbled as she scrambled to her feet. "I should get dressed."

She regretted leaving the warmth of White Wolf's embrace, but she felt it was what she deserved for being so complaisant with him. He was her captor, for heaven's sake, not her betrothed. She should not be sitting about in the sun cuddling with him and revealing her innermost secrets. The chill breeze cooled her body where White Wolf had warmed it. Quickly gathering her clothes, she moved to the other side of the rock and dressed.

Her clothes had benefitted from their ducking. Much of the accumulated dirt from their journey had been washed from them. Rachel herself felt cleaner. Since the weather was beginning to grow a bit warmer, perhaps she would ask White Wolf if she could bathe occasionally — without her clothes. Only her shoes had not dried, but since they were the only ones she had, she slipped them on. It would take too long for them to dry. She knew White Wolf wished to begin travelling again as soon as possible.

After she had donned her clothes, she returned to the other side of the rock. White Wolf stood leaning back against the boulder. His face was turned up to the sun's rays; his eyes were closed.

Arrested by the sight of this man in repose, Rachel stopped in her tracks. He was magnificent. Proud, brave, and wildly handsome. Rachel's heart quickened its beat; her breath caught in her throat. This was the man who had taken her hostage, who had saved her life. He had touched her in passion and made her aware of feelings she had not known she possessed. A warmth, different from that of the sun's, seeped through her body.

Stop it, she scolded herself. Don't be a fool. He is your captor. He wants you only for your ransom. Getting herself under control, she took a step forward.

"I am ready," she announced. She held out the folded deerskin and the wolf pelt.

When White Wolf heard her voice, he opened his eyes and turned to her. His thoughts had wandered aimlessly as he waited for the woman to dress, but always they had somehow returned to a vision of her in the village of his mother's people. He had seen her planting the maize, tanning hides, cooking meals. He had seen her laughing with the women, dancing around the fire. He had seen her big with child. His gaze raked over her now, coming

118

to rest finally on her parted mouth. She was pleasant to look upon, this woman. His visions had pleased his heart. Her pink tongue came out and wet her lips. The muscles of his groin tightened. No, he told himself. Those visions were not meant for him to enjoy. Blinking his eyes to wipe away his wandering thoughts, he straightened and accepted the deerskin and wolf pelt from the woman.

"The ducking has improved you, English," he said. "It is pleasant to see your face no longer covered with dirt."

Rachel sucked in her breath at the backhanded compliment. It was all she had needed to return her to reality. When White Wolf had first opened his eyes and looked at her, she had felt mesmerized by the heat in his gaze. It was as if he held her bound to the spot where she stood. She would have bent easily to his will had he wanted it. Then he had blinked and spoken his words. It was as if that warmth in his gaze had not existed. Now, her temper took over her wayward emotions.

"I would not be so dirty if we were not traipsing through the woods day after day," she snapped.

"The warrior meets his fate calmly and does not complain," he said.

"I am not a warrior," she stated.

As he returned the deerskin to his pack, he said quietly, "Neither does a warrior's woman complain."

Rachel hesitated, wondering if she had heard him correctly. When he straightened again and looked into her eyes, she knew she had. "I'm not a warrior's woman, either," she told him.

"That is right, English, you are not." Hefting his pack over his shoulder, he turned away. "Come, we have spent enough time in this place. The Megwah could find

119

us." He began walking along the bank of the stream.

Rachel was rather disconcerted with his quick agreement that she was no warrior's woman. It pained her somehow that he had not contradicted her. Then realizing the direction of her thoughts, she gave herself a mental shake. Of course she was no warrior's woman, especially not that warrior's. What in the world had she been thinking! He was arrogant and cruel and heartless and he was already way ahead of her. Grinding her teeth together, she began to run to catch up to him. Someday, she would teach this . . . this cad, this savage, this heathen a lesson. Someday.

# Chapter Nine

It was another two nights before White Wolf allowed a fire. During that time, they had eaten only a few of the balls of pemmican supplemented by acorns and ground-nuts which the foraging squirrels had not found. By the time White Wolf brought back a turkey to cook over their first fire in days, Rachel was weak from hunger. She was positive that her captor was trying to starve her to death.

When the turkey was cooked and she had broken it in half, she settled down to devour her portion. After she had taken two quick bites of the hot meat, White Wolf put his hand on her arm to stop her from taking another. She cast an angry glance at him.

"Eat slowly," he told her. "You have not had much food. You are not used to it."

"I know that," she snapped. "You've been trying to starve me." She took a bite of turkey.

"I have been saving you from the Megwah, English."

"Hmph," was all she said as she took another bite of meat. Swallowing, she told him, "That was only an ex-cuse so you wouldn't have to hunt."

"I have not eaten either."

"Well, you redmen can go for days without eating. Everyone knows that. You're different than we are."

White Wolf's eyes narrowed dangerously. This woman's manners had fled with the arrival of the turkey. "Of course," he agreed quietly. "We have horns and a tail and cast evil spells on all the white men."

Intent on her meal, Rachel missed the cold fury in his eyes. "No, no," she said impatiently. "Not that. But you are different. You can walk forever without getting tired, and you can move as silently as a cat, and you have no fear of death."

"We can do those things because we learn them from birth, English, not because we are something other than men."

"Still, no white man can do those things no matter how much he practices. That proves you are different," Rachel shrugged as she took another huge bite of turkey. She was not interested in this argument. She only wanted to eat.

Furiously, White Wolf knocked the meat from her hand and sent it flying back into the fire. Taking her by the arm, he swung her about to face him.

Rachel was just as incensed that he should do such a thing. "Why did you do that?" she yelled. "You horrible man! That was the first decent food I've had in days and now it's gone!" She glanced longingly at the flames devouring her piece of turkey.

White Wolf gave her a little shake, gaining her full attention. "What I have done, English, I have done to keep you alive. I am a man, like any other. I do not have horns or a tail or cast evil spells. I hunt and track better than any white man because I have been taught to do so. I have not allowed fires because the Megwah would have been able to smell them and would have known someone else was near their hunting ground. I told you to eat slowly so that you would not be sick. If you wish to be stupid and eat more, the meat is there, near the fire. I will not stop you from taking it. I thought you were different from other white women, but you are not. All you can see is what you wish to see. Dark Eagle was right. You cause nothing but trouble. I cannot swallow my anger any longer."

Rachel stared up into those blazing eyes and felt his fury to her very soul. Shame at what she had said and how she had acted welled up inside of her. Tears of remorse filled her eyes and spilled over down her cheeks.

"I'm sorry," she whispered brokenly. "I didn't mean to hurt you. I know you have been keeping me alive." She turned her face away to hide from his accusing gaze. "It's been so hard," she sobbed.

White Wolf's heart tightened in his chest. Until now, the woman had shown the courage of a warrior, but even a warrior felt fear. Softly his hand moved up her arm and, across her shoulder to the back of her neck. With a gentle tug, he pulled her body against his and wrapped his arms about her protectively. He waited as she cried out her pain and sorrow and fear against his shoulder.

Rachel's sobs racked her body. White Wolf's shoulder was warm and comforting. As much as she did not want to appear weak before this man, she found she could not stop the tears from flowing. It was as if his sudden anger at her had broken through the dam she had built around her emotions. Only after a long time did her tears stop running. As she caught her breath and sniffed, she realized her face was pressed tightly against his chest and his strong arms held her. She felt the heat of embarrassment

123

flood her face, and she tried to push away from him.

"No," he commanded softly. "You will not run away like a frightened doe."

Rachel remained unmoving for a moment longer, then once more she tried to push away from him.

"Please," she entreated. "Let me go."

White Wolf pulled back from her slightly, but did not release her. With one large hand, he forced her to look up at him. His long fingers splayed across her cheek; his thumb hooked beneath her chin. She could not have turned away even if she wanted.

"It is time for you to understand why you are here, English," he told her.

Becoming angry that he would not let her go and a little bit afraid that he would try to kiss her, Rachel said coldly, "I am not simple. I understand why I am here. There is no reason for you to explain it to me."

One sculpted black eyebrow shot up at her words. "Then explain to me why you are here," he challenged.

"Because—because you want to . . ." Embarrassed, she tried to turn away, but he would not let her. The most she could do was lower her eyes.

"That is not why I took you, English."

The tone of his voice drew her gaze back to his face. His lips were quirked upward in the tiniest of smiles. Those demonic blue eyes had turned warm like the sky on a summer's day. Resisting the pull to fall into the depths of those eyes, she lowered her own, only to have her gaze catch on his chiseled mouth. The memory of how those lips had felt on her flashed through her body. She suddenly wanted him to kiss her again. No! she told herself. No, not that, not ever again. She squeezed shut her eyes to erase his mouth from her sight, but she could

124

not erase the feel of his strong arm about her or the touch of his fingers across her cheek. Her skin tingled wherever his body pressed.

"Closing your eyes does not take away your want, English," he murmured.

Her eyes flew open. "What want?" she demanded. "I do not want you. You are a . . . Well, I do not want you."

"Of course not." His thumb gently scraped across her lips once, twice. "It is good you do not, for, you see, that is not why I took you."

Rachel blinked as she tried to reconcile his words with his actions. His thumb was very distracting.

"Why?" Her question came out in a hoarse croak. Clearing her throat, she asked again, "Why did you capture me?"

In amazement, she watched his eyes turn cold. His thumb returned to its original position beneath her chin. The angles of his face sharpened as he stared hard into her eyes.

"I took you because you are my revenge, English. I saved you from Dark Eagle, and I saved you from the wolves for that reason. You will come with me to New France, and there you will remain."

Rachel blinked as the enormity of his statement sank into her brain. Not actually understanding, needing some clarification, she searched a moment to find her voice.

"Forever?" she murmured.

"Forever."

A coldness gripped Rachel's insides at White Wolf's ruthless words. For some reason, she had not really believed in being kept forever a prisoner in New France. She had presumed that somehow she would be returned

125

to Deerfield, to her friends and familiar surroundings. Now, she knew that was not to happen. This man who enticed her so gently, who confused her mind and her body with his touch, who had ripped her from her home, would keep her a prisoner for the rest of her life.

"No," she whispered desperately.

"Yes," he contradicted. His eyes narrowed dangerously. "You are my revenge. Yes, English, that is the way it is to be."

"I hate you," she spat.

"I know you do."

Rachel broke away from him and quickly moved to sit on the other side of the fire. Hugging her legs, she rested her chin on her knees and watched the man who had so ruthlessly decided to use her for his own purposes. She saw him calmly reach for a chunk of turkey and munch it. He acted as if nothing had happened, as if he had just informed her it was going to snow instead of telling her she would never be going home. Turning her head, she gazed at the darkness beyond the firelight. Escape was impossible. She knew that now. The man who held her prisoner would always find her no matter how many times she tried to get away or how clever she was.

A movement across the fire drew her attention. White Wolf was pulling the deerskin from his pack. She knew what that meant. He glanced up at her with those demonic blue eyes.

"It is time to sleep," he announced.

Without a word, Rachel pulled her cloak tighter about her shoulders and curled up where she was. Determined to shut out the fiend not far away, she closed her eyes.

"Here, English."

Rachel's eyes snapped open and she sat up. Balefully,

she glared at her captor. His impassive gaze merely watched her. She hated him. After informing her of his cruelty, he expected her to sleep with him? He was a beast — worse than a beast! He was the Devil incarnate! In barely contained fury, she leapt to her feet and faced him.

White Wolf stood as the woman stood. He knew well the signs of a cornered animal. She would either attack him or take flight. He watched her eyes flick to the forest and back again. There was no doubt in his mind that he would be able to catch her should she decide to try to flee, but he sincerely hoped she would not. The past few days of little food had sapped his strength more than he would admit to the woman. He did not relish the idea of chasing her in the dark through the forest. Neither did he like the thought of fighting off the attack of a woman turned wild-cat.

"Come, English," he commanded softly.

His words appeared to make up her mind for her. She briefly closed her eyes and clenched her jaw. When she looked at him again, the anger in her gaze had been dampened and veiled. Woodenly, she moved around the fire to stand before him.

"Someday, I will take *my* revenge," she told him defiantly.

"I will live for that day, English."

In satisfaction, he watched the startling effect of his seductive words on her. Her lips parted and a slow blush crept into her cheeks. Once again, her want was plainly visible in her eyes. Rage quickly replaced it and then was gone as she masked her emotions.

He pointed to a spot on the pine branches at his feet. With an angry glare, but in silence, she lay down where he indicated. White Wolf lay down next to her, covered them both with the deerskin and pulled her up against him. Her body was stiff with rage.

Curling his knees beneath her bottom, he allowed himself a tiny smile. He had accomplished what he had wished. When the woman began to cry and he had held her close, the warmth and softness of her had been almost his undoing. He had desperately wanted to kiss her again, to feel her passion.

But she was not for that. He had told her bluntly what she was to him in order to make her hate him. He was drawn to this woman, wanting her as a man wants a woman. He knew that her hate of him would place a barrier between them that he would not be able to cross. It would keep his mind clear for the purpose of this journey and not cloud it with soft feelings for this woman.

They would not reach their destination for many suns. His honor had suffered enough because of this woman. He would not allow it to be snuffed out completely by a woman with hair of hidden fire and eyes the color of the blue spruce.

Hearing the woman's even breathing indicating she was asleep, he closed his eyes. Despite the troubles she caused, he was pleased with his choice. Each day, this woman challenged and enticed him. Truly, she was a worthy enemy.

Rachel awoke with a start. For a moment, she savored the warmth of White Wolf as he lay next to her. His breathing came and went softly against her neck. She allowed her eyes to wander slowly over the campsite as she erased the cobwebs of sleep. It was still dark, but dawn was not far away. A few birds who had not been afraid of spending the winter in the cold twittered in their early morning ritual. All appeared no different than on other mornings. Then she remembered. For her, this day was the beginning of an endless captivity.

Suddenly, the warmth beneath the deerskin was suffocating. She eased herself away from White Wolf so as not to awaken him. Gently, she rolled out from under the deerskin and went to sit on the other side of the cold ashes of the fire. The wind was blowing its last breath before the dawn stillness, and she raised her face to it to cool her flushed cheeks. When she felt her emotions begin to calm, she let her gaze fall on the sleeping man not far away.

This was the first time she had been able to study her captor. Always before, she had been too angry, or too frightened, or too embarrassed to do more than peek at him. And then there were those times when all she could see were those demonic blue eyes. But now, now she could look at him all she wished.

As she watched, the gray of dawn slowly sculpted him out of the darkness. He had rolled onto his stomach when she had left him, and the deerskin had fallen away from one leg. That leg, exactly like the other, was long and appeared well-shaped beneath the deerskin leggings he wore tucked into high, soft, deerskin boots. He wore a linen tunic beneath one of deerskin. Both of these had ridden up during his sleep. As it became lighter in their camp, Rachel realized she could see the bare skin between his belt and the top of his legging. His breechclout draped itself scantily across his bottom. A shadowed hollow defined itself below his hip where the top of his thigh merged into the hardened muscle of his buttock.

Rachel had the urge to run her fingers across that hollow. Clenching her fists, she quickly repressed the urge and told herself how much she hated the man and what a Jezebel she was for even wanting to do such a thing in the first place.

The deerskin beneath which they had slept covered him to his shoulder. His head rested on his arm, and his face was turned towards her. It was a strong face with a broad forehead, high cheekbones and long, straight nose. His eyebrows were black slashes above his closed eyes and his mouth was finely chiseled. She remembered well the feel of those lips on her own, how they had ignited strange, powerful feelings inside her. She gave her head a little shake. No. Never again.

This man who slumbered so peacefully not far away was the most beautiful man she had ever encountered. Yes, she admitted, beautiful was the correct word. His form, his grace, his strength all combined into the closest thing to perfection in a man she had ever seen. Yet all that beauty housed a heart of stone. He was cold and ruthless. Why else would he have captured her with the sole intent of never allowing her to return home?

Pain shot through her at that thought, and she shut her eyes to try to block it out. Having lived through the deaths of both parents, she was not one to dwell on what might have been. She had learned to accept the inevitable. Yet that did not mean that she would not fight to improve her situation. As this man's prisoner, she vowed that he would not find her a congenial travelling companion. There were ways she could make his life difficult. After coming to that decision, she opened her eyes and found the piercing gaze of her captor resting on her.

She stood up and deliberately walked into the woods.

Let him think what he wanted, she decided. There was no reason for her to ask his permission for anything, not any more. She was not in his debt for saving her life any longer. He had not done it out of compassion for her, but because she was only a means to satisfy some dark need that raged in his soul. How could she be grateful for that? Better to have let Dark Eagle or the wolves have her.

There was a small, swift running brook not far into the trees. Here, Rachel performed some haphazard morning ablutions in the cold dawn air. When she finished, she returned to their camp at a leisurely pace. White Wolf looked up from honing his hunting knife when she entered the clearing. She could feel his eyes on her as she went about her chores of breaking camp. When she had finished, she stood waiting for him to lead off into the woods to begin their journey once again.

He took his time completing his task. When he was done, he stood and slipped the knife into its sheath at his waist, collected his bow and quiver of arrows where they hung on a branch, and faced her.

"What I told you last night changes nothing, English," he said quietly.

"It changes everything," she contradicted in a low, furious tone.

Before she said anything else that might jeopardize her safety, she pressed her lips together and turned away. She wanted to rage at him, scream at him in her anger and frustration, but she felt she could not. The fury in his eyes when he revealed his true purpose in capturing her struck fear into her. She sensed she was the captive of a man who would stop at nothing to attain his goal. There was no doubt in her mind that he would keep her alive until the end of the journey and possibly even after that, but there was no reason for him not to torment her along the way.

She had decided that morning that if there was to be any tormenting, she would be the one to do it. No more would she be curious about his people. There would be no more hesitant discussions, no more sharing of their separate lives. She would only speak when spoken to, and perhaps not even then if she did not feel like answering. He would learn she was not to be taken lightly.

White Wolf had remained silent for the space of three heartbeats after her statement. She could feel those devilish blue eyes looking at her. Finally, she heard him say, "Come, English." She turned her head just as he began to walk into the woods. Obedient for now, she followed. There had been no indication in his command that her statement had made any impression on him. There was no anger beneath his words because of her contradiction, not even any curiosity.

Well, why should there be? she asked herself. You are nothing to him, only a means for him to gain his revenge. And he is nothing to you, only the man who captured you. You were a fool to develop any soft feelings for him. He is a savage. Remember that.

That tiny voice which occasionally disturbed her serenity decided to let itself be heard then.

He is more than a savage, it said. He is much, much more.

The hours of their journey turned into days and the days into weeks. Rachel spoke little and White Wolf spoke even less. She slept with him beneath the deerskin only because it was warm and would have been foolish not to do so. She had learned that lesson in those few nights after he had kissed her.

The weather remained cold and dismal as they travelled further north. Spring took its time coming to the mountains through which they journeyed. White Wolf was determined that this woman would not arrive at the village of his mother's people as ignorant as when he took her from her people. Even though she refused to speak to him, he forced her to learn the ways of his mother's people. He taught her to start a fire with a special rock that made sparks when it was hit against pebbles of another type of stone; he taught her to set rabbit traps. She became more proficient at skinning and cleaning game, and much better at cooking it over an open fire. She even was able to blaze a trail through the forest after he told her which direction he wanted to go. He watched with pride as her spirit and her body strengthened.

One evening, several weeks after what Rachel referred to as their quarrel, she was wandering aimlessly around their campsite. She could not go far, for they had stopped on a small cliff near the foot of a mountain. A wall of rock protected them at their backs and trees curved down one side. The other side was open to the breathtaking view, and the tops of evergreens growing below their perch acted like a hedge at the front of the cliff.

She was restless, even after a gruelling day of hiking through the mountains. The sun had not quite set, and its orange glow reflected off the hunting knife which White Wolf was honing. Not wanting to watch his graceful hands, she turned away. His deftness left her disgruntled. Her plan to torment him had backfired. Instead of being able to gain satisfaction at his anger or exasperation, she had been exposed instead to his bottomless patience. He had become her teacher, making her appreciate the ways of his people. And he did it with few words.

She was frustrated at his reaction to her plan, and she wanted to yell at him. She wanted him to yell back. She wanted to talk with him. She wanted to converse with another human being, to voice her thoughts and have someone respond to them.

White Wolf's bow and quiver of arrows hung from a low branch. For some reason, they caught her attention. She had never really looked at them until now, always taking the weapons for granted since they were such a part of him. She gingerly touched the intricate design of quilling that covered the basket quiver. It was beautiful and must have taken someone a very long time to do. About twenty arrows stuck up above its rim, but it could hold many more. Then she turned to the bow. If she stood it on its tip on the ground, it would not quite reach her shoulder. It was an odd configuration. There was a single, thin, braided cord of animal sinew which was the string, but the bow was made of two supple pieces of wood connected at the grip. She ran her fingers over the smooth wood.

"Would you like to learn how to use it, English?"

Rachel jumped at the sound of his voice so close behind her. She had not heard him move, yet he stood scant inches in back of her. Turning her head, she saw him watching her. There was no mockery in his eyes, only curiosity. She gave a tiny nod.

At her assent, he lifted the quiver and bow from the branch and strode to the far end of the small cliff. Pulling an arrow from the quiver, he nocked it on the bow.

"Come here, English." As he said that, he lifted his arms for Rachel to scoot under. When she was before him

134

and surrounded by his arms, he showed her where to place her hands and how to stand. Covering her hands with his, he helped her pull back the bowstring.

"Sight down the arrow and pick the spot where you want it to go," he told her.

"The spot of pitch on that fat tree," she said.

"Then let it go."

Rachel released the bowstring and immediately realized the reason for the double bow. It enabled the bowman to send the arrow at a great speed and distance without a tremendous amount of strength. She watched the arrow fly straight and true towards the tree she had picked out. It stuck, quivering, just above the spot of pitch.

"I almost hit it!" she exclaimed, very pleased with herself.

" 'Almost' will not catch meat for your empty middle or kill your enemy," he observed.

"Oh." She immediately felt very stupid.

"Come, English," he cajoled. "It was good for the first time. Try again."

Rachel thought she heard laughter in his voice, but decided she had to be wrong. This man never laughed. Even so, she was more determined to do better. Once again, she pulled back the bowstring with White Wolf's help and sighted down the arrow. Letting it fly, she watched nervously until it landed with a thwack in the middle of the spot of pitch.

"There!" she said triumphantly. "I hit it!"

"So you did," he agreed. "Try again."

Rachel tried again and again. Sometimes she hit her target, and sometimes she missed. Each time, White Wolf explained to her what she had done right and what she had done wrong. She was so intent on learning how to shoot with the bow that she forgot White Wolf's arms were about her, helping her. It was not until dusk had descended making it too dark to see the target that she realized she was in such close contact with her captor. His body surrounded her; her back was pressed against his hard chest and stomach; his arms encircled her.

"That is enough, English."

His deep voice rumbled in her ear, sending sudden shivers along her spine. Rachel did not move. Her hands were caught beneath his and a tingly warmth radiated up her arms. She dared not breathe for fear of making this moment disappear, for she discovered that she liked the feel of him around her. As he gently withdrew, she felt the merest touch of his lips across her ear. The sensation was so light and so swift she thought she had imagined it. Perhaps she had.

As he hung the bow from a branch, she asked, "May I try again tomorrow?"

He turned and regarded her across the flames of their campfire. "Perhaps," was his noncommittal answer. Rachel tried to read his thoughts, but as usual, those damnable blue eyes told her nothing. With a shrug, she went to sit next to the fire.

The tips of her fingers burned where she had held the bowstring, and she realized she had raised blisters. A small sound of dismay must have escaped her lips, for White Wolf looked up from his seat on the other side of the fire. Without asking her what the problem was, he commanded, "Come here, English."

She moved around the fire and knelt beside him. Taking her hand in his, he very lightly drew the blade of his hunting knife across the blisters. Then he squeezed the fluid from beneath the sore puffs of skin. Rachel sucked in her breath at the pain. White Wolf scooped up a handful of clean snow and held it across her fingertips.

"Your fingers will be sore for a few days," he told her. "Do you still wish to shoot with the bow tomorrow?"

Rachel glanced down at her fingers then back up at him. Gazing into those bottomless blue eyes, she had the feeling his question was more than curiosity. She felt that it was a test of some kind.

"Yes," she said. "I want to learn."

He gazed at her a moment as if searching her thoughts. Finally, he gave a quick nod of agreement and withdrew his hand from hers. Picking up an arrow he had laid beside him, he began to examine it.

Rachel keenly felt the loss of his touch on her hand. Despite the pain he had inflicted by cutting her blisters, she had welcomed his ministrations. Getting up and moving to the opposite side of the fire, she watched as he checked each of the arrows to be sure that the flint tips had not been damaged. Some, he sharpened; others, he returned to the quiver as they were. His fingers tested the shafts, felt the tips, caressed the feather flanges. His hands moved with sureness and grace. Rachel knew how those hands felt, and an odd jealousy of those slim shafts of wood took hold of her.

How ridiculous, she scoffed to herself when she realized what direction her thoughts were going. Remember what you are to him: only his revenge. You are nothing to him. He is nothing to you. He is beneath your contempt. Why, he probably would not know the first thing about proper manners in Boston society.

As she stiffened her spine and turned away from the hypnotic movements of his hands, she gave a loud sniff of

137

disdain. When they finally reached New France, she would show those miserable French and their savage allies that she had been bred a lady. She would prove to this redman what an ill-bred lout he really was.

Even as she made these arguments to herself, the thought niggled at her that her captor would not care if she had been taught court etiquette, that he might even laugh at her efforts to prove it. That is, if the man ever laughed at anything.

# Chapter Ten

During the days that followed, Rachel reminded herself again and again that her captor was a mere savage. Her fingers healed quickly because of his ministrations, and for that she was grateful. Yet, with his arms about her as he instructed her in the use of his bow, she found it necessary to repeat constantly in her head that he was a heathen. The innate gentility in his manner towards her contradicted her thoughts; the touch of his hands on her bare skin muddled her mind.

At the end of each day, despite the gruelling journey that took them through the mountains, she found her nerves wound tighter than a shuttlecock and sleep difficult to find. When White Wolf joined her beneath the deerskin for the night, the nearness of his body fed her agitation. Knowing only that he was the source of her unrest but not why, she silently cursed him as he led her on their journey. Her anger and frustration grew with each hour of each day.

They were moving through a pine forest at the foot of a mountain. It had snowed the night before, not much, just enough to leave a few more inches of pristine white on the ground. Since the winter was slowly giving way to spring, the snow was wet and sticky. It hung heavily on the branches above their heads.

Rachel was in a terrible mood. The snow was just deep enough that it came over the tops of her shoes at every step. Her feet were wet and cold, wetter and colder than usual. She doubted that she would ever be warm and dry again. And she blamed her misery all on the tall, broad-shouldered heathen who stepped lithely on the path ahead of her.

She hated him. She hated his grace, the way he seemed to belong in the forest. She hated the way he appeared to know everything. She hated his long-fingered hands and the way they made her feel as they covered hers on the bowstring. She hated his face, the lines and planes and angles that gave it such masculine perfection. But most of all, she hated his eyes—those clear, blue, fathomless pools that saw everything and gave away nothing.

Not fair, she told herself for the hundredth time that day.

Looking down, she watched her shoes in irritation as the snow caked across the toes. Suddenly, she had an idea, an absolutely, marvelously, wonderfully wicked idea. She scooped up a handful of snow and shaped it into a ball. Before she could consider the ramifications of her action, she let it fly — straight at the broad back of the man in front of her. The snowball had its own idea of where it wanted to go, however. Instead of landing harmlessly in the middle of White Wolf's back, it curved over his head and came to rest on a branch weighted down with heavy snow. The impact of the snowball was enough to dislodge the snow and allow it to plunge through the air to the ground. Except that it did not all land on the ground. Most of it fell directly on top of White Wolf.

Slowly, he turned to face her. A cone-shaped mound of white sat squarely on his head. Half in horror, half in hysterical amusement, Rachel clapped a hand over her mouth. She had never seen this man look less dignified than he did at that moment. Before she could stop it, laughter bubbled up and escaped in a giggle.

White Wolf's eyes narrowed. "Do you want to play, English?"

Rachel shook her head.

"I think you do." As he said this, he brushed the snow from his head with one hand and scooped some from the ground with the other.

Rachel took a step back.

As he straightened, he was forming the snow into a ball. When he began to move towards her, Rachel squealed and fled in the opposite direction. The snowball whacked harmlessly into a tree next to her. Rachel scooped up some snow and tossed it back over her shoulder. Because she had left it loose, it scattered and some landed on her prey. Another snowball landed harmlessly next to her. She laughed in delight. She had scored twice while White Wolf had missed her completely.

Dodging around a tree, she tried the same tactic with the snow again with equal success. This time, White Wolf was ready for her. At the same time she threw her snow, he threw some at her. It sprayed over her face and caught in her hair. Sputtering and giggling, she ran off into the woods with White Wolf close behind. As she glanced over her shoulder, she realized he was not there any longer. Cautiously, she looked around. He was nowhere to be seen. Step by step, she moved among the trees.

As she came around a particularly large pine tree, she saw White Wolf standing a few feet away. He casually tossed a snowball in the air and caught it again. What made Rachel stop, however, was not his presence or even the fact that he had a snowball. What arrested her was the fact that he was grinning like a little boy. He was enjoying himself!

Emotions too numerous to name suddenly swamped her. His grin was the most beautiful sight she had ever beheld. It made him irresistible. Befuddled at the sight of this usually impassive man actually having fun, she completely forgot that they were having a snowball fight. When White Wolf pointed to a branch above her head, she automatically looked up. It was not until she saw the snowball land and the avalanche of snow begin to fall that she realized her folly. By then it was too late. A deep, male laugh was muffled by the impact of snow on her head.

With a shriek, she wiped the snow from her face and tossed a chunk of snow at him. She bounded off into the trees before he could retaliate. White Wolf was not far behind. His footsteps pounded closer and closer. Laughing in delight, she glanced over her shoulder. He had disappeared again.

Rachel stopped and listened. All she could hear was her own breathing. The forest was quiet. Hesitantly, she took a step back in the direction she had come and peered about. There was no sign of him. She could not even find any footprints which might suggest where he had gone.

"White Wolf?" she queried.

Only silence.

She walked a few more paces.

"Hello? White Wolf?"

Still no answer.

One more step.

"I know you're there."

Another step.

Before she had time to speak again, she heard a shout come from her right and a form launched itself at her. With a screech of delicious fright, she recognized White Wolf as they both fell into a snowdrift. Laughing, she gazed up into his face as he lay above her.

His eyes were warm with amusement. The hard lines of his mouth had softened into a grin. She was struck again by the proud beauty of the man and the transformation that had come over him during their game. Her gaze caught in the hypnotic blue of those eyes, and she felt herself drowning in them. She watched, mesmerized, as they darkened in color to the same shade as the ocean on a clear, bright, summer day. Slowly, his grin faded. His expression became intense, searching.

Rachel could not think. Those eyes held her mind captive with their heat. All her senses were centered on his gaze. Instinctively, her tongue slipped out and wet dry lips. She knew what was coming, what she wanted. Yes, she wanted it. She wanted him to kiss her, to make her come alive. Nothing else mattered.

When his head dipped towards her, her eyes fluttered close. At the soft touch of his mouth against hers, a sigh escaped her lips. He teased her with tiny butterfly kisses. Rachel's fingers clutched at his deerskin tunic. His tongue gently outlined her mouth; he nipped softly at her bottom lip. When Rachel was about to scream in frustration, he took possession of her mouth. Her lips parted for him as his tongue slipped inside to taste the sweetness.

Rachel's arms slipped about him, holding him close as

she floated on the zephyr breezes of sensation. Her body throbbed with exquisite feelings that she had not known were possible. Time stood still and her surroundings faded away into nothing. All her awareness was focused on the man who kissed her.

His mouth slipped away from her lips and down her jaw. As Rachel caught her breath, she felt his tongue make lazy circles on the sensitive spot below her ear. She turned her head to allow him access.

The thought of denying this man what he wanted never entered her mind. Her fear of him, her dislike, her contempt, all faded away before the truth of his touch. All her preformed notions about this man were gone, sizzled to cinders in the heat of his kiss.

She felt his fingers at the ties of her nightdress, and then a coolness as he pushed her clothing away before his warm lips covered the tip of her breast. A sharp thrill ran through her body at his touch. Gasping with pleasure, her hand held the back of his head as his tongue teased and his lips suckled. Mindless, she allowed him to do as he wished, for she knew in her woman's heart that this man who touched her so intimately was no savage and no ordinary man. Somehow, in some obscure way, their souls were connected.

Her hands roved over his back as he took possession of her other breast. His thumb teased one as his mouth claimed the other. Throbbing, exquisite sensations built within her. A tiny, mindless moan escaped her lips.

Slowly, he withdrew. Opening her eyes, she saw him gazing down at her with an odd expression. The awful thought that she had done something to cause him to stop knifed through her mind. Anxiously, she watched him.

With gentle movements, he pulled her nightdress and

cloak closed. Confusion made Rachel immobile. She could not understand what was going on. White Wolf brushed a stray hair away from her face with a strange, half-smile. As his gaze met her eyes, the smile faded.

"English."

His word came out in a strangled whisper. Then, in a fluid motion, he rolled off her to his feet. Rachel watched as he strode away into the trees in the direction of the path they had left.

Slowly, Rachel got up and brushed the snow from her clothes. She was perplexed as she followed White Wolf's footprints back to the path. Why had he stopped? What had she done that had made him back away? Perhaps in her innocence of men she had done something wrong. Perhaps the fact that she was a white woman disgusted him. Or perhaps because she was English. Perhaps he had been testing her in some way. Perhaps she had failed.

Yet, it had not seemed like a test. Their kiss had appeared to come naturally, as a result of their play. And White Wolf had seemed to enjoy it. At least, until he stopped.

She did not feel the awful wrenching guilt that had plagued her after the first time he had kissed her. There was none of the anguish she had felt at the betrayal of her body in her response to him. This time, she had wanted him to kiss her, had reveled in his touch. Yet, the sensations he had awakened in her body confused her. While he had been with her, those feelings had taken her over, engulfed her. Now that he was no longer touching her, she felt unfulfilled, bereft of something wonderful.

And it had been wonderful. His kiss, his touch had been gentle. He had made her feel cherished. It was not at all the action of a man who wanted her only for his re-

145

venge. She was confounded by that, for he could have done anything to her. Her control over her emotions and her body had fled the minute he had kissed her — fool that she was. Rachel's cheeks burned at the memory of her wanton response to his touch. Despite his gentleness, he was still her captor, she his prisoner. She could not allow her heart to overrule what she knew in her mind to be true.

White Wolf stood waiting for the woman as she emerged from the trees. Searching her face for her reaction to what had just taken place between them, he noted the high color in her cheeks and her lowered lashes. Embarrassment became her, he decided. Embarrassment and loving.

She was very pleasing to look upon. Beautiful. Yes, he admitted it, beautiful. Her lips were red and full from his kisses. The memory of that soft mouth yielding to him set his blood racing. He could have taken her. He knew that. It would not have been difficult. She was so innocent, so trusting, so warm and inviting. He could have had her. Willingly. With an effort, he forced himself not to think about it. It was not to be. He knew that, also.

She was with him for another reason, a promise he had made when he was very young. For that reason, he would keep away from the woman. He would not allow her to entice him with her eyes the color of the blue spruce or with her laughter that reminded him of the tinkle of water over rocks in a mountain stream. He would not lose himself in her hair of hidden fire. No, he would not. For at the end of this journey, she would no longer be his.

He turned and started off through the forest. Rachel followed. She remained silent, yet there were questions that burned in her mind. She had seen the searching look he had given her, and the flare of heat in his eyes before he masked it. He wanted her, yet he had backed away when she had given him the opportunity. There was something hidden within this man that drove him, something that ate at his soul. Sometime before they reached their destination, she meant to find out what that was.

They camped that night beside a tiny mountain brook. Everything was the same as before, yet there was difference. She saw White Wolf's eyes on her when he thought she was not looking, and she sensed a restlessness in him that was unusual in a man who before had emanated only impassive calm. As she cleaned up the remnants of their supper of rabbit, she decided the time had come to find out what secrets lay behind those devilish eyes.

Sitting down across the fire from White Wolf, she hugged her legs and rested her chin on her knees. She watched him a moment as he repaired the string on his bow. His head was bent over his work; his fingers moved nimbly.

Finally getting up her courage, she asked, "Why did you take me for your revenge?"

White Wolf's head snapped up and his eyes glittered in the firelight. Rachel had the impression that he might lunge at her across the fire. The feeling lasted only a moment, for he soon lowered his head to continue working on the bowstring. When Rachel thought he might ignore her completely, he put the bow aside and gazed at her.

"What do you wish to know, English?" he asked. His voice was flat and almost discouraged her answer.

Swallowing her misgivings, she plunged on, "Why did you take me for your revenge? Why me and not someone else? What is it that you seek revenge for?"

The corner of White Wolf's mouth lifted slightly. "Which question do you want me answer?"

"All of them."

He raised an eyebrow indicating the folly of her response.

"All right," she acquiesced. "Then tell me why you chose me."

"Because you were there, English."

"I don't believe that."

"Believe what you wish."

Rachel shook her head vigorously. "No. You wanted me. Just me. You saved me from Dark Eagle, and you saved me from the wolves. You took no other prisoners."

"You do not know if I took other prisoners."

"All the men watched over their own prisoners. You only watched over me."

White Wolf merely gazed at her, daring her to come to some conclusion. Rachel was not that brave, nor that foolhardy. She could not bring herself to do that, not even in her own mind. Grudgingly accepting defeat on that score, she decided to press him on another.

"Then what is it you seek revenge for?" she asked.

"That does not concern you," he stated.

"It most certainly does," she contradicted. "Since I am the means of your revenge, I think it concerns me a great deal."

White Wolf stared at her for the space of ten heartbeats. Rachel thought he would not answer. Anger flashed brightly in his eyes before he turned his head and stared off into the growing darkness.

"A warrior does not speak of his pain," he finally said in a low voice. "It is a sign of weakness."

Rachel's heart constricted at the obvious torment he

148

felt. Yet, now that she had him talking, she did not want to let the opportunity die.

"It is not weak to tell your prisoner why you have taken her," she prodded gently.

He turned back to face her across the fire. His eyes met hers briefly, then focused on a time and place that only he knew.

"Long ago, when I had not seen so many winters," he began, "I lived with my father and my mother and my sisters in my father's house. In my mother's village, there was a girl, the daughter of a brave warrior. She was pleasing to look upon and a good girl, who helped her mother and learned well what she would need to know to become the woman of a warrior. It had been in my thoughts to make her my woman when I had proved myself worthy and gathered enough skins and a wampum belt large enough to present to her family.

"One day, this girl came to my father's house to visit my sisters. While she was there, a ship, an English ship, sailed up the river. It carried the chief of a place where many English lived, the village called Boston. It also carried many men. When these men came ashore, they swarmed over my father's house like many bees. My mother and sisters had hidden themselves, for my father had travelled to Quebec.

"One of these men found this girl whom I had planned to ask to be my woman. She had not been able to hide herself well. This man also thought she was pleasing to look upon. He picked her up to take her back onto the ship. When my mother saw this, she ran out to try to help the girl. The man hit my mother and she fell.

"I had been out hunting to bring home something for my mother to cook that would please this girl. When I returned, my sisters told me all that had passed. My mother was dead and the girl whom I had thought to make my woman was gone, taken by the man on the ship."

White Wolf's eyes focused on Rachel once again. They burned in their intensity. "The girl was taken to Boston. No one ever saw her again. She is dead to me, just as my mother is dead. Just as you will be to all who know you."

Rachel stared at him. She was speechless in the face of White Wolf's rage. Compassion for him at his loss flooded through her. She understood his wanting to take revenge for something so vile. How much he must have been hurt to have carried his pain for so long!

Yet the cruelty of his revenge repulsed her. The attack on Deerfield had included people who were innocent of the death of his mother and the abduction of his intended. She certainly had not had a part in any of it despite the fact that she had once lived in Boston. Why he had chosen her was still a mystery. Suddenly, she was struck by the irony of the situation. A smile crept across her face and hysterical laughter bubbled up from within her.

White Wolf stiffened at her laughter. Among warriors, it was a sign of bravery to laugh in the face of death, but he felt that this woman was finding something in his tale truly funny. Perhaps, she was laughing at him. That was the ultimate insult. Jumping to his feet, he stormed around the fire to where she sat.

Rachel saw White Wolf coming at her and knew he was furious, yet she could not stop laughing. As he stood towering over her, all she could do was sit where she was in hilarity. Roughly, he grabbed her by the arms and hauled her to her feet. His eyes blazed in his dark face. She should have been afraid, but she was beyond that.

Giving her a shake that rocked her head back on her neck, he growled, "Why do you laugh?"

Rachel just shook her head and laughed. His fingers dug into the soft flesh of her arms, but she felt nothing.

He shook her again. "Why?"

"Because," she gasped amidst her laughter, "it's so funny."

"You dare to laugh at me, English?" White Wolf looked about ready to cut out her heart.

Forcing herself to regain some control, she looked up at him with a grin. "Don't you see?" she said. "Your revenge has not worked. You have chosen the wrong woman. There is no one who cares for me. Not really. My family are all dead, and there is no man who will mourn my disappearance. There is no one."

White Wolf flung her back to the ground. He glared down at her. "You laugh at me." His voice was cold, murderously so.

Rachel shook her head. "No, not at you. At the situation." She caught her bottom lip between her teeth. Had she pushed this man too far? Would he kill her now? Hesitantly, softly, she told him, "I would never laugh at you."

His eyes narrowed at her, then he gazed off into the darkness above her head as his thoughts whirled inside his head. What the woman said about her family was true. She had told him that before, when they had sat together in the sun as they waited for her clothes to dry. The woman did not speak falsely. It was ironic that he had chosen her, a woman who had no family and no man who cared for her. He glanced down at her. She had stopped laughing. Sadness clouded her face and darkened her eyes. When their gaze met, she stood before him.

She reached up and touched his cheek. "I'm sorry," she whispered. "I did not mean to hurt you."

White Wolf felt a rush of feeling for this woman at her gesture and words. He wanted to clasp her to his chest and bury his face in her hair of hidden fire. And he wanted to beat her until she cried out for mercy. Knowing he should do neither, he stepped back from her.

"Sleep, English," he told her. "The morning comes swiftly. We have far to go."

Rachel watched as he turned on his heel and disappeared into the woods behind him. She had made a mistake in laughing. She knew that. This was a proud man who held her captive, one who would lash out at someone who injured his dignity. He remembered insults and repaid them in kind. Now that he realized that she was worthless to him, would he murder her here, in the middle of nowhere? Would he find the rest of his friends and return her to Dark Eagle? He had placed himself in jeopardy because of her, and she had just proven that his efforts had been for nothing. What would he do?

With a sigh, she realized that her worrying would not bring an answer. She would have to wait for White Wolf to answer her questions. Pulling the deerskin out of his pack, she lay down on the pine branches and curled up. As he had said, the morning would come soon. All she could do was sleep.

Once again, White Wolf found himself sitting in a tree in the dark forest because of the woman. Once again, he had wanted to run until he dropped and knew he could not. With his eyes closed against the sight of her through the trees, he raged against her. She had laughed at him.

Laughed! At him! Others who had done that had found swift pain their immediate companion. Yet, he had restrained himself with this woman, this woman with the courage of a warrior.

She had dared to laugh at him. No, that was not so. She had laughed at the situation. She had showed him his mistake and had been able to laugh in spite of what he had told her. His revenge was meaningless for there was no one who cared for this woman. No one who cared.

That thought caused a twinge of something foreign to him. What was it that he felt? Impatient, he pushed the feeling aside. He did not want to look deeply into his heart to decide what it was. The woman had laughed at him. What was he to do with her? He should kill her. She was his enemy. He had every right to do so. He should have let Dark Eagle have her, or the wolves. But that was past. She was with him now, and she had laughed at him.

He placed his hand over his cheek where she had touched him with her fingers. He could still feel the softness of her caress, hear the pain in her words. With a low growl, he flung out his hand and slammed it into the tree trunk. She was a wicked spirit come to torment him. So what was he to do with her?

Opening his eyes, he peered through the trees to the flickering light of the campfire. He saw the woman curled beneath the deerskin. The memory of her warm body soft against his own as they slept stirred the muscles in his groin. Her eyes, changed to the color of the deep sea after he had kissed her, haunted him. Her hair of hidden fire made him want to lose his fingers in its depths.

He shook his head and turned his eyes away from the woman. If he kept on this way, he would soon be as crazy as the loon. So what was he to do with the woman? He did not know. All he knew was that he would keep her with him. If nothing else, she relieved the boredom of the journey.

# Chapter Eleven

Rachel awoke alone the next morning. Yet she knew she had not slept the whole night by herself. The deerskin still held the extra warmth of White Wolf's body.

Puzzling over the strange happenings of the night before, she rolled over onto her back and gazed up at the treetops and the sky beyond. The sun had topped the trees already. It was much later than when she and White Wolf usually started their day's journey. Panic flooded her a moment as the thought shot through her brain that he had left her stranded in the wilderness. Her eyes probed the little clearing where she lay and a sigh of relief escaped her lips. There was his pack hanging from a branch, and not far away, his bow and quiver of arrows.

Getting to her feet, she headed into the trees to take care of her morning needs. Since it was so late, she had the feeling that White Wolf would want her to be ready as soon as he returned from wherever he had gone. No doubt he would be in a surly mood after her stupidity of the night before. As much as she regretted her actions and felt guilt over them, she was not looking forward to whatever punishment he might have decided to inflict on her.

She washed quickly in a mountain stream that gurgled by not far from their camp. On her way back to the clearing, a strange noise arrested her. Standing absolutely still, she listened intently. She had not been mistaken. The deep baritone of White Wolf's singing echoed through the trees from the other side of the camp.

Intrigued, she followed his voice. The sound of the mountain stream accompanied his singing. As the trees thinned, she stepped out upon the narrow flood plain of the stream and stopped. Before her in the morning sun stood White Wolf, his back to her, barefoot and stripped to his breechclout, his arms outstretched, palms up, his head thrown back to the sky. Beads of water glistened on his shoulders, and rivulets ran down his back from his long, dark hair.

The winter's cold still hung in the air, and Rachel shivered just looking at him. Surmising he had just emerged from the stream, she marvelled at the control he had over his body's demands for warmth. And it was a magnificent body, all muscle and hardness. Broad shoulders tapered down to a lean waist and hips. Strong, straight legs ended in narrow ankles and well-shaped feet. She remembered the feel of that body as it lay above her, how well it seemed to fit with hers. A deep curl of excitement made her suck in her breath. She wanted to look at him forever.

His chanting began once more and she listened. It was a glorious sound, a mixture of long and short syllables that meshed perfectly with the gurgling water. Then it ended, suddenly, leaving the memory of the last note echoing in the air.

He dropped his arms, turned and bent to pick up his clothes. That was when he saw her. Rachel did not know what to do. She was embarrassed for spying on him in such a private moment, yet she could not have moved had she wanted to, so mesmerizing was his song.

Slowly, he straightened, waiting, watching her. Biting her bottom lip in trepidation, Rachel moved forward out of the trees. She took a few steps towards him and stopped.

"I . . . I heard your singing," she began.

He said nothing.

"It was beautiful."

He still said nothing.

"Were you praying?"

He gave a short nod.

"I did not mean to pry."

He remained silent.

She glanced away from those searching blue eyes as she tried to think of something else to say. Taking a deep breath, she turned back to him. Inspiration had struck.

"I was not laughing at you last night," she said quickly before she lost her nerve. "I understand the pain you felt at losing your mother and the girl who was to be your wife."

He started to say something, but she held up her hand to stop him.

"I know, a warrior does not speak of his pain," she told him. "But I understand. I know what it is like to lose people you love. I understand how you want to lash out, to hurt someone. I know why you came to Deerfield." Without warning, tears filled her eyes. "I understand why you took me."

Before he could say anything, she turned and fled back to the camp.

When White Wolf returned shortly after, Rachel was

waiting for him. She had scattered the ashes and gathered his belongings and made sure that everything was ready for them to leave. As he entered the clearing, his eyes quickly surveyed the area and came to rest on Rachel as she stood with his bow and quiver in her hands and the pack on the ground next to her. When he approached her, she held out his weapons to him. He took them, slung his bow across one shoulder and the strap of the quiver across the other, but he did not move. He just looked at her.

Rachel gazed up at him, wondering at his odd behavior. His eyes probed hers, and she felt herself falling into the depths of those devilish eyes. The world around them seemed to fade away.

"English," he finally spoke. "You have been sent to me by the Great Spirit, perhaps to be a thorn in my side, perhaps to teach me. As the sun-spirit awoke this day and climbed to his seat in the sky, I spoke with the Great Spirit and asked what I should do with the woman with hair of hidden fire."

He paused there. A tiny smile curved his lips.

Rachel was intrigued by this change in his manner. Was he no longer angry with her? Curious, she asked, "What did the Great Spirit say?"

His smile broadened. "That is not for me to tell you. You will have to discover that on your own." He turned and started across the clearing. "Come, English, walk beside me on the rest of our journey."

Rachel picked up the pack and hurried to catch up. Matching her strides to his, she walked next to him. Befuddled by his sudden openness with her, she nevertheless was not about to let this opportunity for conversation slip by.

"Do you pray to the Great Spirit often?" she asked.

White Wolf glanced down at her. "When I feel the need."

"Oh."

They walked a few steps in silence.

As long as White Wolf had changed in his manner towards her, Rachel decided to make clear something that had been bothering her. Taking a deep breath, she said, "Just because I understand why you took me does not mean that I like it, you know."

White Wolf grunted.

"I mean, it was not the men from Deerfield who attacked your home. It was men from Boston."

"They are all English," he stated flatly.

"But the people of Deerfield are innocent."

"The people of Deerfield have settled on land that does not belong to them. *You* settled on land that did not belong to you." White Wolf halted and swung about to face her.

"It most certainly did! My father had a deed. You had no right to attack our village."

White Wolf's hand snaked out and caught her by the nape of her neck. His fingers tangled in her hair, holding her head still, making her captive to his gaze. "I had every right to attack *your* village," he sneered angrily. "It was never *your* village to begin with. It was not *your* land. The land belongs to all creatures, not this man or that man, not this country or that. You say you understand why I took you, but you understand nothing.

"Yes, I took you for my revenge, but I also took you so that you would learn about the People. And you *will* learn, English, even if you die trying. The English are weak and know nothing about the land. I can live on my

159

own for many moons with what the Great Spirit provides. Can you, *English* woman?"

He released her suddenly, and Rachel fell back a step. Fearfully, she gazed up at him. His eyes blazed and his face was dark in his anger. Despite the fact that he might murder her right there, her own anger began to surface.

"You know I cannot live on my own," she retorted. "I don't want to be out here in the wilderness. It was not my choice. If you want me to learn about the People, then you will have to keep me alive. But be aware that when we come near civilization, I plan to escape. I will not be punished for something in which I had no part."

"You had a part, English. You were born of the wrong people, those who have no right to what they take."

"How dare you say such a thing! Your friends had no right to take the villagers from Deerfield. *You* had no right to take *me!*"

"I had every right. You are here now. That gives me the right."

Rachel could stand no more of his arrogance. Wanting only to punish him in some way, her hand flew out to slap his face. Before it connected, he caught her wrist in a steely grip.

His eyes narrowed dangerously. "Do not ever try to strike me again," he warned coldly. "You are my revenge, but you are also my enemy. I do not hesitate to kill my enemies."

He dropped her wrist and stared hard at her a moment before he turned and strode off. Rachel rubbed where his fingers had held her as she looked at his retreating back. Even though he frightened her down to her toes, she was still angry at him. His arrogance was insufferable. How was she ever going to be able to keep from kicking him or

160

scratching his eyes out? she wondered, because that was just what she wanted to do. She wanted to pummel him until he was black and blue and he realized how overbearing he really was.

With a sigh, she began to follow him. There was nothing she could do. She could not kill him even if she wanted to, because she would not be able to live alone in the wilderness. She could not kick him, or scratch his eyes out, or pummel him black and blue, because that would bring his wrath down on her. And he was much stronger than she. She could only follow him and do as he wished.

A sense of loss welled up in her as she remembered White Wolf's easy manner of a short time ago, and the warmth he had displayed the day before in their snowball fight. She wanted to see more of that man, the one who could laugh and the one who could tease. And the one who could make her forget everything with his kiss. After the fight they had just had, she doubted she would see that side of him ever again.

The day passed uneventfully. White Wolf spoke little, and Rachel spoke not at all. When night came, they slept together beneath the deerskin. Rachel did not want to, but she knew the folly of sleeping alone in the cold. They had travelled far that day, farther than they had previously, so she did not take the trouble to worry much about the nearness of White Wolf's body. Sleep claimed her almost immediately.

Their anger with each other slowly ebbed over the next several days. Rachel realized how difficult it was to remain angry with someone who was her only means of survival. Besides, White Wolf seemed to have forgotten their argument after that first day. Although he did not tease her or smile at her, still he treated her kindly and renewed her lessons with the bow and arrow. Her aim had improved immensely. When White Wolf pointed out a rabbit just off their path and handed her his weapons, she was able to kill the animal. Rachel was ecstatic. They ate it that night in companionable silence.

White Wolf watched the woman pick the last bits of meat from a bone of the rabbit she had killed. He smiled to himself at her pride in her accomplishment. He was proud, too. The woman had proven herself worthy.

The angry words they had exchanged days before echoed in his head, but not in the way of enemies. Neither had they exchanged words in the way of friends. Rather, they had exchanged ideas of two people from two different worlds. Yet, the woman would come to see the truth. He could feel that. Even though her thoughts were not his, he sensed a oneness with her spirit. She was learning the ways of the People.

He thought of the body cloaking that spirit and his blood quickened. He wanted to possess her. From the first, his need had grown. He knew she also felt this need. The want had been in her eyes. When they had touched, their spirits had touched. He had not planned on this happening when he took the woman. He had wanted no ties to the woman who would be his revenge. Yet, he knew when the time came to give this woman over, he would feel the loss.

The woman looked up at him and smiled as she licked her fingers. Her eyes danced. Firelight flamed in her hair. He felt a stirring between his thighs. He could possess the woman. For her people, that would be the ultimate shame: to have him, a redman, possess an English woman. For his people, it meant more: he would be taking her as his woman. The decision was his to make. If he told her nothing, she would not know of the meaning to the People. She would know only that she had been touched by him. He wondered if she would feel shame.

At the end of their journey, another decision awaited him. If he possessed her body, would he still use her as his revenge? The thought had been in his mind to send whatever woman he took as prisoner to his sister. In the home of her husband, his sister could do as she wished with the woman. Yet now, he was unsure that was what he wanted. His sister had mourned long and bitterly for their mother. If he sent the woman to her, she would use the woman cruelly. Would that be just punishment for this woman who had proven herself so worthy?

He watched as the woman cleaned up the remnants of their meal and tossed the remains into the fire. For a moment, she was obscured as the flames leapt to consume the bones and fat of the rabbit. In those flames, he saw the vision he once had of this woman in the village of the People.

His eyes sought out the woman as she moved among the shadows. She had been right to laugh that night when he had told his story. He saw that now. His anger was directed more at himself than at the woman. It had been a trick of Gluskapi, the Trickster Spirit, to have him claim this woman who had no family as his revenge. Still, she was his prisoner even though she had no one who would mourn her. He had the right to do with her as he pleased. He would make the decision about sending her to his sister when it was time and not before. For now another decision had been made.

He pulled his pack closer and rummaged inside. At the bottom, where he had left them, were the pair of moccasins he had made. They were from rabbits he had killed at the beginning of the journey. He had not known he had been making the moccasins for the woman, yet now that he held them in his hand, he saw they would fit only her slim feet. Rummaging again inside his pack, his hand closed over the short, narrow band of wampum he had brought with him. It would fit nicely about the woman's wrist.

The woman had settled on the pine boughs near him. Casually, he reached over and placed the moccasins and tiny wampum belt in her lap. It was the custom for a man to gift the parents of the woman he was claiming in accordance with his wealth and the standing of the woman's family. Here, in the forest, all he had were the moccasins and the meager string of wampum. The woman had no family to whom he could present his gifts. He could only give her this poor offering.

Surprised, Rachel looked down at what White Wolf had placed in her lap. Gingerly, she touched the smooth leather and ran her fingers over the soft fur on the inside of the moccasins. She picked up the string of purple and white shells and examined it.

The bracelet was lovely. The shells had been ground and shaped into tiny cylinders and strung on animal sinew. The deep purple beads at each end were matched closely in color. White shells formed a picture of what could only be a wolf in the center of the bracelet. Laying it on her lap, she turned to the other gift.

The moccasins were beautifully made. She realized these were what White Wolf had been working on all those nights when they had sat by the campfire. She had watched him clean and dry the skins, had helped to carry the frame on which he had stretched them. Assuming that whatever he was making was not for her, she had paid little attention to what he did. Now, overwhelmed by this gift, she could only gaze up at him in wonder.

"For me?" she asked.

"Yes." Having answered, he appeared to busy himself with something in his pack. It was not the way of a man to seem anxious to see if a woman accepted his gift.

Thrilled at receiving such a wonderful present, Rachel immediately pulled off her poor, worn shoes and tried on the moccasins. They were an exact fit. Sticking her feet out before her, she turned them this way and that to get a better look at them. Then jumping up, she walked about a bit to see how they felt. She had never had anything so comfortable on her feet. As she sat down again next to White Wolf, she tied the bracelet about her wrist. After admiring it a moment, she placed her hand on his arm. He turned to look at her.

"They are lovely. Thank you," she told him.

"Then you accept my gift?" he asked.

"Well, of course. Why wouldn't I accept it?" she wondered.

White Wolf looked deep into her eyes. He sensed the woman did not know why he had given her the gift, why she had accepted it. But he knew. Soon, she would also know.

He shrugged. "It is a poor gift."

"It is a wonderful gift," she contradicted. "Because you made it."

White Wolf's heart sang at the woman's words, but he kept his face from showing what he felt. He wanted to possess this woman now, but he knew it was not the time. It was too soon. There was more for her to learn.

"You do me a great honor," he said.

Rachel gazed at him a moment, at his solemn face, his serious blue eyes. There was more to this man than his being a savage, a redman, her captor. She felt drawn to him, more than to anyone else in her life. The thought that they would separate when their journey ended shot through her and brought her pain. Somehow, she could not imagine herself not following him through the woods or sitting across the fire from him. She could not imagine not curling up against him beneath a deerskin at night. Climbing to her knees, she knelt before him. Her eyes were level with his as he watched her. Leaning over, she placed her lips softly against his, her hand caressed his cheek.

When she pulled back, she smiled hesitantly. "I just wanted to give you something, too."

White Wolf reached out and touched the woman's cheek. Her skin was soft as down beneath his fingers. He traced the outline of her quivering lips. Her beauty entranced him; her bravery thrilled him. This woman would be as wild as the ocean when she came to him, as gentle as the summer breeze. But not now. Dropping his hand, he turned to his pack and pulled out the deerskin.

"It is time for sleep, English," he announced.

Without protest, Rachel curled into her usual position against his chest. She could feel the slow, rhythmic thudding of his heart. A sense of peace encompassed her. When they finally parted at the end of their journey, she felt she and White Wolf might be friends. The idea made her smile to herself. Who would have thought she would be friends with the man who had swept down onto her village and carried her away into the wilderness?

# Chapter Twelve

The next morning a cold drizzle was falling when Rachel awoke. White Wolf was already up and moving about the camp. Not wanting to emerge from beneath the warm, dry deerskin into the chill and damp, she huddled down and tried to pretend she was still asleep. White Wolf had not been fooled.

A hand grabbed the deerskin and pulled it off her. "Come, English," a deep voice prodded. "We have far to go today."

Rachel groaned and curled tighter into a ball. "I don't want to," she complained. "It's too wet and cold."

"The river is wet and cold, English."

Rachel opened her eyes and glared up at White Wolf's face far above her. "You wouldn't dare throw me in the river."

His eyebrows shot up and a smile curved his lips.

With a grumble, Rachel climbed to her feet. A warm feeling glowed in her middle at his teasing. As much as it seemed incredible, she really liked this man.

"A woman can't even get a few hours of sleep without

167

someone coming about and waking her up," she mumbled as she headed off into the woods to take care of her needs. As she washed at the tiny brook that fed into the river White Wolf had referred to, she marvelled at the change in their relationship. Never would she have imagined that she would actually be teasing with her captor. It was beyond her comprehension. All she knew was that she enjoyed every minute that they spent in easy companionship.

When she returned to their camp, White Wolf was waiting for her. Impatiently, he watched as she carefully packed her moccasins away and donned her old shoes. He had already packed away the deerskin and scattered the ashes of the fire. Seeing she was finally ready, he turned and started off.

White Wolf kept up a gruelling pace that day. It was midafternoon when he stopped at what appeared to be a cave. Ducking beneath the bare branches of a large bush, he disappeared into the opening. Rachel quickly followed.

Inside, the cave was dark, but wonderfully dry. She did not see White Wolf immediately, but she heard him rummaging among the rocks. When he stepped into the dim light near the cave's entrance, he held another pack in his arms.

"What's that?" Rachel demanded.

"You ask too many questions, English," he replied. "We will spend the night here. Start a fire."

Rachel was tired and cold and grumpy. Taking offense at White Wolf's observation about her curiosity and at his abrupt tone, she stormed back outside the cave to gather wood. Everything was wet and soggy. She did not have the patience or the energy to find dry wood for a fire.

168

Those pieces she brought back into the cave were, at best, damp.

Using the flint from White Wolf's pack, she tried several times to light the fire. Her cold fingers were clumsy; the twigs and leaves she used for kindling were damp. All she wanted was to curl up and go to sleep. White Wolf had pushed her hard all day, barely allowing her any rest. She was exhausted.

Finally getting a spark to settle on a leaf, she blew on it to coax it into a flame. After a tiny, brief flash, the spark died in a plume of smoke. Once again she struck the flint. This time, it slipped and scraped across her fingers. With a cry of vexation, she threw the flint down.

"A child could do better, English," White Wolf told her impatiently.

"Then you do it!" she exclaimed, jumping to her feet.

Without waiting for his reaction, she fled out of the cave. For some reason, his words had cut deeply. Tears gathered in her eyes and blurred her vision. Stumbling across the uneven ground, she moved quickly away from the cave. She did not want to be near that awful man. He had been a beast all day, urging her on, making her hurry. As soon as they had started out that morning, his attitude had changed. His teasing manner had abruptly given way to taciturn silence. What had she done to make him change so swiftly?

Slowing down to a walk, she sniffed and wiped her eyes. She was acting like a child. He was probably tired, too. Shaking her head at herself, she stopped and took a deep breath. She would go back and apologize.

Having made that decision, she looked around to see where she was and how to get back to the cave. A rustling in the brush behind her drew her attention. Swinging about, she saw a huge brown bear on its hind legs not two arms' lengths away. It waved its huge front paws at her and gave a loud growl. Rachel could not move. Opening her mouth to scream, she could only emit a tiny squeak. As the bear lunged out with one paw, she jumped back and tripped over a rock. Falling hard on her backside, she finally found her voice.

White Wolf heard the woman's scream just as he got the fire lit. It had annoyed him that she had gathered damp wood, especially after all he had taught her, all he thought she had learned. The thought had crossed his mind that perhaps she was not worthy after all. Perhaps he had been wrong in choosing her. Then he realized that she was still learning. It was good for her to be off by herself, to calm her thoughts before coming back to the fire. The circle about the fire was a place for peace, not for angry words. Then he heard her scream.

Rising to his feet, he stood and listened. There was no other sound. Then, faintly, the growl of the bear reached his ears. Without hesitation, he ducked out of the cave and followed the woman's path. It did not take him long to find her. She was sitting on the ground and staring up at the huge bear that towered over her. It swayed back and forth, swinging its paws with those deadly claws and revealing the huge, sharp teeth in its open mouth. With one swipe, the animal could cut the woman to pieces.

White Wolf gave a shout and jumped to one side of the bear to gain its attention. It swung its huge head around in his direction.

"Move away slowly," he told the woman. "It will not harm you."

Rachel scooted back as White Wolf directed, then scrambled to her feet. In horror, she watched the awful dance that was taking place before her. White Wolf had circled about to keep the bear's attention on him and away from her. Occasionally, he would jump forward to within a handsbreadth of those deadly claws and then back again. The only weapon he had was his hunting knife, which he waved constantly back and forth. The bear followed the movement of the shiny object before its eyes.

Suddenly, White Wolf picked up a short branch that lay on the ground and tossed it at the bear. As the bear grasped for the branch, White Wolf lunged forward and seemed to be enveloped by the bear's embrace. Rachel gasped and covered her eyes. She did not want to watch the mutilation and death of White Wolf. His presence had become as much a part of her as the forest through which they travelled. Not to have him with her was beyond her comprehension.

The sounds of the struggle attacked her ears. She could hear the awful growls of the bear and the labored breathing and shouts of White Wolf. As long as she could hear him, she felt safe. She knew he would protect her as long as he was alive. After what seemed a lifetime, she heard a scream of anguish and the falling thud of a body hitting the ground. Then there was silence.

Carefully, she peeked through her fingers. White Wolf stood panting over the dead bear. He was covered with blood, but whether it belonged to him or the bear she could not tell. He finally raised his head and looked at her. His blue eyes were bright, and a small smile curved his lips. In relief, she grinned back at him. As she hurried towards him, he swayed and steadied himself on a nearby tree. It was then she realized not all the blood belonged to the bear. Three even gashes in his shirt ran from beneath

171

his arm, across his ribs to his chest. Blood was staining his shirt dark.

"You're hurt!" she exclaimed as she rushed to his side.

He shook his head. "Just scratches," he said. He stepped over the bear's leg and stopped as his equilibrium deserted him. Taking a deep breath, he started walking again. "The bear has to be skinned, meat cut up." He swayed again, and Rachel ducked beneath his arm, taking his weight across her shoulders. "Just scratches," he repeated.

Rachel said nothing. She knew the claws of the bear had inflicted more than mere scratches. The shirt beneath her hand where it hugged his waist was soaked with blood. Keeping her worst fears at bay, she concentrated only on getting White Wolf back to the cave before he fainted.

The effort drained the last of White Wolf's strength. As they entered the cave, his knees gave way beneath him. He sank to the ground, and leaned wearily against the cave wall.

"The bear has to be skinned, meat cut up," he repeated weakly.

"Of course," Rachel agreed soothingly. "I'll take care of that as soon as I've seen to your wounds." Silently, she decided the bear would be food for the animals of the forest.

White Wolf shook his head. "Just scratches," he said a third time.

"Umhmm." Rachel thought that either he was being particularly thick-headed, or his wounds were worse than she thought and he delirious. "Even so, I think I should wash them and bandage them. You could get an infection."

White Wolf shook his head, but he allowed her to help

him lay on the spruce branches they had cut for their bed. When Rachel helped him pull off his deerskin and linen tunics, intense pain flitted across his face before he was able to control his features.

Rachel bit her bottom lip to keep from gasping at what she saw. Three parallel gashes ran across his body exactly where his shirt had been cut. One was not too deep, but the other two sliced down to his ribs. They would have to be sewn.

"You need to be stitched," she told White Wolf. "Otherwise, I don't think . . ."

White Wolf looked at her, his eyes intensely blue with his pain. "Do what you have to," he said, straining to keep his voice steady. "I do not want to go to my ancestors just now." He managed a tiny smile, then closed his eyes and turned his face away. "You will find what you need in those." He motioned weakly at the packs.

Rachel rummaged through both packs. Inside one, she found a small package containing dried herbs, several porcupine quills, and thin strings of animal tendon. In the other, she found a hollow gourd drinking cup, and a large, heavy basket, along with another deerskin and a four-point Hudson Bay blanket. The blanket was of the highest quality, and could only be traded for a great number of the thickest and best beaver skins. The basket, she realized, was woven tightly enough to hold water.

Satisfied that she had everything she needed, she told White Wolf she was going to fetch water, then ducked out of the cave to the little stream that trickled down over the rocks just outside the cave entrance. After filling the basket with water, she ripped several long strips from her nightdress and washed them as best she could in the stream. Her last task involved searching for dry oak leaves. Then she reentered the cave.

White Wolf lay as she had left him, with one arm flung up over his eyes. Settling herself beside him, she lightly touched his shoulder.

"Do what you have to, English," he murmured.

Gently, she washed the blood from his wounds, grimacing in sympathy every time a shudder of pain ran through him. Although the gashes still bled freely, she could now see more clearly where she had to stitch. Threading one of the quills with a tendon string, she began to close the cuts across his ribs.

It was an agonizing process. She hated inflicting more pain on White Wolf, but she knew that if she did not close his wounds, he might die from loss of blood. He did not utter a sound during the whole process. Occasionally, Rachel would glance at his face, but only the quivering of a muscle in his jaw indicated the intense pain he was feeling. When she finally finished, she was drained. Sitting back on her heels, she took a deep breath. White Wolf did not move. Softly, she placed her hand on the arm he had flung across his eyes.

"It is done," she said.

He nodded weakly, but that was all the response he made. Deciding that he did not want her interfering with the extreme control he was holding over himself, she turned to examine the herbs. Some, she recognized as having medicinal qualities. She would need fresh water to boil them. Picking up the basket again, she went outside.

The rain had stopped and the clouds were breaking up, revealing a bright blue sky. The sun was just beginning to slip behind the trees. Tomorrow would be a beautiful day. Tomorrow, she might be alone in the wilderness. Shaking off her morbid thoughts, she emptied the dirty water from the basket and refilled it. Then she went back inside the cave.

White Wolf was watching her when she entered. His face was drawn in pain, but he was lucid. He even attempted a smile.

"I told you, they were just scratches," he said.

"Of course," Rachel agreed, "and we've just been on an afternoon stroll in the garden." She stood over him and shook her head. "Men. I will never understand why the good Lord ever made you so stubborn."

"We are not being stubborn, English. We are being brave." As he finished speaking, a spasm of pain tore through his body.

Rachel dropped to her knees beside him and placed her hand on his brow. His skin was hot. It was as she feared; he had developed a fever. Opening the packet of herbs, she put some into the gourd along with a little water. Mixing it together with her fingers, she made a poultice. As gently as she could, she spread it across his wounds.

As the herbs seeped into the gashes, White Wolf sucked in his breath painfully. When she had finished, he released a painful sigh. "If it does not cure me, it will kill me," he observed.

"It won't kill you," she told him. She pressed the oak leaves softly over the gashes.

He endured her ministrations in silence, then shivered. "Cold, English. Come warm me." He reached out for her, but she evaded him.

"No, I have to bandage your wounds." She retrieved the rest of the strips of cloth she had torn from her nightdress where she had left them to dry by the fire. Helping

175

White Wolf to sit up, she wound them about his middle to protect the gashes. By the time she had finished, he was shivering violently. After getting him comfortable once more, she covered him with the Hudson blanket and the deerskin, then crawled in beside him to add her body's warmth to that of the fire and the blankets. After suffering through every spasm of the chills with him until the sun's rays were low enough to slant into the cave entrance, she finally felt him drift into sleep.

Satisfied that she had done everything she could for him and that he would sleep for a good while, she gently disengaged herself and got up. After cleaning up the cave, she took his hunting knife and returned to where the dead bear lay. The animal was huge. But White Wolf had killed it by himself with only the knife she held in her hand. She knew what she had to do.

It was quite dark by the time Rachel returned to the cave. She had accomplished her task. She had partially skinned the bear and cut off the claws to provide White Wolf with a trophy of his victory, and she had taken some meat to provide them with food for the next day or two. After washing the blood from her hands and arms in the little stream, she went into the cave to check on White Wolf.

He had thrown off the blanket and deerskin in his sleep and lay outstretched on his back. His face and chest was covered with perspiration. She was worried about the fever, but she was more concerned about his wounds opening and beginning to bleed again. After checking the bandages and satisfying herself that there was only a spotting of blood, she fetched cool, clean water to bathe him and bring down the fever.

As she wiped a wet cloth across his chest and arms, Rachel tried to ignore the urge to stare at White Wolf's body. There was no hair on his wide chest, nothing to hide the latent strength in that broad expanse. Muscles rippled beneath satiny skin. She remembered the feel of that hard chest pressed against her, those steely arms wrapped about her. She wanted those feelings again.

Rachel wriggled guiltily. She should not have such thoughts, especially about this man. He had told her she was only his revenge. She meant nothing to him. Yet, during their journey, she had seen that this was an honorable man who could love just as strongly as he could hate, and who could laugh as well as cry. In their weeks together, he had not mistreated her. On the contrary, he had been generally kind to her. Although his manner at times had been less than gracious, he was, after all, her captor. Even so, she knew there was a gentle side to this man. She had glimpsed it occasionally, particularly in his kisses.

Rachel's face flamed at the memory. Never had another person been able to arouse such strong feelings in her. They were wonderful feelings, but frightening. Did other women feel as she did? she wondered. Or was there something wrong with her? Should a woman have those feelings?

She remembered her own parents when her mother was still alive. They would laugh and talk and occasionally, when she came upon them unexpectedly, she might find them kissing. Her mother never seemed to feel guilty at how she was acting. Perhaps that was how people in love acted.

Rachel froze with the damp cloth suspended above White Wolf's forehead. Because she had these feelings with White Wolf, did that mean she was in love with him?

She shook her head. No, that could not be. This man was an Indian, a heathen. He came from a totally different culture. He had attacked her village, had taken her captive. He had told her she was his revenge. She glanced down at his face. Yet, he was more than that.

When she had seen him fighting the bear, she had covered her eyes, not to hide from seeing the gore, but so that she would not have to witness his death. The idea of not having him beside her in the wilderness was something she did not want to contemplate. He was more to her than someone to keep her company and help her stay alive. His loss would be devastating to her. It would open a hole in her heart.

White Wolf groaned in his sleep, and Rachel continued to bathe him with the cool cloth. This man, who had torn her away from everything that was familiar to her, had somehow become precious to her. She did not know how that had happened, or when. When next he kissed her, if he ever did, she would welcome his touch, his caress, as a woman should welcome her lover.

As she continued to wipe his face to bring down his fever, she shook her head at herself. She was a fool, she told herself. She had not fallen in love with any of the men in Deerfield and the surrounding towns. No, she had fallen in love with a man who called himself White Wolf. A small, satisfied smile curved her lips. Prudence would be appalled and Mistress Whitson would be scandalized if they ever found out. A giggle erupted in her throat. She would dearly like to see their faces when they were told.

White Wolf's fever suddenly turned to chills as shivers racked his body. Rachel tossed down the cloth she was using to bathe him and quickly pulled the blanket and deerskin over him. After feeding the fire with more wood, she once again crawled beneath the blanket and held him close to give him her own body's warmth. Soon the shivers stopped and he slept peacefully. Rachel herself drifted into a light doze. It had been an exhausting day.

At sunrise, Rachel was already up. She had slept little, for White Wolf fluctuated between fever and chills. He was still sleeping, quietly at the moment, so Rachel walked to the cave entrance and looked out. It was going to be a beautiful day. The sky was clear and the sun was a bright yellow ball as it rose above the treetops. Spring was finally making an appearance.

Turning back into the cave, she decided she would take the time while White Wolf slept to cook some of the bear meat for herself and make some broth for him. By the time she had finished, he was awake. His eyes were bright with fever as he watched her in silence.

"I made some broth for you," she told him as she held out the gourd.

He struggled to sit up. Rachel rushed to his side to help him.

"I can sit on my own, English," he snapped.

"Don't be silly," she scolded. "You are injured and ill. My helping you won't lessen your bravery."

He grunted at her, but accepted her help nonetheless. After sipping at the broth, he glanced at her. "You have taken meat from the bear," he observed.

"Yes."

"And the skin?"

She nodded to the corner where she had stored it. "Over there." Reaching behind her, she scooped up the claws and spilled them into his lap.

Approval shone in his eyes. "You are becoming a true member of the People, English."

179

A warm glow enveloped her at his compliment. Not wanting to give away her feelings just yet, she told him, "Drink your broth."

He chuckled and did as he was told. Handing the gourd back to her he said, "We will continue our journey when the sun is high in the sky."

"We will do no such thing," she contradicted. "You can not even walk. We will stay here until you are well. *Then* we will continue our journey."

"I can walk," he grumbled.

Gently, Rachel pushed him back to once again lie on the branches. "You cannot even sit up," she said. "Now, go back to sleep and regain your strength."

"A warrior does not need an overbearing woman telling him what to do," he complained.

Rachel laughed and sat next to him on the branches. Placing her hand on his shoulder, she said, "This warrior has been telling this woman what to do for weeks. It is time I had a turn telling you what to do."

White Wolf's eyes met hers, and suddenly the touch of her hand on the bare skin of his shoulder was warmer than the fever that claimed his body. He reached up and drew his fingers across her cheek.

"When I am healed . . ." he began, then yawned.

Rachel smiled. The fever had weakened him more than he cared to admit. The fatigue that invaded his body would keep him quiet until his wounds had healed enough for them to continue their travels.

"When you are healed, we will speak of it," she told him.

He mumbled something she could not understand, then he was asleep.

Late that afternoon, he awoke again. This time, his fever was high. Rachel helped him drink more broth and fed him a bit of meat. When he had finished, he fell weakly back onto the branches.

"You are kind to me, English," he said. "Why?"

Rachel was not about to tell him the real reason she was so concerned about his health. "Because I need you to keep me alive until we reach civilization," she told him lightly. She sat next to him and placed a cool cloth on his hot forehead.

He reached up and grabbed hold of her wrist. His grip, although weakened by his illness, was not loose. "There is more," he said darkly. "You keep me alive to turn me over to your English friends."

"Don't be silly. How can I reach them? We are miles away from any English settlement."

"You lie!" His eyes burned feverishly bright.

Although Rachel knew he did not have the strength to really hurt her, still his words and attitude frightened her. She shook her head. "No, I don't lie. You know I speak the truth. You brought us here. You should know there are no English anywhere about us."

"They follow us," he muttered. His eyes moved vaguely about the cave. "They follow us," he repeated. His eyes fluttered close, and soon he was sleeping.

Rachel disengaged his fingers from about her wrist and stood up. Leaning weakly against the rocky wall next to her, she gazed down at White Wolf. She wondered what had made him accuse her of contacting his enemies, and what had made him say that they were being followed. Perhaps he was reverting to the cold, suspicious man who had first taken her prisoner.

Shaking her head at her thoughts, she decided it was only the fever that made him think of such things. Yet, that last morning when they had set out, something had made him hurry her along. Something had worried him. Glancing about the cave, she reassured herself of the placement of his bow and quiver of arrows and his hunting knife. If someone was following them, whoever it was would have to get past her first. Feeling much better, she went out to fetch more wood for the fire.

# Chapter Thirteen

That night, White Wolf's fever became dangerously high. Rachel remained awake bathing him with cool water from the stream. Twice, she had to venture down to the water to refill the basket, and each time, she found herself looking over her shoulder to see if there might be someone skulking about in the trees. She saw no one, and told herself how silly she was for being afraid. Yet, there had been something that concerned White Wolf, something that had made him accuse her. However, having someone following them was not her major worry. The man who had stolen into her heart needed her full attention.

Two days passed, but Rachel was barely aware of the passage of time. White Wolf absorbed her completely. She was either bathing him with cool water or wrapping him in warm blankets. She ate sparingly, saving the meat from the bear for broth to force between his lips. As dawn of the third day of his illness blushed across the gray sky, White Wolf's fever broke, and he settled into an easy sleep. Exhausted, Rachel bathed him once more, then curled up beside him and slept herself.

It was midday when she awoke. White Wolf still slept soundly. Rising quietly so she would not disturb him, she ate a small portion of the last of the bear meat, then, with a glance to reassure herself that White Wolf was still all right, she ducked out of the cave and headed towards the stream.

Spring had finally overcome the hold of winter on the land. The sun was warm, and birds twittered in the trees. Although the branches were still bare, buds had begun to swell on the limbs. Rachel smiled and hummed to herself. The world was a beautiful place.

When she reached the stream, she quickly undressed and walked into the cold water. The stream was icy, but she did not mind. It was the first chance she had to bathe properly. Even though she had no soap, still, the water washed the grime of the journey from her. When she emerged, she felt wonderfully refreshed. It was with a shudder of distaste that she put her old, travel-worn clothes back on. She wanted to wash them, but she did not dare leave White Wolf alone any longer. At least it was warm enough for her not to have to don her cloak. Dragging her fingers through her hair, she untangled it as best she could, then fluffed it to help it dry quicker. Letting it fall free down her back, she headed back to the cave.

When she entered the cave, it took a moment for her eyes to adjust to the dimness. As she became acclimated to the change in light, she saw White Wolf leaning weakly against the wall of the cave and watching her.

"You shouldn't be up," she scolded him as she rushed to his side. Placing her arm about him in support, she urged him back to the bed of branches.

"Where did you go?" he asked, as he allowed her to help

him sit.

Grinning mischievously up at him, she teased, "Did you miss me?"

His hand grabbed her arm with surprising strength for one who had been ill. "Where did you go?" he repeated furiously.

Suddenly frightened of this man, Rachel sat back on her heels and gazed up at him with wide eyes. "I went to bathe."

White Wolf's eyes studied her face, then went to her damp hair. Tiredly, he dropped his hand and looked away. "I thought . . ." His voice trailed away.

Rachel's eyes narrowed suspiciously. "What did you think?" she demanded.

He shook his head. "It does not matter."

"It does. What did you think, White Wolf? That I had left you? Abandoned you here? Is that what you thought?"

"I took you as my revenge. It would have been easy to leave me here and escape."

Rachel jumped to her feet and stalked to the other side of the cave. "How could you believe such a thing? You saved my life. I could not leave you to die."

He did not answer, and he refused to look at her.

"Do you think because I am not of your people that I am without honor?" She did not want to mention that it was not only honor that held her there with him. "You are a fool if you think that."

His head swung about to face her and his eyes blazed. "If I were not as weak as an old woman, I would make you take that back, English," he growled.

"I would not take it back, because right now it is true. Your people are not the only ones who have honor. My

185

father taught me that life is precious. Any life, no matter whose it is. I could not leave you to die."

There was a long silence while neither moved or said anything. Finally, with an exclamation of anger and frustration, Rachel busied herself with cooking the last of the bear meat for his meal. Even though she knew he was too weak to take care of himself, she wanted to leave him on his own for being so ungrateful and callous to believe such a thing of her. She had sewn his wounds, bandaged him, bathed him during his fever, fed him. And all she got in return was suspicion. She should take his hunting knife and run it through his ungrateful heart. With a jerk, she turned the meat over the fire.

White Wolf watched the woman at the fire. Her words had struck his heart. When he had awakened and found her gone, he had felt a terrible loneliness, such as he had never felt before. Then he had felt betrayed. He had saved this woman's life many times, and she had repaid him by escaping at the first chance she saw. His rage had boiled up inside him and turned him blind to all else. He had sworn he would track her and find her, then he would beat her until she could no longer stand. Perhaps, he would even kill her. No woman would make a fool of him. Especially this woman.

But he had been a fool. When she had entered the cave, smiling and smelling of spring, his anger had overcome his relief at seeing her. He had suspected her of the worst treachery. For that morning when they had set out before reaching this cave, he had discovered that someone was following them. He did not who it was, although he had an idea. He had thought the woman had met the man who followed them and made plans with him. He knew now that was not the truth. Now, he had to take back his angry words to her. If she would let him.

"English." His voice floated to her out of the shadows. She did not answer. The meat was done. Taking it from the fire, she took it to him and held it out on the stick on which she had cooked it. He took the stick, but his eyes watched her face, not what he was doing. With his free hand, he gently caught her wrist.

"English, I am sorry," he told her. Giving a tug on her wrist, he pulled her down next to him. "You are brave, like the warrior, and kind. I am wrong to accuse you."

Rachel's heart swelled at his apology. This was a proud man who sat before her. She knew how much it cost him to say he was wrong. It had hurt deeply to have him accuse her of running away. Tears suddenly flooded Rachel's eyes. Embarrassed, she turned her head away.

He reached up and caught a crystal drop that slowly ran down her cheek. "Why do you cry?"

"Because," she sniffed. "Because . . . I don't know." She shook her head and shrugged. Drying her eyes, she turned back to him. "Eat the meat. You have to get back your strength."

White Wolf smiled at her and took a bite of the meat. "Bear meat," he observed. "You took the meat of the bear. You did well, English." His eyes travelled about the cave and he spotted the skin of the bear and its claws lying in a neat pile. Now, he remembered. The woman had taken the skin and claws for him. He grinned. "You learn quickly."

Rachel blushed at his words. His praise meant more to her than anything she had ever heard.

White Wolf finished his meal and tossed the stick onto the fire. "I feel stronger already," he announced.

"There is no more meat," she told him. "I will have to

187

hunt for food.

"My warrior," he teased. With his finger, he wiped a tear that still clung to her cheek. "So brave and so delicate." He reached up and touched Rachel's hair. "Beautiful," he whispered. "Hair of hidden fire."

His eyes bore into hers, capturing them in their blue depths. Rachel found herself unable to look away. That mesmerizing power that had first sent shivers chasing down her spine held her completely. Then, when she had first been caught by those eyes, when this man had first taken her captive, all she had wanted to do was run from him. Now, she did not want to look away, she did not want to move. All she wanted was to gaze into those blue eyes.

White Wolf's hand slipped down onto her shoulder, then down her arm. His palm covered her hand where it lay on the branches. His fingers entwined themselves with hers. He raised their hands, interlocked, palms pressed together, fingers enmeshed.

"You will be my woman," he told her.

A surge of excitement shot through her body at his words. "Yes," she answered in a whisper.

With his free hand, he unlaced the neck of her nightdress and her bodice. Gently, he pushed them from one shoulder. His fingers lightly caressed her bare skin. Rachel felt a burning heat wherever he touched. His hand slipped around to the back of her neck, and slowly, inevitably, pulled her towards him. His fingers tangled themselves in her hair, holding her head still.

When their lips met, a flash of feelings exploded inside her. His mouth claimed hers in the ancient way of men and women, and Rachel allowed him to claim it. Her lips parted invitingly as he teased them with his tongue, then it slipped between them.

A deep throbbing started somewhere in her middle and spread outward through her whole body. His kisses always did that to her, and she marvelled that, each time, the throbbing was just as intense as the last time. She would have thought her body immune to him by now, but it was not so. Hungrily, she kissed him back, wanting these crazy, confusing feelings.

His arms slipped about her, pulling her against his chest, and then falling back with her onto the pile of branches. Rachel clung to his shoulders, vaguely aware of the strength, the warmth beneath her fingers. Her attention was centered on her mouth, his mouth, and what he was doing to her. Wanting to give him the same sensations she was feeling, she hesitantly ran her tongue about his lips. He pulled back slightly and grinned.

"You learn quickly," he repeated.

Rachel gave him a satisfied smile.

Sitting her up to straddle his hips, he reached up and pulled her nightdress and bodice back off her shoulders. "You have beautiful skin," he murmured. "As soft as the fur of a baby rabbit." His fingers traced the line of the hollows of her shoulders and came to rest where her clothes came together between her breasts. Looking up, his eyes burned into hers. "Undress for me."

Rachel hesitated only a moment before she pulled off her bodice and undid her nightdress down to her waist. Slowly, she pushed the nightdress from her shoulders and arms, revealing herself to him. Reverently, he reached up and cupped her breasts in his hands. His thumbs softly moved back and forth across her nipples. Tingles of excitement radiated through her at his touch. It felt wonderful, but he had kissed her there before, and she wanted him to do that again.

As if reading her thoughts, he pulled her forward and took one rosy bud into his mouth. Flames of heat shot through her. Her eyes closed in ecstasy. When he moved to the other breast and sucked and tickled with his tongue, she moaned low in her throat.

White Wolf reveled in the feel of the woman's body. She was firm, yet soft and warm. Her high, round breasts beckoned to be touched and loved. He knew she had never lain with a man, yet she opened herself to him without question. Her trust in him made him proud. She made his blood race through his veins. Truly, he had chosen wisely. He had wanted to possess no other woman as much as he had wanted to possess this woman. She was his woman. She had said so.

Rolling over, he lay above her. Rachel could feel his throbbing manhood hard against her hip. His body covered hers, pinning her where she lay. Before, she would have felt threatened; now, she welcomed the heavy hardness of him upon her. He fit there, as if he had been made for her.

Moving off her slightly, White Wolf undid her skirt and pulled that and the nightdress off her. Except for the moccasins he had made for her, she lay naked before him. White Wolf let his gaze wander over her body, the narrow waist, flat stomach, the flare of her hips, and long legs. The sight of her laying passive, waiting, beneath him sent a rush of exhilaration through him. She was as he had pictured her. Her body was perfection, as it should be belonging to a woman with hair of hidden fire.

The air was cool against Rachel's body, and a tremor ran through her. But whether she shivered from the cool air or his heated gaze, she could not tell, for his eyes devoured every inch of her. Watching him look at her brought a fresh rush of excitement to her. Her breathing, shallow and quick before, became ragged and caught in her throat.

Was she being completely shameless in allowing this man such liberties? she wondered. Shouldn't she keep some piece of clothing on her? Shouldn't she at least pull the deerskin over her? He reached out and ran his hand lightly over her breast and down across her flat stomach. His touch sent tremors through her. Sighing, she decided there could be no shame in something that felt so wonderful.

His fingers stopped at the triangle of hair where her thighs came together. As he bent forward to claim her mouth once more, his fingers entered her womanhood. She shook her head and tried to tell him no, but his mouth covered her lips, and the sweet shafts of pleasure that ran through her from his touch confused any coherent thoughts she might have had.

Clinging to him as if she were drowning, she was aware only of him, of this man, what he was doing, what he was making her feel. She knew that whatever he did to her could not be wrong. She trusted him. When he nudged her thighs apart, she willingly obliged. She would open herself to him.

Softly, he murmured something in his Indian language in her ear. She did not care what he said. It was the sound of his voice that was beautiful. Her arms went about him tightly, hugging him close. She felt something warm nudge at her, then he was inside her, filling her. It was wonderful. She moved her hips against him.

He thrust against her movement. A sharp pain made her cry out. Her eyes flew open, and she gazed up at him in confusion and anguish.

191

"Shush," he soothed. "It is over. It will not hurt again."

He kissed her cheeks, her eyelids, her mouth. His hand found her breast and he teased its tip. His lips moved from her mouth, to her jaw, to the pulse that throbbed at the base of her neck. He sucked at each heartbeat.

His caresses worked their magic. The pain retreated and was once again replaced by her pulsing need. She wriggled her hips. It did not hurt. She wanted him, more, something. What, she did not know. She only knew this man could give her whatever she needed. He lifted his head and smiled down at her. Then, capturing her mouth once more, he thrust into her.

Rachel rode the spiralling sensations he created, higher and higher, until he shuddered above her and an intense sweetness pervaded her whole body. White Wolf growled deep in his throat, then collapsed onto her. She held him tightly clutched to her. With a contented sigh, she stroked his hair. She was this man's woman now. He had taken away her maidenhood, and given her something much more wonderful in return.

White Wolf rolled off her and pulled her close against him. He groaned once in pain, but when she tried to move away, he held her tightly. She did not argue. Within a heartbeat, she felt him go to sleep. Smiling, she pulled the blanket over them, and she allowed herself to join him in dreamland.

White Wolf still slept soundly when Rachel awoke. It was midafternoon. Gently, she disengaged herself from his arms and rose. She smiled down him. In repose, his face was not harsh. She saw laugh lines about his eyes that she had never noticed before. This was not the face of a cruel man, but of one who had known cruelty. Rachel reached out and softly touched his cheek and ran her fingers across his lips. He smiled in his sleep.

Quickly, before he awoke, she dressed, took his bow and quiver of arrows and slipped out of the cave. She had to find and kill something for their supper.

By the time she returned to the cave, the sun was setting. White Wolf was awake and sitting, waiting for her by the fire. He had gathered more wood, and he poked at the burning embers moodily.

"Look what I have for our dinner," she greeted him as she entered the cave.

He glanced at the fat partridge she held up, grunted and turned back to the fire.

Disappointed in his reaction to her prowess with his bow, she dropped the bird in a corner and put away his bow and quiver. "I guess you are not feeling very well," she observed.

"I am well," he said.

Rachel frowned at him and went to collect the partridge so she could clean it before cooking.

"It is the man's job to hunt for food," White Wolf declared. "It is the woman's job to gather wood and tend the fire."

"You have been ill. You cannot hunt."

"I can hunt."

"Well, I can, too," Rachel informed him heatedly. "Using the bow might open your wounds again. I have spent days caring for you. I am not going to allow you to hunt just because you believe it is your job. That is stupid."

White Wolf climbed to his feet, rather quickly for one who still had stitches holding his wounds closed. Towering over her, he demanded, "Are you saying I am stupid?"

"No. I am saying your idea is stupid. This morning you could barely stand up because you were so weak. How do you expect to use a bow in your condition?"

"A man hunts until he is dead."

Rachel ground her teeth together in frustration. This man was being impossible. "Fine. You hunt and you soon will be dead, because your wounds will open again and you will bleed to death. Don't expect me to care for you again, because I will probably be dead, too. I will be lost in this forest and die of exposure or the wolves will get me or a bear. Then you will be with your ancestors and I will be with mine, and all because you had this stupid idea that only a man hunts."

After her long speech, she took a deep breath, tossed the partridge at his feet and flounced to a corner of the cave where she plopped herself down. She had met the same set of mind in Deerfield. No young man had been brave enough to ask for the hand of a woman who was willing and eager to perform tasks they considered *man's work*. She did not want to be a man; she just did not see anything wrong in her hunting or plowing a field or building a table. Her father had encouraged her to do the things that pleased her, that expanded her mind. Did that mean she was less of a woman? No, she told herself forcefully. She also enjoyed cooking and needlework. And someday, she wanted to be a mother.

When she had given herself to White Wolf, she had not realized he thought as he did about a woman's role. Because he had taught her to use the bow, she had been lulled into believing that he was different from the other men of her acquaintance. How wrong she had been!

A chuckle snapped her head around, and she glared in

White Wolf's direction. What did he find so funny? she thought furiously. She watched as he picked up the partridge and sauntered over to her. Crouching down, he smiled into her eyes.

"I would not want the wolves to have you, English," he told her in a voice filled with laughter. "I did not save you from them only to let them have you in the end."

"I was not being amusing," she said with an affronted sniff. "Do not laugh at me."

Schooling his face into seriousness, he went on, "A man hunts for his woman, for his family. It is the way of the People. When a man is injured and cannot hunt, another of the People will provide for his family. If there is no other man, it has not been unknown for a woman to hunt. When a man is stupid, it is the duty of his woman to tell him so."

Rachel searched his face. Even though his eyes smiled at her, she knew he was no longer laughing at her. He had apologized to her and acknowledged that she was his woman. Her heart swelled with happiness.

He held up the partridge. "Since you hunted, I will clean and cook this fine bird."

As he started to rise, Rachel put a hand on his arm, stopping him. "White Wolf, I have something to ask you."

He waited expectantly.

Nervously, she licked her lips. "Please, do not call me 'English' any more. My name is Rachel. Rachel Linton."

"Rachel," he repeated, except that he pronounced it 'Rachelle.' "It is a beautiful name. But, to me, you will always be my 'English'."

Rachel blushed at his intimate gaze and warm words and watched him move to the entrance of the cave where he knelt and began plucking the feathers from the bird.

Perhaps she had not been wrong about White Wolf after all, she thought as she went to throw another piece of wood on the fire. He was different from other men.

That night when Rachel changed the bandage on White Wolf's wounds, she realized he was healed enough for her to remove the stitches from his side. It was a painful, uncomfortable process, but White Wolf remained mute the whole time.

When she had finished and was winding a clean bandage about him, he observed, "You know much of healing. Who taught you?"

"My father was a physician," she said as she tied off the strip of her nightdress that served as dressing for his wounds. "He taught me many things."

White Wolf nodded his understanding. "Is that why no man had claimed you for his woman? Because they were all afraid of your healing powers?"

Rachel laughed, surprising herself that his questions did not bother her. "No. All the young men I knew thought it was the man's place to hunt and the woman's place to gather wood and tend the fire."

White Wolf glanced at her sharply and saw the teasing, mischievous glint in her eyes. Narrowing his eyes, he told her, "They probably also thought a woman with a sharp tongue would cause them much trouble."

Rachel cocked her head to one side and grinned up at him. "What do you think, White Wolf? Do I cause you much trouble?"

White Wolf's hand snaked out and caught the hair at the back of her head. "You cause me a great deal of trouble, English. But I know how to punish a woman who does not know her place."

As he slowly dragged her towards him, she asked in a

husky whisper, "How do you punish such a woman?"

"Like this," he said, then made all other conversation unnecessary as he covered her mouth with his.

Much later, when they were curled together in each other's arms, White Wolf told her, "We will leave here tomorrow."

"But we can't," Rachel objected. "You're not strong enough to travel."

"Strong enough. We cannot stay here any longer. I must reach the village of the People."

Rachel was silent as an ache penetrated her heart. When they reached White Wolf's village, she would no longer be his woman. She would once again become his hostage, his revenge.

"How long will it take us to get there?" she asked.

"When the moon is full, the People will greet us."

Rachel tried to remember what phase the moon was in. It was a half moon. It would take them about a fortnight to reach his village. Two weeks. Fourteen days. That was all she had left with him. A wolf howled from somewhere deep within the forest, and she shivered.

White Wolf hugged her tightly. "The wolf will not come in here," he said soothingly.

The wolf was already here, she thought to herself. "Love me, White Wolf," she whispered.

He smiled down at her. "You were just telling me I was not strong enough to travel. Do you think I am strong enough to chase away thoughts of the wolf again?"

"You heal quickly," she told him as she ran her fingers lightly across his chest. She marvelled at the way her touch made his male nipples pucker "I want to test your strength, to see how far you can travel tomorrow."

"I think it will be a test of your strength, English. How

far can you travel after a man has loved you well?" He rolled her onto her back and braced himself above her.

With wide eyes, Rachel told him in mock seriousness, "I don't know. No man has loved me well."

"No man, English?" he demanded. With a growl, White Wolf swooped down on her mouth to prove her statement false.

# Chapter Fourteen

"Rachel."

A deep voice called to her and something tickled her ear. With an annoyed groan, she rolled over and pushed the vexing tickle away.

"Rachel."

This time, the voice was louder and something warm and wet outlined her ear then continued down her neck. Vague, sweet memories made her smile, and a sound like a contented purr came from her throat. But she still did not want to wake up.

"Rachel."

This time, painful nips on her shoulder made her complain and open her eyes. White Wolf crouched above her and grinned at her.

"It is time to greet the sun, lazy one," he told her. "You cannot sleep all day."

Through drowsy eyes, Rachel drank in the sight of him. He was so beautiful, especially when he smiled at her as he was doing. And she was his woman, at least until the moon was full.

Sensuously, she stretched and smiled back at him. "I don't think I've ever slept so well."

White Wolf laughed and stood up. Putting his hands on his hips, he remarked, "I am not surprised. If I were not such a strong warrior, you would have worn me out last night."

Rachel sat up and hugged her knees. "If you were not such a strong warrior, I would not have become your woman."

"You speak the truth, English," White Wolf agreed with a grin. He turned and started out of the cave.

"Where are you going?" she asked.

"To bathe," he flung back at her over his shoulder.

With a small exclamation of dismay, Rachel scrambled to her feet, began to rush after him, then realized she was totally naked. Grabbing her cloak, she hurried out of the cave. "Wait," she called to his bronze back. "You can't bathe. Your wounds will open."

"My wounds will not suffer. If you are so concerned, come bathe with me."

Rachel stopped short when she heard his invitation. The idea of bathing with him made her toes curl, both in fright and anticipation. The feel of his body beneath her hands when they had made love convinced her that it was not just his face that was beautiful. The glimpses she had of him had not been enough; she wanted to see more. Without any more hesitation, she rushed after him.

White Wolf was plucking at the bandage about his middle when she caught up with him. He turned to her in exasperation.

"Did you purposely tie these bandages so that I would be unable to take them off myself?" he demanded.

Rachel chuckled and reached to help him. "I tied them

the way any good physician would have — so that a strong warrior would not be tempted to go without them."

As the knot came free, White Wolf's arms dropped about her. "Will I have to punish you again, English?" he asked with a lecherous grin.

Rachel tilted her head back and smiled into his eyes. "You may punish me all you wish," she told him. "I will never be an obedient woman."

He shook his head in mock dismay. "What will I do with you then? I can do this . . ." He bent his head and nipped at her ear. "Or this . . ." He tickled her neck with his tongue. "Or this . . ." He brushed his lips across her mouth. "Or maybe this . . ." His thumbs found the tips of her breasts and teased them.

Rachel's eyes closed in rapture. Waves of pleasure coursed through her at his touch.

"No," he decided. "None of those."

He dropped his hands and stepped back. Rachel's eyes snapped open at the loss of his touch. He was grinning mischievously at her. Dropping his breechclout from about his waist, he reached out and pulled the cloak from her shoulders.

"A bath is what the woman needs," he declared as he grabbed her hand and pulled her into the icy water of the stream.

As the freezing water lapped about her ankles, then her knees and finally about her waist, Rachel let out a gasp and a squeal. A strong hand pushed gently against her shoulder and she fell backwards completely into the water. Gulping for air, she shot to the surface.

"Oh! Ow! Oh!" she sputtered, not being able to say anything more coherent. The cold water had taken her breath. Shaking the water out of her eyes, she saw White Wolf standing before her, laughing.

"Punishment," he nodded in satisfaction.

"Unfair!" she exclaimed as she splashed him.

Laughing, he turned away from the spray and splashed her back. A water fight ensued. They were finally both laughing so hard they could barely stand in the swiftly running stream. Rachel ended the fight by ducking under the water and then running onto dry land.

"Coward," he called teasingly.

"N-not so," she stuttered through chattering teeth. "S-Smart. I kn-know w-when I am b-beaten. And wh-when I am-m c-cold. H-Hurry out-t of-f th-the w-water and w-warm m-me."

As she wrung out her dripping hair, she watched White Wolf wade further out into the stream, make a shallow dive, and swim a few strokes. A catch in his strong, graceful movements was the only indication he gave of being injured. Even though he was stiff from his wounds, he reminded her of a sleek otter as he turned towards the bank where she stood.

Rising out of the stream, he advanced towards her. The sun glistened on his water-slicked skin. Except for the three, long, angry slashes across his ribs, he was perfect. Rachel felt the curl of sensation that she had come to recognize as desire for this man. He was magnificent, like one of the gods of Greek mythology that her father had taught her about.

Her eyes travelled over his body, drinking in every detail. When she came to that part which had given her such pleasure the night before, she had to hide a gasp of surprise. It was soft and shrunken and did not look at all how it had felt. Her gaze flew up to his to see if he had been able to read her thoughts. She did not wish to make

202

him angry. He had not seemed to notice. In order to turn her thoughts away from his manhood and its odd transformation, she concentrated instead on the small leather bag which hung from a cord about his neck. She had noticed that he never removed it.

When he was near enough, she asked him, "What is in that little pouch?"

He fingered the bag gently. "It is my medicine bag. A charm to keep away evil spirits."

"What is in it?"

White Wolf paused as he considered if he should tell this woman. Deciding she had a right to know because she was his woman, he answered, "Every warrior wears one. When a boy reaches a certain age, he must pass a test of strength. At the end, he will find a relic of the animal who will be his spirit guide for the rest of his life. This, he places in his medicine bag, along with any other small things that he believes will help him keep strong."

"Oh." Rachel reached out and gingerly touched the well-worn leather. "What do you carry in yours?"

"That is not a question for the woman of a warrior to ask," he chided.

"I am sorry. I did not mean to pry." Dropping her eyes, she found herself again staring at his shrunken manhood. With a mortified gasp, she turned away and concentrated on wringing out her hair.

"English." His voice held laughter.

She peeked up at him from beneath her lashes. White Wolf grinned at her. "Did you believe it always is swollen with pleasure?" he asked.

Rachel's cheeks flamed. She knew immediately he was not speaking of his little medicine bag. "Of course not," she choked.

"Near you, it probably will be."

The heated flush crept down her neck. She kept her eyes on the ground.

"Unless there is some cure you know of to relieve the swelling," he suggested.

Rachel glanced up at him sideways. "I might be able to find one," she told him softly.

"Ah, I thought you might." He took her hand and placed it on his growing manhood. "Do you think you could find the cure now?"

"Now?" she squeaked. "Here? In the open?" She looked wildly around.

"Why not? Do you expect visitors?" White Wolf searched the area with his eyes.

"No, but . . ."

He raised an inquiring eyebrow.

Beneath her hand, she felt his manhood stir and swell. She gasped as it grew firmer and larger.

"It needs only your touch to awaken it," he murmured as his mouth swooped down to capture her lips.

Rachel's hand was caught between them, but all her being was centered for the moment on his sweet ravishing. Nothing else mattered except what this man was making her feel. When he jerked away from her suddenly, she was so giddy that she swayed into him. His body stiffened, and he faced into the tiny breeze.

"What is it?" she asked when her senses had stopped reeling. "What's the matter?"

"Smoke," he answered shortly. "There is smoke in the air."

Rachel sniffed, but could smell nothing.

"There is someone who follows," he said. He bent to scoop up their pieces of clothing, but a grunt of pain escaped his lips. He put a hand on her arm for support as he rose. "We must leave quickly."

"You should not travel," Rachel told him as she placed her hand over his. "Your wounds . . ."

". . . will not kill me," he finished. Taking her hand, he led her swiftly back to the cave.

As they hastily filled the packs and cleaned the cave of all evidence of their presence, White Wolf berated himself for his lack of caution. He had known there was someone who followed, yet he had allowed himself to become foolish. The woman had enticed him with her beauty and her warmth. She was not at fault. It was he who would bear the guilt if they did not reach the village of his mother's people in safety. His illness had made him weak in spirit as well as in body. He had chosen to forget that he was White Wolf, that everywhere there was danger. He wanted the woman named Rachel, but she must learn what it meant to be the woman of a warrior.

Soon after, they were travelling through the forest. Rachel had a feeling that White Wolf knew who it was that followed them, but she also felt that he would not tell her. His face was grim as he led her through the trees. The teasing sensual man who had made love to her and played with her in the stream was gone, replaced by the taciturn, impassive woodsman who was her captor. Yet, all was not as it had been before. Now, she followed him willingly, afraid of the danger to him as well as to herself.

That night, when White Wolf had her light a fire, she asked, "Won't this tell whoever is following us where we are?"

"He knows," White Wolf answered shortly.

Rachel got the fire going and began feeding pieces of wood onto the flames. "Who is it?" she wanted to know.

205

Casually, she pushed a spit into the pheasant that White Wolf had killed for their supper and placed it across the fire.

"Why do you think I know who it is?"

Rachel turned to look at him. "You know," she stated.

White Wolf's hand cupped the back of her neck and began to draw her close. "It does not matter," he murmured. His eyes fastened hungrily on her parted lips. He was amazed and pleased that she was able to read his thoughts so well, yet he was not about to tell her all he knew. She was a stubborn woman, and he knew the only way to get her to stop asking him questions was to confuse her mind. He enjoyed confusing her mind.

Just before their lips met, Rachel whispered, "The pheasant. It will burn."

"I burn, English." His hand slipped under her cloak and covered her breast. He felt her nipple pucker beneath his touch. "Put out my fire."

As his mouth captured hers, Rachel moaned with desire and leaned into him. Her arms slipped about him and held him close. When his tongue softly caressed her lips, she parted them in invitation. As her mind sank into the whirlpool of delicious sensation that he always created, her last coherent thought was her knowledge that White Wolf was evading her question. With a mental smile, she decided she would let him evade any question he wanted if he did it in this manner.

Much later, sated by love and full stomachs, they lay together beneath the deerskin and watched the flames of their campfire. Rachel's back and bottom were pressed intimately into the curve of White Wolf's body. His hand lightly cupped one breast.

Rachel smiled in contentment. The grave doubts and

feelings of guilt she should have had with becoming White Wolf's woman were absent from her mind. Here, beneath the stars, among the trees, with only the sounds of the animals to keep her and White Wolf company, the rigors of society's strictures were far away. When she finally returned to civilization, it would be time enough to worry about the opinions of others. For now, all she was concerned about was White Wolf and his safety.

"Tell me of this person who follows us," she said.

Again, White Wolf told her, "It does not matter." His voice was a rough rumble in her ear.

"It does matter. It is someone who wants to harm you." She flipped over so that she was facing him. Realizing too late that she had made a mistake in doing that, she tried to ignore the hardness of his body against the softness of hers. "Who wishes you harm?"

He grinned slyly at her. "No one that I can see." His hand cupped her bottom and pulled her into him.

Rachel pushed against his chest and wriggled back. "Don't change the subject. There is someone out there who wishes to do you harm. I want to know who it is and why he is following us."

White Wolf rolled onto his back and closed his eyes. With a tired sigh, he said, "Do not nag me, English, or I will give you back to the wolves."

A pain so sharp it made her gasp shot through her at his words. She thought she had meant something to him. That was why she had allowed him to . . . Evidently she had been wrong. She was only a female body for him to use. When he tired of her, he would do away with her. Pulling back from him, she slid to the very limit of the covering of the deerskin.

Feeling her move, he opened one eye and peeked at

her. At the same time that his hand reached out to pull her back, he said, "It was a jest, English. Come back here and warm me."

Rachel resisted only the length of a heartbeat before she slithered cautiously back to him. Despite his gentleness during their lovemaking, his comment had sharply reminded her that this man was not of her world, that he came from an uncivilized society.

When she was settled once again against him, he told her, "The one who follows will not harm me."

"Then why are we running from him?"

"I run from no one," he said fiercely.

"Pardon," she mumbled at his insulted tone. "Why did we have to leave the cave quickly?"

"I wish to return to the People. You will be safe there."

His hand stroked her arm, and she could feel her body relax against him. His concern for her safety wiped away any fears she had of his doing away with her.

After a long pause in which Rachel's eyelids had begun to grow heavy and she had almost succumbed to sleep he spoke again. "The one who follows us," he told her, "wants only to be sure that we return to the village of the People."

His reassuring words made no impact on Rachel's love-fogged, exhausted mind. Mumbling some incoherent syllables, she drifted into comfortable sleep.

A man stood on a small precipice on the bald face of the mountain and gazed out over the dark land spread before him. The moon had risen and cast its light over the forest, hills, and valleys. Huge black shadows transformed the wilderness and gave it a distinctive nighttime identity. Somewhere in the distance, a wolf howled.

The man's eyes scanned the distant blackness, where

the horizon was marked only by the absence of the stars. His face was set in hard, determined lines. He had travelled far this day, but the fatigue that should have claimed him was not evident in his taut muscles or decisive stance. He would find those he sought.

His gaze searched back and forth across the dark land spread out before him. He was close. He knew it. The distance of one sun, maybe two, that was all. Finally, a satisfied grunt emerged from deep in his throat. There, beneath the star that marked the tail of the Big Bear, he found what he sought. A thin column of smoke, lighter than the surrounding blackness, rose upward above the trees before it curled and spread in the night wind.

He watched the smoke a long time before he turned his back on it and walked the few paces to where he had piled dead leaves and twigs. Striking a spark, he lit the debris and started his own campfire. It chased away the dark, and its flames warmed him. Yet, he paid little heed to its heat. His discovery occupied his thoughts. The pain of betrayal knifed through his chest; the coldness of love turned to hate froze his heart.

He was the one to bring this man before the People. The only one. The People would decide. White Wolf was out there with the woman. What he had done could mean banishment from the circle of the People. The man who had once been his brother would be as if dead to all the People.

The man threw back his head and faced the stars. They told him nothing. A cry of anguish, frustration, and rage ripped from his very soul and echoed against the night.

Dark Eagle!

The thought immediately woke Rachel, and she bolted upright beneath the deerskin. Blinking, she sought White Wolf beside her, but he was not there. It was still dark, not time for them to begin travelling again. Searching the immediate area of their camp frantically with her eyes, she finally saw his shadow next to a tree. He seemed to be holding himself upright with one hand propped against its trunk. Quietly, she rose, wrapped the deerskin about her, and approached him. His back was to her. She reached out and tentatively touched his shoulder.

"White Wolf?" she asked softly.

"Go back to sleep." His voice was low and sounded strained.

"What is it? What's wrong?"

"Nothing." He turned to face her. "I heard a sound, but it was nothing." Again, he put his hand on the trunk of the tree.

Rachel sensed there was more to his wakefulness than what he was telling her. She tried to study his face in the darkness, but it was useless. She could see nothing. Knowing he would tell her only what he wished and when he wished, she turned and started back to the pile of boughs that was their bed.

"Come lie with me," she urged.

"Soon." His answer was distant as if he were far away and not standing just a few paces from her.

Rachel stopped and turned to face him. He was looking back, into the black forest beyond the clearing again. The name that had awakened her surged through her mind once more. Dark Eagle. He was out there. He followed them. Fear crawled down her spine.

White Wolf had told her that whoever followed them wanted only to be sure that they reached his village. Yet, his manner suggested there was something he was not telling her, that there was some danger involved in this deadly race. Why did Dark Eagle wish to be sure that they reached the village? What secrets would be revealed upon their arrival? White Wolf had separated from the rest of the captors to save her. He had gone against what Claude Donat had told her was the decision between the two men to punish her. Had White Wolf broken some law of his people? Would he be savagely punished for saving her? What would become of her once they reached the village? Would she be given to Dark Eagle as his reward for bringing the outlaw to justice?

Questions tumbled across her brain as she stood staring at White Wolf. He had told her she would be safe when they reached his village. Yet she felt there was danger there, too.

"Why do we have to go to your village?" she asked. "Why don't we go someplace else?"

White Wolf's head whipped around as he faced her. She felt his eyes burn into her.

"You speak foolishly, woman," he snapped. "There is no other place to go, not for me, not for you."

"But it is dangerous to go there." She made her words a statement of fact.

"There is no danger."

"Then why are we running from whoever is following us?"

"I do not run like the frightened deer. I run like the wind, hurrying to get where I must go."

"I know who follows us. It is Dark Eagle. You betrayed him by rescuing me, didn't you?"

211

White Wolf did not answer. Instead, he turned his back on her and returned to staring out into the blackness.

His silence was his answer. Contrary to the fear she had just experienced, a tiny thrill raced through her and made her toes curl inside the moccasins he had made for her. In rescuing her, he had stated that she meant something to him, more than his agreement with Dark Eagle. Perhaps, at the time, it was only that she was a valuable hostage, the means of his revenge on the English. Yet he could have had his revenge by leaving her to the wolves. He had not. Instead, he had betrayed the man who was of his own people.

Pulling the deerskin tighter around her shoulders, Rachel moved to the pile of branches and lay down. White Wolf would tell her nothing more. Yet, by his silence, he had proven her correct. There was enmity between White Wolf and Dark Eagle, something that could only be resolved in their village.

She had no idea how the resolution would take place or what the outcome would be, whether it would be civilized or savage. But she knew that she was intricately involved in both the problem and its solution. Helplessness overwhelmed her. She could do nothing to stop the inevitable flow of events, nothing except escape. Even if she wanted to, she knew White Wolf would not allow that to happen. Despite his recent gentleness and their lovemaking, he would be very sure that she entered that village with him, either by force or by her own free will. Even though she had tried to forget, she was still his prisoner.

White Wolf heard the woman settle herself on the branches. She would not ask him anything more this night. Her words had been true, her questions like arrows hitting their mark. She saw into his heart as if it lay bare upon his chest. There was something about this woman that was powerful. He smiled a grim smile. Her power had made him break his vow to himself, to his mother who was with her ancestors. It had made him betray Dark Eagle and the People. He had saved the woman, taken her in passion. Now, in shame, he returned to the village of his mother.

He should have left the woman to die with the wolves; he knew he could not. There was a bond between them, he and the woman, something that held him, drew him to her, stronger than his own will. She had saved him when he had been injured by the bear. She could have left him to die; she did not. The bond held her, also.

He listened to the sounds of the night beyond the clearing. There had been one sound, from far away, barely heard, that had awakened him and brought him to stand at the edge of the trees. It had been a cry that tore through him with its intensity. He knew it had been Dark Eagle, accepting his pain, mourning the loss of his brother.

There would be suffering that would have to be endured at the village; White Wolf knew that. Yet he felt that after its passing, both he and Dark Eagle would be stronger. He hoped they would not be enemies. If he reached the village of the People first, if he could talk to the wise one, Hunting Dog, he thought he might be able to heal the pain of Dark Eagle. That would give him great happiness.

He would carry his own shame in silence in his heart. The Council would decide what would be done. If he was to be banished, then let it be so. He had known what he had done at each step. He accepted his fate.

The weakness of his body which he had felt upon first

arising washed over him. His wounds throbbed painfully. He had pushed himself this day, forcing himself to travel far and quickly in order to stay ahead of Dark Eagle. His body was not ready for such punishment. Yet he had to reach the village first.

Sleep, he decided, was what he needed. Walking back into the clearing, he stood a moment over the sleeping form of the woman. Rachel. The rift between him and Dark Eagle would be made wider or resolved because of her. Either way, he would have her, this woman with hair of hidden fire.

# Chapter Fifteen

Rachel had not been asleep when White Wolf came to stand over her. Knowing Dark Eagle was out there, somewhere, tracking them relentlessly, kept her watchfully awake. She sensed the deep concern of White Wolf, but knew he would not talk to her about it. It was not his way. All she could do was remain silent and follow him.

She sat on the cold earth now as the sun lit the gray shroud of dawn. She had fallen asleep only when White Wolf lay with her beneath the deerskin. The security of his hard strength and warm body finally lulled her to rest. But thoughts of their pursuer nagged at her and kept her from blessed unconsciousness. She had awakened with her heart pounding, her blood racing, her lungs gasping for breath. Fear invaded her dreams as a huge monster. Realizing that fear had chased away all possibility of sleep for her, she had risen and kept watch over White Wolf, who needed sleep much more than she.

His sleep was deep, testifying to his exhaustion. She had seen the way he had leaned against the tree trunk for support, had seen him stop in midstride to regain his equilibrium. Not wanting to let on that she had observed his weakness, knowing he was a proud man, she had feigned sleep when he returned to lie with her. Yet, she knew how much the day's quick journey through the wilderness had sapped his strength. It was too soon for him to be demanding so much of his wounded body.

He sighed and rolled towards her in his sleep. A grimace of pain crossed his features. His eyes opened and she watched him glance about as he took in his surroundings. When that bright blue gaze finally settled on her, she smiled brightly.

"Good morning," she greeted him. "Did you sleep well?"

He rubbed a hand across his eyes, then searched the sky and the sunlight gilding the treetops. "It is late," he announced as he began to sit up. A catch in his fluid movement made the muscle jump in his jaw; his hand went to his side.

Rachel supported his back as he sat up the rest of the way. "You shouldn't try to move so quickly," she told him. "You will tear open your wounds."

He shook off her hand and growled something that she was glad she could not understand. "Why did you let me sleep?" he demanded angrily. "We should be far from here."

"Because you needed the rest." Rachel's tone indicated that she was offended by his ungrateful attitude.

"Do not clothe me in your woman's weakness." His blue eyes sliced into her.

Rachel scrambled to her feet and backed away a step as if she had been burned. "If you believe that, then you are a fool." Turning her back on him, she struggled to keep the tears from falling. His words had hurt, more than she wanted to admit.

She heard him stand, heard the breath catch in his throat at the painful stiffness of his wounds. Every nerve cried out for her to turn around and face him. She could feel his anger emanate from him like the hot rays of the sun, but she refused to give in to her fear. Turning her back on him while he was enraged was either the bravest or stupidest thing she could do; she hoped she was not being stupid.

She felt his hand on her shoulder. Terror slipped through her and she flinched away. She had given herself to him, yes, but still she knew so little about him. He was a redman, a savage. What did she know of the ways of his people, of how the men treated their women? Perhaps the men beat their women. It was certainly not unheard of in her own society. She had been a fool to allow him to possess her.

"Rachel."

Her name was a whisper on his lips. His tone made her turn slowly to face him. Unsmiling, his eyes searched her face.

"We should be far from here," he said again. "We have to start our journey now. We must reach the village of the People quickly. I will deal with my pain. Do not make me weak." He reached out and drew his fingers down her cheek. "The one who follows will sense my weakness and strike at you. You will be safe in the village."

Although his words were not exactly an apology, still, Rachel felt a warm glow. He did care about her enough to want to protect her. Nodding her acceptance of his words, she turned to gather their few possessions together while White Wolf took care of his needs. It was not long before they were travelling quickly through the forest.

They shared a sense of urgency. Their words were few; their steps swift; their rests infrequent. Rachel watched White Wolf closely for signs of fatigue caused by his injuries, but he showed none. Not wanting to repeat her mistake of trying to take care of him, she did not question his gruelling pace. She herself had no wish to fall into the grasp of Dark Eagle.

That night, when they lay together beneath the deerskin, White Wolf's lovemaking was sweet and gentle. His actions more than apologized for the harsh words he had spoken that morning. Rachel fell asleep exhausted, but with a contented smile on her lips.

The following days all seemed to run into each other in a haze of flight through the wilderness by day and sweet, wild love at night. Rachel lost track of time. She knew that soon they would reach the village and her days with White Wolf would come to an end. Each night when the moon rose, she would look to see how much it had swelled. Then, one night, her heart seemed to shrivel in her chest. The moon was round and full. She would have one more day, possibly two, with White Wolf.

When he reached for her beneath the deerskin, she placed her hand on his chest and pushed him onto his back. She wanted this night to be special, something they could both remember. Straddling his hips, she leaned over him and flicked her tongue across his chest above the bandages that still protected his wounds. She marvelled anew at the smoothness of his skin, like taut satin over coiled springs. When she straightened and ran her fingers over where her tongue had just been, she caught the expression of soft amusement in his eyes.

"You learn quickly, English," he told her.

She smiled back at him. "I've had a very good teacher."

Leaning over him again, her hands framed his face and she took his mouth. Her tongue teased the outline of those chiseled lips, then sucked and nibbled at them. White Wolf lay compliant beneath her, urging her on with his own tongue. Finally, she plunged between those inviting lips, feeling, stroking, arousing and being aroused. Breaking away to gasp for breath, she trailed her tongue across his jaw, down the sinew of his neck to his male nipple. Curious about his reaction, she sucked on the hard nub. A barely audible gasp came from deep in his throat.

Straightening once again, she allowed a triumphant, sensual smile to curve her lips. His answer was a look filled with heat and hunger. Raising herself above him, she impaled herself on his shaft. This time, it was she who gasped as her eyes widened with the intense pleasure. His hands came up and cupped her breasts, now swollen, the tips tight and aching to be loved. Her eyes slipped closed as she concentrated on the feel of the man she surrounded, who surrounded her.

He began to move within her; she matched his rhythms. Clutching at his shoulders, her neck arching back, she rode him as sensations of pleasure spiraled her away to another world, taking him with her. She lost herself in the web of heat they erected around themselves. Suddenly, violently, the heat, the other world, exploded in a blinding, whirling maelstrom of pleasure that pulsed and throbbed forever. When it was finally over, she collapsed on top of him like a limp flower.

His arms came about her and held her tightly. Her hands snuggled beneath him. Neither wanted to move, to disengage themselves, one from the other. What they had experienced had torn apart their souls and put them together again in some new formation that neither was willing to explore. They wanted only to float in the aftermath of the warm glow that remained from their trip to another world. Sleep came quietly and carried them into their dreams.

Rachel was awakened by the deerskin being yanked off her and a hand pulling her to her feet. Groggily, she opened her eyes and tried to gather her wits.

"What is it?" she mumbled through the fog of sleep. "What is going on?"

"Get dressed," White Wolf ordered. "Hurry."

The coolness of dawn slapped her skin and made gooseflesh rise all over her. She hurried to obey him. When she was dressed, again she asked, "What is going on?"

"The one who follows is near. Come, take care of your needs as we travel."

White Wolf slung his bow and quiver across his shoulder and picked up one of the packs. Before Rachel had a chance to question him further, he had set out across the field of tall grass where they had made their camp the night before. Grabbing the other pack, she hurried after him.

She was quiet as she followed White Wolf. Her thoughts were a mixture of apprehension and regret. Dark Eagle must be very close indeed if White Wolf was so concerned. Fear crawled up her back, and she nervously glanced over her shoulder. All she could see was the tall grass gilded by the rising sun, and beyond, the dark trees that marked the forest. There was no sign of movement; no sign of humanity. Berating herself for her foolishness, she realized that if Dark Eagle were close enough to be seen, he would be confronting them instead of skulking in the woods. The thought calmed her only a little. She wanted very much to be within the confines of the village where White Wolf had said she would be safe.

As she hurried along, sadness washed over her, drowning her fear. Upon entering the village, her life would change. No longer would she be White Wolf's woman. She would become his hostage once more, his prisoner. He would send her to the French, those vile people, for his ransom and revenge.

Indecision created havoc in her brain. If she hurried and kept pace with White Wolf, she would lose him sooner; if she trailed behind slowly, she would lose her life. She studied the broad back of the man who strode before her. There was no answer in his resolute steps, in his proud carriage. The dilemma weighed heavily on her. Love or life? She could not make that decision. Blocking out all thought, she concentrated on putting one foot before the other.

They stopped to rest only twice, once in the late morning and once in the late afternoon. The terrain had not been difficult to traverse, but their pace had been quick. Rachel sat catching her breath and looking around her. The countryside was different from what they had been travelling through since that dark morning when White Wolf had swept down onto her home. They had left the mountains behind. Having skirted the northern tip of a large lake, they sat on rocks at the edge of a swamp that stretched away to the south. The dry browns of winter still colored the wetland, but a faint, yellow-green blush that haloed the scrub announced that spring was on its way. Birds twittered and flew from bush to bush. The distant sound of rushing water came sporadically on the light breeze.

White Wolf stood up suddenly and gazed across the swamp. He appeared to be listening for something. Rachel had heard nothing unusual. Only the far cry of a whippoorwill had echoed across the marsh.

"Come," he said. "Walk only where I walk."

Rachel watched him head unerringly into the thicket of brambles and bushes that grew on the drier parts of the morass spread before them. With an apprehensive frown, she hesitatingly followed.

She tiptoed and hop-stepped from dry spot to dry spot. The spring thaw had made the ground wet and spongy. Tiny rivulets and larger brooks crisscrossed between minuscule islands. Bushes and undergrowth clogged the dry land making passage almost impossible. If it were not for White Wolf's forging a path, she would have been hopelessly tangled and desperately lost. By the time the sun was low in the sky, she was ready to collapse.

"Please," she panted. "Can we rest for a while?"

White Wolf glanced back at her. Grabbing her hand, he pulled her through the bushes to stand beside him.

"We are there," he announced as he pointed to a canoe that lay on the shore of a wide stream. Gesturing at the water, he said, *"Pigwaduk."*

Rachel glanced around, then up at him in confusion. "I'm sure there must be ducks around here, but where are the pigs?" she wanted to know.

White Wolf flashed her a grin. "No pigs or ducks," he told her. *"Pig-wa-duk.* It means 'bent stream'. It is the name of the water."

"Of course," she mumbled. "How stupid of me. Everyone knows that."

"Everyone who lives here knows that, English. Now you know it, too. Come, I will take you to *Ne-gan-o-den-ek*, the village of the People."

He led her through the rest of the undergrowth to the shore of the stream. After helping her into the canoe, he pushed off and climbed in after her. Rachel was grateful for the rest, and she appreciated being able to travel without having to move. It was a luxury to sit and watch the shores of the stream pass silently by.

"Where did the canoe come from?" she asked.

"From the village. We have been watched. The People know we are coming."

Rachel was not sure she liked the idea that they had been observed, yet she welcomed the transportation. "I would like to thank whoever left the canoe."

"Then thank the village, for no one will ever say that he was the one who left it. It is the way of the People."

They rode quietly after that. White Wolf paddled noiselessly in the rear of the canoe, and Rachel sat in the bow and enjoyed the ride. As they rounded a curve in the stream, she heard White Wolf make a perfect imitation of the call of the whippoorwill. The song was answered from the stream's shore far ahead. She realized that they were being watched as White Wolf had mentioned. His birdcall had been a signal to whoever was on shore that he was a friend, coming in peace.

Soon after, the stream widened into a river. Across the water sat an island, and on its shore was a village with tendrils of smoke from cookfires rippling up from dome-shaped houses. People moved among the buildings; children played and dogs barked. It was a peaceful scene. One that disguised the horror that Rachel knew she would have to face.

They skimmed across the water, seemingly propelled by a giant hand that swept them along. When Rachel remarked upon this fact, White Wolf was quick to enlighten her.

"It is *Kwel-bejwan-osik,* where the waters turn when they meet," he said. "At high water, the current runs toward the island; at low water, it runs away from it. It is high water now."

Marvelling at the idea that these people had a name for all of the oddities of nature, she soon was distracted by a sound of whooping and yelling coming from the village. As she watched, the people began to gather on the rocky beach. They waved their arms; some waved bright blankets in the air. Rachel had no trouble understanding what was taking place. They were welcoming home a brave, beloved warrior.

As the canoe sped closer to shore, Rachel was able to study the inhabitants of White Wolf's village. They were a handsome people, tall and straight, their features striking. She understood now how White Wolf had received his wild beauty — all except those devilish blue eyes, for all of his people were dark- eyed. Even from this distance she could see that.

"You must have many warriors in your village," she observed. "The men from the attack could not have made it back here before us."

"There were few from this village who joined the war party," White Wolf told her. "Most of the warriors came from Caughnawaga near Mont Réal."

Now Rachel understood why the group of French soldiers and Indians had wanted to take the hostages to Montreal as Claude Donat had told her.

The canoe scraped on the sand. Boys eagerly ran forward to pull it out of the water. As Rachel and White Wolf climbed out of the craft, they were soon surrounded with happy, noisy, curious villagers.

Rachel and White Wolf became separated by the crowd. Chattering among themselves, the women converged on her. They stared and pointed, making her feel self-conscious and uneasy. Gingerly, they reached out and touched her hair. Rachel remained perfectly still, not wanting to insult or annoy them, but feeling the fear rising within her.

When the women discovered her hair felt like any other hair, they began pulling at it; those who could not reach her hair began pulling at her clothes. The change in the women's manner from curiosity to violence was so swift that she was unprepared for it. With a cry, she backed away, but they surrounded her. Trying to protect her head and face with her arms as best she could, she twisted and turned out of the reach of some of the women only to find herself closer to others. Hands clawed at her.

"No! Stop!" she cried out in panic and pain.

A loud command came from White Wolf, and the women immediately ceased. They backed away several paces as he spoke sharply to them in their native language. Finally, one woman of about middle age stepped forward.

White Wolf turned to Rachel and explained. "You will go with Corn Woman. She will feed you and see to your needs."

As he started to turn away, she blurted out, "But—"

Angrily, he swung back towards her. "Do not question. Just go." Pausing for a moment as if trying to decide about something, he added in a softer tone, "I will come for you later."

His attention turned from her and he searched the crowd of women. Finding the woman he sought, he walked up to her and spoke a few quiet words. Suddenly, the woman cried out in anguish and tore her tunic. Falling to her knees, she scooped up dirt and rubbed it into her hair and over her face and arms. A group of old women surrounded her and escorted her back into the village. Rachel was curious about what had occurred, but she thought it might have something to do with a warrior who had been killed in the attack on Deerfield.

White Wolf remained motionless as the small group of women disappeared among the huts. When they were out of sight, Rachel watched him stride away up the beach towards one end of the village. A few of the men followed, but most dispersed in various directions. The woman he had indicated as Corn Woman gestured for Rachel to go with her. Rachel accompanied her up the beach and into the village.

Corn Woman was not quite as tall as Rachel, but age had not bowed her. Her back was straight and her bearing proud as she led the way across the rough sand of the beach. A single thick, dark braid sprinkled liberally with gray hung halfway down her back. It was held at the bottom with short strips of rawhide in which tiny bird feathers had been tied. Her deerskin tunic and skirt were well made and intricately decorated about the hem and sleeves. She was obviously a woman of high rank within the village. Rachel wondered what her connection was to White Wolf.

The woman led her past several of the dome-shaped houses which Rachel now saw were sided with strips of birch bark sewn tightly and intricately together with thin roots. A hole in the middle of each roof allowed smoke from the cookfires to escape. Corn Woman stopped before a house towards the middle of the village. Its pieces of bark covering were skillfully sewn with more intricate stitches than many of the others. Holding up the skin which covered the entrance, she motioned Rachel to enter.

Rachel ducked into the dim interior. She was amazed at the coziness that greeted her. The inside walls were decorated with hangings and pictures painted directly on the bark. Low platforms piled with furs and blankets ringed the circumference of the house. In the center of the floor, a fire burned, and hung over the flames was a clay pot from which emanated a delicious smell. Corn Woman motioned for Rachel to sit on one of the platforms, then she spooned some of the food that had been cooking in the pot into a wooden bowl and handed it to Rachel along with a wooden spoon. Thanking her, Rachel accepted the meal.

It was a fish stew flavored with vegetables. Upon tasting it, Rachel found it delicious and finished every drop. While she ate, Corn Woman busied herself with sewing some skins, but Rachel noticed she glanced up often to see how her guest enjoyed her cooking.

As Rachel handed the bowl back to the woman, she said with a smile, "I know you don't understand me, but that was the most delicious meal I've ever had."

Corn Woman said nothing as she accepted the bowl, but Rachel could tell she was pleased. The woman went back to her sewing after wiping out the bowl. Rachel sat and watched her for a while, wondering what White Wolf was doing and when or if he was coming to get her. She tried to tamp down her fears. Except for the overexuberance of the women on the beach, she had been treated well. White Wolf had even protected her from the women. Surely, if he meant her harm, he would not have saved her from the mob.

Outside the hut, the village suddenly became quiet. A scratching sound on the outside of the hut and soft words were spoken indicating the presence of someone. Corn Woman rose and went out. Curious, Rachel followed and stood just outside the entrance to the hut.

A group of old women entered one of the huts across the open space in the middle of the village. From one end of the village, elderly men were proceeding towards the same hut. The leader banged on a small drum and chanted mournfully. The group of men stopped outside the hut across the village, and they were joined by others of the village, both men and women. Rachel caught a glimpse of White Wolf near the front of the crowd. When all had gathered, the old man who banged the drum began to chant once more and the people joined in. The chanting went on for a while, then ceased. Slowly and in silence, the people drifted back to their own homes. Rachel noticed their faces reflected intense sadness.

On his way back to wherever he had gone before, White Wolf saw Rachel standing outside the hut of Corn Woman, and he approached her. His expression was grim.

When he stopped before her, Rachel asked, "What is going on?"

Glancing back across the village at the hut he had just left, he answered, "The People are helping the mother of Deer Stalker mourn her son."

"Was he killed in Deerfield?" she wanted to know.

White Wolf's eyes grew hard. "It was the shot from your firestick that killed him."

228

Rachel fell back a step before the fierceness of his tone. "Oh," she gulped.

White Wolf looked away, turning the intensity of his emotions away from her. Sighing, he murmured, "It is the way of enemies, English. Deer Stalker died as a warrior should die." He motioned to the hut behind her. "Go now and sleep. The sun has closed its eyes. Soon it will be going on in darkness." Abruptly, he walked off.

Rachel wasted no time in obeying him and ducking back into the hut. Corn Woman entered soon after. Outside the hut, Rachel could hear the sounds of people calling back and forth, of conversations rising and falling, the sounds of a peaceful village heading into the night. Corn Woman lit several split sticks of pitch pine for light inside the hut so she could sew.

Soon the exertions of the day and the sensation of a full middle made Rachel's eyes grow heavy. Not even her concerns about her future or the whereabouts of White Wolf could keep her mind alert. Desperately, she tried to stifle a yawn. Corn Woman happened to glance up at that moment. Seeing that Rachel was tired, she motioned for her to lie down on the platform where she sat. Rachel did not need much urging. She reasoned that she would be able to deal better with her precarious situation if she were not so tired. Curling up on the soft furs, she was soon asleep.

The old man sat puffing on his pipe and staring into the fire. He had hoped he would not have to lead the mourning song when his warriors returned from their war party. He was getting too old to lead the mourning song. It was time it was sung for him. But the runner had arrived at his lodge with the news of the death of Deer Stalker and the arrival of the one called White Wolf. The death of a brave warrior was bad, but the lonely arrival of the one called White Wolf was a worse thing. Warriors were not supposed to return from war alone.

Patiently, he waited. The spirits had warned him that something was not right. There was bad blood between two brothers. He had looked through the sacred smoke into the sacred fire. Again, he had seen the woman of cold fire. She had been the center of this evil, but also the center of great good. This woman had come with the one called White Wolf.

A soft scratching on the outside of his lodge signalled that someone wished to enter. He knew who it was — someone who was in great pain, who needed his advice. Pausing a moment to summon the spirits for help, he bade the person enter.

White Wolf ducked through the opening and quietly sat opposite the old man. He watched the shaman — the old man's eyes were half-closed — puff several times on his pipe. Respectfully, White Wolf waited a few moments before he spoke. The time gave him a chance to gather his thoughts and his courage for what he was about to tell the old man seated across the fire from him.

"Long may you live, grandfather," White Wolf began in the language of his mother. "It gladdens my heart to see you. The fire of youth still burns in your eyes."

The shaman's old eyes crinkled at the corners, the only sign of emotion he displayed upon seeing the man seated before him. Nodding, he answered, "The fire of youth has long gone from these eyes, my son, but this old man cherishes your words. Come, sit down at the rear."

White Wolf bowed his head to hide the surge of emotion he felt. The old man had invited him to sit in the honored spot at the rear of the lodge. Hearing the old man speak, White Wolf realized he had been gone too long. He had missed the sound of his voice.

"You have returned unharmed," the old man observed after White Wolf had settled himself at his right. "There will be feasting."

A pain so sharp it might have been physical passed through White Wolf's chest. Raising his head, he looked Hunting Dog in the eyes. "No, grandfather. There will be no feasting. I have brought shame to the People. I have done wrong to Dark Eagle."

The shaman said nothing. His old eyes searched the face of the son of his daughter. He saw great pain reflected there. "What you have done, you have done. There will be feasting because a son of the People has returned. Then the Council will decide."

White Wolf shook his head. "No, grandfather. I will not stand before the Council. I will leave the village. It is the only way."

Hunting Dog lay down his pipe with two hands on the ground before him. "Tell me of the woman."

White Wolf almost smiled. It had always been the way of the shaman to end a disagreement by speaking of something else. Hunting Dog usually won those disagreements, but not this time. White Wolf could not allow the People to split themselves into two opposing groups, one on his side, one on the side of Dark Eagle. It would be better if he left the village of the People. It would have been better if he had left the woman behind in her village.

Drawing a breath, he began, "The woman is a worthy enemy. She is brave, her heart is strong. She has travelled far with me. I took her as my revenge." He stopped, reluctant to say more.

"You hide things in your heart," the shaman accused.

White Wolf faced his grandfather squarely as he said, "She is my woman."

There was no surprise on Hunting Dog's face at his grandson's words. He knew now what the spirits had been trying to tell him. "What of Dark Eagle?"

"Dark Eagle comes on my heels. You may speak with him yourself."

Hunting Dog's eyes opened wide at the rudeness of the son of his daughter. Never had he spoken such words.

White Wolf realized his error and was immediately sorry for his words. "Forgive my sharp tongue, grandfather. I meant no disrespect." His hands clenched convulsively where they rested on his knees. He forced them open and made himself overcome his pain. "Dark Eagle will call the Council together, but that will cause anger among the People. They will fight among themselves. I have wronged Dark Eagle. I admit it and accept my punishment. I will leave the People. There is no need for the Council."

"It is the way of the People to call the Council. It is for the wise ones to decide. Has Dark Eagle wronged White Wolf?" His sharp old eyes bore into the man sitting across from him.

White Wolf bowed his head. "That is for Dark Eagle to say."

Hunting Dog grunted his satisfaction in his grandson's humble words. "This woman who has come between two brothers, where is she?"

"In the lodge of Corn Woman."

"You have made her a guest amongst the People while she is still a prisoner."

"She is my woman."

"She is a prisoner. Lay down a pledge. It is the way of the People. Will you give the Council more to wag their tongues at? When the sun sits in the trees tomorrow, there will be feasting. The woman will be offered to the People as a prisoner. If you wish to take this woman, you will lay down a pledge." Hunting Dog's eyes narrowed in speculation. "Has this woman made the brave White Wolf weak? Has she wiped the memory of the People from your heart?"

White Wolf stiffened at the rebuke. "No, grandfather. The memory of the People is strong in my heart."

"Then what strong medicine does this woman have that makes White Wolf, the brave warrior, go against the laws of the People?"

White Wolf gave a tiny half smile. "Hair of hidden fire."

"Strong medicine," the shaman agreed. "Bring the woman to me before the Council is called. I will see this woman myself." He took a pipe, decorated with carvings and feathers, from a shelf behind him. After packing it with aromatic tobacco, he lit it with a glowing stick from the fire. "Now, we will smoke the sacred pipe."

# Chapter Sixteen

Rachel walked along the riverbank beside Corn Woman. It was early morning and they were returning from bathing at a tiny, secluded inlet away from the village. Corn Woman had been gracious to her and had again shared a meal with her. Rachel appreciated her hospitality, but she wondered what had become of White Wolf. She had not seen him since he had left her after the mourning for Deer Stalker.

As they neared the village, she saw White Wolf walking towards them. She almost ran to greet him, but her footsteps faltered when she saw the stern, closed expression on his face. Apprehension slithered through her. Something was not right.

He stopped before them and spoke to Corn Woman. She glanced at Rachel, then nodded and walked away. Rachel was not sure what was happening. Uncertainty changed to fear as Rachel glanced up again at White Wolf's face. It was cold and hostile. He had once again become her captor, the same man who had attacked Deerfield and dragged her through the village, the same man who had told her she was his revenge.

Taking hold of her wrist, he tied the end of a strip of rawhide to it. It was as if they had never spent all those weeks together in the wilderness, as if they had never made love.

"What are you doing?" Her bewildered question came out in a husky whisper.

White Wolf glanced at her with those frosty blue eyes and dropped her wrist, now attached firmly to the rawhide. Holding on to the loose end, he turned and started back towards the village. Rachel had no alternative but to follow.

With a couple of quick steps, she caught up with him and placed her hand on his arm. He swung about on her.

"Why?" she asked. "Why are you doing this?"

"You are my hostage, my revenge," he told her coldly. "You know this." He paused for a moment, weighing his next words. "Show your courage, English."

Rachel dropped her hand and lifted her chin. A coldness had settled in her chest in the vicinity of her heart. "Of course," she told him. "How silly of me to forget what I am to you."

When White Wolf turned and started towards the village once more, Rachel followed with her head held high. She had made a mistake in believing that White Wolf would put aside his idea of revenge. How could she have been so foolish?

As they walked through the village, women and children began to follow them. As the crowd grew, they became vocal and began laughing and yelling. Some of the more audacious children took up long branch switches and hit her with them. White Wolf did nothing to stop them.

The women became bolder and bolder. They closed

around her, pulled at her clothes and hair, and poked at her with sticks. Hundreds of claw-like hands reached out for her. It was like a nightmare, but it was reality.

"No!" she cried as she twisted and turned out of the reach of the women. "Stop it! Stop it!"

Her cries went unheeded.

White Wolf brought her to a post stuck in the ground at the far end of the village. The women followed and harassed her the whole way. At a sharp command from White Wolf, they backed away. He made Rachel face the post, then pulled her arms about it and tied her wrists together.

Someone from the crowd hit her in the back with a clod of dirt. The yelling and laughing started up again as others threw dirt at her. White Wolf was also hit. He turned on the nearest woman and growled something at her. The others immediately dropped the dirt in their hands and backed away. After assuring himself that the women would not throw any more dirt, he checked that Rachel's bonds were strong enough that she could not escape.

Swallowing her pride, Rachel pleaded, "Please, don't do this to me."

White Wolf raised those devilish blue eyes and stared at her solemnly. "Show your courage, English," he repeated, then he turned and strode away through the crowd.

Before the women pushed around her again, Rachel caught a glimpse of him at the edge of the crowd. He was standing aloofly away from the commotion, his feet planted firmly, his arms crossed at his chest. His cold blue eyes stared at her. There was not the slightest indication that he even knew who she was. He looked at her as if she were a creature beneath his contempt. As she watched, he turned on his heel and strode away.

Rachel's legs suddenly could not support her any longer. Slowly, she sank to the ground and leaned her cheek against the rough post. She did not care that some of the women still poked and pulled at her. The pain they caused was nothing compared to what she felt inside.

A cold hand clutched at her heart. She had been a fool to trust White Wolf, to allow him to touch her in passion, to let him use her body for his savage lust. She was nothing to him, only his prisoner, his revenge.

Her fate was now very clear to her. She would become the slave of this tribe of savages. They would use her for their entertainment, and when they grew tired of using her for that purpose, she would be killed. She understood now what White Wolf had meant when he had told her she would never return from New France. Terror at what lay ahead and rage at herself for what she had done twined together in her chest and weighed down upon her. Nothing mattered any more. Nothing. Not food, nor water; heat, nor cold; pain, nor pleasure. She was a lump of flesh that would slowly fade into nothingness.

As the women realized they would get no more response from her, they slowly drifted away. Finally, Rachel was left alone in her misery. Through dull eyes, she watched the life of the village. Women cooked on fires in front of their huts, or tanned skins, or sewed clothes, or performed the hundreds of little tasks involved in day-to-day living. Men sat in small groups and talked; some headed down to the beach with nets and traps; others disappeared beyond the village to hunt. Children gathered wood and placed it in a pile in an open area in the middle of the village. The smaller children played among the huts with the many pet dogs. It was a peaceful, happy scene, and Rachel hated it.

As the morning crawled by, Rachel noticed that food was being gathered into the middle of the village where earlier the children had placed the piles of wood. The men returned from fishing and hunting. Two deer were skinned; a large central fire was lit and the carcasses were placed over the blaze to cook. It did not take much of Rachel's imagination to realize that a feast was being prepared. Keeping her eyes on the ground, she turned away from the happy atmosphere of the village. She did not want to contemplate what role she would play in this celebration.

Noticing two moccasined feet not far away, she could not help the tiny surge of joy that flashed through her. Closing her eyes tightly to banish the feeling, then opening them again, she slowly raised her head. She could not allow White Wolf to see any of her emotions. She did not want his pity, if he was capable of it, and she could not deal with his contempt.

The face she saw made her gasp. It was not the one she expected, that deep in her heart she longed to see. Staring down at her was the cold, cruel visage of Dark Eagle.

Their eyes met and locked. Terror slipped through her and made her tremble. This was the man who had found their trail and followed them, who had wanted her scalp, her death. Now that White Wolf had turned his back on her, there was nothing to prevent Dark Eagle from taking what he wished.

Dark Eagle spoke something to her in his native language. When he finished speaking, he raked his eyes over her, and a frigid smile curved his lips. Turning abruptly away, he sauntered off. A quiet laugh as icy as a winter blast floated back to her.

"Dear God in Heaven," she muttered. "Save me from that madman."

"Perhaps He has, my child."

Startled, Rachel swung her head around towards the sound of the voice. Standing beside her was a man dressed in the black, flowing robes of a papist priest. He was not very old, but his face showed signs of much past hardship. As she stared at him, he crouched beside her.

"I am Father Lisle," he introduced himself.

Rachel blinked away her shock at discovering another white person in the Indian village.

"I come from the mission. I was summoned by—" He broke off his sentence abruptly, then continued, "Someone told me that a white woman had been brought to the village as a prisoner. Is there anything I can do for you, child?"

Rachel hesitated. She had heard all her life that papists were spawns of the Devil. How could she ask one of these evil men for help? Mutely, she shook her head and turned away.

"Please, don't turn away," he pleaded gently. "I will not harm you. You are English?"

Rachel nodded, but she still would not look at him.

"I am also English."

Rachel snapped her head around and stared at him. "You are English? Then why . . .?" As her words trailed off, her eyes strayed to his priestly clothes.

He smiled. "I was captured by the Indians when I was twelve. They sold me to a French priest who cared for me and taught me everything he knew. I came to love him like a father, and I wanted to honor him. When I was

239

twenty, he sent me to France to become a priest." He shrugged. "So, here I am."

"But how could you become a papist and go against what your real father believed?" Immediately, she realized she might have insulted him. "I'm sorry. I did not mean to pry."

"You do not have to apologize. I understand. Would you like some water?"

He dipped a gourd into a clay pot sitting on the ground beside him and held it out to her. At her nod, he put it to her lips so that she could sip from it.

When she had finished, he said, "Now, tell me how you came to be here."

Despite the fact that he was a French papist priest now, at one time he had been English. Rachel felt the need to tell someone of her troubles, and this priest had at one time been English. This was a bond between them. She told him of the attack on Deerfield, of how White Wolf had rescued her from the wolves, and how they travelled the rest of the way by themselves. Leaving out their intimate relationship, she told of White Wolf saving her from the bear and her care of him after he was wounded. She told how Dark Eagle had followed them. And she told of how she was White Wolf's revenge.

Father Lisle gazed at her in sympathy. "You have had a difficult journey. I fear it is not over yet."

"What do you mean?"

He glanced at her bound wrists. "You are a prisoner here. I don't know what will happen to you. I heard that you were the one to kill Deer Stalker. I know of White Wolf's need for revenge."

A cold hand gripped Rachel's insides at the priest's words. "Please, can you help me escape?"

Father Lisle shook his head. "I am sorry. I can't."

In despair, Rachel turned her head away.

"It's not what you think," the priest told her. "I know White Wolf. I cannot betray him by releasing you. I can only talk to him."

Anger at this traitorous Englishman suddenly surged through her. "You would allow me to be savagely murdered by these people rather than betray one of them? What kind of priest are you? What have these French devils done to your mind, Englishman?"

Father Lisle's reaction to Rachel's biting questions was only sadness. "I'm sorry I cannot explain more. All I can tell you is that we are all God's children, French and English. It is not God who created boundaries. I will speak with White Wolf. He is honorable. Take heart in that. One thing more: no matter what these people do to you, do not cry out. They respect bravery more than anything else." He rose and picked up the clay water pot. "God bless you, child."

Rachel watched him walk away and disappear between two of the Indian huts. A wild rage pumped through her. The French had again reached out and wounded the English. They had taken an Englishman and turned him into a French priest, a child of the Devil. Determination joined her anger. No matter what these savages did to her, she would not die. Somehow, she would escape and get to New France. There, she would seek her own revenge.

Just before sunset, some of the villagers began gathering in the open area in the middle of their huts. One of the men began beating on a small drum. At the sound, more of the Indians appeared from their huts. Soon, the open area was crowded with talking, laughing people.

241

Food was passed around and hungrily devoured.

Rachel watched all this from her lonely spot at the far end of the village. The delicious smells that wafted her way on the evening breeze made her mouth water. Her stomach grumbled hungrily, for she had had nothing to eat since very early that morning.

Reluctantly, she searched for White Wolf. Even though she tried to tell herself she did not care if she saw him, still she could not keep herself from watching for a glimpse of his tall form. As much as she berated herself for being a fool, she seemed to be obsessed with him.

It was not until the meal was over and the women had cleared away the bowls and dishes that she finally saw him. The villagers were sitting in a circle about the great central fire. A few of the men began beating drums, shaking gourd rattles and playing reed whistles. White Wolf stood in the center of the clearing near the fire and began to speak.

Rachel could not understand him, but she did not need to. The firelight played across his strong, handsome features. A headband decorated with quillwork and beads stretched across his forehead and held back his freeflowing, long, black hair. A handful of turkey and eagle feathers stuck up from the back of the headband. His muscular chest was bare except for the medicine bag which hung from a cord about his neck. Three dark stripes slashed down across his ribs where his wounds had barely healed. The leggings he wore were fringed; his breechclout was bordered with beadwork. On his back was his silvery wolf pelt. Rachel could not tear her eyes away from him.

He finished speaking and began moving in time to the music. It did not take Rachel long to realize that he was acting out the attack on Deerfield, her capture, and their trek through the forest. Mesmerized, she watched his graceful motions.

Suddenly, another male figure appeared on the far side of the fire. Rachel could not see who it was, but when White Wolf noticed him, he stopped dancing and stood perfectly still. The other man jumped high into the air and gave a loud shout. It was then Rachel realized it was Dark Eagle.

The music faltered for only a moment, for Dark Eagle immediately began to dance, telling his version of the events. White Wolf remained where he was for the space of two heartbeats before he quietly slipped through the crowd of villagers and disappeared into the dark. Rachel tried to follow his retreating form, but the night closed around him.

She turned her attention back to Dark Eagle. The villagers appeared to enjoy his performance as much as that of White Wolf. Even Rachel had to admit to herself that he was a powerful performer.

When his dance was over, the tempo of the drums changed. The villagers rose from their seats, formed themselves into two circles—the men on the inside, the women on the outside—and began to dance with a shuffling step. Off-key singing accompanied their movements.

The dancing and singing seemed to go on for hours. Slowly it built in intensity, becoming more emotional as it went on. Rachel huddled beside the post and tried to make herself small. She reasoned that if no one noticed her, she would be able to avoid becoming part of their entertainment. However, that was not to be.

As the celebration reached its height, a dark figure detached itself from the crowd and moved towards her. Only as it came close, did she see it was Dark Eagle. Standing over her, his teeth flashed in a cruel grin. Rachel felt her blood turn cold. In one fluid motion he pulled his hunting knife from his sheath, bent down, and cut her bonds. Taking her by the arm, he dragged her to her feet and pulled her after him in the direction of the crowd.

The people parted to allow them into the middle of their circle. Dark Eagle raised his arm and shouted something. At the same time, he twined his free hand into her hair. When he finished speaking, the woman who was Deer Stalker's mother came forward. Ashes covered her head, face and clothes. In her hand was a willow switch. As she called something out, she whipped Rachel across the back. The people murmured their approval. Again, she called out and whipped Rachel, and the people approved. Five, six more times, she repeated the process, each time whipping harder and faster. Finally, with a loud yell, the woman waved her arm at the crowd. The people converged on Rachel. Once again she was subjected to the torture of being poked, pulled at and slapped. Several of the women had also acquired willow sticks, and they used these to whip her.

Rachel covered her face with her arms, and tried to move out of the way of her tormentors, but she could not go far. Dark Eagle had seen to that by holding her by her hair. No matter where she turned, a hand or stick was there to hurt her. Biting down on her lip, she kept silent, remembering the words of the priest. If she could convince these people of her courage, then perhaps they might let her go. Tears streamed unchecked down her cheeks at the pain and humiliation.

Suddenly, something large and heavy landed at her feet. All the noise stopped, and the Indians backed away. Drying her eyes with the backs of her hands, Rachel glanced about. Standing back at the edge of the circle was White Wolf. His eyes were not on her, but locked with Dark Eagle.

Slowly, Dark Eagle untangled his hand from her hair. White Wolf said nothing for a moment, then pulling his eyes away from the other man, he made an announcement and pointed at what he had thrown at Rachel's feet.

Glancing down, Rachel saw it was a blanket made of beautiful beaver skins. Rolled inside it was a bow and several arrows, along with the bearskin she had taken from the animal that had attacked her and a large belt of wampum of intricate design. A bundle of blue cloth tied together by the corners had landed beside it. One of the women crept forward and untied the cloth. Inside was a hunting knife, a delicately carved wooden box, and four silver spoons.

Rachel did not have time to wonder where he had acquired such expensive items. With a motion of his hand and a command in his Indian language, he motioned for her to go to him. She saw that his stern features would allow no disobedience. Reasoning that White Wolf was a better master than Dark Eagle, she did as he commanded. When she was standing before him, he took her wrist and raised her arm high above her head, showing the villagers that he held her. Then turning on his heel, he pulled her through the crowd to a small hut that stood near the opposite end of the village from where she had been bound to the post. Raising the deerskin flap that covered the opening, he motioned for her to enter.

Rachel ducked through the entrance and glanced

about the interior of the hut. It was very similar to that of Corn Woman. One low platform bed lay snugly against the far wall. It was covered with many fur blankets. Several bows hung from the wall supports, and a musket rested against the wall near the doorway. The walls were not decorated as in Corn Woman's hut, but the panels were sewn together as tightly and neatly. This hut, she surmised, was White Wolf's home.

Not quite sure what he expected of her, and not sure of her own feelings, she wandered past the small, central fire and turned to face him. Inside her, anger and hurt warred with an almost uncontrollable urge to fling herself into his arms for comfort. She could not do that. He had betrayed her, given her to the villagers to torment, allowed Dark Eagle to ridicule her. He was a savage, a beast.

He moved a step towards her; she backed away.

"Don't come near me," she told him. "Don't touch me."

"You are my woman."

"I am nothing to you except your revenge," she spat.

White Wolf's heart twisted in his chest at her pain. He knew this time would not be easy. All day he had remained in the sweat lodge to cleanse his spirit and to speak with his spirit guide about how he should talk with the woman when the time came. He had also remained hidden so that he would not have to look upon her in her misery. He had waited impatiently for the sun to sink below the trees. His only weakness had been to send for Father Lisle to come and comfort her, but he had learned that the priest had not been successful. The woman, he had been told, bore as large a hatred in her heart for the French as he bore for the English. Perhaps she should have been born a warrior.

He studied her now. Even in her bedraggled state, she was magnificent. Her head was high, and her eyes flashed fire. The rough treatment of the villagers had not dampened her spirit. Although she stood before him, dirty, scratched, and in rags, she was as proud as any warrior. He wanted to reassure her; he could not.

He bent and picked up a small clay pot containing water, walked to the sleeping pallet and sat down. "Come, sit here." He motioned to the spot beside him. "I will wash your wounds."

It was only as he mentioned them that Rachel could feel the sting of the scratches and welts on her hands, arms, across her back, and down her cheek. Realizing she must look like something that had been in a cat fight, she shook her head and turned away.

"English, sit here." His tone of voice did not allow disobedience. When Rachel turned towards him, he added, "Please."

Hesitantly, she settled beside him on the pile of furs. She sat only close enough for him to reach her, not so close that their bodies touched. Knowing what his nearness did to her mind, she was careful to keep her distance.

He took one of her hands in his and gently washed it with a piece of cloth he had dipped in the water. Softly, he cleaned her arm and the ugly scratches that showed dark red against her pale skin. Like a woman in a trance, Rachel watched the movements of his hand. She did not dare raise her eyes to look into his face. His devilish blue gaze could make her do things she thought herself incapable of doing; it could make her forget everything. He had hurt her deeply; she had to remember that.

"Why did you give me to Dark Eagle and the villagers?" she finally asked in a husky voice.

"It is the way of the People," he said. "You are my prisoner. You are the killer of Deer Stalker."

"How could you do such a thing? The way your people treat prisoners is so . . . so . . ."

"Uncivilized?" he finished for her with more than a trace of anger in his voice.

"Cruel," she corrected firmly. "Your people treat prisoners cruelly, as if they were animals."

"How do your people treat their prisoners? I have seen warriors who have returned from your prisons. They are no longer men. They have been kept in tiny rooms with no light and very little food or water. Here, a prisoner has a chance to become a member of the People. He or she may be adopted by one of the families. The cruelty that you speak of is a test of bravery. A true warrior welcomes the pain in order to prove himself worthy."

Rachel could see she was not going to win this argument, not in one night of discussion. The ways of his people were too much a part of him. Yet, the hurt of his abandonment still remained. "But I . . . You . . . We . . ." She could not bring herself to pronounce that ultimate intimacy which they had shared.

White Wolf smiled and reached for her other hand. "You are trying to say that we touched in passion," he offered.

Rachel's silence was her answer.

"You are still my prisoner," he told her. "One has nothing to do with the other."

Rachel's head snapped up and she glared at him. "One has everything to do with the other. I would not have . . . if I had thought you would not protect me. You saved me from Dark Eagle and you saved me from the bear. Why wouldn't you save me from the villagers?"

"I did." He began washing her face. As she opened her mouth to say something, he told her, "Hush, now, while I clean your face." As long as she was prevented from speaking, he decided to explain. "It is the custom of the People to give all prisoners to everyone. If a warrior wishes to keep a prisoner, then he must pay a pledge to the tribe. I paid for you. You will remain here, in my lodge, as my prisoner."

Rachel realized her mistake in allowing him to touch her so intimately. He would use her until he grew tired of her, then, soiled and degraded, he would sell her to the French. "As your whore, you mean," she mumbled.

White Wolf's eyes suddenly shot blue sparks. Grabbing her chin, he made her look at him. "You are my woman," he rumbled. "If that does not please you, I will give you to Dark Eagle. He will not touch you in passion, I assure you. It was his mother's son whom you killed."

Rachel stared at him as her brain reorganized his words into something she could understand: Deer Stalker, whom she had killed, had been the brother of Dark Eagle. She closed her eyes to shut out that intense gaze and the visions of Dark Eagle's revenge for killing his brother. She shivered. White Wolf had never been truly angry with her, but she felt that he was very close to that now. In his rage, he could be capable of doing almost anything, including handing her over to Dark Eagle. The idea of White Wolf losing his temper frightened her more than all the bears in the forest ever could.

He dropped his hand. "Is Dark Eagle your choice?"

She knew there was no choice. No matter how much White Wolf had hurt her, she could never take Dark Eagle in place of him. Rachel shook her head, but kept her eyes tightly closed. She did not want to look at him, to see his handsome face hard with fury. All she wanted was to be comforted, to be told that everything would be all right. She wanted to know that White Wolf would not discard her when he decided she had fulfilled his need, that he would not turn her over to the French to fulfill his revenge.

"English, open your eyes," he told her.

Slowly, fearfully, Rachel obeyed.

"Your eyes change to the color of the pine tree when you are troubled — or when I touch you in passion," he murmured. He reached up and drew his fingers down her cheek, then trailed them down her throat to where her nightdress had been ripped open.

Rachel felt a tremor run through her at his touch. No, she told herself, he cannot do this. She should not let him. She was angry with him. He had hurt her deeply.

"Your lips are as soft as a butterfly's wings." His hand slipped to the back of her neck. He began to draw her closer.

Stop, she scolded herself. Don't let him do this. Her eyes were held by his steady gaze.

"You taste like honey." His hand tangled in her hair and held her motionless.

Don't do it! she screamed in her head. You are his prisoner, his revenge. She could not move.

"You are my woman," he whispered against her lips.

Rachel's eyes closed and a sigh of contentment slipped from her as he captured her mouth. Her good intentions were wiped away with his touch. Shivers of excitement coursed through her. When he teased her lips with his tongue, she allowed him entrance. Her mind went blank and all thoughts of running, of denying him, fled before his gentle onslaught. She was hungry, starved for him, for his touch, his passion. Limply, she clung to him.

Something inside her head nagged at her. Something made her realize what she was doing. Pushing against his chest, she jerked away from him.

"No," she whispered brokenly. "No." Jumping to her feet, she fled to the opposite side of the hut. "Don't touch me."

White Wolf rose to his full height and faced her. His eyes blazed in fury. "Does my touch shame you, *English?*" His once tender name for her was a snarled insult on his lips.

"Yes. No." She shook her head in confusion. "I don't know."

"You don't know?" he repeated incredulously. "You do not know if my touch shames you, an Englishwoman?"

Rachel felt the raw emotion underlying his words. She did not want to hurt him, but neither did she want to leave herself open to future pain. Taking a breath, she tried to explain.

"It is not what or who you are that shames me, but what you have done."

"What is that?" he growled.

"I am your prisoner, your revenge. You told me that yourself. I cannot . . . I can't . . . I can't make love with you."

"You already have."

"I know." Wretchedly, she clasped her hands before her and twined and untwined her fingers. "But I can't, not again."

"Why not?"

Reluctant to say any more, she remained silent.

White Wolf strode around the fire and grabbed her arm. Giving her a little shake, he repeated, "Why not?"

"I can't tell you."

He dropped his hand and folded his arms across his chest. With narrow eyes, he asked for a third time, "Why not?"

Rachel kept her eyes lowered. She could not tell him that he had become an important part of her life, that his giving her to the villagers had made her realize that she meant nothing to him. Despite his tenderness when they were together, she was still his prisoner, his revenge.

The silence between them grew. She knew he was waiting for an answer, and she sensed that he would not move or allow her to move until she gave one to him. Finally, she raised her eyes to his.

"You gave me to the villagers," she told him quietly.

A frown darkened his brow. "It is the way of the People. I told you that. And I laid down a pledge for you. You will be safe here with me."

She nodded, but only to appease him. There was nothing left for her to say. She could not tell him of her feelings and lay herself open. She could not give him that power over her. It would be too painful when he rejected her. Wanting to put some distance between herself and his powerful body, she walked to the other side of the fire.

White Wolf knew her nod was only to end the argument. Angry that she had not revealed what was truly in her heart, he asked, "Do you not believe that I will keep you safe?"

"Of course you will," she answered quickly, angry that he would not let the argument die. "Why wouldn't you? You told me I was your revenge. You will keep me safe until that is satisfied. And you will use me as you wish, whether I like it or not."

White Wolf strode around the fire and stood before her. "I do not use you," he growled. "I have treated you well. When we touched in passion, I did not force you. You wanted it, English." His hand snaked out and caught her hair at the back of her head. "You wanted it, as you want it now. I took you as my woman; you agreed. There is nothing to your anger. Nothing but air."

Rachel opened her mouth to disagree, but he gave her hair a tiny jerk of warning.

"Nothing," he repeated, then he took possession of what he believed was his.

Rachel could not fight off the sensuous plunder of her mouth. His hand, tangled in her hair, held her still. When his fingers slipped beneath her clothes and found her breast, her knees barely supported her. Yes, she wanted him. She could not deny that. But at the same time, she knew that she was losing something of herself. Even while her arms clung to him and her body yearned for his possession, a part of her was pulling away from him and closing on itself. Before she had thought that sometime she would be able to share all of herself with him, but now she knew that was not possible. He was her enemy; he always would be. She would always have some part of her that she would have to keep hidden.

He dragged her down to the sleeping platform and lay above her. His body held her immobile, but she did not care. His hands and mouth were everywhere. Tiny fires ignited every place he touched. The argument, her hurt pride, the raw wound of his betrayal of her were burnt to cinders in the heat of their passion. Rachel was aware only of what he did to her. Somehow, her clothes were suddenly gone, torn easily from her. She held him tightly against her, loving the feel of his bare skin against her nakedness. Then he entered her, quickly, sharply thrusting, giving her no chance to deny him. Like a leaf caught in the current of a river she rode the tide of his motion, the whirlpool of desire. Sucked down, down into its depths, she hit bottom with an explosion of sensation and lights and emotion. Her scream of release and his growl of pleasure mingled in the joining of their mouths.

In the aftermath of their lovemaking, she lay, wilted and spent, against him. Too tired and too emotionally drained to move, she allowed him to hold her. In this night of anger and passion, she had learned again how dangerous he was, how vulnerable she was. Despite her anger and hurt, he had been able to arouse the fires of desire in her until she was mindless. His power over her was frightening, bewildering. Something bound her to him that was stronger than any rope or rawhide cord. She knew this would always be so, no matter what he considered her to be — his woman or his revenge. Wiser now, she knew she could not expect sweet words or commitments from him. She would have to guard her heart.

# Chapter Seventeen

Rachel was abruptly awakened the next morning when White Wolf pulled the fur blankets from her. The cool air raised gooseflesh all over her and made her curl up and protest wordlessly.

"Go away," she murmured. "I want to sleep."

"The sun is high. It is time to bathe. This morning you will meet Hunting Dog."

Rachel rolled onto her back and gazed up at him. "Who is Hunting Dog?" she wanted to know.

"One of the wise ones." White Wolf's eyes caressed her body, then he turned away. "Do not entice me, woman. There is no time."

Rachel had not meant to be seductive, but she had become very comfortable being unclothed in White Wolf's presence. As she rolled off the sleeping platform, the idea struck her that perhaps White Wolf was as affected by her as she was by him. The thought was comforting in the aftermath of the night before.

Picking up her clothes from where White Wolf had tossed them when he had ripped them from her in passion, she realized that they could no longer be used as clothing. They were rags, but they were all she had to wear. With a sigh, she laid them out on the sleeping platform. As she tried to piece them together, White Wolf placed a bundle next to them.

"You will wear this," he told her.

Curious, Rachel unfolded the bundle. It was a long tunic made of soft, white deerskin and decorated around the bottom with beading in a beautiful pattern. Beneath the tunic was a pair of leggings made of the same deerskin. A headband with fine quillwork completed the outfit. Rachel was astounded at the wonderful gift.

"They're beautiful," she breathed. "Thank you."

White Wolf ducked his head curtly. "Hurry," he told her. "Hunting Dog wishes to see you before the Council is called."

Rachel threw her old cloak about her shoulders to cover herself, picked up her new clothes, then hurried out of the hut to go bathe.

Excited at the prospect of being able to wear something new, she forgot her curiosity about Hunting Dog until she was returning to White Wolf's home. Only then did she begin to wonder about this person whom White Wolf had called a "wise one." By the time she stood before the deerskin flap covering the opening into White Wolf's hut, she could not keep her knees from knocking.

From the way White Wolf spoke of this man, Hunting Dog, she deduced that he must be very powerful, more so even than White Wolf. She knew White Wolf was a powerful man in his tribe from the way he had dressed at the feast the night before. Except for Dark Eagle, none of the other men had been wearing as many feathers, nor had the decoration on their clothing been quite so fine. Yet he spoke of Hunting Dog with reverence. Perhaps he was a medicine man. She shivered. She had heard of those men and the strange things they did. Giving herself a mental shake, she decided she could not worry about what she did not know.

As she raised her hand to push back the flap, it was pushed back for her, and White Wolf emerged into the daylight. Startled, a gasp escaped her and she fell back a step.

White Wolf frowned a little. "Where is the brave woman who walked with me for many suns?" he asked.

Rachel took a deep breath and forced a smile. "I'm not frightened."

"Good," he nodded, then his eyes ran over her. Pleasure in what he saw made his mouth turn up at the corners. "You look like a woman of the People," he approved.

A warm feeling burst inside her at his compliment. Blushing, she bowed her head. "Thank you," she murmured.

Guiding her by the arm, he urged, "Come. We will go meet Hunting Dog."

They walked to a lodge not far from White Wolf's. When he scratched lightly beside the door, an old man's voice came from within. White Wolf ducked through the opening and bade her follow. Rachel found herself in a hut similar to White Wolf's, but with the difference that there were many strange objects hung from the walls, objects that Rachel did not wish to look at too closely. The central fire gave off the sweet smell of burning tobacco. Beside the fire, sitting cross-legged and leaning against a propped-up, decorated board, was an old man. His face was stern and lined and weather-worn; his straggling gray hair was held back by a simple leather cord. His deerskin tunic hung on his slight, withered frame. But in spite of his obvious age, his eyes were bright and piercing beneath thin gray brows.

At their entrance, Hunting Dog motioned with his hand and an old woman rose from the shadows. As she passed White Wolf on her way out of the hut, their eyes met and a look of affection passed between them. Rachel did not need to be told that Hunting Dog and his woman were very close to White Wolf.

White Wolf sat across from the old man and motioned Rachel to sit beside him. When they were settled, the man spoke to White Wolf in his strange language, and White Wolf answered him. The two men conversed for a short time, then White Wolf turned to her.

"Hunting Dog wishes to know if you are comfortable in my lodge," he said.

Rachel was taken aback at the question that spoke of courtesy and concern for others. She had not expected it from a man whose people tore at prisoners as if they were nothing. Unable to find her voice, she nodded.

"Hunting Dog wishes to hear you speak, Rachel," White Wolf told her.

"Tell him I am comfortable," she answered.

When White Wolf had translated, the old man said something else.

"He asks if he may feel your hair," White Wolf said.

Puzzled at the request, Rachel only looked at him.

Understanding her confusion, he said, "The People are very polite to each other, Rachel. It is only with enemies that they show cruelty."

Rachel glanced from White Wolf to Hunting Dog. The old man's sharp eyes watched her. Deciding she was in no danger, she got up and knelt next to the old man.

Hesitantly, she held out a thick braid to him.

Hunting Dog gently took hold of the braid and felt it between his fingers. Then he placed his hand on her head and ran the palm down the length of her hair. His touch was surprisingly soft. Glancing at White Wolf, he said something.

"Hunting Dog says a woman with such hair must have strong medicine," White Wolf translated.

Hunting Dog said something else. White Wolf hesitated before he told her, "He says that only a woman with strong medicine could . . ."

"Could what?" she prompted. She was amazed at the look of embarrassment that crossed White Wolf's face.

Staring at a spot above Hunting Dog's head, he finished, ". . . could make White Wolf take a woman."

Rachel smiled with pleasure and her eyes met those of Hunting Dog. In that glance, a bond was formed between the old man and the young woman.

Hunting Dog again spoke. White Wolf answered him, then translated.

"Hunting Dog asks that you tell of the deeds of White Wolf and Dark Eagle, of that which happened when your village was attacked."

Sitting back on her heels, Rachel gazed at White Wolf. "Should I tell him everything?" she wanted to know. "Even of killing Deer Stalker and your saving me from the wolves and running away from Dark Eagle?"

"Everything."

"Should I tell him about how I tried to help one of the men escape from you?"

"Everything."

At her dubious look, he reassured her, "You will not be harmed, Rachel. You are safe. You have my protection."

Turning back to Hunting Dog, she saw the expectant look in those piercing eyes. Nothing, she knew, would escape his gaze. He would notice the inflections of her voice and be able to detect when she was leaving something out or not being completely truthful. Settling herself more comfortably, she began her story.

Much later, when Rachel's voice was hoarse from her long story, the three people inside Hunting Dog's lodge were silent. She had finished her story, and White Wolf had translated it for her as she spoke. Hunting Dog sat puffing on a pipe with his eyes half closed. Finally, he spoke.

"Hunting Dog says you have the courage of a warrior," White Wolf told her. "He says that you will stand before the Council and tell your story."

Rachel almost groaned aloud at the prospect of telling it all over again in front of many people, but she sensed she should not. "What is the Council?" she asked instead.

"It is a gathering of all the wise ones and all the warriors of the village," White Wolf said.

"Why would they want to hear my story?"

"Because Dark Eagle will call them together and accuse me of what I have done."

"What have you done?"

Pain passed swiftly across White Wolf's face before he once again held tight control over his emotions. "I have betrayed Dark Eagle," he told her slowly. "Betrayal to the People is like lying. The punishment for lying is to be cast from the village of the People."

Rachel felt his pain as keenly as if it were his own. "But you did it to save me!" she exclaimed.

He shook his head. "It does not matter. The Council will decide."

Hunting Dog said something and White Wolf answered him. A drum began to beat somewhere out in the village.

Turning to Rachel, White Wolf said, "Hunting Dog says your spirit is strong. You will tell the Council what you know. You will convince them that there was wrong on both sides."

"What did you say to him?" she asked.

"That the decision of the Council does not matter. I will take you with me when I leave, and the People will always remain in my heart."

When Rachel and White Wolf emerged from the hut of Hunting Dog, men were beginning to gather in a circle beneath an ancient tree at one side of the village. Some women sat on the outside of the circle, not part of the Council, but close enough to hear what was being said. As they crossed the open space in the middle of the village, Corn Woman emerged from her hut. White Wolf told Rachel to go with her.

As the two women made their way to the circle, from the corner of her eye, Rachel noticed the people stop and step back. Turning, she saw Dark Eagle approach. White Wolf had remained just outside the hut of Hunting Dog. When Dark Eagle saw the man he had pursued through the wilderness, he stopped short.

The two men stared at each other, neither moving or saying a word. The villagers around them remained motionless, watching, wondering what these two who had become enemies would do. Finally, White Wolf nodded at Dark Eagle, acknowledging his presence. There was no answering nod from Dark Eagle. He merely began walking towards the Council's circle as if he had not stopped. Once he had moved on, the rest of the people continued to walk.

Finally, all were gathered. White Wolf and Hunting Dog sat next to each other in the inner circle. Dark Eagle also sat in the inner circle, but opposite them. Hunting Dog lit a carved pipe decorated with feathers. After holding it aloft, he took three puffs and passed it to the warrior beside him. Each man puffed on the pipe and finally it came to White Wolf. After he had puffed on it and passed it to Hunting Dog, he stood and began to speak.

Rachel could not understand what he said, but she enjoyed listening to his voice and watching him. He stood proudly and his voice rang across the clearing. When he had finished, Dark Eagle stood and spoke. Rachel assumed they each were telling their version of what happened in Deerfield and afterward in the wilderness. Occasionally, the people would turn and stare curiously at her, but their attention did not remain on her for long.

When Dark Eagle finished, others got up and spoke. Since Rachel could not understand any of what was being said, her attention soon wandered. It came as a shock, finally, when she heard White Wolf call her name. Glancing up at him, she saw him standing in his place and motioning for her to rise.

"You will tell the People the story of how you came to be at *Neganodenek,* the old town, the village of the People," he said.

Standing slowly, Rachel glanced about at the waiting faces, then back at White Wolf. His face was stern and impassive, showing nothing of his feelings. Her gaze slipped to Hunting Dog, and she thought she saw him give a tiny nod of encouragement. Looking back at White Wolf, she took a deep breath and began.

White Wolf again translated for her. At first there was

polite silence from the Indians, but soon she could tell that they became engrossed in her story. Occasionally some would murmur or nod. Not wanting White Wolf to be banished from his village, she tried to emphasize those times when he had saved her from Dark Eagle. What she received for her trouble was a dark look from White Wolf. When she finally finished, there was quiet as the people digested what they had been told.

Corn Woman lightly touched her arm and motioned for her to accompany her. Rachel followed her across the open space of the village to White Wolf's hut. Corn Woman motioned her to enter, then she returned to the Council. With a last glance at the circle of men and women, Rachel ducked into White Wolf's hut. She supposed that since she was not a member of the tribe, she would not be allowed to sit in on the decision of White Wolf's future.

It was not long after that she heard the sound of the Council dispersing. The flap of the hut was pulled back and White Wolf entered. His face was grim.

"What did the Council decide?" Rachel asked.

White Wolf did not answer immediately. He stood just inside the opening and gazed around the interior of his home. His eyes reflected a deep pain. Without looking at her, he ordered, "Come," and turned and ducked outside.

Curious, Rachel followed. When she emerged into the sunlight, she saw the villagers staring solemnly at the hut. Hunting Dog stood before her with a burning branch in his hand. Not knowing what was about to happen, she glanced at White Wolf, but he just pulled her to one side.

No one moved for the space of ten heartbeats, then the

crowd parted. Dark Eagle appeared carrying an armful of his possessions, among them the bow to which he had attached the lock of her hair. Without a glance to the right or left, he walked to the opening of White Wolf's hut and dumped the things there on the ground. As soon as he had stepped back, Hunting Dog touched the burning branch to the pile then to White Wolf's hut.

Rachel gasped in horror and clamped a hand over her mouth. The villagers were so quiet, she did not dare say anything. She could sense the intense sorrow of the people around her. From White Wolf, all she could feel was an icy, rigid self-control.

The hut and all it contained burned quickly like a tiny inferno. The pile of Dark Eagle's possessions were soon consumed in the flames. When the fire began to burn itself out, the people started to wander away. All but Dark Eagle.

White Wolf had watched his lodge go up in flames and had felt his heart cry. It had been his home when he had stayed with his mother's people. Corn Woman, the sister of his mother, had built it for him with the help of other women of the People. Inside, were many memories of good hunts and quiet talks. Now, he would have to carry all those memories in his heart.

He glanced at Dark Eagle, his brother. Although the Council had decreed that his lodge not be burned, Dark Eagle had been told that his best possessions should be added to the fire. Anger still flamed hotly in Dark Eagle's heart. The punishment of the Council had only fanned it higher.

White Wolf's eyes turned to the woman beside him. Her expression told of her horror and the pain she felt for him. It told of her fear of what would be her end, her lack of trust in him. She did not know of the other home which beckoned him. Now was not the time to tell her. She had to learn to trust him.

A sudden movement from Dark Eagle caught his eye. As he whipped his head around to face him, his friend let out a yell and jumped before him. He held his hunting knife in his hand.

The crowd backed away from the confrontation between the two men. Corn Woman pulled Rachel back by the arm and made her go with her to her hut. Rachel, sensing that she should not interfere, nevertheless went reluctantly.

"You betrayed me, brother," Dark Eagle accused White Wolf in the language of their mothers. "You have betrayed the People." He threw his knife down so that it stuck into the earth. "Only death will bring peace between us."

"I will not fight you, my brother," White Wolf told him quietly. "We have been punished for the wrongs we have done to each other. Let the trouble die."

"It will only die when one of us dies. You betrayed me. You saved the woman. You and I had made a pact to leave her for the Great Spirit."

"My spirit brother came to me in a dream and said I should save her. Her hair has strong medicine. She is a worthy enemy."

"She killed the one who is now mourned. She entered the circle and struck me. She deserved to be punished."

"She was your enemy. Should not an enemy strike?"

"She is a witch-woman. She will bring evil down on us."

"There will be no evil. The evil comes from two brothers who fight."

Dark Eagle stared at the man who was once brother to him. The color of those eyes mocked him. They were the eyes of the white man. He had known this man all his life. He was of the People. Yet, those eyes told of who else he was.

"A brother who betrays a brother is brother no more," Dark Eagle said.

"You will always be my brother," White Wolf told him. "The woman should make no difference. She is brave, like the warrior. She could be of the People."

"She is not of the People. Why do you protect her?"

"She is my revenge."

"She should be killed, slowly, painfully, for what her people did to the mother of White Wolf, for what she did to the son of my mother."

"Her people will suffer when she is not returned to them. They will know pain when they discover what has happened to her."

Dark Eagle said nothing. Despite his anger, he felt a lightness begin to take hold of his heart. He sensed that perhaps his brother had not failed him. Perhaps taking the woman as his revenge was a great coup. If this was so, then White Wolf was truly worthy of being chief of the People.

"What will her people discover?" Dark Eagle finally asked.

"I have made her my woman."

Dark Eagle could not speak. His throat closed on any words he might utter. He knew the contempt in which the English white man held the People. For a man of the People to take one of them as his woman was to shame the white man. It was the act of a man worthy to be sagamore of the People. His brother was truly worthy, worthier

266

than he, Dark Eagle. Finally, dropping to his knees, throwing his head back to the sky, he let out a wail of anguish and guilt.

"I have wronged you, my brother," Dark Eagle cried. Pulling the knife from the ground, he began to draw the blade across his chest to indicate his grief.

White Wolf reached out and grabbed his wrist. "No," he said. "Do not wound yourself. It is better that we stand and face each other as brothers." With a slight pressure, he urged Dark Eagle to stand. "I will need you beside me to lead the People."

Dark Eagle stood and dropped the knife. Joy filled his heart at his brother's words. "We will gather another war party and attack the English," he stated.

White Wolf shook his head. "No. Not now. It is time for me to go away, to visit the land of my father. The People need a time for peace. Care for them, my brother, until my return."

Turning, he headed for the lodge of Corn Woman where Rachel awaited him. He would explain to her all that happened so that she would understand the People better. Now that she was his woman, she should know of the People, their ways and customs. Tomorrow would be soon enough to travel the river to the land of his father.

When White Wolf entered Corn Woman's hut, Rachel jumped to her feet. Her eyes searched his face to gauge his mood and travelled over his body to see where he was injured. Seeing that he was calm and at peace, and there was not a hair out of place, she was elated, but puzzled. Corn Woman discreetly ducked out of the hut, and White Wolf settled himself before the fire.

"I smell venison stew," he observed. "I am hungry."

Rachel, who was wildly curious about what had taken

place, picked up a bowl and ladled some stew into it. Instead of asking about his confrontation with Dark Eagle, however, she exercised tremendous self-control and said instead, "I am sorry about your home being burned."

White Wolf shrugged. "It was the decision of the Council. There will be other lodges, other weapons."

Despite his nonchalance, she knew he felt deeply about the loss. Changing the subject to the one that nagged at her, she asked as she handed the bowl of stew to him, "What happened between you and Dark Eagle?"

Taking the bowl from Rachel's fingers, he glanced up at her and growled, "A woman should allow a man to eat before she expects him to talk."

Exasperated at his refusal to satisfy her curiosity, Rachel plopped down on the other side of the fire. She knew he would not say anything until he was ready. Impatiently, she watched him eat his meal.

When he had almost finished, he said without looking up, "You will sleep in the lodge of Corn Woman tonight."

"Where will you sleep?" Rachel asked before she could stop herself.

White Wolf glanced up at her with a smile crinkling the corners of his eyes. "Will you miss my touch, English?"

Rachel felt the heat rise in her cheeks and turned away. Stupid, she scolded herself. You will lay bare your heart if you are not careful.

Casually, she said, "I am only concerned about your safety."

White Wolf went back to his meal, but she saw an amused twinkle in his eyes before he lowered them. When he had finished eating and she had cleaned his bowl, he sat with her and explained all that had happened: how the burning of his lodge was his punishment for betraying Dark Eagle, and how the burning of Dark Eagle's most precious possessions was that man's punishment for wanting something he was not supposed to have, namely her. He told her how Dark Eagle had confronted him and of how they had solved their differences, and of Dark Eagle's anguish over their anger with each other. He hinted that it would be appropriate for her to show some sign of grief over her killing of Deer Stalker. Then, to Rachel's delight, he related some of his boyhood, how he and Dark Eagle had grown up together and been the best of friends.

When he had finished, Rachel placed her hand on his arm. "Thank you for sharing that with me. I think my people could learn a lot from your people. Betrayal and lying are the worst things we can do to each other."

White Wolf said nothing but she could tell he was pleased.

"Now that your lodge has been burned, where will you live?" she wanted to know.

"We will travel down the river when the sun is high above the trees again. I will not return to the village of the People for many moons."

"But where will you go?"

"Quebec."

"Oh," Rachel said, downcast. Quebec was in New France, and New France was where the other prisoners were to be taken, according to Claude Donat. White Wolf would sell her to the hated French and then be out of her life forever.

White Wolf's eyes narrowed. "Do you not trust me, English? Do you think you will die of starvation before you get there?"

269

"No, of course not. You will keep me alive so that you will be able to use me for your revenge." Anger at his lack of feeling for her made her words barbed.

"I have already used you for my revenge," he told her coldly.

The meaning of his words did not register in her brain until he was standing over her. Before she could scuttle out of his reach, he had her by the arms and had hauled her to her feet.

"You are my revenge, English, but you have not denied me. You no longer have the right to be angry."

The blood drained from her face as she realized the truth he spoke. He was right; she had not denied him. She had allowed him to touch her, to possess her. She, an Englishwoman, had become the whore of this redman. What had she done?

As she tried to pull away from him, he held her tightly and forced her to look at him. "You are my revenge, but you are also my woman. You can not deny either, English. And you can not deny me."

His mouth came down hard on hers. Rachel tried to block out the dizzying sensations he made her feel, but it was no use. When he drew her tightly against his body, she did not have the will to fight. He pulled her down with him onto the sleeping platform. She followed like a ragdoll. Pushing up her deerskin tunic, he entered her. She was ready. Her body accepted him as if he had always been a part of her. Their release came swiftly, hard, together.

When she was once again aware of her surroundings, he rose above her and gently pushed the hair back from her face. "You are my woman, English," he whispered. "You cannot deny it." Brushing his lips across her mouth, he stood. "You will sleep here tonight. Do not miss me too much." With a twitch to his lips, he was gone.

In a fit of frustration, Rachel picked up the wooden bowl he had eaten from and threw it at the deerskin flap that fell across the opening as he left.

# Chapter Eighteen

The next day, White Wolf and Rachel walked through the village to the riverbank. As they passed the huts, the villagers emerged and followed them. By the time they had reached the riverbank, practically the whole village was gathered. White Wolf was not being expelled from his village, but was being given a great send-off.

Dark Eagle stood at the front of the crowd. After what White Wolf had told her of the relationship he had with the man, Rachel felt she understood him better. She decided that if she was to spend the rest of her life in New France, she did not want Dark Eagle as her enemy.

Leaving White Wolf's side, she walked up to Dark Eagle and stood before him. His dark eyes bored into her. She had thought long and hard about how she would demonstrate her grief over killing Stalking Deer.

Steeling herself for what she was about to do, she reached out and placed her fingers around the hilt of his hunting knife that stuck out of the sheath at his waist. His hand clamped over hers. Calmly, she looked up into his eyes. Somehow, he understood that she was not going to harm him. Releasing his grip, he allowed her to pull the knife from its sheath. Taking the blade, she cut a lock from her unbound hair and held it out to him.

"Strong medicine," she said, even though she knew he could not understand her. "May it keep you safe."

As Dark Eagle took the lock of hair, a murmur of approval ran through the crowd. When she handed his knife back to him, handle first, a cheer went up. Grinning with pleasure at the success of her action, she turned and skipped down to where White Wolf stood waiting by their canoe. He said nothing, but the pride in his gaze conveyed all he felt.

After motioning her into the canoe, he pushed it onto the river and jumped in himself. Several men jumped into other canoes. They would escort them during the trip. As they caught the current, White Wolf let out a yell. It was answered from shore, then the villagers began to sing. Their song accompanied them until the village was out of sight.

Rachel enjoyed the canoe trip on the river. The water was calm and the current helped to carry them along. White Wolf had told her that they would reach their destination the following day. He would not enlighten her about what that destination was, but she was not concerned. She was safe until she reached Quebec.

Several times they were forced to paddle to shore and carry the canoes around falls and rapids, but the trip went quickly. That night, the men with them killed a turkey and several rabbits, so they had plenty to eat. When it came time to sleep, Rachel and White Wolf shared a beaverskin blanket. Rachel enjoyed feeling White Wolf's hard body pressed against hers as she drifted into sleep. She had missed sleeping with him while they had been in the village.

The next day dawned wet. A fine drizzle fell from the clouds and mist blanketed the river. The weather did not seem to hinder White Wolf and the men. As if it were a perfectly clear day, they launched their canoes and the party set out once more. By midday, the mist had dissipated, but clouds still hung heavy in the sky.

All along the river they had passed isolated farms that had been cut out of the wilderness on the riverbank. The houses were all similar, being made of stucco over wooden frames, having long frontages and steep, low roofs. The land that had been cleared for farming was narrow and stretched back a good distance at right angles to the river. By the middle of the afternoon as they rounded a point of land, another spot of civilization appeared.

Several buildings stood in a clearing that stretched far back from the riverbank. As they drifted closer, she could see that one was a house made of whitewashed stucco. The steep, low roof was tiled. Three stone chimneys rose above the roof, one at each end and another at the back of the house. Several windows were aligned across the front on either side of the doorway.

A smaller house stood a short walk away. This was made of the same materials, but it had only one stone chimney. A barn of wooden planks stood between the two houses, and a small log building sat on the other side of the large house. Between the log building and the large house was a small, dome shaped edifice that seemed to be made of stones and plastered with clay. There was a small opening in the middle of one side, and Rachel realized this was an oven. Chickens pecked at the ground in the open area between the houses and the river. Several sheep grazed in a fenced-in field behind the barn along with a cow calmly chewing its cud. The fields behind had been plowed and were ready for planting.

As they neared the shore, Rachel heard a man shout. *"Le seigneur! Il est ici!"*

The lord? she asked herself. Who was the man referring to? Glancing about at the men in the canoes, she could only assume she had misunderstood. It had been quite a long time since she had practiced her French with her father.

The canoes scraped against the river bottom as they approached the bank. A man hurried to pull their canoe onto dry land and steady it.

*"Mon seigneur,"* he panted. *"C'est bon de vous voir."*

Rachel had not been mistaken. The man spoke to White Wolf, telling him it was good to see him.

When they had climbed out of the canoes, Rachel observed to White Wolf, "That man called you 'lord'."

White Wolf shrugged. "The man knows who I am. I visit often." After helping to pull the canoe higher onto the riverbank, he asked her, "You speak French?"

Rachel nodded. "My father taught me. He said it was good to know the language of the enemy."

"Your father was a wise man." He turned and started towards the house. "Come. A meal has been prepared for us."

Rachel walked with him and the others to the house.

Inside, the damp of the day was dispelled by a fire burning on the flagstone hearth. The chimneypiece was made of fieldstone and covered the whole end wall of the house. The room they entered was the main room of the house, with a long trestle table, several chairs with rush seats, a spinning wheel, a loom and several cupboards. Hooks stuck into the chimneypiece held a large variety of

275

cooking utensils and pots. The floor was of hewn boards that had been rubbed and scrubbed so much they were smooth. The walls were plastered and whitewashed. A middle aged, pleasant-looking woman glanced up from stirring something in a pot hanging over the fire and greeted them warmly.

White Wolf turned to Rachel. "This is Marie, and her husband Charles you have already met. They care for the house and farm and trading post when the owner is not here. If there is anything that you need, let Marie know and she will get it from the store."

"I could not do that. I have nothing to trade for goods," Rachel objected.

White Wolf flashed her a quick smile. "My credit is good. Get what you need."

They sat at the long wooden table, and Marie served them and Charles, and then joined them. The Indians who had accompanied them took their dishes outside to eat. Marie had made a delicious clam chowder and fresh bread. Rachel had two helpings.

During the meal, White Wolf recounted his adventures to Marie and Charles, with the couple interrupting only occasionally to exclaim or make an appropriate comment. White Wolf delicately left out his intimate relationship with Rachel, for which she was very grateful. She realized the couple would learn about it eventually, but she did not feel comfortable in announcing her position.

When they had finished eating, White Wolf told her, "I have a surprise for you." He took her to a door off the back of the main living space and opened it. Inside was a bedroom with a huge, four-poster bed hung with dark red embroidered woolen hangings. In one corner was a hand-carved wooden chair with a cushion to match the bed hangings and against one wall was a tall wardrobe. Several large, brightly colored, woolen braided rugs lay scattered about the floor. A large fireplace dominated the back wall. But what drew her attention more than the fine furnishings was a large wooden tub in the middle of the floor.

Before she could say anything, Charles excused himself from behind her and walked past carrying two buckets of steaming water which he poured into the tub. Marie followed with two more. Rachel turned to White Wolf with shining eyes.

"A bath!" she exclaimed. "A hot bath! Thank you."

White Wolf smiled down at her. "I thought it might please you."

After the tub had been filled and towels laid out, she quickly undressed and climbed into the tub. A sigh of pure pleasure escaped her lips as she sank into the steaming water. White Wolf had stood watching her and now he sauntered over and dropped something into the water. Rachel caught it before it sank to the bottom.

"Soap!" she cried with pleasure. Sniffing it as she made suds in her hands, she murmured, "Mmmm. Bayberry. It smells wonderful." Rubbing the soap down her arm, an absolutely wicked idea entered her head. Coyly glancing up at White Wolf, she asked, "Will you join me?"

White Wolf, enjoying the sight before him, shook his head and smiled with reluctance. "I have to speak with Charles about some matters and make arrangements for our trip to Quebec."

"Oh." Rachel could not keep the disappointment out of her voice.

White Wolf traced his finger through the suds on her

arm. "I will bring you pleasure tonight, English," he told her softly. "Enjoy your bath."

When White Wolf had left the room, closing the door behind him, Rachel was suddenly aghast at how she had just acted. What was she thinking to invite him to share a bath with her? Why, the very idea was indecent. What had she become?

His woman, that little voice inside her head answered.

Shaking her head to get rid of that little nagging voice, she proceeded to bathe and to try to ignore the disappointment she felt at White Wolf's rejection of her invitation.

When she had finished bathing and had dressed once more, she emerged into the main room of the house. Marie was working at the spinning wheel. When she saw Rachel, she smiled and stopped the wheel.

"*Le seigneur* asked me to take you to the store," she said to Rachel in her native French. "Do you understand?"

Rachel nodded and answered in French, "Yes, I speak your language."

"Good. It is good to speak with another woman. Charles does not understand about cooking and sewing the clothes. All he talks of is the farm and the animals and the store."

She led Rachel out the door and across the yard to the small building that housed the trading post. This was not as grand as the house itself, being made of logs with thatching covering the roof. The chinks between the logs were filled with mud and straw. The inside of the building was one room with a small stone fireplace at one end. Shelves covered the walls, and these were piled with smaller articles such as cloth, tools, and small wooden canisters of gunpowder and shot. The floor was littered with barrels of flour and various grains, dried fish and meat, hard biscuits, and crates of muskets and large tools. Bundles of animal skins were piled in a corner.

Without hesitation, Marie walked to several shelves and pulled out various items. On the table in the middle, she placed a brush and comb, a handful of hairpins, and a small hand mirror. Beside these, she piled a bolt of white linen, a bolt of red wool which she replaced with one of blue, and a bolt of creamy muslin sprigged with pink flowers. Going to a corner of the room, she opened a chest and pulled out a large handful of several different types of lace. This she also placed in the growing pile on the table. Placing her hands on her hips, she surveyed what she had collected.

"What else?" she asked of herself. Glancing at Rachel, she said, "If there is anything else that you wish, just take it." She gestured to the crowded interior.

Rachel was stunned at what Marie had gathered. Speechless, she just shook her head.

Marie came out from behind the table and took Rachel by the arm. As she steered her around the shelves, she told her, *"Le seigneur* was very specific. He told me you were to be given anything that you needed, anything that you wanted. You must not be shy, *madame."*

Rachel stopped and turned to face Marie. "I am not . . ." Feeling the heat rise in her cheeks, she swallowed and plunged on. "I am not *madame.* I am not White Wolf's wife."

Puzzled, Marie tipped her head to one side. "You are not? But he said you are his woman. Is that not his wife?"

"Yes. No." Rachel's face blazed in embarrassment.

Marie paused a moment as she watched Rachel's discomfort. "I am sorry. I should not pry, but I think perhaps you do not understand *le seigneur.* Did he not gift your family with many great things?"

"I have no family. He and his warriors attacked my village and took me and my friends prisoner."

"Ah, poor little one," Marie nodded. "That is very sad. But, then, did he not gift you with many great things?"

Rachel shook her head. "No."

"With nothing?"

Rachel began to shake her head again, then stopped. The moccasins she wore were a gift to her. White Wolf made them himself. And the wampum bracelet. And the deerskin dress, and leggings, and headband, these were all gifts. Then there were all those wonderful things that Marie had pulled from the shelves and piled on the table.

"Ah. So. He did give you gifts," Marie observed. "It is the custom of a Penobscot man to gift the family of the woman he takes as wife with many great things. If the family and the woman accept the gifts, then she becomes his wife. Since you had no family, the gifts went to you. Did you accept them?"

Joy swept through Rachel at Marie's explanation. She remembered how White Wolf had acted when he had placed the moccasins and bracelet in her lap. He had seemed unconcerned about her reaction to his gift, almost as if he were trying to hide his deepest feelings. But in fact, he had asked her to marry him in the custom of his people, and she had accepted!

Marie watched the happiness spread across Rachel's face. She nodded in satisfaction. "Good. It is well I explained. Now, what else would you like?" She gestured to the full walls of merchandise.

Rachel wandered about the store, touching a tool here, fingering a piece of cloth there. Finally, her eyes fell on a bright green spot of color in a corner on a shelf behind a stack of bolts of brown and gray wool. Reaching behind the bolts, she pulled out a thick, folded piece of green silk.

"Oh," she murmured. "It's beautiful."

"It would make a beautiful gown," Marie agreed.

Rachel shook her head and decisively put it back where she found it. "No, it is too much. I couldn't ask for that." Seeing that Marie was about to argue with her, she took instead a bolt of pale blue muslin.

Marie placed a card of needles and several spools of thread on top of the pile. "Tomorrow, I will help you make some clothes," she said. "You will need more than what you are wearing when you go to Quebec. The women there are very fashionable, *très chic.*"

Rachel looked at the bolts of material she and Marie had gathered and wondered when she would be able to wear the clothes that would be made from them. Since she was White Wolf's woman, wouldn't she be living in his village? she wondered. Shouldn't she wear deerskin? Yet the tunic she wore was the only piece of clothing she owned. She supposed she needed something else to wear.

When the two women emerged from the store, the sun was sinking behind the trees. Soon the men would want a meal. Rachel and Marie hurried to the house to prepare the food. It would be a cold supper tonight of bread and cheese and ale. Just before they entered, one of the Indians who had accompanied Rachel and White Wolf from the village caught up with them and held out four large trout he had caught. Marie took them with a grateful smile and her thanks.

Laying the fish on the table, she observed with a little laugh, "It will not be a cold supper after all. Men will always take care of their stomachs, no matter who they are or where they come from."

Rachel helped Marie clean the fish, then she set out the dishes and bread, cheese, and ale while Marie cooked the trout over the fire. Marie chattered about Quebec, and what Rachel would find there. Rachel learned that it was quite a cosmopolitan town, with ships arriving constantly in the good weather and canoes full of Indians coming and going. She discovered that the Governor of New France, the Marquis de Vaudreuil, was particularly fond of wearing the latest fashions which arrived from France.

The town itself had what was called an upper and lower town. The lower town sat on the river bank, and this was where most of the common folk lived and worked. The upper town sat on cliffs high above. Here were the governor's grand house, and a large Jesuit seminary of priests, and a convent of Ursuline nuns. Rachel was astounded at the influence which the Roman Pope and his church had on the town. Marie told her that guarding the town from hostile forces was a high wall with many gates. The town, she said, was magnificent.

By the time Marie had finished telling her about Quebec, the men arrived, hungry and ready to eat. Marie placed the sizzling trout on the table. Once again, the men who had accompanied Rachel and White Wolf down the river took their food outside to eat.

As the food was passed around the table White Wolf announced, "We will leave for Quebec in eight days. Charles and I will have the fields plowed and planted by then." He turned to Rachel. "Did you find everything you need at the store?"

With shining eyes, Rachel nodded. "Everything, and much more. Thank you."

White Wolf gazed at her a moment while he tried to puzzle out the reason for her glowing expression. Finally, he just nodded and turned to discuss something about the planting with Charles.

Rachel listened to the conversation and wondered about why he would be so concerned with the plowing and planting of the owner's lands. Finally, she asked, "Why do you take care of the fields here?"

Three pairs of eyes swung in her direction. No one said anything for the space of two heartbeats. Rachel looked expectantly from face to face, not knowing the reason for such blank looks.

White Wolf suddenly picked up a piece of bread and broke it. Casually, he said, "I have an agreement with the owner. When I am here, I help to take care of his lands." He popped the bread into his mouth and went back to eating.

Marie began chattering about all the material she and Rachel had picked out and the wonderful clothes they were going to make. Puzzled, Rachel looked around the table at the averted faces. Something was very odd, but she could not figure out what it was. Pushing the idea aside, she concentrated on her own meal and a plan that had been forming in her head all afternoon. Tonight, she would truly become White Wolf's woman, because today she had learned she was truly his wife.

Rachel sat in the padded chair in the corner of the bedroom. The room was dark except for a small fire on the hearth to chase away the nighttime chill. She waited for White Wolf, who had gone outside to sit with his friends from his village. Marie and Charles had already retired for the night. Rachel had learned that they lived in the smaller house on the property. Their children were grown and married, some already with families of their own, so the house was adequately large enough for just the two of them. They seemed very content with each other, and happy. Rachel began to wonder what the future held for her and White Wolf, if they would be as content with each other, if they had a future.

She heard the outside door open and close. Only the creak of a floorboard indicated White Wolf's progress across the floor. Slowly, the unlatched door of the bedroom swung open, and White Wolf stood in the frame.

"You are not asleep," he observed.

Rachel stood up and took two steps towards him. "I waited for you."

He entered the room and halted before her. "Did you miss my touch, English?" he teased.

"Yes."

Her simple, truthful answer seemed to surprise him.

Reaching out, she untied his belt and let it drop to the floor. "I want you to touch me," she whispered. She slipped her hands up under his tunic and ran her fingers over the skin of his chest. "I like touching you."

He caught his breath at the feel of her fingers on his body, but otherwise did not move. His eyes glittered in the firelight. He wondered what had happened during the day to change her attitude. Ever since he had given her to the People as a prisoner, he had felt her close herself off from him. The openness she had showed him when he had taken her as his woman had been hidden away from him. Now, suddenly, she was opening herself to him again. What had Marie told her to change her mind?

She pushed up his tunic and he cooperated by stripping it from his body. Her hands glided over his skin, then her mouth followed. A stirring between his thighs indicated his readiness. This woman could entice him above all others. He wanted to give in to her, yet he needed to know the reason for her sudden openness. Placing his hands on her arms, he held her away from him.

"Why are you doing this?" he growled.

Her eyes filled suddenly with tears at his apparent rejection. "Don't you want me to do this?" she asked brokenly.

"I want to know why," he told her in a gentler tone.

Rachel backed up a step and hugged her arms about herself. Unsure whether she should tell him what she learned from Marie, she said nothing.

"English," he prompted.

Turning away, she stared down into the fire. "Marie explained to me what it meant when you gave me the moccasins and the wampum bracelet. I did not understand before. I realize when you gave me to the village, it was something you had to do, something that was expected of you by your people, but it hurt. Now, I know it was probably something you did not want to do. All I am trying to say is that I will be your wife. I just did not know that was what you were asking."

There was silence in the room when she finished speaking. Afraid that she had spoken aloud something that he had not wanted to admit, she did not move. She barely breathed. As she waited for him to say something, she began berating herself for being a fool. Here she was opening herself to him once again. How could she be so stupid? she wondered, not for the first time.

285

She heard him moving behind her, but she did not turn around. When she felt his hands run up her thighs beneath her dress, she jumped a little in nervousness. His fingers curled around her hips and he pulled her back against him.

"A man does not always know how to speak what is in his heart," he murmured in her ear. "Many times, it takes a woman to speak the truth."

Upon hearing his words, she closed her eyes in happy relief and allowed her head to fall back against his shoulder. Perhaps, she was not so stupid after all. Her body certainly did not think so. She loved the feel of him, the hardness of him, the strength of him. His fingers splayed across the front of her thighs; his thumbs teased the edges of her secret triangle. She leaned weakly back against him.

"My woman," he whispered and turned her around to face him.

His fingers magically undid the lacings of her leggings and they fell to the floor. In a single motion he swept her tunic over her head. Rachel realized he had already divested himself of his own clothing as they came together in a tight embrace. Lovingly, she gazed up into his face and traced the outline of his smiling lips.

"You are my man," she answered him.

Unable to hold off any longer, their mouths came together hungrily. Sucking, licking, biting, they tasted of each other as if they had been starved. Rachel's knees turned to water and she was glad of his strong hold on her. Nothing, nothing was as wonderful as his kiss.

Needing to breathe, they broke apart. He swept her up into his arms and carried her to the bed where he laid her in the middle of the soft, woolen coverlet. Before he stretched out beside her, he allowed the hangings to fall closed. They were ensconced in their own wonderful cocoon.

Coming together again, their hands and mouths roved over each other's body. They could not get enough of each other. Wild murmurings and hot pantings were their only language.

Rachel had no thought but of the man who was her man. He was everything, everywhere. Her mind was a confusion of sensation; her body responded to his every touch. When he finally entered her, waves of passion washed over her. Surprised at what had happened, she blinked up at him. He only smiled down at her and began moving within her. Surprise slipped into desire as she matched his rhythm. The tidal wave of exquisite pleasure finally broke, carrying them both on its crest until it ebbed, leaving them sated and quiet once more.

Rachel lay exhausted, wrapped securely in White Wolf's arms. As she drifted into sleep, she thought: Wicked.

*Wonderful!* that little voice inside her head yelled ecstatically.

# Chapter Nineteen

The next morning Rachel awoke alone in the huge bed. Smiling in contentment, she rubbed her hand across the space where White Wolf had slept. After last night, she was most assuredly his woman. Warmth rose in her cheeks as she remembered her wanton response to his touch and her wicked advances. Would she have behaved so with some farmer's son from Deerfield? She thought not.

The sound of pots and pans from the kitchen drew her attention. Realizing that Marie was already at work, she quickly rolled out of bed and dressed. Brushing her hair with her new brush, she braided it, then walked out into the kitchen.

*"Bonjour!"* Marie called gaily from where she stood in front of the hearth. "Did you sleep well?"

"Very well, thank you," Rachel answered with a blush.

"Ah, *le seigneur*, he is a passionate man, yes?"

Rachel's face turned pinker.

Marie chuckled. "Do not fret. My Charles, he is a passionate man, too. It is good for a man and woman to make the love. It brings them together and makes the babies, eh?"

Rachel was now bright red. Yet, despite her embarrassment, she wondered how White Wolf would react to her having his baby. Would he want a son or daughter from the woman whom he had taken as his revenge? And what of her own feelings? She suddenly knew she wanted very much to have his child.

Wanting to change the subject, she asked Marie, "Where are White Wolf and Charles?"

"They are in the fields." She handed Rachel a basket. "Please, go fetch eggs from the barn. The men will be back soon for breakfast."

As Rachel took the basket and walked out the door, Marie was already slicing bacon from a huge slab. Rachel entered the barn and quickly found where the hens roosted. She collected over a dozen eggs. As she was walking back to the house, she saw White Wolf and Charles heading across the fields. She stopped for a moment to admire the easy grace of the man who had taken her to wife. Pride swelled her heart. He was magnificent, and he was hers. Realizing the men were coming back from the fields for breakfast and that she still had the eggs in her basket, she hurried to the house.

When White Wolf entered, Rachel looked up eagerly from slicing bread. Their eyes met and held for a moment before White Wolf's gaze warmly slipped down over her body. Rachel felt its heat clear down to her toes. Shyly averting her eyes, she returned to her task. She did not hear him come up behind her. Only when his lips brushed across the back of her neck did she know he was there.

"Tonight, English?" he whispered.

She gave a tiny nod, but did not dare look at him. Very aware of the presence of Charles and Marie, she was afraid her need would be written all over her face. How, she wondered, could such a simple gesture and such simple words make her ache for the feel of him?

Somehow, Rachel got through the meal. She congratulated herself on her ability to act quite normally. She kept her hands to herself and did not give in to the urge to reach out and touch White Wolf, who sat at the head of the table to her left. She did not allow her feet to come into contact with his beneath the table. She did not stare at him. She did not grin idiotically. Her only problem was the constant blush in her cheeks and the heat she felt that was totally incongruous with the cool morning air.

When the meal was over, Marie asked Rachel to fetch water from the well and asked if Charles could remain a moment to help her move the heavy table. When White Wolf offered to help Charles, Marie refused, then shooed him back to the fields. Rachel and White Wolf left the house together.

When the door had closed behind them, White Wolf took Rachel's hand and ran with her to the barn. Once inside the dim interior, he pushed her against the wall. Before she could breathe or think, his mouth was possessing hers. Her arms slipped around his neck, and eagerly, she kissed him back.

When they finally parted enough to catch their breath, he whispered, "I have been waiting for that since I woke this morning."

Rachel smiled. "I love having you kiss me." She reached up and traced his mouth.

Catching her hand in his, he groaned. "I cannot wait until darkness." He pressed against her. "You see? Already I need you."

Rachel wriggled her hips. "I need you, too."

From outside, Charles called. White Wolf grimaced at the voice. Rachel giggled.

"You laugh at me, woman?" White Wolf asked with mock severity. "You will not laugh so tonight. I promise you."

Rachel giggled again. "I cannot wait for your punishment."

"Wicked woman," White Wolf growled, then swooped down on her mouth once more.

He left her quickly, then. She leaned limply, dreamily against the wall. It did not seem possible that the cold, hard, impassive man who had swept into her village was now the source of her happiness. A shaft of sunlight burst into the dim barn. That was how White Wolf had come into her life, she decided. He had burst into her dreary existence and brought her light. With a smile on her face, she picked up the bucket where it had fallen from her fingers and went to fetch water for Marie.

The day passed more quickly than Rachel could have believed possible. She helped Marie with chores about the house, then they went out into the field to help the men sow seed where the land had been plowed. Late in the afternoon, she and Marie began cutting and piecing the material they had taken from the store so that they might make clothes for Rachel. After the evening meal, the four of them sat about the fireplace. Marie and Rachel sewed while Charles and White Wolf played chess. Rachel was amazed that her husband, whom she had first assumed to be an uneducated savage, knew the game. That night when they retired to their four-poster bed, she was again amazed at the heights of passion she achieved in White Wolf's arms.

They remained at the trading post for a week. Rachel had come to learn that the land belonged to a seigneury, a French version of a feudal manor house. The lord owned all the surrounding land, and the farms she had seen on the trip down the river were all worked by tenants who paid rent and owed fealty to the lord. Some of the tenants came and consulted with White Wolf, and once, he was called upon to settle a dispute between two farmers who claimed the same calf.

Rachel found the situation very confusing. Every day, she learned new things about White Wolf. She realized that somehow, he was very important to this seigneury, but every time she asked him about it, he was evasive with his answer. Even Marie would not satisfy her curiosity. Realizing that White Wolf would explain to her only when he was ready, she let the matter drop. It was not important enough to argue over. She assumed that since White Wolf was such an important man with the Penobscot, then the tenants of the seigneury also relied on him for leadership.

The night before they were to leave for Quebec, Rachel lay awake in White Wolf's embrace. Their love-making had been slow and easy, an exploration of each other's bodies. Physically, she was tired, but her mind was filled with questions and apprehension about what lay ahead in the city of the governor of New France.

Breaking the contented silence, she asked White Wolf, "Why do we have to go to Quebec?"

"I have to go," White Wolf answered.

"But, why?" Rachel persisted. "Why can't we stay here? Or in your village?"

"You know why we cannot remain in the village, English. Dark Eagle needs time to heal from the wrong I have done him. It is best if I stay away."

"Then why can't we stay here?"

"The governor wishes to speak with me. I promised that I would bring you to Quebec."

Rachel was silent for a moment as she fought the pain his words brought. "You mean you promised to bring back your revenge," she corrected.

"Yes." His answer was direct, but contained no vindictiveness. He raised himself up on an elbow and gazed down at her. "You have nothing to fear, Rachel." He brushed a stray hair out of her face. "You are my woman."

Rachel said nothing. When White Wolf again lay down, she snuggled up to him. She did feel safe with White Wolf, yet something still bothered her, something that remained at the edges of her mind. Deciding finally it was only her own silliness, she pushed the vague apprehension away and went to sleep.

The next morning, they were up and ready to leave before dawn. The other Indians, who had come with them from the village and had been out hunting during the week, would accompany them. They were already waiting beside the loaded canoes when White Wolf and Rachel emerged from the house. The several dresses

293

which Rachel and Marie had made and the rest of the bolts of cloth had been wrapped in several layers of deerskin and oilcloth for protection on the journey. Rachel shook hands with Charles and gave Marie a hug and kiss.

*"Bonne chance, mon amie,"* Marie whispered tearfully in Rachel's ear. Good luck, my friend.

Rachel, not trusting her own voice, gave her a little squeeze, then turned and followed White Wolf to the canoes. As the canoes slipped into the river, the sky was beginning to brighten in the east. Rachel waved one last time to her new friends, then faced forward into her future.

The trip to Quebec would be easier than the trek from Deerfield to the village of White Wolf's people. Most of the journey would be by canoe. White Wolf told her they would be in Quebec before the next new moon. Rachel calculated that would be not quite two weeks. She resigned herself to another long trip.

They travelled back up the river, but before they reached the village, they turned off into another river. White Wolf told her this was *Sebesteguk,* the almost-through river. It was the short way to Quebec. Rachel appreciated that they were going the short way, for they would have to spend less time in the wilderness, but it would also mean they would be arriving in Quebec sooner than if they went the long way.

The day passed slowly for Rachel. The excitement of starting out soon gave way to the boredom of sitting still in the canoe and watching the riverbank slide past. During the afternoon after a brief stop, White Wolf gave Rachel a paddle and showed her how to help propel the canoe along. She soon discovered muscles she had never known she had. Paddling, which seemed so easy and effortless when White Wolf did it, was very hard work, she discovered. That night, exhausted, she fell asleep almost as soon as she had eaten her share of wild goose and corn mash.

The next days were the same as the first. On the fourth day, after portaging the canoes through a stretch of woods and steep hills, they came to a huge lake. This, White Wolf told her, would take them almost all the way to Rivière Chaudière which they would follow to the Rivière St. Lawrence and then to Quebec. It seemed to Rachel that they would reach Quebec much sooner than she had calculated — something to be grateful for and something to fear.

A week later, they entered the wide St. Lawrence. Rachel was overwhelmed by the size of the river. Their tiny canoes were dwarfed in its expanse. Realizing for the first time just how fragile their transportation was, she was very glad to see signs of a town on shore in the distance.

As they neared, she could finally see the town that Marie had so colorfully described. It was, indeed, built on two levels, with a lower town and an upper town on the high cliffs above. Impressive buildings and spires rose up from the upper town. The buildings in the lower town were simpler, being of only one or two stories. Several ships lay at anchor near docks reaching out into the river. Smoke rose from chimneys. Dogs barked. Sailors sang as they loaded or unloaded ships. They headed their canoes toward shore just above the town where the riverbank sloped gently down to the water. Several boys ran to watch curiously. White Wolf called one of them over and spoke with him a moment before the boy grinned and nodded and ran off. Rachel was too glad to be finally on land and able to stretch her legs to pay much attention. Several of the other boys came over looking to help, and White Wolf had them unload the canoes. After saying goodbye to the Indians who had accompanied them, he escorted Rachel into the town. The boys followed with the packs.

Rachel was enchanted with the town. They wandered through narrow streets and wide avenues, but what she found most charming were the tiny lanes that were not streets at all, but walkways that contained steps from one level to another. It was not until they stood next to the flight of stairs that clung precariously to the cliff that she realized just how far above her the upper town actually was. This flight of stairs was not charming at all. It was higher than any building she had ever seen.

Pausing before the bottom step, she gazed up to where the top step was lost in the glare of the sun. She had never seen such a long flight of stairs, much less climbed one. The idea caused an uncomfortable fluttering in her stomach.

From behind her, White Wolf teased, "Is the brave Englishwoman afraid of a few stairs?"

Rachel gulped. "I have never seen such a long flight of stairs. Is there another way to the top?"

"There is, but it will take us out of our way and we will be late for dinner."

"Oh," was all she said in a tiny voice as she surveyed the steps once more. Taking a deep breath, she placed her hand on the railing and her foot on the bottom step. Without looking anywhere but at her feet, she began her ascent. Finally, after an interminable time, she stepped once more onto solid ground. Feeling White Wolf's firm presence behind her, she breathed a sigh of relief. She resolved to avoid that flight of stairs as much as she could while she was in Quebec.

They set out once again, side by side. They passed a group of very large, impressive buildings. An orchard and gardens lay to one side, and in the center was a church. White Wolf told her that this was the Seminary, where the Jesuit priests lived.

Just as they neared the edge of the property, Rachel heard a familiar voice call out, "Rachel! Rachel Linton! Is that you?"

Rachel stopped and swung about. Standing behind her was Reverend Williams, escorted by a soldier. As Mr. Williams began to rush forward to greet her, the soldier held him back by the arm. White Wolf motioned to the soldier to release the man. Mr. Williams hurried forward and gripped Rachel's hands in greeting.

"Rachel! It really is you!" he exclaimed. "How are you faring? Are you well?"

Rachel laughed with pleasure upon seeing someone from Deerfield. "I am fine, Mr. Williams, thank you. And you and your wife and children? How do you fare?"

A shadow passed across his face. "My dear wife did not finish the journey, I am afraid, and my children are being held by the Indians and priests who are trying to seduce them to their heathen ways."

"Oh, I am so sorry, reverend. I did not know." Sympathy flooded her at the thought of those children, from big to small, with no mother.

Mr. Williams waved a hand as if to dispel the gloomy thoughts of both of them. "It is the will of God," he declared. "My children have a deep love for the Bible. They will not forget their catechism. I only fear for the young ones, Eunice especially. She is so timid. But it is the will of God," he repeated. He stood back a step and perused her from head to toe. "But you, Rachel, I never thought to see you again, child, and now, here you are. What you did was so very brave. What happened to you?" He stole a quick glance at White Wolf who stood back, glaring at him. "Has any harm befallen you, child?" He looked pointedly at her deerskin dress. "You look so . . . different."

Smiling, Rachel assured him, "I am unharmed, Reverend, honestly I am." She turned to indicate the man behind her. "This is White Wolf. He has protected me and brought me here. He saved me from the wolves when I was left in the forest."

"Well, I am certainly grateful for that. But your mode of dress . . . Have you turned from the ways of God? Have you taken up these heathen ways? These Jesuit priests are constantly trying to turn our neighbors to popery and Romish superstition."

"I have done nothing of which I am ashamed," she said.

The reverend sent a sideways glance to White Wolf and lowered his voice. "But has he disgraced you in any fashion?"

Rachel dropped one of Reverend Williams' hands

and placed her hand on White Wolf's arm. Smiling into those impassive blue eyes, she told the reverend, "I am White Wolf's woman."

There was shocked silence from Reverend Williams, then he blurted, "Oh, my dear girl, how you must have suffered!"

Rachel looked at him in surprise. "I have not suffered at all, reverend. I have been quite happy."

Mr. Williams glanced at White Wolf's dark face. Realizing the man's anger was just below the surface, he did not argue with her but said instead, "We must speak of this Rachel. I will ask if I may visit you."

"You may come to visit if I have White Wolf's permission to receive you, reverend, but I will not change my mind. I will remain White Wolf's woman."

"But my dear girl, think of your poor, departed father, may he rest in peace. What would he say?" Reverend Williams persisted.

White Wolf spoke then in the man's own language. "He would probably thank me for saving his daughter from the wolves and wish her happiness."

At hearing this Indian speak fluent, educated English, Reverend Williams's mouth dropped open and his eyes popped. Rachel bit down on a giggle.

As White Wolf took her arm to lead her away, she told Reverend Williams, "It was good to see you, Mr. Williams. If you see any other of our neighbors, please wish them well for me."

"I will pray for you, Rachel," the reverend called before the soldier with him nudged him on his way.

Rachel and White Wolf walked for a while before he said, "I do not like that man."

299

"He means well," Rachel told him. "He is only thinking of my safety."

"I will keep you safe. His prayers will not help. I would ask that you do not receive him."

Rachel stopped and placed her hand on White Wolf's arm. "Please, don't ask me not to see him. He is from my village. I would like to hear the news of my friends."

White Wolf searched her face for a moment before he reached up and drew his fingers down her cheek. "You have never asked me for anything, English. How can I refuse?"

Rachel almost threw her arms around him in gratitude, but she remembered they were standing in the middle of a street. With glowing eyes, she told him, "Thank you."

"Just remember that you are my woman. You belong to me, now, and my people, not to that man."

Rachel grinned impudently. "How could I forget?"

White Wolf's gaze narrowed. "You are a wicked woman, English," he teased.

"I know," Rachel nodded in mock sorrow. "Will you punish me, now?" She peeked up at him coquettishly from beneath her lashes.

A slow smile spread across White Wolf's face. "Severely," he told her. "Tonight."

"Oh, dear," Rachel sighed. "Then I will have the rest of the afternoon to worry about what you will do to me."

"Waiting is part of the pleasure, English," he told her with a chuckle as he began walking again.

Rachel knew he spoke the truth from past experience. Skipping a few steps to catch up to his long-legged stride, she questioned him about the various buildings they passed. She was amazed at the number of churches in the town. It seemed everywhere she turned there was another magnificent cathedral or small wooden chapel.

She was also amazed at the people they passed. Women and men of wealth wore clothes of fine cloth, decorated with laces and ribbons. Those of the middle class were also well-clothed. Even the servants who scurried through the streets on errands for their masters had bits of lace or ribbon trimming on their clothes. Yet, Rachel and White Wolf were not the only people clothed in deerskin. Many Indians roamed the streets, and men dressed like Claude Donat, the *coureur de bois,* mingled in the crowds. Priests in their robes and nuns in their dark habits strolled among the populace. Rachel became dizzy with trying to see everything. This town was far from the sleepiness of Deerfield, or the strangeness of the village of the Penobscot.

White Wolf finally turned into the courtyard of a small stone house. Before he could knock, the door was flung open and an older woman whose face was framed by a lacy dustcap stood smiling at him.

"*Mon seigneur!* You have come!" she exclaimed in French.

She stepped back and allowed them to enter. The interior of the house was dim but pleasant. They stood in a small parlor that stretched off to the right. The walls were paneled in dark wood and some were plastered and whitewashed. Bright tapestry covered the cushions of chairs and a sofa. To the left was a round polished table and several chairs. The furniture, Rachel decided, had been brought from France. Before her was a narrow set of stairs leading to the upper floors.

She and White Wolf had barely stepped through the door when a young, attractive woman of about Rachel's age burst from a closed door at the back of the parlor. Her dark curls bobbed beneath a tiny dustcap, and her full figure strained at the chemise tied loosely across her bosom. Skidding to a halt before them, she curtseyed to White Wolf.

*"Mon seigneur,"* she panted in the same language as the older woman. "We have been waiting for you." When she stood, her dark eyes roved over White Wolf, then landed with curiosity on Rachel.

White Wolf smiled indulgently at the girl, then turned to Rachel. "This is Madame de la Roche and her daughter, Celeste. They take care of the house. I stay here when I am in Quebec." To the two women he said, "This is Rachel Linton."

Rachel waited for him to add that she was his wife, his woman, anything, but he did not. And she did not like at all the way Celeste looked at him. This situation would need watching.

Celeste showed her to a spacious, airy bedroom upstairs where a large bed dominated the room with floral embroidered bed hangings and matching draperies on the windows. Two velvet-covered chairs sat before a tiled fireplace, and a large wardrobe hulked beside the door. A washstand stood in one corner.

"You may refresh yourself before dinner," Celeste told her. "Perhaps by then, your things will have arrived." She gave a disparaging glance to Rachel's attire, then turned and left.

Alone, Rachel walked to the window and looked out.

Below, the empty courtyard swept out to the quiet street. Whose house was this? she wondered. Did it belong to the same man who owned the seigneury? What was White Wolf's relationship to him? What was White Wolf's relationship with Celeste? This last question weighed the most heavily on her mind. Realizing the stones of the courtyard would reveal nothing, she turned away from the window with a sigh.

She walked to the washstand to refresh herself after the trip. Her thoughts remained dark. Despite the brightness and gaiety of the town, she felt a weight pressing down on her. This was the home of the French, whom she despised. Being surrounded by them made her tense and somewhat fearful. She had not felt like this with Charles and Marie because there had been only the two of them, and they had been very kind to her. Yet, here, in the town that had spawned her hatred of these people, she could not forget what the French had done to her.

Her bundles of belongings arrived then, delivered by two of the boys who had met them on the riverbank. They were adorable urchins with wide dark eyes and impertinent manners. Rachel wished she had something she could have given to them. Touching their hands to their forelocks, giggling, they scurried out the door. Rachel heard Madame de la Roche admonishing them downstairs. She turned to unpack the bundles and in the wardrobe she hung her two dresses and a third that was unfinished.

While she was checking to make sure there had been no damage to any of the cloth she had brought with her, a panelled door she had not noticed opened in the wall

303

across from the foot of the bed. White Wolf stood in the opening.

"Are you pleased with your room?" he asked.

"It is lovely, thank you," she replied. She caught a glance of another bed with dark hangings behind him, where he had come from.

His eyes travelled over the room. "I am glad you like it. It belonged to someone special." His voice was distant, as if he were reliving old memories.

Rachel said nothing, but she was curious about who that person might be.

Coming out of his short reverie, he smiled and said, "If you are not too tired, I would like to show you more of the town."

Rachel smiled. "That would be very nice."

He told her he would meet her downstairs, and returned from where he came, closing the door behind him. Rachel finished rearranging her hair, then she hurried downstairs.

The front door stood wide and outside was an open carriage with two horses. White Wolf came up behind her.

"I thought you might like to ride in the *calèche*," he told her.

Taking her by the hand, he drew her outside, then helped her climb up onto the single seat that sat above the splashboard at the front. White Wolf climbed up beside her. Snapping the reins, he urged the horses forward. Rachel watched his expert handling of the animals and wondered at the mystery of it all. This man was a constant source of amazement to her. Where had such a grand vehicle come from, and where had he learned how to drive one so masterfully?

Her curiosity was soon forgotten in the sights of the town. They drove past the Château of Saint-Louis, which was the residence of the Governor, the convent of the Ursuline Sisters, and the hospital, the Hôtel-Dieu. The Seminary, where the papist priests were housed and where she had met Mr. Williams, stood on the edge of the cliff overlooking the river far below. They passed other houses, not quite so grand, but still comfortable and similar to the one where White Wolf had taken her. Many other people, dressed in fine clothes, were also out riding in their carriages. Many of them greeted White Wolf gaily. Despite her dark feeling of earlier that afternoon, Rachel could not help but be swept up in the excitement of the town.

They returned to the house at sunset. White Wolf had surprised her on the ride by stopping at a shop called *au Bien Chaussé,* a cobbler's, and ordering several pairs of shoes for her. Then he had stopped at a tailor's for gloves, and at a hatter's. Rachel was overwhelmed with his generosity and his sudden cosmopolitan attitude. How had this man, whom she knew as a woodsman, learned of such things as fashion?

Befuddled, she was very quiet as he helped her down from the seat of the *calèche.* Her silence remained as, after a short rest, she sat at the dinner table and was served by Celeste. The meal, consisting of fresh haddock, asparagus with onions, fresh bread and finished off by preserved walnuts, was delicious, but she only picked at her food. Her questions tumbled about in her head. Reticent still about prying into White Wolf's past, she kept quiet, not wishing to voice her doubts

305

and fears and disturb their tenuous relationship.

White Wolf sensed her pensive mood and did not try to disturb it. He knew the day's events had raised many questions in her mind, but it was too soon to answer them. In time, when they had become more comfortable with each other, he would tell her all she wished to know. For now, all he wanted was to be with her and have her cuddle next to him.

When dinner was over, they sat in quiet companionship before a small fire. The excitement and wonders of the day soon took their toll on Rachel. Curled up on a silk-tapestry-covered sofa next to White Wolf, she soon feel asleep. Gently, he carried her upstairs and laid her on the bed. Undressing her, he slipped her beneath the covers, then slid in next to her. He stared up at the ceiling as he held her close and listened to the soft sound of her breathing.

She had learned much about him this day that had puzzled her. Yet, she had asked him nothing. It had always been so with her, since that day he had taken her from her village. She would watch and wait for answers to be revealed to her and then decide what she should do.

What, he wondered, would she do when she discovered the rest of his identity, the other half of his heritage? He knew of her hatred of the French. She had admitted it freely, almost proudly. Would she be able to suppress that hatred in order to live here with him in New France?

He did not know. Like Rachel, he would watch and wait for the answer to be revealed.

# Chapter Twenty

The next day, Rachel discovered a small garden behind the house. She took the dress she was sewing out there to work on while White Wolf called on several people he had told her he must see. He was very vague about who it was he was going to visit, and Rachel did not feel she should pry. There was so much of White Wolf which he kept to himself. She hoped that in time he would come to share more of himself with her. A vague uneasiness assailed her about this reticence on his part, an uneasiness that she had not felt while they had travelled through the wilderness. She attributed it to being surrounded by so many French.

That morning, when she awoke, White Wolf had still been lying beside her. He smiled tenderly at her when she opened her eyes. They had made love slowly, gently, only at the last giving way to unbridled passion. She had felt better afterwards, more secure, safer, but still a sense of disquiet lingered at the edges of her mind and remained with her even now in the quiet solitude of the garden.

Madame de la Roche appeared at the kitchen door.

"Mademoiselle Rachel," she called. "You have some visitors. I have shown them to the salon."

Puzzled about who would be coming to see her, Rachel thanked her and put aside her sewing. Walking swiftly through the kitchen and past Celeste who was sullenly stirring a pot over the fire, she stopped before the parlor door. Two men rose when they saw her.

Rachel's mouth dropped open as she recognized them. "Enoch Cooper, Israel Putnam!" she exclaimed as she rushed forward. "You are here in Quebec!" She took one of their hands in each of her own and gripped them in pleasure. "Yesterday, I met Reverend Williams, and today I find both of you here in this very house. I thought never to see anyone from Deerfield ever again."

They grinned back at her. She bade them sit and asked Madame de la Roche, who was hovering just outside the parlor door, to bring some refreshment. When they were all settled, she asked, "How did you ever find me?"

Israel looked a bit sheepish as he said, "I saw you out riding with that Indian yesterday and I followed you. I hope you don't mind."

"Not at all," Rachel assured him. "I am so happy to see you."

Enoch had been studying his surroundings, and now he observed, "This seems like a pretty fancy house for an Indian to live in."

"We are just staying here for a while," Rachel told him, but the statement mirrored her own thoughts. Impatiently, she pushed her doubts away.

Madame de la Roche brought a tray with a decanter of claret, a small pitcher of water and crystal glasses.

When she had left, Rachel stared thoughtfully at the tray. Crystal and wine? she thought. How wealthy was the man who owned this house?

In order that she would not appear ungracious, or reveal her own misgivings, she quickly poured wine and water into each of the glasses and offered it to her guests. As they sipped, she asked how the men fared and about the other people of Deerfield who had been taken captive.

Most, she discovered, had survived. Some had arrived in Quebec and were being housed by tradesmen's families. A few of the children had been adopted by their Indian captors. Others were in Montreal. Reverend Williams had been to see the Governor about arranging ransom so that the people might return home.

"That's why we've come to see you, Rachel," Israel said finally. "It will be months, perhaps years, before ransom can be raised and an exchange made. We want to escape and give Governor Dudley in Boston enough information so that he can mount a counterattack on the French."

"Sh," Enoch warned as he glanced about suspiciously. "Not so loud. Do you want every Frenchie to know what we plan?"

Rachel thoughtfully put her glass on the small table before her. "I do not think either Madame de la Roche or her daughter understand English. What is your plan?"

"We want to steal some canoes and sail up the Chaudière River, and then head overland to the coast where we can get a ship to Boston," Israel said eagerly. "But we need supplies and a guide."

"I don't see how I can help. I have nothing to give

you," she told them.

"You came with the Indian. You can help us get the canoes." Enoch looked pointedly about the room, at its rich furnishings. "You can probably help us get supplies, too."

Rachel shook her head. "I don't know. I've only just arrived in Quebec. As I said, we are just staying in this house. White Wolf knows the man who owns it. I don't know how long we will be here."

"But you have to help us," Israel pleaded.

Rachel shook her head. "I can't. Not now. My hus—White Wolf is friendly with the French. I do not wish to betray him."

"But he attacked our village!" Israel exclaimed.

Before Rachel could say anything else, Enoch placed his hand on Israel's arm and put his glass down suddenly on the table. His eyes darted to the door, then back to Israel. "We have to get back. We are expected to work for our keep, and we have been gone too long as it is." He stood. "Come on, Israel. Rachel will help if she can. She's loyal to her own people and won't forget them." With a stern expression, he turned to Rachel. "We'll wait for word from you. You can reach me at the bakery on Rue Sous-le-Fort in the lower town."

After they left, Rachel returned to the garden and her sewing, but she made little progress. Her thoughts rushed about, chasing one another inside her head. A return attack on the French was an intriguing idea. Certainly, it would help repay an old debt she felt she owed the French. She knew that the information Enoch and Israel could provide the Governor of Massachusetts would be helpful in planning such an attack. Yet, by helping the two men, would she be betraying the

310

trust of White Wolf? She was his woman now, and by that very fact she should feel loyal to him and his people. His people had been wronged by the English; there was no doubt in her mind about that. Yet, would she be propagating the wrong by helping the two Englishmen? She did not know. She just did not know.

White Wolf did not return until just before the dinner hour. As they sat at the dinner table, he told her that the governor, the Marquis de Vaudreuil, had invited them to a gathering at the Château de Saint-Louis in three days. Celeste happened to be clearing dishes at the time, and Rachel noticed a pout appear on those full lips. She resolved to speak to White Wolf about the girl. But in the meantime, she had to make something suitable to wear.

She watched him lean back in his chair at the end of the meal with a glass of claret in his hand. He twirled the stem with his long fingers. A vision of him in brocade and velvet, with lacy jabot and cuffs spilling over his coat suddenly leapt to the forefront of her mind. Blinking, she looked at him and saw he still wore the fringed deerskin tunic with which she had become so familiar. Beneath the table, she knew his lean legs were encased in deerskin leggings. What, she wondered, had caused the odd picture to appear in her mind?

"Madame de la Roche told me that you had visitors today." His voice broke into her thoughts.

"Yes, two men from Deerfield," she said, as the thought crossed her mind that Madame de la Roche was watching her and reporting on her activities.

"It is strange that they were able to find you so quickly after we arrived."

Rachel looked hard at him. What was he implying?

she wondered. Did he suspect the true nature of the visit of Enoch and Israel? Casually, she said, "They saw us out together yesterday and discovered we were staying here. They came only to bring news." She decided she was not telling a lie, for they had brought news—news of their plan to escape. Yet, she found she did not like evading White Wolf's questions.

He smiled then. "I am glad you have had visitors," he told her. "I promise not to leave you so much alone tomorrow."

Rachel smiled back and the tension left her body. "Thank you," she said. "I missed you today."

He leaned across the table and reached for her hand. "Tell me how much you missed me, English," he whispered.

A delicious shiver ran through her at his seductive words. "I can show you much better," she smiled.

They rose from the table together and met at the doorway. Their hands found each other and their fingers entwined. Quickly, they climbed the stairs and entered her room.

"I missed you today, too, English," he murmured as he framed her face with his hands.

His mouth captured hers and all thoughts were banished from their minds except of pleasuring and desire.

The next two days passed quickly for Rachel. Using the pink-sprigged muslin and white linen, she worked feverishly on a dress that would be suitable to wear to the Governor's house. Madame de la Roche helped, but Celeste seemed to have other more important things to do. By the morning of the party, the dress was almost completed. Rachel held it up and examined it closely. It was pretty, she decided, but not quite as grand as she would have wished. After all, she was being invited to dine with the Governor, who, in spite of being French, was still an important person. With a sigh, she tossed it over her arm, gathered her needle and thread and headed down to the parlor to sew.

About the middle of the afternoon, a knock came at the door. Since Madame de la Roche and Celeste were not about, she went to answer it. A young man stood on the threshold. He was delivering some of the shoes, gloves and hats which White Wolf had bought her on their expedition a few days earlier. Before he drove away, another wagon drove up to the house. This was driven by a middle- aged woman, who hailed Rachel gaily.

Nimbly, she climbed down from the wagon and a young boy jumped down from the back. Together, they pulled a long bundle from the back of the wagon.

Coming to the door, the woman asked, "You are Rachel Linton?"

At Rachel's nod, the woman said, "Good. I am Madame Bonner. *Le Seigneur* asked me to deliver this to you." She and the boy held out the bundle. "May we come in?"

Puzzled, Rachel nodded dumbly and showed them to the parlor. The woman laid the bundle down on the sofa and untied it. A dress of shimmering green silk and white lace popped out of the covering. Shaking it out, the woman held it up for Rachel's inspection.

"There. What do you think?" she asked.

"It's lovely," Rachel breathed in awe. It was the most beautiful dress she had ever seen. Behind the woman, still lying on the sofa, was an underskirt of pale yellow silk that would go perfectly with the dress along with several petticoats.

"Good. I am glad you like it." The woman looked critically at the dress and then at Rachel "I do not think it will need much adjustment. It seems it will fit."

"Do you mean this is for me?" Rachel asked, dumbfounded at the gift.

"But of course!" Madame Bonner exclaimed. *"Le seigneur* said it was for the young woman staying here. He described your hair, and your size. He was very specific about the size." She grinned and winked at Rachel. "He is a devil, that one, yes?"

The heat rushed into Rachel's face and she lowered her eyes. She was amazed at how these French were so open about such intimate matters.

"Ah, this is new to you, eh?" Madame Bonner sympathized. "It is good to be modest. Some of these young girls are so bold. Well, enough. To work. Let us try this gown on you and see what needs to be done." She turned to the boy. "Go wait outside, Michel."

As the boy scampered eagerly out of the house, Rachel helped the woman gather up the dress and the bundle and showed her upstairs to the bedroom. There, she discovered the woman had also brought along all the necessary undergarments. She tried on the gown and discovered it was almost a perfect fit. Only the waist needed to be taken in a tiny bit.

After Madame Bonner made a tuck here and took a stitch there, she declared the gown finished. Turning to face the mirror which hung between the two windows, Rachel was delighted at what she saw. The dress was the most magnificent creation she had ever owned. The low bodice and white satin stomacher trimmed with white lace revealed the swell of her breast. The tight

314

bodice showed off her tiny waist. The color made her eyes iridescent.

"You will be gorgeous tonight," the woman announced proudly. "You will have all men's eyes on you."

Dumbfounded that White Wolf should gift her with such an outrageously expensive dress, Rachel said nothing. She was quiet as Madame Bonner helped her remove the dress and hang it in the wardrobe with her few other articles of clothing. After offering the woman some refreshment, which she refused, Rachel escorted her to the door.

When the woman had gone, Rachel returned to her room and opened the wardrobe door. She just stood there and gazed at the dress. Questions followed one another through her mind. How had White Wolf been able to afford such an expensive item? How had he known about such a thing as fashion? Shaking her head, she gave up trying to find answers. It was too much for her to decipher. The man who had taken her as his woman was too complex for her to decipher. Happily, she went back to examining her new gown.

A knock came at her door not long after, and Madame de la Roche and Celeste entered carrying a tub between them. It was time for Rachel to bathe and get ready for the Governor's dinner party. She did not hear White Wolf come back to the house, but Madame de la Roche told her he had returned and was himself dressing for their outing.

Madame de la Roche arranged Rachel's hair and then helped her into her dress. All the while she chattered and exclaimed about how lovely Rachel would look. Celeste remained sullenly in the background. When Rachel was finally attired in her new clothes, she turned slowly to face herself in the mirror. A strange woman stared back at her.

Her hair was piled high on her head with several lovelocks hanging down over one shoulder. Her eyes sparkled a bright blue-green. Her dress made her appear as if she were a member of the king's court.

Madame de la Roche examined her critically. "Good," she said. "You are almost ready." Pulling a tiny box from her pocket, she opened it to take something out. "Here, this will finish you and make you the envy of all the women." She stuck a tiny, heart-shaped patch just below the corner of Rachel's mouth.

At that moment, the door connecting the two bedrooms opened. Rachel turned expecting to see White Wolf. The person she saw barely resembled the deerskin-clad man who had captured her and brought her to Quebec. Her mouth fell open. He was dressed in a black velvet coat and breeches trimmed with gold embroidery. A lacy, white cravat foamed at his throat. His waistcoat was of pale yellow brocade trimmed with gold lace. White silk stockings embroidered with tiny gold clocks hugged his legs, and his shiny black shoes had buckles of silver. A simple lacy cuff showed beyond the sleeve of his coat. His hair was his only revolt against high fashion. Instead of being curled and waved, it remained long and straight, although he had trimmed it.

Coming out of her shock, Rachel moved before him and curtseyed low. "My lord," she teased. "You do me honor to visit."

White Wolf reached down with a smile and steadied her while she stood. "You are beautiful, English," he told her. "Come, our carriage awaits."

He escorted her down the stairs and out the door. In

the courtyard, a barouche stood waiting with its roof up and a driver in the high front seat. White Wolf handed her into the vehicle, then climbed in himself. Giving an order to the driver, they started off.

As they rode along, White Wolf pulled a box out of his pocket and handed it to Rachel. "This might go well with your gown," he told her.

Rachel opened the box and discovered a pearl collar with a diamond clasp and matching pearl earrings. "Oh, my," she breathed. "They are lovely."

White Wolf fastened the pearls about her neck and helped her with the earrings. When she had finished, he brushed his lips across hers. "They are not as lovely as the woman who wears them," he whispered.

Rachel smiled and blushed her thanks, and placed her hand in his. Although part of her was thrilled at the new clothes and jewels, still another part of her was dark with doubts and questions. No Indian would be able to afford such things, much less care about them. Who was this man who rode beside her in such elegance?

There were other carriages arriving and discharging their passengers when White Wolf and Rachel arrived at the Château de Saint-Louis. The huge house was lit brightly with lamps and thousands of candles. Entering the foyer, Rachel gazed about her in wonder. All the women and men were clothed in silks and satins and velvets. This was no gathering of poor simple colonists, but of wealthy landowners and merchants. A footman was announcing each of the guests as they entered the large salon off to one side. White Wolf guided her in this direction.

When it came time for them to enter, the footman

announced, "Monsieur le Comte Etienne de la Lupe et Mademoiselle Rachel Linton."

Rachel glanced about for Monsieur le Comte to appear at the same time that White Wolf began to lead her into the throng of people. Suddenly, she came to the realization that White Wolf *was* le Comte de la Lupe. Her White Wolf, the man who was of the Penobscot Indians, was a French nobleman!

Stopping dead in her tracks, she stared up at him. "You are French!" she gasped.

White Wolf's face was stony as he gazed down at her. "Keep walking and smiling, English," he told her. "Do not embarrass yourself. I will explain later."

As if in a dream, or a nightmare, Rachel walked the length of the room to meet Governor de Vaudreuil. People greeted White Wolf as they passed. Then she found herself curtsying before an older gentleman dressed in pale blue brocade.

"So, this is the lovely English captive I have heard so much about," the Governor gushed as he bowed over Rachel's hand. "It is a pleasure to meet you, my dear. You must tell this noble savage of yours to bring you to Château de Saint-Louis often. Beauty such as yours must not be hidden in the forest."

Rachel murmured an appropriate response, then lapsed into silence as White Wolf and the governor exchanged pleasantries. White Wolf's speech was smooth and glib, the speech of a courtier, not of a man of the wilderness. Somewhere, somehow, he had been exposed to court etiquette to go along with his noble title.

As they moved away into the crowd, she stiffened when he placed his hand on her arm. Turning on him, she said, "I wish to leave."

"We will stay," he told her. "You will mind your manners and behave. This gathering is to honor the men who returned in triumph from New England and to introduce you to the society of Quebec."

Rachel could not believe what she was hearing. "You would have me remain at a celebration for those who destroyed my home?! It is no wonder that I hate the French. You are more savage than the savages themselves."

White Wolf's face froze at her words. "Beware what you say, English. I may still use you as my revenge."

Rachel lifted her chin in defiance even as tears gathered in her eyes. "I would welcome the act, sir, for I find sleeping with the French more distasteful than sleeping in the pigsty."

White Wolf's eyes glittered with his rage. Before he could answer, a man approached and greeted them. Rachel lapsed into icy silence. She had blundered badly by allowing White Wolf—no, Etienne—to take her as his woman. Having been appalled at his savage need for revenge, she should have realized he was more than a simple woodsman. Only the French with their devious minds would want to do something so cruel. She had learned of the French through her own experience. She should have known better. She had been incredibly stupid.

Somehow, she was able to get through the evening. She talked and ate and danced as if she had not a care. Faces blurred into an indistinct haze and names were just so much gibberish on her ears. Too proud to allow others to see her pain, or her fear, she kept a smile pasted on her face until White Wolf—Etienne—escorted her out into the night and to their waiting carriage.

As Rachel was escorted out of the ballroom by Monsieur le Comte de la Lupe, a man with strange, black eyes emerged into the ballroom and watched her leave. "She is a beauty, is she not?" he murmured to Governor de Vaudreuil who stood next to him.

"Most definitely," the governor agreed. "De la Lupe has found himself quite a woman."

"I wonder . . ." the man with dark eyes said. "I do not think Mademoiselle Linton was happy tonight."

The governor glanced at the man sharply. "What are you plotting, Renaud? You know de la Lupe will slice you to pieces if you touch his woman. He will not stand for your toying with the *mademoiselle.*"

Benignly, Renaud smiled at the governor. "I do not intend to toy with her, Philippe. Mademoiselle Linton and I have some unfinished business."

"What unfinished business could you possibly have with the *mademoiselle?*" the governor demanded. "She is an English prisoner from a tiny village where you have never been."

Renaud's brow lifted arrogantly. "Are you so sure I have never been there, Philippe? Where do you think the information came from about this insignificant village in New England? I have been watching Mademoiselle Linton for some time."

"Beware, Henri Renaud," de Vaudreuil warned. "I will not countenance any of your perversity."

Renaud's face darkened threateningly. "I have served you well, Governor Monsieur le Marquis de Vaudreuil, and have completed tasks and been to places that other men would refuse. You have no power over me." His eyes strayed to the door through which Rachel had disappeared. "I will enjoy finishing my business with Mademoiselle Linton."

The ride from the Château de Saint-Louis to the house was made in cold silence. Rachel struggled to keep the tears from falling. Hurt and rage boiled within her. How, she kept asking herself, could she have been so stupid, so blind? How could she have allowed herself to be seduced so easily?

The words of Reverend Williams came back to her. The French wanted only to convert the hostages to their way of thinking, to their popery and idolatry, to make them allies against their own English Queen Anne. The French were murderers, cruel and devious. She knew that from her own experience. And she, fool that she was, had allowed herself to be seduced by one of them. What had she done by becoming White Wolf's woman?

Blessedly, that little voice inside her head remained silent.

# Chapter Twenty-one

White Wolf was so enraged with Rachel that he did not trust himself to speak. He had saved her several times, had cared for her and kept her alive in the forest, and with one announcement from an insignificant footman, one admission of who he was, she turned on him savagely. Her insults had cut deeply. And she had behaved like a puppet before the governor and his gathering. Just because one Frenchman had caused her anguish did not mean that all Frenchman were cruel and devious. Did she not know that? Could she not understand that he would not harm her? Had he made a mistake in taking her as his woman? Perhaps he should have sent her to his sister in France as he had first planned. At least, if Rachel were out of his sight, she would not make the blood rush through his body with need.

The barouche arrived at the house. In silence, they climbed the stairs to the bedroom. The man called White Wolf, also known as Etienne, Monsieur le Comte de la Lupe, crossed the room, took off his coat, and tossed it on the bed. Walking to the window, he stared out at nothing. He forced his anger back into the recesses of his heart. It had not been Rachel's fault that the evening had turned into a disaster. She had been open with him about her feelings for the French. He had dreaded this moment when Rachel would discover who he was. In his heart, he had known what her reaction would be, and for that reason he had kept his other identity a secret. He could feel her rage as she waited for an explanation. Turning slowly, he faced her.

Rachel watched him. Her eyes devoured his lean body, the hard, muscular frame. He was elegant, suave, handsome. She wanted so much to put her arms around him, to press herself against him, but he was her enemy once more. He had betrayed her with his silence. She was furious and hurt.

"How could you not tell me?" she demanded. "Why did you keep your true identity a secret?"

"It is not my *true* identity," he told her, trying to remain calm. "I *am* White Wolf of the Penobscot."

"But you are French. You are a count. I heard how you were announced. You are not White Wolf. You are Etienne."

"I am Etienne," he admitted. "But I am also White Wolf. My father was the son of the fourth Comte de la Lupe. He came to New France for an adventure, and decided to remain. When his father died, he inherited the title. Now that he is also dead, I am the sixth Comte de la Lupe.

"My father was given a large seigneury, a huge tract of land that was let out to tenants. He built the house where we visited. Marie and Charles are caretakers while I am away. When my father came to this country, he met a native woman, Silver Feather, and took her to wife. They had three children. I am the only son and the eldest. Hunting Dog is my grandfather. When he dies, I will probably be elected sagamore of the Penobscot."

Rachel stared at him as she tried to assimilate all this information. The man before her was White Wolf and also Etienne. He was Penobscot, but he was also French. Why had he not told her? Why had he kept his identity a secret? His silence hurt more than anything.

"You betrayed me," she whispered in pain. "You lied to me. You led me to believe that you were not French, even when you knew I hated them. How could you do that?"

"Does that make me different?" he demanded. "Because I am known by another name, am I a different man?"

"You are French. I hate all Frenchmen."

"You are being ridiculous. All Frenchmen are not the same."

"I do not know that. The French have always been the cause of pain in my life. A Frenchman murdered my mother when she discovered that he was a spy. He vowed to return to kill me and my father for turning him in to the authorities. Because of that threat, we were forced to move from our home in Boston to Deerfield, where the French swept into my life again and destroyed everything I knew. I despise them. What else am I to think of the French?"

He shrugged, hiding his guilt behind a facade of nonchalance. "The French and English are at war. It was unfortunate that you happened to live in Deerfield when it was attacked, but you are English. If you are loyal to your English Queen Anne, then you must suffer the consequences."

"You coldhearted, savage bastard," Rachel rasped.

Anger turned his face dark. He gripped her arms and shook her. "Be careful of your words, *English*. You are in enemy territory."

Rachel jerked free and faced him squarely despite the rage flashing in those blue eyes. "I am very well aware of that. You have threatened me enough with never leaving here. But what causes me more distress than your threats is that I have lain with the enemy."

A stony coldness replaced the rage on his face. "Remember that it was the enemy who brought you such delight. What Englishman was man enough to make you scream in pleasure or pant with desire?"

Rachel gasped at his crudeness.

"How can you be shocked, English? You know it is the truth." His hand snaked out and caught her by the back of her neck. His fingers tangled in her hair to keep her still. "Shall I prove that it is a Frenchman who brings your body to life?" Without waiting for an answer, he captured her mouth.

Rachel had no time to evade him. Her struggles were useless against him. She found herself wanting to stop pushing against him, wanting to lean into him and feel the hardness of him. Only a small reserve of willpower kept her from slipping into his web of desire. Finally breaking free, she glared up at him. Without thinking, her hand whipped out and cracked across his cheek.

The blow turned his head. When his eyes met hers

once again, his mouth curled in a cold smile of possession. "You are my woman, English, my revenge. It is too late to return to your puritanical English ideals. Not even your Reverend Williams can change what already has happened."

"I hate you," she spat.

Etienne bowed his head in acknowledgment. "So be it. It changes nothing. You will spend the rest of your life among the French." Turning on his heel, he disappeared through the connecting door into the next room.

Rachel sank down onto the bed. Next to her was the coat White Wolf—no, Etienne—had removed. In a fit of rage, she picked it up and flung it across the room. It landed, forlorn and crumpled, across the corner of the wardrobe. What was she to do? she wondered. She was trapped. The man to whom she had given herself, the man who had become part of her life, was now her enemy. The pain of his deception ripped through her, and she doubled over. Tears escaped from beneath her closed eyelids and dripped, unheeded, onto the skirt of her lovely gown.

How could she escape this prison? What could she do to free herself from the French? She could not leave the town on her own. It would be suicide to try to return to New England through the wilderness. No ship leaving Quebec would take an Englishwoman.

Suddenly, she bolted upright. Enoch and Israel! They had come to her for help to escape. She would help them, and they could help her. Even if she could not leave Quebec, at least she would be able to get information to Governor Dudley in Boston so that he could mount a counterattack on the French. She would be able to exact some revenge in that way.

She sniffed and dried her eyes. Somehow, she would have to lull Monsieur le Comte de la Lupe into believing that she had accepted her fate. It could not be done immediately, for she had been too enraged for him to believe that she would give in so quickly. No, it would take several days. Gradually, she would make him think she had accepted the French as her own people. Meanwhile, she would contact Enoch and Israel and let them know she would help.

Etienne sat in his room with his feet up on a small stool and stared into the fire. His hands, resting on the arms of the chair, were clenched into fists. He had not wanted to remind Rachel of her position as his prisoner and his revenge, but she had forced him to it with her cutting remarks and vile insults. Normally, he would have been able to shrug off such words, but coming from her, they enraged him. He had lost his temper, said things and acted in ways he should not have. That was something he had been taught not to do. She had made him lose his self-control. Hunting Dog would be displeased to hear of it.

Suddenly feeling confined by the restrictive breeches and stockings he wore, feeling contaminated in the silk shirt with its lace, he jumped up and pulled the clothes from his body. Finding his deerskin tunic and breechclout, he put them on and sat cross-legged before the fire. He needed to think, to decide what to do about the woman, Rachel Linton.

She had looked so lovely tonight when he had first

seen her. Her eyes had sparkled and her hair had blazed with its hidden color. As soon as she had realized his other identity, the blush had drained from her cheeks. Her reaction had been the one he had been dreading. Perhaps, when he had discovered her hatred of the French on their journey, he should have kept to his original plan and turned her over to his sister. One, hating the English, and the other, hating the French, would have expended their abhorrence on each other. Instead, he had turned the fool and made Rachel his woman. What was he to do with her?

He could see no lessening to her feelings about those people who had so wronged her. For that, he could not blame her. Yet, it had not been he who had killed her mother, or threatened her or her father; he had not ordered the attack on Deerfield. For him, the attack could have just as easily been on Hatfield or Greenfield, two neighboring villages. Why could she not understand that?

They were enemies once more. Although the bond of their passion held them, he knew she would try to help the other hostages in Quebec escape. She might even try to escape herself. She would need to be watched.

The idea of Rachel trying to escape made his heart twist in his chest. Despite her feelings about him and the French, he found he did not want to lose her. She had become special to him. He enjoyed waking beside her in the morning and going to sleep at night with her cuddled against him. He liked watching her when she sat across from him at meals. Her quick mind pleased him. Her passion delighted him. She had become part of his life.

She would not leave him. He would not allow it.

The following morning, they met at the breakfast table. Celeste, who served, noticed the strained atmosphere. As she retreated to the kitchen after completing her duties, Rachel noticed sourly that the girl was singing.

The meal passed in silence. It was only at the end that Etienne announced he would be away from the house all day. Despondently, Rachel nodded. Pain lanced through her at the sound of his voice. Why could it not have been different between them?

"You may ask Madame de la Roche to accompany you on a stroll if you wish," Etienne told her just before he left.

Rachel's heart jumped at his words. Schooling her face so as not to show her excitement, she glanced at him and murmured, "Thank you."

With a curt nod, Etienne was gone. Rachel noticed that he had not bestowed his usual farewell kiss on her as he left, but she pushed away her hurt. She was too busy planning how to get Madame de la Roche to the bakery on the Rue Sous-le-Fort where she could contact Enoch and Israel.

The morning dragged by. Rachel had spoken to Madame de la Roche about going for a walk through the town, but she had been told it would have to wait until afternoon. When Madame finally came out to the garden to announce that they could leave, Rachel was ready to scream from frustration.

As they strolled through the square which looked out over the lower town and the river far below, Rachel heard someone calling her name. Looking about, she saw Prudence Whitson leaning from an open barouche. Her blonde curls bobbed from beneath a pink bonnet, and she waved a pink-clad arm.

"Rachel! Oh, Rachel!" she called. She told her driver to stop. Before her carriage halted, she was out and running towards Rachel. "Oh, Rachel! It is so good to see you!"

Rachel was enveloped in flounces of pink muslin and white lace as Prudence hugged her.

"It's good to see you, too, Prudence," Rachel smiled. "You're looking very well. How are you faring?"

"Oh, Rachel! I've met the most wonderful man! After that dreadful march through the mountains and such, I thought I might die. Those savages made us walk so far and starved us. My poor skin suffered so, I thought I would never get it soft again. But when we reached Montreal, I met Captain de Beaucours, and he was so-o-o gallant. We fell in love and he asked me to marry him!"

Rachel laughed. Prudence would always end up with the handsomest or most gallant of men. Rachel wondered about brave, strong Aldridge whom Prudence had left behind in New England, but decided it was best if she held her tongue on the matter.

"That's wonderful, Prudence," Rachel told her. "I wish you all the best."

"We are on our way to visit Governor de Vaudreuil. Isn't that exciting?" Prudence gushed.

"Yes, it is. I met him last night. He is very charming."

"Oh." Prudence drooped the tiniest bit in disappointment when she discovered Rachel had been presented before her.

"What happened to Elspeth?" Rachel asked. "Is she all right?"

Prudence waved her arm airily. "Oh, Elspeth was adopted by some French family in Montreal. They dote on her." She looked closely at Rachel and whispered, "What ever became of you and that savage with the blue eyes?"

"Oh, we had many adventures, but, as you can see, I am unharmed," Rachel answered vaguely. To herself she added, Unharmed on the outside.

Before Prudence could question her further, the young man who had been riding in the barouche with Prudence came up beside her and touched her elbow.

"Come, *chérie,*" he murmured in Prudence's ear. "We must go."

Prudence giggled. "Did you hear that?" she asked Rachel. "*Chérie.* Isn't that the sweetest thing you ever heard?" Turning to the captain, she blew him a kiss. He helped her climb back into the barouche "Goodbye, Rachel," she waved. "Come to visit us in Montreal if you can."

Rachel watched them drive off. She wondered what Mr. Williams would have to say about Prudence and her French soldier husband. Prudence was obviously very happy. Would the reverend try to make her return to her English ways and spoil her happiness? She hoped not.

Madame de la Roche spoke then. "Your friend seems quite happy. It is good that *some* of the English have been able to find happiness with us."

331

Rachel glanced at her sharply. Was there some hidden meaning beneath the woman's words? Did she know of the great chasm that had opened between her and Etienne? Madame de la Roche smiled guilelessly at Rachel and began walking.

"Come, *mademoiselle,*" she said. "You wished to see the lower town. We must hurry if I am to get back in time to cook dinner for *le seigneur.*"

They crossed the square and walked along the clifftop for a while before following a steep, winding road that curved down to the riverbank. Although this was easier to traverse than the stairs, it took longer to get to the lower town. There would not be much time left for searching for the Rue Sous-le-Fort.

As it happened, they soon passed the street Rachel was looking for. Casually, she remarked to Madame de la Roche, "What is down here? Let us go this way."

Madame de la Roche shrugged. "It is nothing but bakeries and pastry shops."

"Oh, let's just wander past them. I love the smell of fresh things baking," Rachel said.

They had walked partway down the street when a man carrying a large sack of flour almost knocked them down. Indignantly, Madame de la Roche began to berate him for his clumsiness. He dropped the sack at his feet and straightened to apologize.

"Enoch!" Rachel exclaimed. "It is you under all that flour."

Enoch bobbed his head. "Rachel," he acknowledged. He turned to Madame de la Roche. *"Pardon, madame,* for being such an oaf. I did not see you."

Madame de la Roche sniffed and turned away. In that instant, Rachel met Enoch's eyes and nodded quickly. Enoch nodded back in satisfaction.

*Tomorrow,* Enoch mouthed silently.

"Come, *mademoiselle,*" Madame de la Roche prodded. "The man has work to do."

"It is good to see you Enoch," Rachel said. "You seem busy. We won't keep you."

She and Madame de la Roche turned away and continued their walk. It was late afternoon by the time they returned to the house. Etienne was still not home, so Rachel went to her room and closed the door. She had to think.

The meeting with Enoch had gone so smoothly that she had been elated. Now, however, dark thoughts assailed her. Doubts crowded into her mind. What she was about to do would widen the rift between her and Etienne. It would mark forever the difference between them. She was declaring herself, once and always, to be English, forever the enemy of the French.

The thought depressed her. Last night, when she had made up her mind to help Enoch and Israel, she had been reacting to White Wolf's betrayal of her. Now, in the light of day, now that she had set the events in motion, she was not so sure this was what she wanted to do. She had missed sleeping with Etienne, of feeling his hard body pressed up against her. She had missed his smile of greeting in the morning. She had missed his warmth and companionship. By helping Enoch and Israel, she would forever be bereft of any closeness with Etienne, for once he discovered what she had done, he would send her away.

"But he is French," she murmured to the looking glass.

He is your lover, that little voice inside her head whispered.

"No," she groaned as she covered her ears and sank onto one of the chairs before the hearth.

The connecting door swung open then and Etienne's voice said, "So, you are here. I thought I heard your voice. Is there something amiss?"

Rachel's head snapped up at his entrance. "N-no," she stammered. "Nothing is amiss."

"Good. Then perhaps you will accompany me to Vespers after our meal."

"Vespers?" Rachel echoed. She knew this was evening prayer for those who were inclined to popery. "No. I don't think I should."

"Oh? Why is that?" Etienne inquired.

"Because I do not believe in the superstitious nonsense spouted by your papist priests."

"I see," Etienne nodded. "I think you should come anyway. Look upon it as a new experience." With that, he backed out of the door and closed it.

Rachel sat back in her chair and stared at the door in the wall as if by her very look she could inflict harm on the man who held her. She knew that if she refused to accompany him, he would carry her to the church, and if she struggled too much, he would bind her. Despite his being French, he was also White Wolf, the woodsman who brought her through the wilderness. Her doubts about helping Enoch and Israel vanished in a puff of heated ire.

After dinner, which was a silent affair, Rachel met

Etienne in the foyer of the little house. Smiling benignly, he held out his arm to her. Stiffly, Rachel accepted it. She would go with him, but she would not be happy about it.

They walked the few blocks to the church and entered. Rachel had never been in a Romish church before and was astounded at the richness of it. The light of a multitude of candles was reflected by the array of gold and silver that decorated the altar of the church.

A bell rang and everyone stood. A priest entered who swung an incense burner. He was followed by other priests in their flowing robes, all of rich satins and silks shot through with threads of gold and silver. Male voices chanted verses in Latin. The pomp and ceremony of the proceedings were so different from the simple services Rachel was used to in Deerfield. When it was all over and they were leaving, Rachel was still overwhelmed by what she had witnessed.

Etienne and Rachel strolled along on their way back home. Noticing her silence, he asked, "What did you think of Vespers?"

"It was all so formal, so ritualized. How can you believe God wants or enjoys all that?" she observed.

Etienne shrugged. "Who knows what God wants? Do you, or does anyone?"

"God wants us to read the Bible," Rachel stated with conviction. "Those are His words. I don't believe that He wants us to worship Him with all that ceremony and richness."

"Perhaps, perhaps not."

"How can you say that?" Rachel demanded. "You pray to the Great Spirit in the woods and wear practically nothing!"

Etienne chuckled. "Who is to say how God wishes that we worship Him? He made many different types of people. Should they not all worship Him in their own way? It is, after all, the same God."

Rachel thought about that. Perhaps he was right. Perhaps Reverend Williams was being too narrow in his views, although he certainly had a right to them. The man walking beside her straddled two worlds, both of whom honored their God in a very different way, both of whom thought theirs was the correct way. Which one was correct? The way of the Penobscot, or the French, or the way of the English? Rachel did not know. But in one thing Etienne was correct: It was the same God.

They arrived home and Etienne escorted Rachel up the stairs. She was surprised that he entered her room with her. A truce seemed to have been struck between them on their walk home from church.

As Rachel pulled off her bonnet and placed it on a shelf in the wardrobe, he came up behind her and placed his hands on her shoulders. She felt his lips nibble at the curve of her neck. A warm throbbing began between her thighs.

Should she allow him what he so obviously wanted? she wondered. Would it be right to make love with this man whom she planned to betray? She had missed his lovemaking, had wanted to feel him touch her.

His hands slipped down to cup her breasts. Achingly sweet, her nipples hardened beneath his touch. Her eyes closed in pleasure.

"A truce, English," he murmured.

Yes, she decided, a truce. She would make love with him. Just this one last time. She had done nothing yet with Enoch and Israel. She had not truly betrayed him yet. His mouth was making her pulse do strange things. It was too late to deny him. He had her bodice undone. His hands were inside her chemise. Yes, she decided as she turned to face him. She would make love with him.

## Chapter Twenty-two

The following morning, Rachel awoke alone in the bed. She stared up at the canopy over her head and thought about the night before. Her love-making with Etienne had been wonderfully satisfying, but it had contained an element of desperation. Both of them had felt it. Both of them knew they craved the touch of the other, yet forces pulled them apart.

Rachel sighed. How could she feel so about a man who was her enemy? she wondered. How could she want him so badly yet at the same time hate him for what he was, for what his people had done to her? She did not know. Sighing again, she threw back the covers and climbed out of bed.

Today, she would hear from Enoch. He would let her know when and where they were to meet to plan the escape. Somehow, she had to be able to leave the house when the time came.

Dressing quickly, she went downstairs. She could hear Celeste and her mother in the kitchen. Their voices were raised in what sounded like an argument, but the words were indistinct. When Rachel entered the kitchen, they immediately quieted. Celeste turned sullenly to cleaning a chicken for dinner, and Madame de la Roche, after giving her daughter a hard look, turned to Rachel with a smile.

"Good morning," the woman greeted her. "Did you sleep well? Monsieur le Comte had to leave early. He had business with the Governor. He said he would be home for dinner." As she spoke, she sliced some fresh bread and placed it with cheese, peach preserve and a large mug of milk on the table in the middle of the kitchen. "Eat, *mademoiselle*. We have already had our breakfast."

Rachel sat before the food but found she had little appetite. Her stomach was tied in knots. Picking at the bread, she said to Madame de la Roche, "Is there anything that I can do to help you and Celeste? I feel I should be doing something."

"So, the high and mighty English lady grows tired of lazing about all day and servicing Monsieur le Comte at night," Celeste sneered.

Madame de la Roche's hand snapped out and slapped her daughter across the mouth. "Celeste!" she exclaimed, horrified. "You will apologize to Mademoiselle Rachel immediately."

"I will not!" Celeste sent a hate-filled look at Rachel. "Until *she* came Etienne liked me best. He was going to ask me to be his wife. I know he was!"

"How dare you speak of Monsieur le Comte with such familiarity! Be glad that he is not about to hear you."

"He wanted me to call him that. He told me so himself. He was going to marry me!" Tears threatened to spill out of Celeste's eyes and down her cheeks.

"He was never going to marry you, you silly girl," Madame told her daughter. "He was arranging a marriage for you with a captain in the governor's guard. But now, since you are so foolish, he may wed you to François Boule."

"But he raises pigs!" Celeste exclaimed.

Madame de la Roche nodded. "Where else would a foolish girl belong who believes she is good enough to wed Monsieur le Comte except in a pigsty?"

Celeste sent an anguished look at her mother and Rachel, threw down her knife, and rushed out the back door of the house. There was silence in the kitchen for a moment, then Madame de la Roche returned to churning butter.

"I am sorry for causing so much trouble," Rachel apologized.

"Nonsense," Madame de la Roche declared. "It is we who should apologize. It must be very difficult for you being brought here among strangers." She shook her head. "My daughter has always had the airs. I knew she was fond of Monsieur le Comte, but I never thought she would go so far. You see, they have known each other all their lives. When they were little, Celeste never paid much attention to Etienne because he was more interested in his Indian friends. But then he was sent to France by his father. When he returned, he had become a man, handsome and worldly. Celeste had eyes for no other. I should have put an end to the infatuation sooner, but . . ." She shrugged.

So, White Wolf had been sent to France to learn the devious ways and charming manners of the French. That explained the appearance of the suave man who escorted her to the dinner party at the governor's house.

Despite her hatred of his countrymen, she could not keep a thrill of excitement from running through her at the memory of seeing him dressed in the height of fashion for the first time. She could not decide which mode of dress made him more attractive—that of the Penobscot, or that of the French.

Rachel poked at the peach preserves on her plate with a piece of bread. Perhaps Celeste still might snag Monsieur le Comte, she thought. When Etienne discovered that she plotted to help Enoch and Israel escape, he would probably want nothing more to do with her. In his anger, he might very well turn to the welcoming arms and soft body of Celeste.

She found she did not like that idea at all. In her mind's eyes she could see Etienne and Celeste together. They were in the room which was now hers. They were kissing. They were rolling about in passion on the bed on which she and Etienne had made love. Rachel squeezed shut her eyes to block out the vision.

She could not think of that. She had decided on her course of action. She had to thwart the French. She had to help Enoch and Israel. Even if it meant destroying herself.

That afternoon, the rest of the shoes and gloves and hats arrived which Etienne had ordered for her. Despondently, she opened the packages. She should have been happy and joyful at receiving so many beautiful things. Instead, her heart was heavy at what she was about to do.

As she was opening the last box which contained a lovely lace fan, Madame de la Roche came to tell her that she had a visitor. With her heart pounding in her chest in anticipation at what she was about to do, Rachel followed the woman down the stairs and to the salon. When she entered, Reverend Williams stood to greet her.

"Mr. Williams!" Rachel exclaimed. "What a pleasant surprise!"

"The governor gave me leave to visit you, child, but only for a short time. How are you faring? Is everything well with you?"

"Everything is fine," Rachel told him as they settled themselves in chairs. A movement behind her made her look about quickly. A handsome young soldier bowed to her then moved back to a corner of the room. Rachel looked inquiringly at the reverend.

"He is my escort," Mr. Williams explained. "I am not allowed to go anywhere without one." He smiled. "The French believe that I could subvert their government here all by myself."

"Then they know you very well, sir," Rachel teased.

The minister chuckled. "Well, perhaps. It does my heart good to see you Rachel. Are you being treated well?"

Rachel nodded. "Quite well, thank you."

"Are you allowed to read your Bible?"

Rachel hesitated. She had never been one to read the Good Book much, even in Deerfield. "I do not have one to read," she finally answered.

"I thought not. I have been allowed to bring one for you." He handed her the book he held in his hand. "You will find Acts of the Apostles, chapter twenty-two, verse ten, most interesting and uplifting."

Rachel thanked him and put the book aside. The minister was always exhorting her to read this passage or that from the Bible. She found his spiritual reliance on it somewhat ethereal and not quite suited to mundane living.

"Have you heard from any of your children?" she asked, changing the subject.

Sadness crossed the reverend's face. "I fear my children are in dire straits. Eunice, my youngest girl still living, is with the Mohawks. Esther has been ransomed by a French family and is living with them, but my two boys, Stephen and Warham, are with the Jesuits and are constantly being abused by them to compel them to turn to the popist faith. They are sorely tried, as we are all."

"Oh, Mr. Williams, I am so sorry," Rachel exclaimed. "Perhaps if I speak with Monsieur le Comte he might put in a word with the Governor to have your children brought to you."

"I have spoken to the Governor myself, child. He is doing all he can. But who is this Monsieur Le Comte?"

Rachel explained the story of White Wolf's transformation into a French nobleman.

When she had finished, Mr. Williams exclaimed, "I knew he was more than a simple savage! You must be very careful, child, that his smooth ways do not turn you from your own people. I know living in his house must be very painful for you. I am sure he has tried to force himself on you without the blessing of God. He will force you to convert to his superstitious ways and marry him in his religion."

Rachel, bowing her head, said nothing. In the eyes of the Penobscot, she was already wed to the man. Yet, in the eyes of the French, and the English, she was living in sin. Who was right, she wondered, and what did Etienne believe? Guilt washed through her for the first

343

time. She had been brought up to give herself to a man only after exchanging vows with him. Had those few words spoken in the cave in the middle of nowhere in front of no witnesses been enough to bind her to Etienne in the eyes of God? She did not know.

"You must be strong, Rachel," the reverend was saying. "You must get down on your knees and pray to God that you may be saved. You must not allow this spawn of the devil who holds you to turn you from the true path. I know your father was not a staunch believer, but he certainly would not want you besmirched by these idolators and disciples of superstition. You must pray."

"I will do my best, Mr. Williams," Rachel murmured. Silently, she wondered how the beauty of what she and Etienne had shared together could be displeasing to God. It was too wonderful.

The guard stepped forward then. Mr. Williams glanced up at him, then said to Rachel, "My time with you has come to an end, I am afraid." He stood. "Remember my words, my child, and read the verse I suggested to you. It will bring you peace."

Mr. Williams and his guard left then. Rachel picked up her Bible and climbed the stairs to her room. The minister's words about her relationship with Etienne weighed on her. Despite the joy she had felt when Marie had explained the meaning of the gift of the moccasins and wampum bracelet, still she could not forget that there had been no vows exchanged between her and Etienne. Was she living in sin or not? She did not know.

Tossing the Bible on the bed, she went to stand at the window and gazed out at nothing. It really did not matter, she decided. Soon, she would betray Etienne, and he would have nothing more to do with her. He would send her away to some other Frenchman, or give her to Dark Eagle. Then she would not be able to worry about sin. She would have to do what she could to stay alive.

She turned away from the window with a sigh. Enoch would contact her today. Somehow, she would have to occupy her mind so that she would not reveal her anxiety. The Bible caught her attention. Reverend Williams twice mentioned a passage from the Bible.

Picking up the book, she turned to the Acts of the Apostles, chapter twenty-two. A piece of paper was stuck between the pages. Rachel read: *Large Warehouse. Docks. Two hours before sunset.*

Excitement and dread ran through her at the same time. This was the message she had been waiting for. Two hours before sunset she was to meet Enoch and Israel and help them plan their escape. If they planned well and carefully, soon the men would be on their way to Boston to bring Governor Dudley help in an attack on the French.

Crumpling the paper in her hand, she glanced down at the open page of the Bible. She scanned to find verse ten. It read: *And I said, What shall I do, Lord? And the Lord said unto me, Arise, and go into Damascus; and there it shall be told thee of all things which are appointed for thee to do.*

Rachel laughed softly. Mr. Williams always had a verse from the Bible for every occasion, even for planning an escape.

Rachel occupied her time for the rest of the day by helping Madame de la Roche with chores about the house. She discovered the woman had been the wife of one of the tenants on Etienne's seigneury. When her husband had died, Etienne suggested that she and her daughter move from the farm and take over the care of his house in Quebec. She had been housekeeper for him for eight years.

When it drew close to the time for Rachel to meet with Enoch and Israel, she debated whether she should say anything about leaving the house to Madame de la Roche, or whether she should just go out without a word. There were good and bad points about each course of action. If she made her intentions known, then Madame de la Roche might forbid her to go out alone, but it would help take away suspicion from her movements. If she left without a word, then she would have the freedom of being by herself, yet her actions would appear suspicious. She finally decided to announce her intention to go out as she was leaving.

Putting on her bonnet and a light shawl, she stopped by the kitchen where Madame de la Roche was bending over a pot over the fire. "I am going for a walk, madame," she said. "If Monsieur le Comte arrives back before me, tell him I will be home in time for dinner."

She quickly turned away and hurried to the front door. As she closed the door behind her, she heard Madame de la Roche calling after her. Rachel ran to the street and ducked around the corner. She would pretend she had not heard the woman.

Rachel made her way to the long flight of stairs which connected the upper town with the lower. She stood at the top and looked down. The height was dizzying, but she did not have time to go the long way about by the road. Taking a deep breath, she began her descent.

After negotiating the long staircase, she discovered

that finding the docks and the warehouse was a simple matter. Wending her way through the narrow streets, she soon came to the river's edge and the several docks which pushed out above the water. The largest of the warehouses was at the far end of the dock area.

Rachel had been so intent on finding her way that she had not paid much attention to the other people she passed. Now, however, she realized that this dock was like any other. It was populated with rough seamen who had not glimpsed a woman for months, *coureurs de bois* who had been living in the wilderness all winter, and sundry other men who frequented the area for their own purposes, legitimate or otherwise. There were few women about, and those whom she saw were accompanied by a gentleman escort. Keeping her eyes forward and quickening her steps, she hurried to the warehouse for her meeting.

It was with a great deal of relief that she finally slipped through the large opening and into the dim interior of the building. Glancing about at the piles of crates and barrels, she wondered where Enoch and Israel were.

"Psst," she heard from her right. "Psst, Rachel, over here."

Squinting in that direction through the gloom, she saw Israel beckoning to her from behind a pile of beaver skins. She hurried to meet him. He led her around the pile and further back into the warehouse. Enoch was standing next to hogheads of wine. A candle, stuck in its own melted wax, lent some light to the area.

"I wish you could have picked a better place to meet," Rachel grumbled as she pulled her shawl tighter about her shoulders.

Enoch shrugged. "It was the only place where we could have some privacy and not arouse suspicion. Israel and I are here to pick up a shipment of sugar for our master."

Rachel frowned. "That is very well for you, Enoch, but if I am discovered here, suspicions will be aroused."

"We're sorry, Rachel," Israel apologized. "Next time we'll try to find a better place to meet."

Enoch threw a disgusted glance at Israel, then to Rachel he said, "You can always say that you lost your way."

Rachel was annoyed at his cavalier manner. "Since it is almost impossible to lose one's way in this town, that excuse will not be believed. Never mind, I am here now. What is it you want of me?"

"You know some of the Indians," Enoch began. "We will need a canoe and a guide. We want to head upriver to Sorel and then into Lake Champlain and then overland to the Connecticut River."

Rachel stared at him. "You are crazy. Both of you. You will die before you reach any of the English settlements."

"That is for us to worry about," Enoch said. "Will you help us or not?"

"I don't know what I can do. I can not speak the language of the Indians, and I certainly can't get them to trust me enough to get one of them as a guide for you."

Enoch and Israel glanced at each other. "We can get a guide ourselves," Enoch confessed to her. "One of the residents of Quebec has offered to help us. What we need from you is information about the soldiers in the town and the Governor's guard. For instance, you can tell us when the guard changes, when it is the least vigilant, and if there will be any holiday celebrations. These would be the best times for us to sneak out of the town."

"Why can't this resident of the town help you with that information?" she asked. "Wouldn't he know these things better?"

"He said that the Comte de la Lupe is an advisor to the Governor, and since you are living with him, you would be able to find out this information quicker," Israel told her.

Rachel looked from one man to the other. Both wore expressions of expectancy. Both were determined to carry out their plan. A feeling of dread overtook her. Something was not right. Their decision to escape, although brave, was foolhardy. In the rush of resentment she had felt against Etienne for his silence about his complete identity, she had agreed to something that would bring these men to harm.

"Are you certain that you want to risk your lives to do this?" she asked them.

Doubt crossed Israel's face, but Enoch declared, "We will not die. We will reach Boston with our information."

Rachel sighed in defeat. "All right. I will see what I can find out for you."

Rachel left them after making arrangements to meet again in four days. She returned quickly to Etienne's house, for the sun was beginning to set. A cool breeze came in off the river, and she hugged her shawl about her. For the first time in many weeks, she felt very alone and frightened. Something about the plan of Enoch and Israel bothered her, yet she could not decide what it was. More than the fact that she would be betraying

Etienne, something caused a feeling of dread to hang over her.

When she entered the house and passed the doorway to the salon, Etienne's voice said, "I am glad to see you, English." His tone, although on the surface sounded friendly enough, had a hard edge beneath.

Rachel stopped on her way to the stairs, turned and entered the room. "I wanted some fresh air before dinner," she said casually as she removed her bonnet. "I did not think you would mind my taking a walk."

"I do not want you wandering the streets by yourself," he told her. "You are not familiar with the town. There are dangers for a woman alone."

"More than what one would find in the wilderness or in one's bed during an attack by the French?" she asked sharply.

Those blue eyes which had become so familiar to her blazed, and he rose to his feet. "You would not be so insolent if you happened upon some of the residents of this town who do not look kindly upon the English. An Englishwoman out alone is fair game for their mischief."

"Are you actually concerned for my welfare, White Wolf?" she taunted, using his Penobscot name purposely. "After all this time and all you have done to me? I am touched by your compassion."

Etienne grabbed her by the arms and shook her. "You will not leave this house alone, *English*," he snarled. "I will not have my *revenge* damaged."

"Have no fear of that, Monsieur le Comte de la Lupe. I would not dream of depriving you the satisfaction of using your revenge to the fullest." Rachel raised her chin defiantly and stared at him with tear-filled eyes. "I am here at your whim, to do with as you please." Jerking out of his grasp, she turned to flee the room.

"Rachel . . ." he called, but she had gone.

He sank down into the chair he had just vacated. Why was it that they were at such odds? he wondered. Why could she not see that he was not like the man who had murdered her mother? His attack on her village had been the result of long years of pain. He had come to see that perhaps he had been wrong in holding his hatred for so long. Rachel had made him see that. Why could she not see that she was doing the same? That her hatred of all Frenchmen was wrong?

He closed his eyes and leaned his head against the chairback. He had taken her to wife in the manner of his mother's people. If he had not felt deeply about her, he would not have done such a thing. Certainly, she must know how he felt about her. Yet, she could not see beyond the fact that part of him was French. Perhaps it would be better if he let her return to her own people when the time came.

No! His hands clenched into fists. He would never let her return. She was his. His woman. She would have to learn to accept him for what he was—Penobscot and French. There had once been gentle feelings for him within her. Somehow, he would have to bring those gentle feelings back. But in the meantime, she was making him as crazy as the loon.

# Chapter Twenty-three

Etienne stood at the window of the small reception room in the Château de Saint-Louis. His arms were crossed at his chest and his feet were planted slightly apart. It was a pose familiar to him, one he used whether wearing deerskin or velvet. Below him, people passed on the street. Some strolled, some hurried past, but he was not really interested in the scene before him.

Behind him, Governor de Vaudreuil and Father Meriel, a spokesman for the Superior of the Jesuits, argued about the fate of the English hostages.

"I wish the hostages ransomed as soon as it is possible," the Governor stated. "I have expressed this opinion to your Superior and His Excellency the Bishop many times. They know my feelings on this."

*"Mon Seigneur,* neither man questions your motives. They are only questioning the wisdom of sending unredeemed souls back into the land of heresy known as New England." The priest's tone was quiet and unctuous.

"I need the revenue. New France needs the revenue from the ransom of these people," de Vaudreuil argued.

"If you priests can not convert these people in the time it takes to send to Dudley in Boston and receive an answer from him, then perhaps you do not know your job."

"Please, *mon Seigneur,* there is no need to be insulting."

"Insulting!" the governor almost shouted. "It is I who am insulted. Neither the Bishop nor your Superior thought my position important enough to come themselves. No, instead they send a mere priest."

"I am only doing as I am asked," Father Meriel said humbly. "Since you would not talk to either Father Superior or His Excellency the Bishop the last time they came to speak with you, they requested that I come to ask you to change your mind. All they ask is that you delay sending the hostages back as soon as you receive word and ransom from Boston. Father Superior and His Excellency the Bishop are merely concerned about the state of these souls. They have no wish to see them burn in Hell for all eternity when there is the opportunity to save them."

"Neither do I wish to see them burn in Hell, father," the governor sighed tiredly. "But you will have to save them in the time you have."

"I am afraid that is not acceptable to either Father Superior or His Excellency the Bishop," Father Meriel answered sadly.

"So be it," the Governor acknowledged. "Since I control the army, I will do what I think best. Tell Father Superior and His Excellency the Bishop that."

Conceding temporary defeat, Father Meriel bowed and left. When the door had closed behind him, the governor asked Etienne, "What do you think? Am I being too stubborn?"

Etienne shrugged, but did not take his eyes from the scene before him. "You might compromise," he suggested. "Keep the English minister and a few others and trade them for Captain Baptiste. Since the English believe Baptiste is a pirate, they will hesitate some time before they agree to release him. The priests will at least have some of the English to torment for a longer period, and you will reap the ransom for most of the hostages." The figure of a woman hurrying down the street caught his eyes. Curls of dark auburn hair showed beneath her bonnet.

"That is an excellent idea," the governor agreed. "I will offer that suggestion the next time those meddlesome priests come to harass me." He rubbed his hands together. "This calls for a celebration. Send for your charming young lady and we shall dine together."

Etienne turned his head, scanning up and down the street. The man he had watching Rachel was nowhere in sight. The vixen had eluded him. Obviously, she was on her way to meet with those English friends of hers.

"I am afraid I must decline your invitation, Governor," Etienne told him as he turned from the window. "I have just remembered a pressing engagement." Bowing quickly, he hurried from the room.

"A pressing engagement?" Governor de Vaudreuil muttered to the four walls. "What could be more pressing than dining with the governor?"

Rachel walked along the street and tried not to run. She had seen the man who dogged her steps, had known that he was there at Etienne's request. It had not been easy outwitting the man and escaping from his watchful eyes. She feared he would find her again and prevent her meeting with Enoch and Israel.

This would be their last meeting. She had come to that decision the day before when Reverend Williams had visited her again and delivered the message that she was to meet with them on this afternoon. Although Enoch and Israel still had not formed a definite plan, she felt she could not help them any longer. She could not betray Etienne. She loved him.

Rachel knew she was running a terrible risk by going to the meeting, but she felt she owed Enoch and Israel an explanation. They had been neighbors in Deerfield; they were English in this town of all Frenchmen. Yet, by going to the meeting, she was tempting fate. The thought of Etienne discovering her deception on this last time made her very nervous. If only she could get this over with and be home before he ever found out . . .

She and Etienne had barely spoken to each other since that confrontation after her first meeting with her English friends. He had not forbidden her coming and going from the house. He had instead had her watched wherever she went. They dined together, but in silence; they slept in separate rooms. Rachel felt the pain of his coldness deeply within her. She missed his warm gaze, the smile that lit up his face. She missed his touch, and the feel of his body pressed against hers as they drifted off to sleep together.

The realization that her hatred of the French had nothing to do with Etienne had come slowly. It had begun when she heard him call her name after their argument. The hesitant, sad note underlying his strong tone had pulled at her heart. She had ignored his call that day, being too frightened of what she was about to do to him and too angry at the words they had exchanged. Yet, slowly, over the next several days, she had come to know that no matter where she was, either in Quebec, in France, or even back in Deerfield, she would always love this man.

She came to the long flight of stairs which led down to the lower town. The many steps had become familiar to her now. Although she still cringed when she stood at the top of them, she could now negotiate them with some speed. Stepping finally on solid ground once more, She gave a quick sigh of relief before she hurried to the warehouse where she was to meet Enoch and Israel.

The dim interior was the same as before. "Enoch, Israel, I'm here," she called. "Where are you?"

The light of a candle flared behind a high pile of crates. "Here," a voice answered.

Rachel pulled off her bonnet as she made her way to the far side of the crates. She stopped and squinted past the glare of the candle. A single figure stood back from the light.

"Israel? Enoch? Is that you?" she asked.

The figure nodded and beckoned her closer, motioning her to be quiet. Rachel moved past the candle.

"Why all the secrecy?" she demanded with a nervous little laugh. "Why are you wearing that dark hat and cloak?"

The man before her stepped into the pool of light. "There is no need for secrecy any longer," he said.

Rachel stared at him. This was no one she knew, yet something was familiar about the man. Suddenly, she gasped and fell back a step. The bonnet fell unheeded from her fingers.

"Henri Renaud!" she exclaimed.

The man bowed before her. "At your service, *mademoiselle.*"

"What . . . How . . . What are you doing here?" she stammered.

"Why, I live in Quebec, and this is my warehouse. Rather, I should ask you what you are doing here."

Rachel fell back another step. "It was a mistake. I was to meet someone, but I think I am confused as to the correct place. Forgive me for intruding on your property." She turned to flee.

Renaud caught her by the arm. "Do not leave, Rachel. There is nothing to forgive. I offered the use of my warehouse to your two English friends, but alas, I fear they will have no more use for it."

"What have you done to them?" Panic turned her cold.

"I have done nothing to them," Renaud chuckled. "It is only that their dream for escape will not become reality. Their plans have encountered a setback. You did not believe that I would actually help two Englishmen escape, did you?"

"You were the resident of the town who was helping them!" Rachel accused. She tried to pull her arm out of his grasp.

"Of course. When I saw you at the Governor's ball, I thought we might conclude our unfinished business."

"I have no business with you, you murderer!" She struggled to free herself from him. Fear had clotted in her middle.

"Do not struggle so. I do not wish to hurt you — yet."

He laughed a cold, evil laugh. "Do you know, your mother tried to struggle, too. She would not stop. A pity, for I did not wish to bruise her. Poor Honora. I wanted her to be beautiful in death. She was a very beautiful woman." As he spoke, he pulled Rachel across the floor to the doorway of the warehouse.

"The murder of someone is not beautiful. You are mad!" Horror made Rachel struggle harder.

Renaud turned his malicious, dark eyes on her and smiled with delight. "Oh, quite mad," he agreed. "But you see, Governor de Vaudreuil enjoys the fruits of my little trips to New England too much, and so he puts up with my little idiosyncrasies." He glanced out the doorway, then back at Rachel. "Come, Rachel, it is safe to leave now."

"No!" Rachel hung back, her fingers clawing for a hold on the wooden wall of the building. "No! I won't go anywhere with you!"

A knife appeared in Renaud's free hand and, almost gently, he placed the point at her throat. "You will come with me." His voice was toneless, evil.

Rachel had no doubt that he would slit her throat right there if she did not comply. If she went with him calmly, then perhaps she might find an opportunity to escape. Etienne might even discover her whereabouts. If for nothing else, he would probably want her back as his revenge.

Swallowing hard and giving her head a little nod, she said, "I will go with you. Please, don't hurt me."

Renaud smiled. "Do you know, your mother said those exact words?" Slipping one arm about her waist, he held the knife to her side beneath her shawl with his other hand. "Come, Rachel. We will walk down to the river's edge as if we were lovers. I think we make a delightful couple, don't you agree?"

Rachel stumbled along beside the man who had murdered her mother. She would have fallen several times had it not been for his tight grip about her. Longing to cry out for help to the few men they passed, she dared not. The point of Renaud's knife pricked her skin where he held it to her side.

They came to a large canoe which had been dragged up onto the shore. An Indian squatted beside it. He was not of the Penobscot, for his dress was quite different from the men of White Wolf's village. When they approached, he stood and steadied the canoe as Renaud forced Rachel to climb in. The Indian and Renaud climbed in after her.

As they slipped out into the current of the river, Rachel craned her neck for a last glimpse of Quebec. Somewhere in that town, Etienne, her love, waited for her. Pain and remorse rushed through her. She had never told him she loved him. Now, she might never get the chance.

At a harsh order from Renaud, she turned her eyes to the front. She would have to repress that pain. She could not allow it to make her weak. Her survival depended upon it. If it was humanly possible, she would escape from this madman. And if she did, one day, she would be able to tell Etienne about her love.


Etienne stood on the road which curved down to the lower town. The roofs of the houses and shops were jumbled together on one side. On the other, the riverbank stretched away to blend into the countryside. Below and in front of him, a couple hurried to the water's edge where a canoe and Indian guide waited.

The thick mass of Rachel's hair was unmistakable. It caught the light of the setting sun and flamed with its inner fire. In all the activity of the town, he had not thought to come upon her unexpectedly like this. He had assumed that he would have had to ask after her and follow her from place to place. Instead, she was there, in person, running from him with some other man.

His hands clenched into fists at his side. He fought to bring the emotions which surged through him under control. Rage like nothing he had ever felt made his blood boil. Pain at her deception gnawed within him. He clenched his teeth against the wild animal cry that clawed for release in his throat. Nothing would make him reveal the power this woman held over him.

He glanced superficially at the man whose arm was so intimately twined about Rachel's waist. The man's dark, wide-brimmed hat and his dark cloak concealed any distinguishing features, yet there was something vaguely familiar about his posture, his gait. Dismissing the man as inconsequential, Etienne turned his eyes once more upon his woman.

They had climbed into the canoe and were setting out upon the river. Rachel gripped the sides of the tiny craft. He remembered her unease when they had first come out onto the river upon arriving in Quebec. The river had opened before them in all its wide splendor. Then, too, she had gripped the sides of the canoe until her knuckles were white. He had admired her courage and self-control in her silence. Now, he hated her for it. She was able to put aside her unease enough to travel upon the river with this other man, the man she had obviously chosen in place of him.

He watched them as the canoe caught the current of the river. She turned once and cast her eyes back on the town she was fleeing. What was that strange expression that crossed her face? Sadness? Or hate? Then she faced front again, towards her new life with that other man.

She was gone. His hostage, his revenge. His woman. Woodenly, he turned to retrace his steps. He would return to his house, but nothing was there for him any longer. There was nothing for him anywhere. No matter where he went he would always see Rachel. Except France. Perhaps in the glittering city of Paris he might find a way to erase her from his mind. But now, he wanted to do nothing. He could not face the idea of preparations for a trip of that length. He could not face anyone or anything. He could not face himself.

# Chapter Twenty-four

Etienne stood at the door of his house and watched the barouche drive away. An audible sigh of relief escaped his lips. The barouche carried Celeste and her new husband, a captain in the Governor's guard. Despite his black moods of the past several days, or perhaps because of them, he had made quick arrangements for the girl's marriage and seen them through to completion. Celeste had discovered Rachel's defection and had tried to replace her in his affections. Although the girl was attractive and very willing, he found he had no taste for her pouting lips or voluptuous curves. He had never really been interested in her, although he had known of her willingness to assuage his needs. Instead of Celeste's round form, he found himself dreaming of a lithe body and masses of hair of hidden fire.

As the barouche rounded a corner and turned out of sight, he became aware of two men who stood across the street and watched him. When they realized that he had noticed them, one nudged the other. Hesitantly, they crossed the street and entered his small courtyard.

Coming to a stop before him, they removed their hats nervously.

"Can I do something for you gentlemen?" he inquired unthinkingly in French.

One of the men cleared his throat. "It is about Rachel," he replied in English. "We are sorry, my lord, we do not speak your language."

Switching immediately to the men's native English, Etienne said, "It is no matter. I speak yours. What is this about Rachel?"

The men glanced at each other. One answered, "I am Enoch Cooper and this is Israel Putnam. We are worried about Rachel."

Etienne looked from one to the other of the men. Both, he knew, were hostages, taken with Rachel from Deerfield. Their faces revealed a deep concern.

"Come in, gentlemen. You ought not to be wandering about the town on your own. You could get yourselves into serious difficulty." He backed away from the door and led them into the salon. After they were all seated, he asked them, "Now, tell me what concerns you."

Enoch had been studying Etienne and he stated, "Rachel said that you are really a French count besides being an Indian."

Etienne glanced at him sharply. He could not decide if he should throw the man out for atrocious manners or laugh at his doubt. Humor won out and his lips twisted in a small smile.

"I am as she told you," he answered.

Israel sent a quelling glance in Enoch's direction. "I apologize for my friend's rudeness. He means no harm. He is only concerned for Rachel."

Etienne raised an eyebrow to hurry them to the point of their visit.

Israel pulled a folded, crumpled wad of blue muslin from inside his coat and held it out to Etienne "We found this several days ago."

Etienne took the clump of cloth. When he shook it out, he saw it was Rachel's bonnet. "How did you gentlemen happen to find this?"

Once again, the eyes of the two Englishmen met. Israel nodded encouragingly to Enoch. "We . . . ah . . ." Enoch searched the room for inspiration. Taking a deep breath, he muttered, "We found it in a warehouse near the docks."

"Ah," Etienne acknowledged and at the same time prompting them to tell more.

Israel glanced with annoyance at Enoch, then looked Etienne in the eye. "We were planning to escape, my lord," he said firmly. "I won't deny it. We are your enemies, after all."

"And Rachel?" Etienne prodded.

"That's the odd part, sir. She agreed to help us, but I don't think she really wanted to. We were to meet with her three days ago, but when we went to the warehouse, all we found was her bonnet."

Etienne did not comment on the length of time it took them to come to him with their anxieties. Instead, he told them, "I am afraid, gentlemen, that Rachel is no longer my concern, nor yours either. It seems that she escaped without your help. I saw her going upriver in a canoe with another man and an Indian guide."

"I told you we should not have trusted him," Israel accused Enoch. "He was too interested in Rachel. Something terrible has happened to her. I know it."

"Nothing terrible has happened to her," Enoch snapped. "She betrayed us. What else could you expect from a woman?"

Etienne was torn between agreeing with the man and tearing out his throat. Instead he asked Israel, "Who is this man you speak of who was so interested in Rachel?"

"Henri Renaud. He owns the warehouse where we met, and he promised us his help to escape."

Etienne gripped the arm of the chair where he sat. He knew now why the figure of the man with Rachel had been vaguely familiar. The rumors concerning Henri Renaud and his treatment of women were wild and numerous. Nothing had ever been proven, yet there was a dark side to the man's personality that Etienne did not like. Slowly, he made his fingers relax. It was none of his concern any longer. Rachel had made her choice.

"I know the man," Etienne told them. "He is devious and will stop at nothing to gain his ends. However, there is something about him that is attractive to women in some base way. Perhaps Rachel found him more appealing than returning to New England with you gentlemen."

"But, sir," Israel blurted, "don't you want her back? Isn't she your hostage? Isn't she . . ."

"Isn't she what, Mr. Putnam?" Etienne growled. "My woman?" He sprang from his seat and loomed over the Englishmen like some predatory animal. "Rachel is no longer my concern. She made her choice and disappeared with Renaud. Let her live with her decision. I believe this conversation has come to an end. The door is not difficult to find." He turned his back and stared down into the cold hearth.

Etienne heard the men rise cautiously from their chairs and move out of the room. Even after the sound of the door opening and closing reached his ears, he did not move. It was all he could do to control the urge to throw something. Henri Renaud. Of all the men in Quebec, why did she have to choose him?

A cold breath seemed to drift across his neck. Perhaps she had not chosen him at all. Perhaps he had forced her to go with him. His eye caught a flash of wrinkled blue muslin on the floor beside his foot. Slowly, he bent and picked up the ruined bonnet.

Would she have gone willingly with the man without her bonnet? Had she lost it in some sort of struggle? Or had she merely forgotten about it in the throes of passion?

With a growl of rage he hurled the bonnet away. She had chosen. She was gone. She would not come back. He knew that. He knew, too, he had probably forced her away. He should have told her how he felt about her, told her he no longer looked upon her as his revenge. But he had not. Now, it was too late. She was gone. She had made her decision.

Yet, a faint sense of danger wafted about the corners of his mind.

Four days had passed since the two Englishmen had come to see him. Four days. Four suns. He sat with his feet propped up on a small footstool before the hearth. A small fire crackled angrily and supplied the only light in the dark room. He had spent all four nights here until exhaustion forced his eyes closed for a short time of sleep filled with visions of a pair of eyes the color of the blue spruce and masses of hair of hidden fire. He would awake in a sweat, expecting to see her near, knowing finally she was not.

Hunting Dog would not have been pleased to discover that he was doing nothing, like the hare sitting, counting the snowflakes. His grandfather would expect him to put the woman out of his mind or go find her. He found he could do neither. For the first time in his life, he was afraid.

He was not afraid of Henri Renaud, nor of the trip to find him. What caused his blood to grow cold was what awaited him when he reached the end of the trail, when he stood before Rachel. Would her eyes betray her disgust of him, her rejection? Or would she be glad to see him, overjoyed to be released from the clutches of Renaud? He did not know. He was not sure he wanted to find out.

A log broke on the hearth and sent up a shower of sparks. A draft, barely detectable, made the sparks dance up the flue. Someone had stirred the air. Etienne became alert, but did not move. Silence descended once more on the room. Only the flames from the burning logs broke the quiet with their hiss and crackle.

Etienne waited for the space of five heartbeats. The moon moved across the sky; the fire blazed. Nothing else happened.

"You have journeyed far, my brother," he finally said.

A shadow detached itself and moved into the circle of light from the fire. "Not as far as you, my brother," Dark Eagle answered. He hunkered down and faced the flames. "Your travels take you beyond the voice of the People. I carry their words."

Etienne glanced sharply at Dark Eagle. For him to come himself with news and not to have sent a runner, the information must be very important and very serious.

"What do the People say, my brother?" Etienne asked.

"They mourn the deaths of two women from the village of Pesadamkik. Their bodies were left on a rock in midstream. It is now known by the People as Psinkwandissek, Scalp Rock."

Etienne jumped up from his chair and stood over Dark Eagle. "Who did this terrible thing, brother? Was it the Megwah or the Kansadakiak, those who are our enemies?"

Dark Eagle craned his neck to look up at his friend. His eyes blazed in anger as he said, "It was neither of those. It was *webalagikws,* a White Eyes. One who crawls on his belly like a snake yet struts like a turkey."

"The families will have their justice. Have they set out to hunt this snake?"

"The families have asked me to come to you. They have asked that you give them justice. This White Eyes lives in this village, where you have your lodge of stone. Your woman is not safe with him here."

Etienne's mouth went dry at the words of his friend. "My woman is no longer with me," he admitted finally. "She has . . . chosen another."

Dark Eagle was silent for a moment. "I hear pain in your words, brother, and I hear doubt. Your woman has strong medicine. Would this snake in the grass try to steal it from her?"

Etienne's eyes strayed to Dark Eagle's bow which he held propped upright on the floor. From its tip swung the lock of hair Rachel had given to him when they had left the village of the People. Would Henri Renaud try to kill her? Was it Henri Renaud who had killed the two women from the village of Pesadamkik?

"Tell me of the deaths of these two women of Pesadamkik," he said thoughtfully. "How did you learn that it was *webalagikws* who murdered them?"

Dark Eagle related the story of how the women were found scalped and left on the rock in the middle of the stream. At first, the People did think that the Megwah or the Kansadakiak had done the deed, but then one of the grandmothers of the village had noticed the women had been abused in ways that not even the Megwah would approve. It had to be a White Eyes. When Dark Eagle explained the abuse, Etienne knew for certain which White Eyes had murdered them. Henri Renaud. The man who had been with Rachel in the canoe.

"I will give the families the justice they ask," Etienne told his friend. "Will you journey with me to find this White Eyes?"

Dark Eagle bowed his head. "I will go with you, my brother."

White Wolf stripped off the coat of dark blue superfine that had fit so perfectly across his shoulders. With that action, he stripped away more than just a piece of clothing. The strictures of French society fell from his shoulders as quickly as his coat. In that moment, the fox, his spirit guide, appeared in his mind. It stood, switching its tail, gazing back at him over its shoulder. It was waiting for him to follow his destiny.

"I will prepare myself," White Wolf announced to Dark Eagle.

Dark Eagle bowed his head once again in acknowledgment. His brother had returned.


Rachel huddled against a tree and stared at the tiny campfire. The Indian guide sat immobile across the clearing. If he had not let out puffs of smoke from his pipe on occasion, Rachel would have thought him a statue. He had been almost invisible during the days they had been travelling. Rachel thought she might somehow gain his sympathy and perhaps his help to escape, but he seemed not to notice her.

She glanced about the small clearing and searched the darkness beyond the light of the fire. Henri Renaud was out of sight. He had gone on his nightly prowl about the woods. She shivered.

Rachel did not know what he did during those walks through the darkness, and she had no curiosity to find out. At some point, there would be the tormented cry of some animal that would echo through the trees, then silence. Not long after, Renaud would saunter back to the camp with a satisfied look on his face.

His return was what she dreaded the most. It was then that he would take notice of her as more than just baggage he was dragging along on this trip. Squatting beside her, he would torment her with his touch, his cruel laugh, his talk of what he would do to her, what he had done to her mother. Hearing his footsteps approach through the woods, she shivered again and tried to make herself small.

He broke from the trees and strode across the clearing in her direction. The firelight caught in his strange, dark eyes and reflected back red lights. All he needed were cloven hooves, horns, and a tail to be the embodiment of pure evil. Rachel wondered if he did not already have those features and was somehow hiding them.

Hunkering down beside her, he ran his fingers along the neckline of her chemise and rested his hand on her shoulder. "Have you thought about what I told you last night, *ma petite fleur?*" he asked seductively. "Did you think about my touch, my hands on your skin, my fingers about your throat?

Rachel ducked her head and turned her face away.

"Did you know that death coming at the moment of climax is the ultimate sexual experience?" he went on. "Your mother found that out. She was magnificent, your mother."

Rachel whipped around to face him. "You are sick!" she spat. "Sick and degenerate! Do not ever speak of my mother again!"

"Tsk, tsk," he chided. "Watch your temper, Rachel. I know you do not wish to observe another poor creature being tortured."

Rachel lowered her eyes in submission. The night before, she had fought him when he placed his hands on her. After he had subdued her and tied her to a tree, he had forced her to watch while he had staked a live squirrel to the ground and disemboweled it before her eyes. By the time she had finished retching, she was too weak to fight him off. The screams of the poor animal still echoed in her ears.

Seeing her capitulation, he smiled evilly. "There, you see? I knew you were a smart girl." He placed his hand on her breast. "When the time comes for me to kill you, you will give me great pleasure."

Rachel clenched her teeth to keep from screaming. Somehow, she had to escape from this madman. Somehow, she had to return to Etienne, even if it was only to tell him she was sorry for betraying him. She kept her mind focused on Etienne — how they had loved, how he had cared for her — as Henri Renaud whispered evil, perverted words in her ear and ran his hands over her body.

Finally, not even thoughts of Etienne could block out what this monster said and did. She had to divert his attention away from his obsession with her. Turning to him suddenly, she asked, "Why do you do these things?"

He sat back in surprise and stared at her. A slow, cruel smile twisted his lips. "Because I enjoy them, *ma petite fleur*. Why else?"

"Why do you enjoy them? What you do is not normal. It is evil." She peered into those dark eyes as black and empty as the man's soul. There was no pity there.

He stood swiftly, towering, menacingly over her. "It is not evil. It is my reward." Placing his hands on his hips, he began to pace before her. "I go through great hardships for His Majesty, King Louis, and His Excellency, Governor de Vaudreuil. If I take a little pleasure from those who are the enemies of France, they do not mind. His Majesty sent me here to do his work. My commander in the army told me so. He said I could do the king's work and have all the pleasure I wished in this new world, that there were hundreds, thousands of Englishwomen and squaws here. He was correct."

Rachel stared up at him. Shock and fear kept her speechless.

He smiled a cruel, secret smile and his eyes focused on something Rachel would never see. "Before we left on this journey, I took my pleasure of two lovely Indian maidens." He shook his head in disappointment. "But they did not scream enough, only at the very end. A pity." He turned his gaze on Rachel once more. His eyes burned into her. "You will be my next pleasure. Do not disappoint me. I expect you to give me as much pleasure as Honora. Do you understand?"

When Rachel did not answer, he prompted, "Well?" At her short nod, he smiled. "I knew you would understand, *ma petite fleur*. Your mother also understood, finally, at the end." He bent close and whispered, "Would you like to know what I do in the woods when I leave you?"

Rachel vehemently shook her head in the negative.

He straightened and gazed at her thoughtfully. "Yes, you are right. It is too soon. You are not ready for those pleasures yet."

Turning suddenly away, he snapped his fingers at the guide. With his eyes lowered, the Indian rose to his feet. Renaud spoke a few harsh words and pointed at Rachel, then at the tree behind her. As the guide moved towards Rachel, Renaud wrapped himself in his blanket and lay down on the ground. Rachel knew he would be asleep almost immediately. It was one of his less threatening habits.

The Indian tied Rachel's arms behind her about the tree. He did this every night for Renaud. Rachel wondered if he knew exactly what Renaud intended to do to her, if he did not care or was completely ignorant of Re-

373

naud's plans. His eyes were blank, showing no emotion.

As he bent over her, desperately she whispered up at him, "Please, help me."

His eyes slid over her and away, back to his loathsome task. As if she had remained mute, he straightened and returned to his place across the clearing. Rachel knew he could not understand her words, but she thought he might have comprehended their desperation.

With a sigh, she leaned her head back against the tree trunk. Even if he had understood her, she knew he would not help her. Two nights ago, when Renaud had been prowling the woods and she thought the guide had not been paying attention, she had tried to escape. He had foiled her attempt as easily and as swiftly as if she had been a child. Her only chance of survival lay in killing both men. The chances of her accomplishing that were almost nonexistent.

Closing her eyes against the tears that suddenly clouded her vision, she compared this captivity with that she had endured with Etienne. She realized there was no comparison. She had been frightened with Etienne, but somehow, she had known deep within her that he would not harm her. With Henri Renaud, she knew her torture and eventual death lay at the end of this journey.

The guide had lain down and was asleep. The campfire still burned steadily, but she knew it would not be long before it died down to only glowing embers. This was the part of her captivity that she dreaded almost more than being tormented by Renaud. Weary from travelling all day, she should have been able to fall sleep. Instead, her mind raced with thoughts of escape, thoughts of dying a horrible death, thoughts of Etienne, her love. Long after both the guide and Renaud had been asleep for hours, did she fall into exhausted sleep.

An exclamation brought her awake instantly. The Indian guide was on his feet, his musket loaded and ready. Renaud was rolling out of his blanket to his feet.

Renaud questioned the guide, and the Indian answered him as he pointed into the trees away from Rachel. Rachel craned her neck and searched the darkness. What was it that aroused the guide? she wondered. A large animal? Hostile Indians? As the two men stood ready to repulse an attack, Rachel felt the shock of the cold blade of a knife slip between her bound wrists and cut her loose. Not daring to hope or breathe, she remained motionless. Could it be? she asked herself. She could not tempt fate. She did not venture to even think his name.

A shout came from the trees across from her, and a figure burst into the clearing. It was Dark Eagle. Another shout came from close by, and Etienne plunged from the darkness. But it was not Etienne. It was White Wolf—White Wolf as she had first seen him, dressed in deerskin, two streaks of red paint slashing down each cheek. Her Frenchman had transformed once more into a man of the Penobscot people.

As she scrambled to her feet, the four men closed to the attack. Dark Eagle lunged at the Indian guide, while White Wolf and Henri Renaud circled each other warily, each with a large hunting knife glinting in their hands. Helplessly, Rachel stood back and watched. There was no weapon for her to use to help.

"So, have you come to rescue your squaw, redman?" Renaud taunted White Wolf. "Do you really think she is worth rescuing now?"

White Wolf did not answer.

"She is very obedient, you know. She will do exactly as you tell her, no matter what it might be." He chuckled suggestively.

White Wolf still said nothing, but the muscle in his jaw jumped.

"A shame I must kill you. I would enjoy having you watch as I take my final pleasure with her."

White Wolf lunged at Renaud with his knife. Renaud jumped out of the way of the deadly blade.

The murderer laughed tauntingly. "So, the aloof White Wolf, the cool Monsieur le Comte de la Lupe, does have feelings. Now I know it will be easy to kill you."

Rachel could not listen to any more of Renaud's insults and threats. Realizing that neither Dark Eagle nor White Wolf would have come after her with only a tomahawk and a hunting knife between them, she stepped into the trees to search for one of their bows which they might have left hidden. She did not have to venture far into the darkness to find what she sought. They had placed their packs and weapons beneath a bramble bush outside the light of the fire.

Rachel grabbed the first bow and quiver of arrows her hand touched. As she stood to hurry back to the clearing, a musket shot rang out. Momentarily paralyzed by the sound and its implications, she remained where she was until the echo died out. Not White Wolf, she prayed. Please, not White Wolf.

Quickly retracing her steps, she entered the clearing. Both Dark Eagle and White Wolf were still alive, and she breathed a sigh of relief. Dark Eagle was kneeling over the Indian guide. His tomahawk came down again and again upon the' man's skull. Only after his anger had been spent did he drop his arm and slowly rise to his feet. Weakly, he stumbled towards a nearby tree. It was then that she saw the black hole in the upper sleeve of his tunic and the shiny, dark blood stain which surrounded it.

As he slumped to the ground, she turned her attention to White Wolf. He and Renaud grappled desperately with each other. Each man held the other's wrist and kept the deadly blades wavering menacingly away from their bodies. It was a bizarre, macabre dance that was being performed before her. Swaying and stumbling, they strained for the advantage. Suddenly, White Wolf's foot slipped on some wet leaves. He went down on one knee. As Renaud's knife arced towards his back, he rolled out of the way. Renaud ruthlessly pursued him.

The sound of White Wolf's labored breathing forced Rachel into action. Nocking the arrow on the bowstring, she sighted down the straight shaft. Her target was the Frenchman who had murdered her mother. Renaud would not remain still long enough for her to get off a good shot. Three times she had him in her sights, and three times he moved away. Rachel's arms shook with nervousness and the unaccustomed strain on her muscles.

As White Wolf and Renaud rolled over and over in the dirt, she relaxed her hold on the bowstring and pointed the arrow to the ground. It was no use. She would not be able to do it. She was too afraid of hitting White Wolf.

Fool! she suddenly chided herself. If you do not kill Renaud, he will kill White Wolf and then you. He is a monster. You have shot rabbits for your supper. Shoot this madman!

Once again she sighted down the arrow. The monster's back was in a direct line. Blanking out all thought, she let the arrow fly.

There was a muffled thud and a gasp. Renaud arched his back as the arrow penetrated to half its length. The hunting knife slipped from his fingers, and White Wolf pushed his lifeless body away.

She had done it. She had killed the man who had murdered her mother. She had exacted her revenge.

The ground tilted crazily then, and she reached out to steady herself against a nearby tree trunk. Swallowing back her nausea, she forced herself to look at what she had done. Slowly, as if in a dream, she walked towards Renaud's body as it lay grotesquely propped up by the protruding arrow. His face was turned towards the fire, his mouth hung slack and his evil eyes stared sightlessly towards the flames. The thought came to Rachel that he was perhaps seeing the fires of hell. She stood over him a moment, absorbing the reality that the man was actually dead. No more would she be driven by the anguish of knowing her mother's murderer roamed free.

The movement of White Wolf climbing to his feet brought her to the present. Guilt and shame flooded her at what she had done to him, at her betrayal of him. Not wanting to face him just yet, she turned to Dark Eagle who sat on the ground and leaned against a tree.

His arm was bleeding freely. He had come with White Wolf to help him save her. Whether it was because of his friendship with White Wolf or something else, she did not care. She only knew she was very grateful to him.

Walking to him, she knelt beside him. He said something in his native language and pointed at the tip of the bow that she still held. Glancing at where he indicated, she realized she had used his bow to kill Renaud. He had tied the lock of hair she had given him to its tip.

White Wolf had come up behind her. "Dark Eagle says your hair is strong medicine," he translated. "The arrow flew straight and true to its mark. He says only a woman of the People could kill her enemy with such bravery."

Rachel looked into Dark Eagle's dark eyes as she said, "Tell him I am unworthy to be a woman of the People. I have betrayed his friend, White Wolf."

There was silence from White Wolf. Rachel could sense his surprise and turmoil at her words.

"Please, tell him," she urged.

White Wolf relayed her words. When he had finished, Dark Eagle shook his head and spoke forcefully.

"He says there is no betrayal where there is bravery and honor," White Wolf told her. "He says that where White Wolf is welcome, his woman is welcome."

Rachel averted her eyes in shame. There was an awkward silence between White Wolf and Rachel as Dark Eagle glanced from one to the other of them. Finally, he spoke again, gruffly.

"Dark Eagle says that while your shame covers you, his blood runs from him like a stream at snow melt," White Wolf translated.

Rachel looked up and smiled sheepishly. As she tore strips from her petticoat to use as bandages, White Wolf brought a deer bladder of water for her to use to wash the wound. She busied herself with cleaning and bandaging Dark Eagle's wound. Fortunately, the ball had gone completely through the fleshy part of his upper arm. When she had finished, he spoke solemnly. Rachel understood that he was thanking her. Picking up his bow, he flashed her a quick, friendly smile and disappeared into the dark woods.

Rachel stood and slowly faced White Wolf across the clearing. While she had been tending Dark Eagle, he had pulled the dead bodies of Renaud and his Indian guide into the woods out of sight. The firelight flickered and played on only Rachel and White Wolf. Opening her mouth to speak, she found she did not know what to say, how to begin.

Tell him you love him, idiot, that little voice inside her head urged.

She ignored it.

"I'm sorry for betraying you," she said instead.

"Not all Frenchmen are alike, English," White Wolf chided gently. "Not all will cause you pain."

Rachel bowed her head. "I know that. Now." She raised her head again and looked at him. "Not all English will cause *you* pain, either"

He smiled. "I know that. Now." His smile faded and he became serious. "My reason for attacking your village was wrong. My revenge should not have been taken out on innocent people."

Shyly, Rachel suggested, "If you had not attacked Deerfield, I would not have met you."

He nodded. "That is true."

An awkward silence settled on the clearing as each wondered how to speak what was in their hearts.

Tell him you love him, idiot! that little voice inside her head yelled impatiently.

Rachel cleared her throat nervously. That little voice had never been wrong before. Perhaps . . .

"I love you," she whispered hoarsely.

White Wolf's face relaxed, and he held out his arms to her. "Come here, English."

Rachel rushed into his embrace. As he clasped her to him and buried his face in her hair, he murmured, "I love you, too, Woman With Hair Of Hidden Fire."

After standing together soaking up the feel of each other's bodies, White Wolf lifted his head and held her away from him. He gazed into those eyes the color of the blue spruce.

"You are my woman," he declared. "Yet, in the eyes of your people, you are not truly my woman. I have given great thought to this. I wish you to be happy, to stay with me until the end of our days. Will you speak the words of promise between a man and woman before Reverend Williams and before a priest?"

Rachel was speechless that he should ask her to marry him in the European manner. She was speechless and wonderfully happy. She could only stare up at him with a dazzled expression on her face.

Not understanding her reason for not answering, thinking she was undecided about her answer, he went on, "It was not right for the English to attack my father's house; it was not right for me to seek revenge on your village. I will go among your people and mine and bring the pipe of peace. If our people are to live together, they must live in peace."

Tears of happiness clouded Rachel's eyes. Swallowing the lump in her throat, she reached up and touched his cheek. "You are a brave, good man, White Wolf of the Penobscot. I love you very much. I would be honored to speak the words of promise before Reverend Williams and a priest. I am your woman."

White Wolf's eyes closed in relief. When he opened them again, Rachel sucked in her breath at their blue intensity.

"You are my woman, English," he stated.

"Yes," she agreed, just before his mouth swooped down on hers and captured what was his.

# Author's Note

Two hours before dawn, on February 29, 1704, a force of fifty French soldiers and two hundred Indians attacked the tiny hamlet of Deerfield in the Connecticut River Valley which lay in the interior wilderness of the Massachusetts Bay Colony. The number of English prisoners carried off from the settlement was one hundred and eleven; the number killed was forty-seven. One hundred and thirty-seven escaped death or capture. The men, women, and children taken captive were herded three hundred miles north to Montreal. During the next two years, some captives were ransomed and returned to their homes and families; some died of sickness or other natural causes. A few, who found the life of the redman more appealing than what they had left behind, were adopted by the various tribes involved in the attack on Deerfield. Four young women converted to Catholicism and married Frenchmen. On October 25, 1706, the last of the hostages, among them Reverend John Williams and two of his sons, set sail from Quebec and arrived safely in Boston on November 21 of that year.